THE HOUR OF TRUTH

The Hour of Truth

A NOVEL BY

DAVID DAVIDSON

RANDOM HOUSE · NEW YORK

Contents

PART ONE: *Laura*   Page   1

PART TWO: *Ernestina*   59

PART THREE: *The Eaglets*   119

PART FOUR: *The Encirclement*   191

PART FIVE: *The Hour of Truth*   243

For My Mother
and My Father

PART ONE: *Laura*

CHAPTER ONE

FROM nowhere, from nothing, could he salvage self-esteem, not even from his heroic stature, his well-made brawn. Standing before Laura, his wife, towering over her but raked by her upturned gaze, he felt himself to be not large but overgrown, not muscular but cumbersome, a cornered behemoth.

"Will," she said, with the low cool voice that had affection in it, patience, concern, everything but respect, esteem, "you *are* in a spin. Will, what're we going to do about you?" Still her bright blue eyes were firing upon him, appraising him, judging him. Any moment he might go crashing down before her, before the keen little huntress who was his wife. Confusedly he reached for the newel post of the hall stairway.

Up ahead the children swung the oaken front door impatiently. "Dad, stop playing statues," said Ann, the older one, taking notice of his stance. "Dad, don't be so pokey," said Betsy.

With a forefinger to her lips Laura silenced them. "Really, Will," she asked, "why *don't* you come to the park with us? For an hour? Half an hour? It'll freshen you up."

"I'm all right," he said. "I'm fine." But he wasn't. All over again he had been made to feel the hidden infirmities in the frame that from the outside looked so powerful, the nicks and scars he had carried in his bones since his football days. A blank cartridge.

"Sweetie, it's Saturday afternoon," said Laura. "You don't have to go at it *that* hard, do you?" She was a handsome girl, it had to be granted, with her fresh skin, the feathery aureole of her tawny hair, her rose-leaf mouth, a creature of the outdoors and sunlight, the kind of girl who goes striding up a mountain all by herself. She was small, but never would she have to be helped across gullies. When for a few years she had worked it had been at a man's job, a graceful one but man's work, as an architect. At one time he had considered it a cause for admiration, this comely strength of hers, hadn't he? Until—until it was borne in upon him one day that it was a strength markedly greater than his own, which to a man was unbearable, or, anyhow, to a man such as himself. "Oh, come on, Will, relax," she said.

He held aloft a handful of legal papers. *Finch vs. Finch.* A new brief, a new start. "This time," he said, "it's got to be right."

"Oh, it will," she said cheerily. "Why wouldn't it?"

He flushed. They were referring in their guarded way—the children must not have their curiosity aroused—to more fiascos than one. This professional, nurse-like tenderness Laura was offering him . . . He must try, in spite of everything, to be a man to his wife. A man, not a patient. He must . . . But no, he was a blank cartridge. Though he stood six feet and one inch tall, though often he had carried a football past plunging shoulders and grappling arms, he had lost his rating. Four weeks ago it had begun, this unwilling celibacy, twenty-nine full days ago, in fact. And night after night, ever since, Laura had gone on searching him with those keen blue eyes, waiting, waiting. . . .

"Will . . ." she began anew.

"I know what I'm doing," he said, sharply now. "This is my baby." Baby. Chagrined by his own evil choice of words, he gritted his teeth.

"What baby?" asked Ann from the doorway. "What's he talking about?"

"Ann," said Laura, "I wish you'd stop calling your father *he.*"

"What should I call him—*she?*"

"Hello, *she!*" cried Betsy.

Laura shook her head severely and they subsided. It was then that she did the worst thing possible. She took hold of him by the forearm. Once again, with her small competent hand, she tried to tug him along—she the mahout, the elephant boy, and he the dumb beast. Exactly, again, as on that rotten night when the fiascos had started. Next, he thought, Laura will be fitting me for a nose ring. Years ago, it occurred to him, his mother must have tugged his father in just the same way through his drunken mists. "Stop it," he rasped, breaking loose.

"Willikins . . ." she said. It was the pet name she had invented for him long ago, on their honeymoon, in the days when he had been "all right," had been fine, had been great, a world's champ in fact. And in those days too, in the flush, then, of their love, he had found pleasure, he had found pride, in her sweet elfin sinews. He had loved to have her rough him about like a sportive Lilliputian at Gulliver—he being utterly confident, in *those* days, that the giant of the two was, of course, himself. "Willikins, we're really going to have to do something."

We, the royal *we,* the language of sovereignty, but not of esteem. Men, from the beginning, had fared poorly in this house of clever women. His mother first, and now Laura his wife . . . They had nursed their husbands, sustained their husbands, endured their husbands, everything but esteemed their husbands. Or was this all just something in his mind? *Was* it? Or on the other hand was . . . Oh, he no longer had the clarity, not here and now, to weigh out the truth of it particle by particle. Instead, he snatched for the warming cup of anger. "Don't coddle me," he said. "For God's sake, don't coddle me."

"All right," she said, still studying him, studying him ceaselessly, perceiving so very much and yet not everything, "all right, Will."

On the record, he had to grant, in the mind of a disinterested jury, she had not said one word which could be deemed offensive. Not ever would she *choose* to hurt him, the felled giant. Yet every single word had reached a vital organ, had murdered over and over again his sense of maleness, of manhood, of adequacy.

Bitterly he turned his back. "See you all later," he said.

When they were gone, when they were out of the house, he stood for a moment in the dark hallway and breathed heavily, alone finally, an escapee. Composing himself, he began to toil up the varnished oak cliff of the stairway, up toward the study. On the first-floor landing he observed that the door of his mother's office, her surgery, stood open. He strode past it determinedly—then inevitably was drawn back. There against the far wall it stood, flashing in the sunlight, the glass case with her surgical instruments. Forceps, clamps, dilators, hypodermics and shears, all so sternly metallic, embedded all in the chest of light and glitter. And also the scalpels, of course, the bright little knives which she could wield so deftly in her thin unhesitant hands. The little knives . . .

Abruptly he turned away, went laboring again up through the dark and silent house to the study, where all the briefs and writs and injunctions in the case of *Finch vs. Finch* were laid out and waiting for him. A new brief, a new start. Fighting off the heavy heat of the June afternoon, he settled himself in a huge soft chair by the window with a bulky maroon-colored law text. *Finch vs. Finch,* that fratricidal tragedy, a cause of crucial importance. Party of the first part, and party of the second part. . . . May it be noted by the honorable Court that the remedy for which my client, as injured party, is herewith appealing—that the easement for which he is praying—the alleviation which he is entreating—the mitigation which he is imploring . . . Where, where did they lie? How, once again, could he be made to feel himself a man?

Through the quiet queasy heat of the city he thought after a while that he heard the telephone ring, but he did not move. It rang a third time, a fourth, but still he refused to get up from his chair, to cross the study and lift the receiver. He did not want to find once again that the phone had rung only in his desirings.

The ringing forthwith stopped.

Just as well, he thought.

The injured party—or parties. Longingly his gaze turned from the telephone instrument to the photo that stood next to it on the desk, to the image of that handsome young corsair with the black curls and the untamed eyes, the old-style youth with the winged collar and the huge cravat.

"My father . . ." he said, racked for the brilliant boy. "Steven . . ." he said, mourning the splendid father he had never seen alive, who had died at twenty-nine, the boy-father, an age already four years younger than that of himself, the posthumous son, becoming each year more and more the junior of his own issue. If only somewhere in this house Steven Harmon had left a message for him—in the way that prisoners write a line of cheer on the cell wall for the successors they never will see but to whose fate they are already linked. If only in this house of silks and scents a cigar could still be found smoldering in an ash tray, a jacket still hanging across a chair. He had given his seed, Steven Harmon, and almost instantly perished, like the resplendent drone from whom, after long fatting, the Queen Bee one day snatches seed, genitalia and life together. Mother, and her little knives . . .

The telephone, he observed, was ringing again, the false one of course, ringing only because he prayed for it to ring, because it had been by telephone, the instrument of urgency, that most of the adventures of his life had started. But lately, and it was deeply disturbing, he had run three, four times a day to the phone to meet not a voice but only a dial tone. Give it up, he told himself. Delivery will not come from the outside—no files baked into a pie. But the horror,

the real one, was the company you had to keep, the cellmate, a man
whose every trait you had long ago come to know too well, all his
stories, his mannerisms, his hopes, his failures. Yourself. *Harmon
vs. Harmon*. It was a brief he could no longer bear to hold.

The phone, he noted, had stopped ringing.

He yawned then and pulled himself up, rung by rung, from
reverie to daylight. *Finch vs. Finch* would not go to trial until the
fall term of New York Supreme Court. Nevertheless, he had insisted on taking home the papers for the week end. He was feverish, of course, to make amends for *Hutchins vs. Webster*. Bad business that. Lousy bad. But, after all, what lawyer hadn't fumbled the
ball once or twice in his life? And I damned well never claimed to
be a mouthpiece. The talk was all talked out of me years ago. By
clever women. I'm a think boy strictly, briefs and contracts. And
damned good at it when I want to be. The clear judicial mind. If
the firm had nobody else handy to argue *Hutchins vs. Webster* they
should have moved for a postponement. His first court appearance
in years—and he *would* have the bad luck to run into a two-fisted
Portia, a perfumed cannonball like Miss Ruby Hopkins, Counselor-
at-law. . . .

Portia, the lovely creature, had not hesitated to drop a couple
below the belt. For the Irish juror in Seat Number Three, a riposte
in brogue and a deft little parable about the two men of County
Cork. For the Jewish juror in Number Nine, a nimble observation
that all was not *kosher* with this witness, and please not to waste
the jury's time with an entire *megilah*. The stratagems of Miss At-
torney Hopkins had involved also the charming of one witness into
complete forgetfulness, the tormenting of another into complete con-
fusion, and the production further of two witnesses of her own who,
Harmon was certain, had not been within five miles of the accident.

Trounced by a girl, he, the athlete-scholar with the Phi Beta
Kappa key across his chest. Tricks, tricks—always, all his life he had
shied away from them as something serpentine, yes, as feminine,
putting his faith optimistically—or timidly?—in clarity of logic,

directness of attack and justice of the cause. For this he had often been considered naïve, which had not troubled him. . . . Trounced by a *girl*. When it was all over she sidled up to him, kitten-like, and measured him from head to toe, admiring openly his soaring height, the wedge-shaped torso. "Counselor," she asked, "can I buy you a drink?"

She had wiped the floor with him, a hundred pounds of frill and wile. "Thanks, but I'll have to take a rain check, Counselor."

She patted him consolingly, then, on the arm. "You're smart," she said, "darn smart on the law, but so scared of getting your hands dirty."

They tell us today that their brains are as good as ours, that women have more stamina, keener senses, greater dexterity, longer life and superior adaptability. Why then should it have rankled so much that . . . ? Behind the shrewd little face of Counselor Ruby Hopkins, he had perceived suddenly the visages of other determined women: of his brilliant and talkative mother; of Laura his wife, with her deadly patience; of the two sharp little females who were his children; of all the mutinous women who these days stalked up and demanded in the words of that booted girl of *The Master Builder,* of Hilda Wangel, "I want my kingdom. The time is up."

Because they had found out that it was not so much, after all, to be a lawyer, a physicist, even a builder of bridges, nowhere near as much as had always been pretended to them, because they knew for themselves now what commonplaces were contained in "a tough day at the office," they had developed a way of saying, "You meet so few real men these days." They were inclined no longer to bring out the slippers-and-pipe at eventide. And in this gloomy old house where he was so outnumbered by females, where the boy who was Father had perished so quickly after being drained of his seed. . . .

No. Nobody had gone after Steven Harmon with a knife. Alcoholism had killed him, not a scalpel. But there was that other little blade, which women carried with them as almost a standard accessory. Lipstick, compact and—mockery. "Oh, now Will, *really!*" his mother had a way of saying, as once she must have said across the table, "Oh, now Steve, *really!*" Even his little daughters, at six and seven, did not go unarmed. It was in the air here, it was an accepted fact in this house, that a man was a target. Only Laura, it was only she, who kept her cleverness sheathed, Laura with her deadly chivalry. The truth, the cold truth, was that she could have her kingdom any time that she chose to reach for it. In the first years of their marriage, while she still worked at her drafting board, she had out-earned him alarmingly. At parties it was to Laura always that their friends turned, while he brought up the rear, the mute dinosaur. Seven years now since she had gone to an office, not since the "temporary" leave when she had given birth to Ann. Her houses now lay hidden, her city of graceful inventions lay locked away inside her desk and inside herself. It was for his sake, of course, that she had done it, to spare him from being merely the husband of his wife, as for so long he had been merely the son of his mother. He should be grateful to Laura, but it was murderous, this gallantry of hers, at one almost with the victorious condescension of Miss Counselor Hopkins asking, "Can I buy you a drink?" —but only after measuring him and deciding that, yes, he would be worth acquiring for a harem of males.

The worst of it . . . It had followed only a few hours in the wake of the fiasco of *Hutchins vs. Webster*. He had emerged from the shower completely nude. At her dressing table Laura had looked instantly about. Again there had pierced him a quick keen appraisal of all his "good points," the stature, the shoulder breadth, the foot-runner's legs. A moment later Laura, of a height hardly to his chin, was nuzzling against him, stroking him, gripping him by the fore-arm, drawing him after her as she backed away toward the bed. If that was all he was wanted for, it had flashed through his mind, as a stud animal, if he was to be ringed through the nose and led off firmly to his duties, the only ones for which he was coddled, endured . . .

Blank cartridge.

Again the telephone was ringing.

In the way of men, he had always prided himself on that kind of prowess, could recall with exactness the time and place and circumstances of all the finest performances. But for twenty-nine days now, and twenty-nine bitter nights . . . That hand on his forearm —if only it had been possible for him to take it as a gesture of simple wifely affection. . . . This was surely the way Laura had meant it, wasn't it? He ought to remember, he must *make* himself remember, how once he had loved to have her tousle him—Laura who was newly his bride—to down him and bestride him in fierce-fond combat. But that was in another era, and that was another Harmon.

Still the telephone rang, the imaginary one, of course.

Must there be a conqueror in every double bed?

It rang and rang.

Laura was beautiful, yes, with her sun-drenched face, her trim and shining body—he must get himself to remember that. And to remember how, in the *beginning,* when she had taken him by the hand he had found it a cause for enjoyment—as in that sweet moment when she had first presented him to the warm bright circle of her family—racing an arm's length before him, drawing him proudly after and declaring, "This is *Will!* This is *Will!*" . . . He recalled too that loving gymnastic of theirs in which she would come running at him from a long start—running full tilt and laughing all the while, *foaming over* with laughter—and fling her whole elfin self high upon his neck, and nuzzle him joyously, her adored giant. And beg him, "Oh, make a muscle, Will! Flex your biceps. Oh, marvelous!" It had been taken for granted, in those days, which of the two was the larger. And it had been a time, too, when those blue eyes, so everlastingly keen, would turn their fire only upon others, and she would whisper to him, "The man's a fraud! He is, isn't he?" And always she had been wonderfully, delightfully, right. . . . But that was a long time ago, a time before his confidence had begun to ebb. Perhaps if he could have got away altogether from this house, and the glitter of his mother's scalpels, and the memory of the tragic boy who was his father. . . . But there had been his mother's steely benevolence—"Now Will, *really*—why, when we have this enormous whole house must you run off to some one-room mousetrap, you and Laura?" . . . Little by little, in this house of women, he had begun to fall back again. Little by little, Laura had gone into the ascendant. And now . . . A man, he concluded, had better marry beneath him. A man *had* to be on top— it was nature's own posture—or he would not long endure as a man.

Still the phone went on ringing. Still . . .

The ringing of the phone, it suddenly came to him, was unquestionably real!

Instantly he was bolting across the study, but telling himself all the while that it could be a wrong number, a call from a playmate of his daughters, a patient of his mother.

"Hello," he said.

"I have a person-to-person call for Mr. William Harmon."

The operator's voice, aloof and monotonous, was so patently like that of a sleep character that quite possibly he was still back there in the chair by the window and only *dreaming* his awakening. "Speaking," he said, deciding to pursue it, hallucination or not.

"Washington calling. Hold on, please."

Washington? Again he became raddled with disbelief. But next, crisp and bright, he heard the voice of Frank Rhodes, yes Frank, the bosom companion of his college days with whom he used to wander each summer as a deckhand but of whom he had long lost track. "Bill," he was asking, and in an instant it surely was Frank, nobody else had this way of opening a subject, "how would you like to play God to fifty thousand South Americans?"

"Where?" Harmon asked. "Where?"

Frank named an obscure little Republic on the western bulge of the continent, one that spilled down from the Andes into the Pacific. He was with State Department now, he said, and he was charged with recruiting personnel for a technical mission. "Bill, I have you down for legal officer and associate director."

Just like that . . . He wanted to laugh. But after all wasn't this the way things were being done these days? Since Pearl Harbor they were even making men *generals* over the telephone.

"I'll need you here in Washington," said Frank, "by Monday noon. Can you make it?"

"Wait," said Harmon, filled suddenly with japery—at Frank, at himself, at the whole hallucination—but falling in, nevertheless, with that private, oblique code of communication that had been theirs since their college days, "wait for baby."

"What more do you have to know?" asked Frank.

"Everything."

"The Good Neighbor in action!" said Frank. Like most fast-moving people, he was given to slogans as a kind of enthusiastic shorthand. "A million dollars for a three-way rehabilitation job in one of their run-down provinces, Alba. Agriculture, public health, public works. Alba's been slipping for a long time; their cocoa went to hell in a plague ten years ago. Last winter there was a border war and Alba was the ball park. We asked everybody to kiss and make up. Our part—we'd patch up the damage and make Alba as good as new. But it can mean more than that." Frank went back to slogans. "A test plant for the Americas. A million dollars buys Alba a future, and a blueprint for the rest of Latin America."

Aloofly still, holding himself in check, not yet to be snared, he asked what Alba was like.

"Tobacco Road," said Frank, "with royal palms. Everything bad, from leprosy to absentee landlords. We figure the job for a year. How are you on the draft?"

"I tried to enlist."

"And . . . ?"

"My football souvenirs." He said this reluctantly, thinking how from the outside he still looked so good to everybody, recalling all the cracks so hidden, and yet so present, in his knees, his elbows and his collarbone. There were times when he expected to give away altogether, like a puppet whose strings are suddenly cut. "They did offer me limited service."

"And . . . ?"

"Who wants to be a Wac?"

"Well," said Frank, "Alba is not for Wacs. I need you, Bill. Latin America was always a subject of yours."

Yes, ever since those sunlit days when he had gone wandering in the southern ports, eaten their strange fruits, learned their stately language. A subject of his. Chess too had once been a subject of his, and Renaissance painting and boats, and string quartets and medieval history. How many skills and knowledges he had let slip away from him. He had been reckoned once to be a youth of great capacities, and even greater promise, but somewhere, somehow, he had lost all the confidence which holds such things together. Each year, of late, he had let himself become more and more ordinary. Under the keen and critical gaze of those clever women who beleaguered him he had grown smaller and smaller.

"Legal officer," coaxed Frank, "and associate director. Say yes."

Tensely—but the question was one which *had* to be put—he asked, "What about families?"

"No dice," said Frank, "not with a child mortality of sixty per cent. Alba is for men only."

For men only. Here it was, wasn't it, everything for which he had been praying—the easement, the alleviation, the remedy? All his heart was for calling a halt finally to the death march of his days, for wheeling in some new direction. "Frank," he begged, "is the job clean? I won't be an errand boy for the dollar diplomats."

"I asked you to play God, Bill, not Satan. This is old stuff. Public Health Service has been cleaning up backward areas for years. Monday noon? I want you to meet your chief of party. Colonel Burling."

Downstairs just then the front door banged open. There followed a clatter of cleated heels on the tiled floor of the vestibule, and the low cool voice of Laura.

"Frank," he said, and he heard his own voice to be tight and tense, "I'll have to call you back."

"South America . . ." Laura repeated. Sitting on the edge of the sofa, she had drawn the children to her in a kind of Niobe tableau.

"Alba is a hole," he said. Still her eyes were searching him—or, again, was it only in his imagination that she was his Inquisitor? "I don't know one good reason why I should take the job."

At the corners of her rose-leaf mouth appeared the most delicate hint of a smile, private and in-looking. It was the smile, he thought annoyedly, with which a woman tells her husband to stop play-acting.

"I mean it, Laura."

"Will," she said, "you know you're packing your bags."

"No!" he said. This was not to be admitted, not under any circumstances.

"South America!" cried Ann.

"Dad," asked Betsy, "will we go by steamship or airplane?"

"Children," said Laura, "I'm afraid Dad will be going alone."

Ann stood instantly agape. "That's mean," she said, "mean and selfish!"

"Wait," said Harmon, "I didn't say I was going." He would not have it look as though he were leaping away at the first call. He would not have Laura think that she knew everything, absolutely everything, about him. "Alba is a terrible place, full of diseases."

"Oh, well," said Betsy placidly, "Granny will stick us full of injections."

Laura drew them in more closely. "Children," she said, "Daddy can't even take *me*."

"Why not?" demanded Ann instantly. "What's so good about *him*?"

Was it the atmosphere in which she had been raised, he won-

dered. Or was it the instinct everywhere for females to make an
enemy of whatever was male? To hack at it and try to bring it
down?

"Alba," said Laura patiently, "is no place for women and children."

"Well, why"—asked Ann, and he was pierced instantly by the
pointedness of her perception—"why does he want to go away to
a place that's not for women and children?"

"He's a stinker!" cried Betsy. "I stink him, the stinking stinker!"

"Children," said Laura, "it's very brave really for your Dad to go
to a place like Alba."

"My hero!" said Ann instantly, flinging wide her arms.

"Hurrah for the flag!" cried Betsy.

Man, the enemy. What a time, thought Harmon, they will be
giving their husbands fifteen years from now. But then, tenderly,
he bethought himself all at once of a little scene of the week before.
They had come to him before supper all streaked with the dirt of
play but their hair doused with some purloined cologne, half tomboy and half coquette, but so heartbreakingly vulnerable in either
role. Inside them too, his daughters, the females from his own flesh,
brewed strifes and storms. With the one hand they would cling to
their dolls, and with the other reach toward the baseball bats, and
never be sure which they really desired. They would know only
that there was nothing from which they wanted to be excluded.

Tenderly he held out his arms to them. "Oh, come on," he said,
"let's have a hug." But silently, icily, they drew back on their
mother. "For goodness' sake," said Laura, gathering them in, "call
Frank back. Tell him you're taking it."

He shook his head. "I don't want the job," he said. "I don't."

Once again, on her lips, appeared that private in-turned smile.

"All right," said Harmon reddening. Awkwardly he stood up.
Awkwardly he walked across the room, sensing upon him all the
while the gaze of his three clever women. Picking up the telephone
receiver, he began to dial.

CHAPTER TWO

THEY swigged beer from the bottleneck, they spat out of windows, they belched freely. They would roister each night in the Washington cafés, then stagger back to their hotel through the blacked-out streets singing in close harmony. They would mull over, the next morning, all the shenanigans of the night before, and shadow-box affectionately among themselves. They had a strong contempt for anybody who was not one of them.

The "Alba Gang". . . . It was like stepping back, thought Harmon, to the locker room, the fo'c'sle, the poker table. He had come, agreeably, upon something he had thought long lost, that raucous camaraderie of men among themselves.

Burling, Ross, the others . . . Their range of languages ran all the way to Chinese, Tagalog and the African bush dialects. They had lived under mosquito nets in half the hot countries of the world and referred to themselves defiantly as "tropical tramps." In the United States they had mailing addresses but no homes. Their wives and their children they had boarded out around the globe. There was not one of them who had not come close on some occasion or other to losing his life under a kris, a bolo, a machete. Alongside such journeyings, thought Harmon, his own had been tame. But they took him in instantly as one of their own. Among the Alba Gang his size counted for something.

By the paper-pushers of the Technical Section they were regarded with open awe. "You're going to Alba?" the paper-pushers would ask, the stay-at-homes dug in behind their Washington desks.

"Why the hell not?"

"Well," the answer was put on one occasion, "you may not all be coming back on your feet, you know."

"Good show!" croaked Colonel Burling in that favorite phrase

he had picked up from the British somewhere in his travels. "First
son of a bitch to fall—I don't care whether it's malaria or VD—
gets a bangup funeral. 'He perished for the Hemisphere.'" (Laura,
of course, would smile. Laura, of course, would say that it was all
swagger.)

Around the Technical Section, in the low wooden building on
Constitution Avenue that had been "temporary" for twenty-four
years, since the first of the world wars, they banded exclusively
together, their shirt collars open and their ties off, their feet on
anybody's desk at all—but tolerated, of course, indulged even, as
gladiator-about-to-die. In the section lunchroom they would turn
their backs on all outsiders, then shout their yarns aloud for the
attention of any who might be eavesdropping.

"This goddamn lady food"—Burling would say—"I could go
right now for a nice tasty dish of fried bees."

"Python stew for me . . ." from Felix Horanyi.

"India?"

"With pepper sauce."

"Gentlemen, have I ever mentioned that when I was on the
Congo . . ."

"Human flesh?"

"It was stringy as hell."

It would amuse them wildly to see the paper-pushers turn green.
(Laura, of course, would consider this kid stuff. Laura would say
they ought to grow up.)

Burling, round-faced and paunchy but with a stiff straight car-
riage, turned out to be an old West Pointer who had left the Army
in the twenties. After Pearl Harbor he had dashed up from Rio,
where he represented a steel firm, to offer himself for reactivation
but had lost patience in the labyrinths of the Pentagon. It could
well be, he granted, that once the Army had let loose the tiger's
tail it was not disposed to grab it again. He carried his jaw thrust
forth like a baseball umpire's, but at the corners of his mouth there

was a perpetual readiness for mirth. Five minutes after Harmon had met him, and they had discovered a mutual feeling for the underdogs of the world, Burling was rattling off a series of tales, genial and self-belittling, that pictured a man who knew all races and climes and was fast on his feet.

In China, related Burling in that gravelly basso, he had once shared a cabin on a river boat with the Young Marshal. During the night a wild storm broke and the Marshal hastily abandoned the traditional impassivity of his race. Planting his middle on a chair he forthwith commanded Burling to instruct him in the arts of swimming. "Billy, I gave him the whole goddamn curriculum. Breast stroke and crawl. Overhand and side stroke. High dive, swan dive, back dive. In Peiping, later, he decorated me with the Golden Carnation." Burling's lips flickered. "The truth is that I've never been in water above my bellybutton." (Laura, of course, would say that it was hardly likely, made up out of whole cloth.)

In Bolivia, it came out, Burling had thrown up a fat contract with the tin operators because of their feudal treatment of their labor. And in Paraguay—his eyes narrowed—a landowner had once invited him on a hunt. Dogs, beaters and all. Halfway into the jungle he learned for the first time that the quarry was to be live Indian peons. The justification, in the mind of his host, was that the peons had run out on a bond of indenture. He had had to resign from that particular safari, said Burling, by force. . . . But a moment later he was deep in a tale of the Sudan and his discomfiture on a very dressy occasion when he had stood abaft a camel and disremembered unhappily that ever since the days of the Prophet camels urinate with a rearward trajectory. (Laura, of course, would say . . .) When he had described Burling in a letter all that she could say was, "He sounds sort of windy, Will, doesn't he?" But she had always had a way—he refused to think about it further—of being disconcertingly right about people.

Now it was July and still they marked time in the sticky heat of

Washington. Rhodes was having trouble filling out the complement. He still lacked a doctor and agriculturist. From the American Ambassador in Chimboya, capital of the Republic, came irritated cables. Anti-American elements, he said, were spreading rumors that the Alba program had been abandoned. He wanted American faces to show in the province at once. Also there were several relevant letters which had been intercepted on their way in from the Republic by postal censorship. "All their glorious promises to rehabilitate Alba," wrote a banker to a friend in Chicago, "have turned out to be the usual *yanqui* bluff. Again they have tricked us."

From another correspondent who signed only "Vicente" came an even sharper letter, one which gave Harmon the feeling all at once that a telescope had ben turned on him from half a world away. "What kind of gods are they planning to ship us in Alba?" inquired Vicente. "The usual Conquistadores of the second class, those Colossi of the North who strut down our boulevards with an oil-company gait? Heaven help us!"

Vicente, speculated Rhodes, was most likely a *Falangista,* one of the Latino fascists who were being subsidized heavily by Franco Spain. As if in answer, Vicente sent another letter soon after. "It is naturally a little difficult for me to picture the dollar diplomats and oil thieves as bearers of light and democracy. But whoever does not automatically sink to his knees as a *yanqui* goes by is labeled a fascist. Long live the Hemisphere!"

The ground was hot under their feet. Each morning they left their bags fully packed in their hotel rooms. But Rhodes, working doggedly from his green metal desk, sweating his seersucker suits into damp bags by each evening, was reluctant to let the party take off without its medical officer and agriculturist. Constantly he was phoning or dictating telegrams or combing the Civil Service lists and rosters of professional societies, always in search of "likely material." For agriculturist he had nothing more than an expression of interest from a homely little man like a scrub oak, Walt Anderson, who was indeed an old tropical hand but was half-committed already to grow food in Hawaii for the Navy. As for medical officer, any doctor who'd ever prescribed a grain of quinine had already been commissioned and rushed to the Pacific. A big operation was working up around a place with a Spanish-sounding name, Guadalcanal. Felix Horanyi, the Mission's economist and anthropologist, knew the place. He'd once done a study of the Solomon Islands artifacts on a grant from Yale.

Horanyi—a Hungarian hussar with a black mustache and three gold teeth that flashed daggers of light whenever he opened his mouth. He had lived a good part of his life in huts, caves, tepees and igloos, and had a way of fixing each expedition by what new tastes he had acquired in alcohol. In Peru it had been *pisco;* in Mexico, *pulque*; in Africa, cactus brandy. And among the Quechua Indians of Ecuador—"*Chicha,* they call it, and the way they make it is for the entire family to sit around a basin chewing boiled rice and spitting the rice into the basin and then letting the enzyme action of the saliva. . . . Ha, it's something delicious!" (Of course Laura would say that he had made it all up for shock effect.)

There had been a few reservations at first about the engineering officer, Fred Ross, a heavy boy with sloping shoulders, whose labors in the sun had given him a permanent scowl. He was only thirty and his highest previous grade in Civil Service had been *second* engineer.

"Hell," Ross came back, "you want a water system, I'll build you a water system. You want a seawall, I'll build you a seawall. What else you want built?"

Burling's lips lifted with amusement. "All right, Jack Dempsey," he said, "I'll take you."

It was inevitable that Tom Mercer—even his boys'-book name was right for it—should turn out to be a product of the Southern military academies. He sat in his chair throughout his interview as though braced for inspection. He snapped to on each question and answered directly to the point. And yet—"My God, sir, ten goddamn years a cadet, sir, and when a real shooting war comes along, sir, they turn me down for goddamn punctured eardrums, sir." He spoke Spanish thoroughly well, though in a kind of cockfight argot, because he'd been knocking around the past couple of years on plantations in the Caribbean. He would be perfect, Burling reckoned, for the thousand and one chores of running camp and handling native labor— "a regular little adjutant."

Burling, Ross, Horanyi and Mercer—world-wise and on their toes. Of course Laura—oh, the hell with what Laura would say. Just as soon as they filled out the team with a medico and a farmer . . . Again there was a letter from "Vicente."

"Suddenly," he wrote, "we are having such a descent of the buzzards upon Alba as not even in the best days of the cocoa boom. The *gringos,* they have heard, will be bringing down a million dollars, ten million pesos. Every day, I am told, the Presidential Palace is jammed with politicos begging for appointments in Alba. Since these jobs do not pay enough, officially, to keep even a midget in tamales, you can imagine, dear friend, what the real attraction must be. How the feathers will fly when the two flocks meet over the corpse of our poor little province, the buzzards from Washington and the buzzards from Chimboya. What excitement! What diversion! Poor Cesar Montalvo, our Eagle of the Andes. Was it for this that he suffered his agony? I must send out for another bottle of brandy."

Vicente—behind the cleverness, behind the satanism could be heard a cry for something lost, for a world that once had seemed more shining. What, speculated Harmon, would he look like? Dark, obviously. Massive. A face with a grin that was not mirthful. "By the way," he asked, turning to Frank, "who is Cesar Montalvo?"

Frank shrugged his shoulders. "One of their presidents. They've had something like fourteen in twenty years."

It was just then that the imperious telephone call came from the

dingy wedding-cake palace on Pennsylvania Avenue. It was the
desire of the Department that the Alba Technical Mission, as much
of it as had already been mustered, proceed that same night to its
field station in the Republic.

There was time enough, just, to phone Laura in New York.
"Well," she said, "have lots of fun, Sweetie."

It was disconcerting that always she could read his most private
intentions. "Fun," he said, stiffening, "is not exactly the point."

She passed this over. "About the trouble, Will—I *know* you're
going to be all right."

All right? Of that there was only one possible kind of test,
wasn't there, one touchstone?

"What I mean, Will . . ."

Between the lines, she was giving him a signal, wasn't she, a
tacit go-ahead? She was hinting, as a modern and tolerant wife,
that for the year he would be away in Alba, if it happened during
that time that his foot slipped . . . or was he only imagining this?

"All I meant to say, Sweetie . . ."

She was presenting him with a shooting license, good only for
the year he would be away, valid only outside the continental limits
of the United States, but a shooting license definitely. He had managed up to now to remain strictly monogamous. As with most
married men, he had come to find that the only other women he
knew were the wives of their friends or the girls at the office. He
had not wanted to conspire against Laura with women who knew
her, or of her. He had not wanted to be searching himself after
the event for lipstick smudges and stray strands of hair. But
now . . .

"Oh, well—you understand," said Laura.

How was this to be considered? As an act of generosity? Or was
it that even of his derelictions—even of these, if any—Laura was
taking charge? He flushed suddenly with new irritation. "Good-
bye, Laura," he said. He was sure that Burling and Horanyi, for
instance, did not wait for their wives to tuck away a shooting

license in the valise. Or—was he being oversensitive? Unreasonable? It was impossible for him, any longer, to be sure. The slate must first be wiped clean. "Good-bye, Laura," he said. It could be, he thought, that he had long lost all knowledge of what his wife really was like.

In the dark of the airfield, on the borders of the city blacked out for war, the motors of the international plane tuned up. There was none, among the twenty passengers, who did not carry a briefcase. Government warriors all.

"Any second now," called Burling from up ahead. Tom Mercer, the "Little Adjutant," had pre-empted the seat beside Burling's and was squirming hotly in every direction. Ross and Horanyi, defying the plane steward's orders, were peering out at the edges of the black-out curtains. For the rest of the passengers this was a solemn moment, a departure into the unknown, the dangerous. But the Alba Gang—their eyes flashed, they nudged each other restlessly, they swore feverishly. "Let's go!" begged the Little Adjutant. "Let's go!"

It came to him, now in the moment of departure, that Alba was hostile country, after all. Not only for all that festered in its swamps, its jungles, on the very air. There was also "Vicente," that arch ironist, to think of—and the "buzzards from Chimboya." It had been predicted, so very freely, that not all of the Alba Gang would be coming back on their feet.

The clatter-clatter of the propellers merged into a single high drone. Then suddenly, with savage effort, like a footrunner drawing on every last cell and nerve, the plane tore down the runway. Ross, the scowling "Jack Dempsey," clasped his hands overhead like a winning prizefighter. Horanyi grinned widely, and bright little daggers flashed again from his three gold teeth. The Little Adjutant danced in his seat.

The plane shuddered.

It was in the air.

"Good show!" boomed Burling.

"We're off!"

"So long America!"

They gibbered with good feeling, were drunk on it. Alba—he wanted to call out—we're heading toward hostile country. But then it struck him, suddenly, that to a wanderer there was no hostile country but his own. It was from his own land alone that a wanderer was in flight.

In Alba, he hoped, he might finally stop feeling the cracks in his bones.

CHAPTER THREE

THAT humans should live like this, that it should be the whole measure of their lives, that they should know no other . . . Angrily, yet with a certain odd pride, he took it all in: the rank, littered mudflat, the half-hundred shanties of cane that waded in the ooze on their stilts, the gray-green contamination that overlay everything, even the waters of the Pacific, and the buzzards, the buzzards. . . . They roosted five and six together on the roofs and fences. They strutted in columns on the oyster-shell causeways. They sallied up to the very doorsteps, as placid, as commonplace, as pigeons in New York. Those black, hunchbacked chickens, compounded of offal and carrion. . . .

In the late afternoon sun, from the porch of their cane tenement —they had screened it immediately on arrival, like soldiers stockading themselves against an enemy—he was gazing out over Puerto Pacifico. A patch of wet desert it was, hardly a town. On three sides of the muddy square, connected with each other by causeways, stood the cane shanties. On the fourth was the crumbled seawall and the Pacific, here so scummy and ill-smelling, not believably the same pure sea that washed Hawaii and Tahiti and all those other sanded isles to the west. Into its heaving mass, pointing like a forefinger, went the long, splintered dock over which Alba sent out its fruits to a world which knew not its name: cocoa and coffee, oranges and bananas. It was only to load and unload that these sick stunted children of the Incas had burrowed here into the mud, sharing their lives with the buzzards. He must take photos of this place, dozens of them, and send them on to Laura. He wanted her to know how bad life could be. Or was it—was it, really, that he wanted her to know how much he, her husband, could put up with?

"See? I told you the *gringos* would come."

"Well? They have screened a porch, they have built a toilet. For *themselves.*"

Outside on the causeway, on the narrow white path of crushed oyster shell, stood two little men, neither of them quite five feet tall, their bronze-colored faces set in metallic folds. They wore patched denim trousers, no shirts or shoes. Their feet seemed to have grown a leather of their own. Either because they had not yet noticed him in the shadow of the porch, or because they did not realize how much Spanish he understood, they went on talking freely.

"Patience," said the eager one. Teofilo, it was, the porter with the resplendent Greek name, lover of God, whom they had just hired for the warehouse. "The *gringos* will bring us a new life."

"*Mierda,*" replied the sceptic. "I urinate on a new life."

"New hospitals," Teofilo went on, doggedly, "milk for the babies, land for the peons."

"And all for nothing? *Mierda.*"

Just beyond them lay the mudflat, a puree of poison in which floated kitchen swill, broken crockery, dead clams and smashed crabs, all the trash of the sea. At low tide, as now, it stank with decomposition. They said that if you went wading in it and had the misfortune to scrape your foot, it could cost you an entire leg within forty-eight hours. At high tide, though, the sea would rush in, and then Puerto Pacifico would become a Venice, a small and rotted Venice.

"Man, man," asked Teofilo, shaking his head, "what *do* you believe?"

"But why should they be so good to us? Why?"

Over by the seawall, on a patch of built-up land, stood a sick little papaya, the one tree in the port, as ragged as a worn feather duster. Daylong the children would bring it cups of water and watch over it like an invalid. And everywhere went the buzzards, complainant and hypochondriacal-looking, jerking their feet upward as from glue when they walked, but bursting into a grand, imperial spread of wing whenever they took to the air, as if blown out by an explosion from within. Pessimistically they clawed all day at whited animal bones and fruit hulls that had been picked over and abandoned a hundred times before. "In Alba," said Maria, the cook, "not even a vulture fills its belly." But they were respected citizens, protected by law, because in all the province there were no other garbage collectors. This morning, on the causeway, he had come across a flock of them obstinately barring the way. For a moment, wondering of what lost corpses their own evil flesh had been formed, he had hesitated. But then he had plunged ahead, on into their midst, thinking all the while that if it were Laura who had to face these carrion birds . . . He must remember, in his first letter, to describe it to her, but only the facts, without seeming to boast.

"Only tell me," the sceptic repeated, "why they're so good to us."

It was the question, thought Harmon, of a jungle dweller, of a man who has found that behind each seeming beneficence lies an adder, or a trap. They had lived for too many centuries, these children of the Sun God, under the heel of conquerors. They had found that living was only a state which must be endured until death. He was speaking, the poor wounded sceptic, from an ancient memory of his race.

But Teofilo, he the believer, the willing one, wagged his head eagerly. "The Mayor says—he read it in the newspaper—because of the Brotherhood of the Americas. What a rich expression!"

"I urinate on rich expressions."

To the right, high high in the heavens, edged with gold by the sun, was a great cloudlike mass which he knew to be the Andes Mountains. To the left was the Pacific. Between them, between these two great splendors, lay the province where he would dwell for the whole next year, a pit of mangrove swamps, choked plantations and a sick fertility. Everywhere, except in the salted mud of the port, something grew—wildly and malevolently, culturing poison and sickness. It was from danger, suppurating danger, that the Sun's children snatched fruits for the tables of the world, and died sometimes with the hand outstretched. The wealth that grew in the trees would go to others, never to themselves. From the labor of many thousands of these starved bodies, a few men would drink champagne.

But still Teofilo persisted, the innocent one, the hopeful one. "It said in the newspaper that the North American mission . . ."

"Mission? What are they, Teofilo—black Protestants?"

"It has nothing to do with religion."

"An oil company!"

"The newspaper said nothing about oil."

"Marines!"

"Where are the uniforms?"

"Then it has no sense. Why, why should they be so good to us?"

Wait, he wanted to say—I can explain it. There are some of us to whom the misery of any man is our own canker. There are some of us . . . But to a jungle dweller, he thought uneasily, it would not be simple to say. It would become involved in magniloquent phrases, like "Good Neighbor Policy" and "Brotherhood of the Americas." It would pass away into "rich expressions." For many years now he had taken it for granted that he was the keeper of every brother who suffered, so many years that he no longer knew how to explain why. He knew only that he wanted Teofilo, the trustful one, the innocent one, to be right. He did not want that innocence cheated.

It was just then that the commotion broke out. From above, from the second floor of the house, came an outcry from one of the servants and a stamping of feet. In his pidgin Spanish, Colonel Burling croaked stern commands. "Outside—*todos*—everybody! *Vámonos!*" There was a mass gallop across the floor, and the slamming of a door, so hard that the entire cane tenement shook.

Harmon opened the door to find a panicstricken horde rushing upon him, all the houseboys, the cooks, the maids. "*Víbora!*" screamed one of the houseboys, Jacinto, the one with the bartender curl on his forehead. "*Muy venenosa!*"

A snake, he translated mentally, very poisonous.

Marching down the stairway in corpulent dignity, absolutely resolved not to be routed into disorderly retreat, came Colonel Burling. "Where's Horanyi?" he demanded. "Where the hell is that snake charmer?"

"Up in Rosales."

"Damn it," said Burling, "damn it to hell."

"What *about* a snake?" asked Harmon. "Can I get in on it?"

Burling compressed his lips, chagrined obviously at a situation that had slipped beyond his, the commander's control. "A pretty little son of a bitch," he said, "all red and green. It's loose in my room."

Harmon found, oddly, that the notion exhilarated him immensely. "I'll tell you," he said, "if somebody'll find me a machete . . ." A ripple of excitement ran up and down his legs. He stood in football style with his hands on his hips, burning for action.

"Absolutely not," said Burling. "We'll wait for Horanyi."

"Hell," said Harmon, "I used to work the fruit boats. I watched how the stevedores used to do it." This was his baby, or had been in the long, long ago. He wanted action. Turning to Jacinto, he said, "Come on, *hombre,* get me a machete."

Still Burling shook his head. "Stay away from it. This is a direct order, Harmon. We'll wait for Horanyi."

But Jacinto came back, instantly, swinging a machete, the yard-long steel cutlass that was the tool-of-all-work for the peon, that cleared brush, plowed the earth, chopped firewood and was known even, in cantina brawls, to have hacked off heads. Hefting it in his hand, feeling himself to be all nerve and muscle, as not for long, as not for so many years, Harmon started for the staircase.

"God damn you, Harmon, come back!" called Burling.

"*Olé!*" cheered the house staff. "*Olé!*"

Up the steps he went, lightly but tensely, reminded all over again that he was an athlete, that he had a body which was equipped to spring, to grapple, to fight.

"Wait!" pleaded Burling from below. "I see Horanyi coming!"

He reached the top step, all flushed with combat now and not to be denied. "No soap," he called down to Burling. "This one's mine." Bit by bit, with his left hand, he edged open the door of Burling's room, holding the machete aloft all the while in his right hand. Suddenly he glimpsed it, just three or four yards beyond the threshold, a splendid jeweled creature lying at full length under a ray of the hard white sunlight that slanted in from the west window. Yes, a pretty little son of a bitch—in the words of Burling—all scarlet and emerald, a Christmas streamer and at least two feet of it. Suddenly he found himself under the gaze of its black diamond eyes.

Before it can strike, he thought, it will have to coil. And before it can coil . . .

He lunged forward then with the machete, all in one sweep, as he had done so often on a quarterback's signal.

"*Ai!*" they shouted up instantly from below, knowing from the crash of the machete on the floor that he had struck, but ignorant still of the outcome, and apprehensive.

The outcome was that on the far side of the broad steel blade a length of the Christmas ribbon quivered hopelessly. And on the near side a forked tongue fell forward desultorily between the hypodermic fangs. "All safe," he called.

Up the stairs, pressing excitedly behind Burling in his dignified strut, they surged.

"Harmon . . ." said the Colonel, glancing at the floor. "Why, Billyboy!"

"*Olé!*" cried the house staff. "A cheer for our snake killer!"

Grinning, he passed the machete back to Jacinto. He tried, suddenly, to recall whether Laura was any good about snakes. It was his recollection that she was not . . . He found, all at once, that he felt wonderful, absolutely wonderful!

CHAPTER FOUR

". . . UP ALONG the railroad are half a dozen other towns where we might have made our headquarters. But Puerto Pacifico, with all I've said about it, is considered the health resort of the province; the salt tides keep down malaria. . . ."

In the light of a naked and flickering bulb he sat in his room and wrote to Laura. It was a letter, he recognized, but fatalistically, which he could as well, or more suitably, be addressing to an acquaintance as to his wedded wife. At no time, it came to him, had he been able to write intimately to Laura. There was that which compelled him always, in his letters, to try to demonstrate that there was yet a different William Harmon from the one she knew too well, a self removed, autonomous and not at her call. Distance, always, had been something to throw about himself as a cloak, a guard—until he was back home again, and a target again for that keen and deadly gaze.

"One week here and the American bathroom gets to seem like a miracle. In Puerto Pacifico sewage disposal is anywhere at all, then wait for the tide to come and get it. Our water supply? Every morning a rusty tank car comes from Rosales, the provincial capital, and the whole town lines up to buy its day's ration. The Borgias could have served this water neat. We neglected at first to chlorinate also our drinking glasses. As a result we're all showing severe symptoms.

"For offices we have the second floor of the Customs House, the only wooden building in town. Our living quarters are a two-story tenement of split bamboo in which an attempt has been made to keep out bugs by plastering the inside walls with old newspapers. On the wall directly in front of me is a sports page with the news that a 'stupendous conflict' is foreseen in the coming basketball match between the Lorca Panthers and the Chimboya Lions as of May 9, 1936. I'm dying to know how it turned out. As of August three years ago Adolf Hitler is demanding the Sudetenland. How do you suppose *that* turned out? On my walls time stands still.

"Just above my cot is a gaudy print of a shrewd old fellow with a white goatee and piercing eyes who makes me think of a Mongolian khan. Cesar Montalvo, the Eagle of the Andes. I'm told by Hector Serrano, our new office manager, that Montalvo was the Abraham Lincoln and first 'modern man' of the Republic. He abolished Indian serfdom (only thirty years ago), built a wonder railroad up the face of the Andes, introduced labor laws, etc. To make sure his work would go on, he sent dozens of the best young men to be educated in England. Montalvo's 'eaglets,' they were called. As a result, most government people in the Republic speak English—in British style.

"Twenty years ago there was one of the periodic revolutions and Montalvo died pretty horribly. Today everybody worships him and there isn't a wall where his picture doesn't hang. A coincidence: next week his son, Marcos, is coming to the province as the new Governor, designated especially to work with us.

"The past couple of days I've been poking my head into the cane shanties of Puerto Pacifico. The possessions are just a little more than you'd find in the cave of an animal: a pot and a pan, a sandbox over which to fry the inevitable beans and plantains, sometimes a hammock for the father. Otherwise everybody eats, sleeps and lives on the bare cane floor. Most often the man of the house introduces his lady not as his wife but as his 'companion,' though four or five children might be festering about the place. It was explained to me tonight by one of our porters, an eager little fellow called Teofilo. A church wedding, he says, cost twenty pesos—about two dollars—and they don't often have that much ready cash.

"In every family there is somebody who is dying. You offer to get them to a hospital and they shrink away. Yesterday at Rosales, going through one of Alba's four hospitals, I saw why. There was just one common ward, and a dog kept running up and down the aisle. The cots consisted of wooden slats and thin straw ticking. Between a girl sick of malaria and a man dying of cancer, a woman had just delivered a child unattended. Another died of tuberculosis with her baby in her arms. Here, when a mother falls sick, her children all go to the hospital with her and settle down in and alongside the bed, chamber pots and all. Hospital records don't exist. The Sisters said they'd 'been eaten by cockroaches.' There was no thermometer. The pharmacy consisted of nine bottles stoppered with twists of paper.

"Yesterday I saw the funeral of a child. The father had knocked together the coffin from scrap lumber. He carried it through Rosales on his shoulder and at the cemetery dug the grave himself. In Alba three out of every five children die by the age of twelve. . . ."

The bulb overhead flickered rapidly and went out. But before he decided to go for his flashlight it came on again, but giving a dimmer light even than before, orange-colored and sodden. The trouble, Fred Ross had hazarded, was at the intake far upriver. One of these days, he had promised, he was going up there to have a look.

". . . Average life span altogether is under thirty, but these people are trained to carry remarkable loads almost from the time they begin to walk. Human burros. Yesterday we saw one of them haul on his back a safe that must have weighed three hundred pounds, but when he set it down he spat blood. We hit an all-time low in illiteracy when Teofilo, the porter I've mentioned, signed the pay-roll. We had to teach him to make an 'X'. He's had to support himself since he was eight, but he talks eagerly of the 'new life' that the Mission is going to bring to Alba and has begged for in-struction in how to write his name.

"Up in the Andes the full-blooded mountain Indians still dress in serapes and salad-bowl hats, as in the tourist folders. But the *mestizos* of the coast, of mixed Indian and Spanish blood, dress like any down-and-outer the world over. Pants; a shirt if they're rich. Their women wear calico dresses, nothing underneath.

"Why—you ask yourself—must human beings live like this? You clench your fist and want to hit somebody, whoever is responsible. Some people blame the border war, but I'm told that Alba was like this even before the invasion last winter. Others blame the cocoa plague of ten years ago when Alba lost its world markets, but I'm told that even in the best times, when the landowners lived in Paris like Argentine beef millionaires, the peons ate only beans and plantains. Right there, of course, is one reason. In the old Spanish tradition, the land is held by a very few rich men, chiefly by a young grandee called Ramón Manriquez who has his finger on practically everything in the province, and their peons grow crops for export, almost nothing for themselves to eat.

"I've mentioned Felix Horanyi, our economist and anthropologist who's done a lot of work before in backward societies. The trouble as he sees it is that these people have simply been left behind. The culture of Spain has died out and so has the Inca. What remains is a poor sick copy of the modern world. A simple culture, says Horanyi, is not necessarily inefficient. The tools of the Eskimo, within their range of technology, are very efficient. The steamships, railways and telegraph of the Republic are within the sphere of modern technology, but badly operated and maintained. (Like my weak, flickering electric light overhead, for instance.)

"The job, obviously, is to try to bring these people a little nearer to the standards of the modern world of which they form a part. At Lorca, where our plane landed last week, we had cocktails with the American consul. On his fourth Martini he asked, 'Why don't you people blow your million dollars on one good marble monument? It'll last a hell of a lot longer.' Well, we know very well that a million dollars is not going to bring that 'new life,' of which Teofilo talks, all by itself. But it can give a push in the right direction. From then on, as Burling always emphasizes in his talks with the nationals, it's up to them to keep the ball rolling.

"On one question, among the Alba Gang, I stand alone. I can't for the life of me make myself wear a tropical helmet. It reminds me too much of lion hunters, pukka sahibs, white conquerors. So I walk in the sun bareheaded, which is a source of great bafflement to our houseboys. A *gringo* without a helmet, they say, doesn't exist.

"Our biggest problem is bugs. There isn't a minute of the day when we're not scratching ourselves. Sandfleas, rat fleas, chiggers, hornflies, gnats, midges—everything that hops, flies, bites. And scorpions. We have a variety in Alba, a gray little chap, whose bite makes the tongue swell to three times normal and brings on rattling chills. But Serrano tells me consolingly that it's fatal only about half the time.

"Love. Kiss the kids for me.

"Will."

It was then finally that he remembered to write the line which was really the whole point of this letter: "P.S. This afternoon I killed a snake."

Undressing, he strung his khaki work clothes up on the rope which he had drawn across the room at the suggestion of Horanyi, that old tropical hand—keeping them well away at either end from the infested walls. From the metal hoop above his cot he pulled down his mosquito net (it hung then like a bridal veil) and tucked it in carefully, all around, under the mattress, leaving only a crevice for an entrance.

Switching off the light, he darted inside.

Instantly he felt a deep sense of shelter. It seemed to him that the gauze walls of his cell were a bar not only against insects, and scorpions and snakes as well, but against all other dangers from the present and woes from the past.

In Alba, this perilous swamp, he felt safe.

CHAPTER FIVE

"THANK you, Señor Associate Director," said the police colonel, bowing himself out. "A pleasure, Señor Associate."

Returning to his desk, Harmon picked up the title plate and gazed at it amusedly. *"Director Asociado,"* associate director, it was inscribed—in a ceremonious Spanish lettering all filigree and arpeggios. When Hector Serrano, the office manager, had presented it to him this morning, the foot-long pyramidal spar, varnished and glittering, he had thought it absurdly pompous. He had accepted it, and with elaborately Hispanic thanks to match, only because Serrano seemed to have his heart set on it.

His token of office. Actually, when Frank had conferred the title on him back in Washington, it had been largely as a form. There was a "line" for it in the Mission's table of organization and it had seemed as convenient to throw it to Harmon as to anybody. A half-fiction then. Yet ever since the plate had begun to sit on the edge of his desk this morning, it had been working a certain spell—as, for instance, with the police colonel, who had stalked in stiffly to demand an explanation in some matter where the Mission, or rather hotheaded Tom Mercer, was woefully in the wrong. But then, taking note of the resplendent little mace, the police colonel had clicked to attention. Morning-long other callers, official and unofficial, had directed themselves, after a hasty glance, not to "Señor Harmon" but to the "Associate Director." A joke—but one with which, in this land of formalisms, it was easier to fall in.

Setting the title plate down again, he plunged back to work, which consisted at the moment of preparing an abstract of the national labor code for guidance of the Mission.

It was not long after that the bullfrog basso of Colonel Burling began to *harrumph* on the other side of the cane wall. "God damn it, Ross," he said. "Three weeks in the province—and all you can show me is blueprints and profiles. I want to see something going up."

"Right!" snapped Tom Mercer, the Little Adjutant.

"Hell," Ross came back, ever the bullyboy, "how can I build you a road without a dragline? How can I move you water without pipe? You give me something to build with, Mister, and I'll build."

"*Me* give *you?* Mister, what the hell kind of an engineer are you?" Always when they felt bellicose they addressed each other as *Mister,* in a sham formality.

"Then it's up to those paper-pushers in Washington. Let 'em ship me a dragline, let 'em send me down five miles of good black pipe, and I'll do you a job."

"Jesus," muttered the Little Adjutant. "Sweet Jesus."

There followed a long throbbing silence during which Harmon could picture the blood flooding Burling's face until it would seem ready to jet from every pore. "Ross!" he roared finally. "There's a war on! You were told to make do with whatever you'd find in the field! God—damn—it!" He spoke each word of the oath separately and passionately. "God damn it to hell!"

What had become, Harmon wondered, of the fatherly comedian of Washington, the genial Falstaff, the urbane friend of the Young Marshal? In Washington everything had promised to be a lark.

"Look, Colonel," replied Ross stubbornly, "I been up and down the coast maybe a dozen times. Three times I flew all the way to Chimboya. This country is a poorhouse, Boss, not a warehouse."

Burling began to pace, and even in Harmon's office the floor rattled under that fierce tread. It was in an interlude of this danger-filled meditation that Serrano, the office manager, came in, short and gray-haired and portly, dressed as always in spotless white polo shirt and white trousers. "Two ladies, *Señor Asociado,*" he said. "They did not ask to see Colonel Burling, but in the circumstances . . ." He motioned archly with his head toward the cane partition.

"Who are they?"

"Do you know the Señora Serafina Bustamente? Our Mammoth of Mercy?" It was a substantial name indeed. With his hands Serrano puckishly described vast arcs about his chest and hips. "The Lady President of the Red Cross of Alba. Also . . ." now he smiled pleasurably ". . . the Señora Manriquez."

"Manriquez?" The name stirred a faint recollection. "Is she anything to the landowner?"

Serrano pursed his mouth with distate. It was evident that he was not on the side of grandees. "His wife. But a nice young lady all the same. Show them in?"

Señora Serafina Bustamente was large indeed, verging evidently on three hundred pounds, the kind of fat woman, fragrant and sparkling, of whom it is always said, "What a pretty girl she must have been." Sailing up like some low-lying galleon, the gray ringlets quivering on her head, she seized both of Harmon's hands emotionally in her own and, with a glance toward the title plate, exclaimed, "What an honor, *Señor Asociado,* to meet you! To think that you and your compatriots have come from so far to rescue our martyr province!"

He bowed. "An occasion even more glorious for me, your happy servant." In Spanish, he reflected, there would never be a simple way for saying *anything*. But already his glance had moved on to her who had lingered behind. She stood midway between the door and his desk, half-smiling but inattentive, as if waiting abstractedly for all the alarums to be done. In distinctly American style she wore a shirt-waist dress of cotton and black-and-white saddle shoes. Her shining black hair fell to her shoulders; it accentuated strongly the smooth pallor of her face.

"Ernestina!" cried the Mammoth of Mercy. "Come, my dove. Come meet the *Señor Asociado!*"

Rousing herself from her half-reverie, the girl came forward. "How do you do?" she asked, in English. There was no trace of accent.

"You're not American—*North* American?" he asked.

"Oh, no," she said, in a rather muted faraway voice. He was surprised that with hair so black she could have eyes so gray. Her cheekbones slanted tautly toward the temples in a way that gave her face a look of tension. "But I went to school in the States. Ann Arbor. I went to the University of Michigan."

The shirtwaist dress, the saddle shoes—out of this tropical swamp, suddenly, had walked a girl of the campus. But her skin was moon-pale and there hung about her an aura that was incongruously spectral.

"Untrue," the Mammoth of Mercy was exclaiming, "that all you *yanquis* have hearts of chromium!" Her plump hands were aflutter and from one of them broke a wild sparkle that was all rubies and diamonds. She was wearing a ring, he found on closer inspection, that was nothing short of spectacular: a cross of rubies set into a disk of diamonds, and the whole thing was the size at least of an American twenty-five-cent piece.

"Solidarity of the hemisphere," he murmured with what he judged to be suitable magniloquence. He brought forward two chairs.

The Lady President lowered her great bulk in the manner of cargo being winched into a hold. A relief shipment, she declared, had only just arrived from her good friends in Chimboya for the poor of Alba.

Since no suitable storage space was elsewhere available, secure against thieves and rodents, she was presuming to ask, in the name of the organization of which she had the honor for the sixth consecutive year to be leader, whether the Mission would permit her to store the crates momentarily in its own warehouse. This was a great presumption, naturally, but if the *Señor Asociado* could see his way clear to . . .

"Delighted," said Harmon, studiedly spare.

From the gray, thoughtful eyes came a flicker of amusement. He found himself pleased, instantly, that he had caused Ernestina Manriquez to smile. But a new outburst just then from beyond the cane wall made both ladies start.

"Harmon told you that?" rumbled the Colonel.

"Boss, I had a motor all lined up in Lorca. I could have had the water works in Santa Ana running again inside forty-eight hours. But Harmon nixed me."

"Why?"

"Some bushwa about politics."

"God—damn—it!" swore Burling, again in three separate volleys.

The ladies lowered their heads studiously. In his swivel chair Harmon braced himself for what was certain to follow.

"Harmon!"

"Yes?" he called back mildly.

"Come here!"

Dolefully he stood up. The office manager, he told the ladies, would arrange for porters to haul the crates from the dock. If there was anything else . . .

Once more the Mammoth of Mercy clutched his hands. "You marvelous, marvelous *yanqui!*" she cried. Again he sought out the gray, thoughtful eyes. For an instant they lit up with an answering smile.

"Hell," raged Burling, "why did you go and louse Ross up on that motor?"

"Hell," he replied, with a trace of japery—he could afford to, he was sure of his ground, "the motor was offered by General Imports."

"And?" Sweat buds had erupted all over Burling's bald crown.

This was something that Burling should know. It had been mentioned only a few days before in a flyer from the Embassy in Chimboya. "They're on the Ambassador's black list. Hell, they're Axis agents."

Burling's harsh stubby hands searched the air for something with which to grapple. "Embassy!" he exclaimed with rich scorn. "How the hell will I ever make a showing on this job if those cookie-pushers won't let me?"

The snub-faced Little Adjutant grimaced as though he had tasted something nauseating.

"Well," said Harmon patiently—he wondered why all this should be necessary, "the idea is that any money we spend with General Imports will go to finance Axis activities down here."

Over the round fleshy face went a look of woe. I didn't realize, thought Harmon, how much he resembles a baby, a large, unhappy baby. "Hell, hell," moaned Burling, "I have a showing to make."

It was a word that was on his lips constantly these days—*showing*. For a moment Burling panted with weighty thought, then aimed one blunt forefinger at Ross. "Tomorrow morning," he ordered, "you're putting on three hundred laborers."

"What for?"

"Line them up in Rosales. Start grading every goddam street and alley in town. Charge it up to malaria control."

"Mister," Ross protested, "those are dirt streets. They'll wash out at the first raindrop."

"I don't give a damn," said Burling. "Stop crossing me up." He whirled about instantly in his swivel chair, turning his back on them all.

"Window dressing?" asked Harmon thoughtfully, addressing himself to the imperious back.

"These monkeys love circuses. We'll give them one." Still Burling refused to face about. "Spades and wheelbarrows provided by us. We pay five pesos a day."

"Hmmm," said Harmon.

Now Burling swung about. "I'm sick of you no-boys!"

"I only wanted to say—" this was his department, he *had* to talk up—"that the code for common day labor . . ."

"Whose goddamn code?"

"The province's goddamn code." He snapped his answer back freely, exuberantly. This kind of sport, after all, was open to anybody, especially if you happened to be right. "It's six pesos a day for common labor."

On the bald crown the sweat buds burst and began to run in tiny streams. "All right," conceded Burling, "but I'm sick, sick, sick of you no-boys. Get out of here now, all of you."

At the door Harmon was struck by a thought. "Boss," he called back, "about lining up equipment . . ."

Burling stood up, full of thunderclouds.

"Would it make sense," Harmon asked, "if we were to work up a list of every engineering firm in the Republic and . . ."

Still Burling scowled.

"My notion—couldn't we draft a circular letter asking about any machines or materials they might be able to spare? For lease or sale, either way. We might even be lucky enough to pick up some black pipe and a dragline."

For one instant longer Burling held back. "Good show!" he boomed finally in that favorite phrase of his. "When can I see a draft of that letter?"

"By lunchtime?"

"Now," said Burling, "we're getting somewhere. The first real idea I've heard from anybody since we hit this hole."

Honestly, thought Harmon, it couldn't be *that* good, could it? Back in the States it would have been strictly routine.

"You're cooking, Billyboy," continued Burling, ever more lavish. "You're on the beam."

Well, he thought, *that* kind of wonder he could dream up any day in the week.

He found her alone in the warehouse—Señora Bustamente was waddling off in diminishing perspective to the dock—alone and gazing despairingly into one of the crates from Chimboya.

"Goodness," she said, fishing up something which turned out to be a tattered chiffon negligee. She let it fall back and fished up a second find, a black taffeta dinner gown that had split into long vertical ribbons. "For the poor of Alba," she murmured, shaking her head.

"With the compliments," he added quickly, "of Marie Antoinette."

She smiled and brushed a vagrant lock of her black shining hair back from her face. "Last month when we asked for food contributions some of them sent—I know you won't believe it, Mr. Harmon—cocktail biscuits and anchovy paste." She spoke in a strange but pleasing voice which was two voices: one muted and substanceless, the other tolling behind it like a bellbuoy in a mist. Though it was bright morning, the bouquet that came from her was shadowy, night-like. "You must despise us," she said suddenly, "the foolish, foolish rich."

He bethought himself instantly of Señora Bustamente's badge of office, the Red Cross ring that was fashioned of rubies and diamonds, but made no answer.

Ernestina Manriquez turned back to the crate. "Do you know," she asked, looking away all the while, "how many banana trees my husband owns in Alba? In Alba alone? Two hundred thousand. And when I think of all the cocoa and coffee and oranges . . ."

A strange girl. "It troubles you?" he asked.

Her answer was not direct. "These countries," she said, "are so full of extremes. There's a cruelty down here that you North Americans can't really understand. Rich toward the poor. Big toward the little. White toward the Indian." She faced about again, brushing a fallen tress back over her shapely head with her hand. "Do you know these countries well, Mr. Harmon?"

"Only the ports. And what I've read."

"When I think back," she said, glancing at him all the while, seeming to plead for his favor, "life in the States looks so wonderfully innocent. So gentle. The football games—the chocolate sodas—the juke boxes. In the States people go on playing for so much longer. Have you noticed at all what kind of clothing our children wear here in Alba? So few of them have children's things. At seven and eight they're grown-ups already—grown-ups in little sizes."

She must spend a good deal of time by herself, he hazarded, alone and in thought. She was so unexpectedly keen, and so self-contradictory. Saddle shoes—moon-white face. Campus girl—lady of sorrows. She lived in one world and dreamed of another. And she was trying so very hard, it seemed, to win approval from him. She was begging him not to think of her as belonging with the Conquistadores.

Her glance, he noted all at once, had darted toward the open doorway. Like a galleon fighting heavy seas, Señora Serafina Bustamente was making her way back along the oyster-shell causeway. "The Mammoth of Mercy," he murmured.

Ernestina Manriquez smiled; it was as though a moon-ray had lit the slanted cheekbones. "How ever did you know *that?*"

"I've heard."

"Oh, poor Serafina," she said with a mingled fondness. "They started it up in Chimboya, the town wits. For years now they've played a game of pinning tags on her. The Gargantua of Good, the Leviathan of Love, things like that."

"Doesn't she ask for it?"

"The cross of rubies? I suppose. But her husband's dead and her daughters are all married off in other countries and she's terribly alone. And in her poor silly way she's trying dreadfully hard to be a modern woman. You have to know Serafina. She could surprise you sometimes."

"How?"

Abruptly the huge bulk of the Lady President corked the doorway. *"Señor Asociado!"* she cried.

He bowed deeply.

In a melodious torrent the Lady President poured out her thanks for his unstinting co-operation in the humane endeavors of the Red Cross of the Martyr Province. The *Asociado,* beyond all expectation, had proved himself great-hearted and noble, humanitarian and Christian. "And Ernestina," she added, in a sudden turn that was astonishingly different, "the boy is no pain to look at! Quick, Ernestina, wrap him up!"

Back in his office, he plunged to work on the circular letter of which Burling had made so much. From the tail of his eye he caught a glitter of the title plate. Associate Director? Well, why not?

CHAPTER SIX

A SIGNBOARD over the gateway read, "Palace of the Provincial Government," but the red-painted decaying planks of the façade were reminiscent rather of a waterfront warehouse. Here and there on the walls, mingling with such bold patriotic slogans as "Long live the Republic!" and "Death to the Invader!" had been chalked obscene words and drawings of nude women. The Palace served also as quarters for a company of Carabineros, the national police, and a number of these, their rifles stacked, lounged within the courtyard. They wore enormous straw hats and loose white uniforms that were like slept-in pajamas. A bugler, practising a high run, blew sour notes over and over again. A tall young Negro, one of the few Harmon had seen in Alba, kept firing unsuccessfully with a slingshot at the buzzards.

Beneath the soft Spanish intonation, the Governor's English was precise and elegant. He had been educated in England, it developed, and served there later in the Republic's legation. "Gentlemen," he apologized, as he seated Burling and Harmon in two rickety kitchen chairs alongside his desk, "the invaders did not leave us much in the way of furnishings."

"Mr. Governor," brayed Burling with the old heartiness, "we didn't come to Alba to drink pink tea."

"I fancy not," smiled the Governor.

On the scratched bruised desk was an electric push bell, but lid and button were gone, leaving only the naked copper spring. All about the room ran open plank shelves upon which lay brown-paper packets, each tied with a red string to which had been affixed a cardboard tag. It looked like laundry long unclaimed.

"Yes," sighed the Governor as he followed Harmon's gaze, "our filing cabinets." But, amid all the dust and decay, he sat clean and fresh in a suit of sand-colored linen. He appeared to be in his early forties. Here and there his brown wavy hair was flecked with high-lights of pure gold; his eyes were a tawny hazel. The Montalvo ancestry, evidently, had stemmed from the north of Spain, remaining unmingled still with Moorish or Indian strains. In New York or London the Governor would have been exactly right.

On the wall behind him, Harmon observed, hung the inevitable portrait of Cesar Montalvo. They seemed, on the surface, to be of two different races, the Mongolian khan and his exquisite Western son. Yet, continuing to study the image on the wall, Harmon found that the Oriental expression of the father lay wholly in the old-fashioned tufts of white mustache and goatee. Piercingly, grandly, but humorously also, the shrewd eyes looked down from the wall, taking charge of everything about. To have had such a father, thought Harmon, with a flare of the old longing. That genial emperor. Aloud he remarked, "One sees as many ikons of Cesar Montalvo here as of Christ."

The Governor nodded somberly. "The parallels are more than one. Do you know how my father died, Mr. Harmon?"

"There was an uprising, I've been told. The landowners and the clericalists . . ."

"They took him from the Palace and tied him to mules. For two hours they dragged him about Chimboya, in the sun. Somebody thought finally of asking, 'Is he dead?' He opened his eyes, Cesar Montalvo, and said, 'No, you hoodlums, and he will never be dead.' They dragged him to the public gardens and made themselves a fine bonfire and . . ." It was an episode which must have crossed the Governor's mind many times these past twenty years, but still it caused him to shudder. "The famous 'Spanish fury.' Why do we do such things? It must stem, I suppose, from our deep Catholic tradition. Over and over we are compelled to repeat the Crucifixion. Study the lives of every hero whom we Latin Americans have ever had. Sucre, San Martín, Bernardo O'Higgins. Even Simón Bolívar, the greatest of all. In their life time we torment them. In their death we deify them."

Behind the young politico, thought Harmon, lurked a moody poet. It was in the tradition—so many of the *Presidentes* had in their youth written quatrains.

Outside, in the courtyard, the ambitious bugler reached a soaring trill and broke. "Well," said the Governor in an instant change of mood, "you did not come here for a philosophic treatise."

"Very educational," boomed Burling.

With his handsome gilded head, Marcos Montalvo gestured toward a window at his right, toward the ragged, dusty palms of the public gardens, toward the huddle of sagging shanties that was the provincial capital. "When I accepted this appointment," he said, "it was as a debt which a son owes his father. If we can do something now to continue his work, to change Alba from a garbage heap to a land where men may live with some dignity . . ."

"Exactly," said Burling.

". . . and where children may be reared with some hope of a future rather than a coffin by the age of twelve . . ."

"Yes!" said Burling.

The Governor leaned forward across his desk. "I must warn you,

Colonel Burling, that Alba also has its *bad* elements. Selfish, greedy, feudal. Hostile to anything North American."

Vicente, thought Harmon, that savage ironist.

"They will try to sabotage everything you do," said the Governor, "steal your supplies, spread vicious rumors." With his even, well-shaped teeth, the Governor bit off a snip of fingernail. "When you run into that sort, please let me know."

Outside, coincidentally, the bugler blew a flourish that was like a call to arms.

"Good show!" said Burling, and they all laughed together.

Now from the breast pocket of his belted khaki jacket, the garment that was the uniform of the old tropical tramp, Burling drew a sheaf of papers. "Mr. Governor," he said, "the projects as worked out in Washington and Chimboya are excellent. But you local people are naturally a little closer to the realities. I would be very happy if you and your people would review these plans and criticize them in any way you see fit."

"Honored. I may keep this?"

Burling passed over the papers, then slouched low in the rickety kitchen chair and stared thoughtfully up at the cracked, stained ceiling. "The bulk of our operations," he said, "will be carried out directly by our own technicians. But there will be many smaller operations in which we will want to encourage, well, local enterprise. Repair of public buildings. Construction of furniture. And so forth. On contract." Into Burling's voice had come a sly ring. "Naturally, we don't want any of these contracts getting into the hands of the 'bad elements.' You yourself, I know, will be best able to advise us on which persons are deserving and which . . ."

Harmon winced. It was such a crude, naked insinuation: name your dummies, Mr. Governor . . .

"The funds," broke in Montalvo, "are a public trust." Over his face had come a quizzical look.

"Oh, nothing out of the way!" said Burling. "Of course not. A sacred public trust." The chair creaked heavily as he rose from it.

"All my life, Mr. Governor, I've dreamed of being able to give a leg up to my fellow man. This is it. I would like some day to be remembered as 'Burling of Alba.' And you, I know . . ."

"Either that," said the Governor, "or these poor devils might just as well cut their throats."

They drove in silence down the rutted highroad of Rosales, on which lay the stark whited jawbones of animals and the hulls of fruits, on which the buzzards, as always, did their melancholy cakewalk. Here and there, alongside the road, cocoa beans had been laid out on immense canvas tarpaulins to dry in the sun. From the beans came the sour odors of fermentation. In time, hulled by the cleaner fingers of machines, powdered and packed into charming cartons, they would find their way to the tables of the world, a steaming confection or bonbons for the tongue. But here, lying by the thousands in the sun, the beans looked only like the droppings of small animals.

On they drove, past the crews of laborers who hacked and filled the hummocky earthen streets to bring them into order, and then, beyond Rosales, into a gray flat plain, so supine and female, stretched out as for ravishment. From the thick knotted covers of the mangrove swamps in the distance rose flights of birds—herons and ibises and egrets, unbelievably white and pure and elegant, the only clean things that had yet shown themselves in this contaminated land. How, Harmon wondered, did they manage to remain so unsullied?

"Boss," he asked finally, his eyes still fixed ahead on the road, "wasn't that a foul ball?"

"What was?" Drowsily.

"That business about contracts. Offering Montalvo the *mordida*, the bite."

Burling, coming awake from his drowse, chuckled. "Billy," he said, "there isn't one single operator in a hot country who doesn't earmark ten per cent of gross profits for the *mordida*. Otherwise you never get your import licenses—your tax reports are put on the pan—you get smothered under currency regulations."

"Yes, yes," said Harmon impatiently. "I wasn't born yesterday. But in the case of Montalvo . . ."

Burling patted him indulgently on the shoulder—and it was so irksome, this heavy cunning, that he came close to pushing Burling right back in the face. "They will talk day and night about their sacred idealism, Billyboy, but the hand is always there."

Tricks, tricks . . . It was supposed to represent sophistication, this kind of cunning, but he had always thought that it looked more like fear. He had met, as a lawyer, many other such sophisticates: business schemers and Broadway characters and racing touts, even gangsters. And they had struck him in some ways as remarkably naïve. Everywhere around them they saw a jungle full of dangers, these toughies, and their money was always up to buy their way out. Of course he had fears of his own—oh, he certainly did— but not these fears, other ones. In matters like these he was willing to take his chances.

"I tell you, Billyboy," went on Burling, still bubbling with self-appreciation, "that if you've helled around the tropics as long as I have . . ."

"Maybe," Harmon broke in wearily, "you've helled around too long."

Burling's reply was most surprising. He remained silent.

As he climbed the steep, shaky staircase of the Customs House he heard two voices arguing in Spanish—one with the orotund periods of the Andes highlands, the other with the cockfight argot of the Caribbean which dropped all final *S*'s.

"*Si, vo' conozco bien, vosotro' lo' mono',*" the Little Adjutant declared. "I know you monkeys inside out. You can't pull a holdup like that on *me*."

"Absolutely," was the answer. "Now go and tell your father I want to talk with him."

"The guy in charge of payrolls is me."

"Come, come, where is your father?"

The dispute, Harmon ascertained, was taking place in his own office. He opened the door to find Tom Mercer ensconced imperially in the swivel chair and declaring, with narrowed eyes, in a manner patently borrowed from Burling, his idol, "Fellow, I give you just five seconds to chase yourself the hell out of here."

"Dear me," said the visitor. He was a large man, Harmon observed, with a head of wild gray hair. He wore a wrinkled suit of tan cotton with sagging pockets, no tie. In his hand, like a burning scepter, he held a black and immensely long cheroot. A king of the hobos, thought Harmon.

"Ah," asked the visitor, taking note of Harmon's entrance, "are you somebody with authority?"

The Little Adjutant bolted up. "Mister . . ." he began.

"Tom," said Harmon, "sit down. Rest your gums." Inquisitively he turned toward the visitor and introduced himself. The visitor accepted his outstretched hand with a kind of royal indulgence. "Hidalgo is my name," he replied. "Lawyer by profession."

Yes, thought Harmon, he had seen the type hanging about the corridors of the magistrate's courts, seedy and rapacious, carrying their offices in their hats. But "hemisphere solidarity," in this instance, demanded politesse. "Señor Hidalgo," he said, "we're colleagues."

"Oh, splendid, splendid," said Hidalgo, seating himself. Out of everything he gathered a kind of private amusement which Harmon found irritating.

"He keeps yapping something about social laws," muttered Tom Mercer. "What the hell, we're giving away a million bucks free to the monkeys as it is."

Monkeys, thought Harmon—"our brothers of the Americas." Inquiringly he turned toward Hidalgo, becoming aware simultaneously of a strong bouquet of alcohol.

"Once upon a time," began Hidalgo, crossing his legs elegantly and speaking in the manner of a story-teller to very young children, "there was a Republic of Monkeys. Now it was the practice in this Republic to work the poor little creatures from dawn to dusk and to reward them for their labors with a little shred of coconut for each. There came finally a great revolution. It was decreed that henceforth the *monkeys*"—he grinned all the while in the direction of Tom Mercer—"that they could not be worked more than eight hours each day, so that they would last a little longer. Also, that when they fell sick, they would receive their shred of coconut just the same, for a little while. All this, Señor Harmon, went by the name of the 'social laws.'"

"Come," said Harmon annoyedly, "let's get down to cases."

Hidalgo's face darkened. "Well," he said, "when your day laborers were paid off today at Rosales, four of them were docked for sickness. The labor code permits three days a month of sick leave with pay."

"Hell," demanded the Little Adjutant, "what's that got to do with the Mission?"

Harmon disregarded him. "Señor Hidalgo," he asked, "just what is your own interest in this matter?"

"My fee!" declared Hidalgo with a broad grin which disclosed remarkably white teeth. "For intervening as counsel to the monkeys, I stand to be rewarded with a substantial molecule of their shreds of coconut."

By nobody, thought Harmon angrily, had he ever been made to feel so foolish—not even by Laura. "Seriously . . ." he urged.

Hidalgo drew brusquely on his cheroot. "The monkeys," he said, "were threatened with jail. They are too frightened to talk for their rights. Reason enough?"

"All right," said Harmon. "We'll abide by the labor code."

Instantly Mercer bolted up.

"Cool off," said Harmon. "This isn't even debatable. It was so agreed by Washington when the program was drafted."

Without a word the Little Adjutant stalked out of the room.

"You yourself," said Hidalgo cheerfully, "are the nicer kind."

Harmon sat down in his swivel chair, his throne of office. "Of what?" he asked, taken in by the urbane smile, momentarily off-guard.

"Imperialist."

Instantly Harmon flushed. "Colleague," he said, "that isn't very friendly."

"Come, come, *Señor Asociado*," said Hidalgo with an ironic glance at the title plate which sat so pretentiously on the edge of the desk, "you are not really pretending that you've come to Alba for purposes of altruism."

That rancid boozy cynic . . . "Well," asked Harmon defensively, "what's wrong about building hospitals and purifying water?"

From one of the sagging pockets of his jacket, Hidalgo extracted a packet of the cheroots. "I don't think you'll want one," he said. Harmon shook his head and Hidalgo lit up with a hand that quivered slightly. "In the olden days," he said, "the Conquistadores came with the cross and the sword. Nowadays they come with hospitals and water. Otherwise the purposes are much the same. Have I been rude enough, *Señor Asociado,* or would you care to hear more?"

There was a lilt to his voice which made of the title something ponderously absurd, absolutely spurious, which turned it into an epithet even more insulting than anything else Hidalgo had said. Irritatedly, protectively, Harmon drew the title plate in closer to himself. "This is your country," he said. "Say what you please."

"*Señor Asociado* . . ." It was insupportable, this open mockery; now Harmon shuffled the title plate down the desk and into his lap, out of sight altogether. ". . . You talk of rehabilitating this miserable little swamp and I'll wager some of you are even sincere about it."

"Is that wrong?" He was sure that on other terms, desperate as he had been, he would not have come here. He had begged Frank over and over to assure him that it was "clean," and Frank had assured him it was.

"Unhappily," said Hidalgo, "you can't possibly succeed. This kind of thing has been tried before, you know, and in a large way, *really* large."

In spite of his resolve to remain aloof, not interested, he found himself drawn in. "Are you talking of Cesar Montalvo?"

Again Hidalgo drew on the gnarled cheroot—that boozy shyster. "What defeated Montalvo," he said, but deeply earnest all at once, even melancholy, "was an old tradition, a terrible one, something stronger even than himself. The tradition of the Conquistadores, I mean. Of Pizarro and Cortez. Plunder. That these lands were to be used for nothing but conquest and plunder. It has been going on for a long, long time, you know. Into the fourth century. Now and then a great spirit comes along who tries to smash that tradition. The trouble—there are simply not enough Cesar Montalvos in these countries to go around. That part of it is *our* fault. I admit it freely. We breed far more Pizarros than Montalvos among ourselves. But, one way or another, the moment your Mission is gone the jungle will start growing back over everything you have done."

Angrily, defiantly, Harmon stood up. The title plate slipped from his lap and clattered to the floor, but he let it lie there. He wanted no part of it—not just now. He didn't even need it. "So we're here on a fool's errand?" he asked.

"Oh, no," said Hidalgo, genial again. "Absolutely not. No Conquistadore is ever really a fool. In the end he manages pretty well to carry out his purposes. Yes, even the Conquistadores of the second class."

Again that scornful phrase. Somewhere, Harmon felt, he had heard it before. . . . "Well," he asked, trying to return scorn for scorn, "tell me what purposes the Mission is serving."

"Oh, you'll have to give me a little time to study that," replied Hidalgo, again with that satanic grin which showed the fine teeth, showed them as some inner part of the man untouched by wear and corruption. "My guess is that your Government sent you here for one set of purposes. You undertook, as individuals, to come to this stinking little swamp for another set of purposes—your private ones."

Damn him—the clever shyster! Damn him! How did he know so much? It was as though Hidalgo had focussed an X-ray machine upon him suddenly and picked out relentlessly every single one of the cracks and scars in his bones that he wanted to forget. Overnight, in Alba, he had been presented with worth, importance, adequacy. And now this rumpot was trying to take everything away from him.

Defiantly, Harmon bent down, retrieved the title plate and, with a clatter, set it back on the edge of his desk.

"I'll tell you," went on Hidalgo, again with that false urbanity—was there no stopping him?—"what the Temperate Zone exports to the tropics is generally its failures. Why should a man, a *successful* man, want to come to a place like this—to the heat, the bugs, the discomforts of every kind? The truth is that successful men do not want these jobs. They are left open, everywhere in the world, to the failures. And the failures take them because it is only here, in countries like these, alongside people even weaker and sicker than themselves, that they can come to feel like men. And to receive rewards all out of proportion to their abilities. When I think, for instance, how many pygmies went out over the centuries to rule India . . . !"

Damn him—damn him!

Stiffly, Harmon strode away from his desk to the window. Blankly he looked out over the mudflat. How much more did he know—this rummy clairvoyant? For a moment Harmon's gaze was caught by the curious play of two buzzards on a rusty rooftop. Methodically, with unwonted delicacy, they kept crossing their long slim beaks—like fencers with foils. It was their manner of lovemaking, he had been told. Instantly, then, he bethought himself of a certain savage characterization. "The buzzards from Washington and the buzzards from Chimboya . . ." Oh, yes, and that other scornful phrase too—"the Conquistadores of the second class . . ." Now he was beginning to remember. It was something that he would be able, in a moment, to use.

Boldly Harmon wheeled about. "Pygmies?" he repeated. "You apply all that to me?"

"Oh, please!" exclaimed Hidalgo. "Present company excepted. Always. I apply it to the boy who was so rude to me a few minutes ago. My guess is that he learned his Spanish by bossing labor gangs in Puerto Rico. True?"

"I don't know." To this fly-blown shyster he would concede nothing, absolutely nothing.

"You will agree"—again with that dazzling white grin—"that back in the United States there would be no such opportunities for him to boss other people, certainly not two or three hundred of them."

Mercer—in the States? He would find his level in life as a shipping clerk probably. Or a gas station attendant. This had to be admitted, but not openly. And Burling?—he was forced to ask himself. And Fred Ross? And what of the Mission itself—which so far, in truth, looked good only from the outside?

But he would admit nothing. Stubbornly he gripped his title plate, held it so tightly that the sharp wooden edges dug into the palms of his hands.

"Cortez and Pizarro . . ." the man went on. *"They,* at least, fought their way into totally unknown country. Against spears and poisoned arrows. That much, at least, must be said for them. But as regards the *new* ones, the invaders of the present day, the Conquistadores of the *second* class . . ." Hidalgo shook his head with sad affability, broke off in mid-sentence and made to go.

Now, thought Harmon. "One moment, please." he asked. Hidalgo, turning about, cast upon him a look that was utterly despondent. "Does your Christian name," asked Harmon, "happen to be Vicente?"

Hidalgo's hand, in the act of raising his cheroot to his lips, paused in mid-air. "Is that of any significance, *Señor Asociado?"*

"Well," said Harmon acidly, "you write very interesting letters."

Hidalgo gave it an instant of thought. Then, through the despondency, there came a flash again of the white, brilliant smile. "I'm considered important enough to be spied upon? *Señor Asociado,* this is very flattering."

This time the dart fell against Harmon impotently. "It's wartime," he said, "and all foreign mail goes through the hopper."

"Well, what do you make of me, Harmon? I'm a fascist?"

"Some people put it that way."

There was a burst of deep, pained laughter. "Oh, my dear young Colossus, I am about as important as a mosquito. Not the anopheles, mind you. No—a non-toxic variety." He stopped laughing abruptly and stood swaying. "Take my word for it, Harmon."

What a disturbing man! The ruin, it must be, of something once much larger, much grander. Of what?

"This much you will have to grant, Harmon. If you've read my letters carefully, you must know that I have as little use for our own native buzzards as for the imported variety. I don't lay everything against the *gringos.* Not everything. In any case, let me thank you for your kindness in the matter of the sick pay. You *are* one of the better ones."

"A better buzzard?"

Hidalgo shook his head with a certain sweet ruefulness. "We will be living together in this swamp a whole year, Harmon. I would just as soon be friends."

As though leaving this for Harmon to think about, he did not offer his hand. Instead, he turned and went away down the narrow cane hallway, lurching slightly as he went, touching first one wall and then the other with his shoulders—but carrying himself, nevertheless, with a kind of magnificence.

A Danton, thought Harmon—a drunken Danton who no longer believed in anything, not even what he was fighting for. A man on his way to some kind of doom.

PART TWO: *Ernestina*

CHAPTER SEVEN

He was waked before dawn, in his cell of gauze, by phonograph music that came mournful but loud from one of the bars across the mudflat. To an ancient and stately measure from the courts of Spain, a piercing tenor sang of the vastness of the world and the smallness of man—of wind and rain, and man's own nakedness.

Across Harmon's room swept a white scythe of light. The revolving beacon of the lighthouse, signalling in a ship. Wednesday— therefore it would be the *Relampago,* the feeble little sidewheeler with the grandiose name *Lightning.* It would be bringing mail, newspapers, supplies and also Walt Anderson, who was joining the Mission as agricultural officer, after all. Things were going better these days—the circular letter had produced a few results—but Anderson would be a much-needed addition all the same.

In the next sweep of light, Harmon held aloft his wrist watch. Not yet five o'clock. Dawn would not come until six, but then *precisely* at six, and almost full-blown, as every day here on the Equator. But already he felt wide-awake and fresh, ready for whatever might come, not, as in New York, wincing against the daylight. He yanked the mosquito netting up heartily from under the mattress and found his flashlight on the camp chair alongside his bed. Then he shook out his bedroom slippers carefully—for scorpions—and switched on the overhead light.

Directly above him, on the second floor, a cot rattled heavily, as if on the march across the room. Burling, it was, engaged in the reflections of waking. All at once his tuba voice blasted out a sardonic reveille. "Up, up you rascals! Rise and shine—and give out that glory, glory!"

"Up yourself!" mocked Harmon. Through the thin cane walls could be heard the characteristic sounds—he knew them so well by now—that marked the waking of all the others. Ross groaned and stumbled about heavily, like a blinded Samson. Horanyi cursed cheerfully in several languages. Tom Mercer took brisk tight steps in all directions.

Piece by piece Harmon drew his clothing down from the line, shook out each garment separately, and dressed. He washed his face in a bowl of gray water. Again on guard against scorpions, he shook out the towel before wiping his face. Never again, he thought, would he take for granted that safe hygienic world of the Temperate Zone, where enemies did not always lie waiting, where every chink and crevice was not an ambush. Here in this over-rich soil, in this incubator air, everything grew with equal fervor: cocoa and microbes, bananas and bacteria, coffee and vipers. If only a frost would once swoop down and sterilize this moist sick warmth . . .

He stretched cozily, yawning aloud, and walked over to the window that was merely a square gap in the cane wall. Over by the dock, torches and flamepots tore holes in the night. At their sandboxes the foodhawkers were broiling fish and brewing coffee. A toylike locomotive of the narrow-gauge railroad squealed and whined as it tugged a string of latticed box cars along the dock. From all sides of the town, men wearing white trousers and, on their heads, burlap sacks in the style of the Arab burnoose—the stevedores of Puerto Pacifico—converged along all the causeways toward the sea. They called tired, sad greetings to each other in the dark.

In the commotion of the ship's docking they heard an American voice call them by name, but it took a moment longer to pick out Walt Anderson at the rail of A-deck.

"Welcome," called Burling, "welcome to the glorious and invincible province of Alba, pearl of the Pacific."

Anderson raised a hand over his eyebrows, visor-like, and surveyed the mudflat on which already the sun was swiftly rising. "From where I stand," he said, "it looks like the anus of the universe."

"From anywhere you stand," said Harmon.

Anderson waved a canvas sack which he said contained their mail—he had picked it up at the Consulate in Lorca. Then he turned to a girl alongside him at the rail, a stocky and breasty maid with broad Indian features, and said something which caused her to giggle convulsively. "How do you like my sweater girl?" he shouted down. Lavishly he patted her on the rump. The girl ran away laughing. Anderson, gazing after her voraciously, tick-tocked his head in time to her retreating haunches.

"Mister," called Burling, "I hope you took precautions."

"Three of them!" replied Anderson with a wild leer.

Between Washington and Puerto Pacifico, thought Harmon, a transformation had overtaken the weatherbeaten, Gothic little farmer. In Washington all his talk had been about seed, soil, livestock. In Washington when he had talked to the stenographers, he had mumbled diffidently, his eyes averted. And now, making his entrance into the tropics, he was cavorting like a supercharged goat.

But then again, as Anderson came down the gangplank, he was buzzing with plans. "Colonel," he said, "I laid over in Washington an extra week so's I could start some seed shipments down. Air priority too."

"Good show."

"Also, I'm getting six acclimatized stud bulls from Ecuador. Holstein crossed with Cebu. For that demonstration farm, I'll want plenty of land. Do I get it?"

"Write your own ticket."

"I hear there's some first-class sisal in these parts. We'll be making hemp inside of three months. Rhodes sends you a short-wave radio as his personal gift. I understand you heroes have been having yourselves a time."

Grouchily, Burling opened his shirt. Across his chest flamed a furious rash, red nodules topped by amber pinpoints. "How about a medical officer?" he demanded. "When the hell is Rhodes sending us a doctor?"

"He was a new prospect, a fellow I knew in Costa Rica. And a ball of fire, too. Meanwhile Rhodes says to make do with the *nacionales,* the local boys."

"The *nacionales!*" spat Burling. "Cover it with banana leaves, *Señor Director*. Make a paste of cocoa powder and cowflops, *Señor Director*. God Almighty!"

"Live in the tropics," said Anderson placidly, "and you itch. God's law." Gazing at the mudflat, its tidal waters now pinked by the sun, he sighed with an odd contentment, then demanded, "Mister, does a man get any breakfast around here, or do you just throw him to the buzzards?"

After breakfast—a tumbler of orange juice for each, but only unbuttered bread and a gummy, bitter coffee—they spread out on the porch with their letters from home. "Hell, hell . . ." Ross kept mumbling as he combed through a thick, blue-tinted packet, "hell, hell." Burling glanced perfunctorily at an envelope with a Brazilian stamp—from the wife he had shelved in Rio?—and turned away to a batch of newspapers from Lorca. He made his way through them haltingly, humming out war dispatches from places with names like Bougainville and Owen Stanley Range. . . . Horanyi, stretched out in a deck chair, held a sheet of pink-tinted stationery before him at arm's length and yawned. . . . What did she look like, wondered Harmon, the wife who bored Horanyi so? And the wife Burling had misplaced in Rio? And that other wife, Ross's, who alone was sighed for? What was it anyhow that joined women in marriage to men who would always be away, to seafarers, engineers, commercial travelers and tropical tramps? They were joined, such husbands and wives, only to be sprung anti-magnetically apart —in marriages to be carried on at a distance, save for the sporadic homecomings for purposes of reproduction. They must come each year to feel ever more abandoned, the Penelopes, ever more the mothers of their children and ever less the wives of these eternal runaways.

Tom Mercer, who alone had no letters from home, sat placidly on a stool alongside Burling and gazed out over the mudflat, a faithful Fido. Anderson, all the while, walked about the house, inspecting everything and shouting with good-natured outrage, "God Almighty! God Almighty!" Several times he stole into the kitchen and said or did things which caused the cooks and maids to shriek.

"Why," she wrote, "did we ever let you do it, darling? The food, the water, your living quarters! And to have to put up with that for all of a year. Is the work as important as Frank Rhodes seems to think? Good Neighbor—yes, I know. But it's all still vague to me, to be perfectly truthful, as to just why the Government had to send all of you off to an out-of-the-way place like Alba in the midst of a world war. Willikins, we certainly don't want you coming home a physical wreck. The whole thing seems to have been set up so hastily and thoughtlessly. Promise me—won't you?—that if it turns out to be more than you really care to put up with, or anybody would, that you won't have any false pride about resigning. If it's going to be a wild-goose chase anyhow . . ."

He was brought to by an all-out blast from Colonel Burling that caused the buzzards outside on the causeway to leap five into the air together. "God—damn—it!" stormed Burling. "Damn it to hell and back!"

"Jesus," muttered the Little Adjutant faithfully. "Sweet Jesus."

Wonderingly, Harmon looked up. Burling, without a word,

handed him one of the Lorca newspapers, holding it between thumb and forefinger like a contaminated object.

"Ministerial Committee Reviews the Alba Program"—ran a bold headline across the front page. It was a deftly phrased communiqué from the cabinet committee to which the Mission had been accredited. While the projects were all admirable in intent, stated the Ministers, many had been drawn in Washington at a distance of four thousand miles from the scene. It was their intention therefore to order some thoroughgoing revisions. Larger sums would be allocated to establishing new industries and repairing public structures. The technicians, further, would be ordered to draft plans immediately for the draining of the mudflat in Puerto Pacifico and . . .

"Hell," said Burling, "if those monkeys think I came down here to be their water boy . . ."

"The jerks," said the Little Adjutant.

"If they have any notion that I'm going to jump through hoops every time they crack the whip . . ."

Anxiously Harmon put down the newspaper. "Look," he asked, "you don't really take this crap seriously?"

Upon him Burling turned a jet of scorn that he supposed was meant to obliterate him. "Well, Counselor, what do *you* think?"

He reminded himself tartly of his conversation with Vicente Hidalgo and what he had learned from it. "That it's mostly an act. They're glad enough to take our million dollars, but there's one thing, you know, that no Latino politician can afford—they don't want it said that they knuckled under to the *gringo* imperialists. Every now and then they have to yell 'Down with the Colossus!' Hell—we can still build the hospitals."

But Burling was not appeased. "God damn it," he grumbled, "to go and needle me like that in the public prints . . ."

"Sure," said Harmon, "but you don't save face in private."

Still Burling refused to be appeased. "The bastards . . ." he rasped. Hands behind his back he began to pace, Napoleon on the bivouacs. The porch quivered and groaned under his footfalls. Ross, off in his own corner, was going through all his letters a second time and mumbling all the while, "Hell, aw hell . . ." Horanyi, holding off yet another pink-tinted missive at arm's length, yawned expansively and again the sun struck a volley of bright little daggers from his three gold teeth.

"I'll show them . . ." railed Burling under his breath. "Right here and now!"

This fat, bratty autocrat, thought Harmon. All that was missing was for him to stamp his foot and roll on the floor. There was not much about Burling that impressed him any more. "Easy, easy," he coaxed. "Calm down." In his hand, all the while, he was holding the letter from Laura—the letter in which she pitied him for being in Alba and urged him to come home.

"Tom," called Burling, wheedling suddenly about. Up bolted the Little Adjutant. "Get a pencil and paper. Never mind—use this." From his pocket Burling took the letter from his wife, turned over the typed sheets to their blank sides and lay them on a magazine for backing. "To the Ministers of Welfare, Public Works and so forth . . ." he began.

"Right," said the Little Adjutant after a moment.

"The undersigned, as chief of a party of technicians sent to this Republic at the expense of the North American taxpaper . . ."

"Hell, hell," said Harmon, becoming ever more irritated, "why rub it in?"

". . . resents the efforts of the esteemed Ministers to make a political football out of the Alba program." Mercer, all the while, raced away with his pencil. "The tactic of criticizing the Mission in the public prints when the Ministers know full well that the budget has always been considered subject to revision . . ." On the peak of his flight Burling suddenly stalled. "Tom . . ."

"The tactic of criticizing . . ."

". . . does not strike the undersigned as meeting the standard of ordinary good manners . . ."

"Jesus," said Harmon, "what Latino can swallow *that?*"

". . . ordinary good manners which the undersigned has a right
to expect. Be it noted, gentlemen, that the members of this Mission,
all outstanding experts in their fields, have each sacrificed incomes
of fifteen to twenty thousand dollars a year . . ."

"Ha!" cried Horanyi amid a new shower of gold daggers.

"Christ," said Harmon. "Be yourself."

". . . in order to place themselves at the service of the suffering
people of Alba. The thought of drafting plans to drain a town which
is under water at high tide can only be taken by the undersigned
as absurdly humorous. The expansion of dry ground in Puerto
Pacifico is a problem of dredging and filling, not of drainage. Our
sense of frustration at receiving orders of such a nature must be
evident."

He paused at this point—for so long that Tom Mercer looked up
and said, "I have it, sir."

As not in many weeks, mirth lifted the corner of Burling's lips.

Here it comes, thought Harmon, another trick.

"Your chief of party, therefore, is left with no alternative," Burling
went on, "but to ask for the immediate relief of himself and the
entire Mission staff, a request in which my associates join me
unanimously."

"Ha!" cried Horanyi zestfully.

Now Harmon's anger exploded. "No!" he shouted. "Hell, no!"
In his hand he crumpled up the letter in which Laura pitied him
for being in Alba.

"Unanimously," repeated Burling.

Vigorously, determinedly, Harmon shook his head.

"Why not?" asked Burling. Coolly now. Mockingly now. With
a thin sour smile that was unbearable. "No nerve, Billyboy?"

"Because . . ." Away into his pocket Harmon stuffed the letter
from Laura with its catalogue of all the miseries of life in Alba,
with all its cogent arguments for returning home. "Because . . ."
But no—his reason was certainly not one that he could tell. It had
been hard enough to admit it even to himself.

"Why not?" repeated Burling.

"You"—he would improvise some other reason—"you just can't talk like that to Cabinet Ministers. It's *their* country." As a rationalization, this had the merit at least of being true.

"Hell," said Burling, "it's my mission."

His mission—that overgrown, tantrum-ridden baby. "Look," begged Harmon, trying yet another tack, "at least talk it over first with the Ambassador. Fly up to Chimboya and see the Ambassador."

"Billyboy," said Burling, "stop wetting your pants. I can call the turns as plain as a square dance. The Ministers get my letter and their liver turns to water. They high-tail it over to the Ambassador, who's an American, remember, and can't lose face for our own crowd. 'Gentlemen,' he says, 'I realize that the tone of this communication is somewhat direct, but we must bear in mind that Colonel Burling is a sincere and straight-spoken man. My advice is to antagonize him no further.'"

Horanyi chuckled.

"Then," said Burling, "I have them by the short hairs."

"Or else," said Harmon—and it was what all along he had been fighting against—"they ship us right home."

"No," said Burling. "They couldn't afford to. They wouldn't dare to. Not on your life."

But the possibility left Harmon profoundly disturbed.

CHAPTER EIGHT

AFTER supper, because there was nowhere else to go, and on a Saturday night, they straggled across the mudflat to one of the *cantinas,* a flyblown little box with rickety camp chairs and wormeaten tables. The owner, a thin melancholy man who was also mayor of the port, wore a mint-and-cinnamon-striped shirt which must have been made over from a frock. *Ai,* he sighed, there was not one single drop of hard liquor to offer the gentlemen. The tax on spirits was so high these days, and the quality so rough, that it was not worth serving. He was in a position, however, to recommend the bottled beer—*riquissima,* very rich.

But the beer, when it came to the table, was warm, because there had been no ice shipment from Lorca in three days; also it was thin and flat.

Walt Anderson, turning for diversion in a new direction, went tomcatting behind the bar after the barefoot waitress. She giggled a great deal but, with a constant eye toward the mayor-proprietor, kept pushing Anderson away. He revenged himself by playing over and over, on a phonograph with a horn, a popular Mexican ditty, *"Tu ya no soplas como mujer"*—"You're not worth a hoot as a woman." Under the table the others slapped their ankles unceasingly in a running war with the sandfleas. The beer gagged them and they abandoned it, all of them, at the halfway mark down the glass, a cause of curiosity to the two or three *mestizos* who regarded them from the corners of the room.

Fred Ross, twisting in his chair, groaned. "That amoeba sure has got me."

"See Dr. Solís at Rosales," urged Horanyi.

"I did." He rubbed his belly woefully.

The Little Adjutant extracted a flea from inside his shirt, crushed it between his nailtips and said, "Try bismuth. Bismuth as usual."

"I don't know," said Ross sceptically.

Ross, the bullyboy, had not flourished in this mangrove swamp, thought Harmon. Every day he filled sheet after sheet with engineering sketches, then crumpled them and threw them away.

"Why the hell," asked Horanyi, "did we let ourselves run out of whisky? Tropics without whisky doesn't exist."

"Two cases coming in from Lorca on Tuesday," said the Little Adjutant.

"Tuesday!" said Horanyi. "I am so far gone I could drink donkey sweat."

"Have another beer," suggested Harmon. *"Riquissima."*

"Harmon, you put this beer in the same class with donkey sweat?"

Saturday night—and stranded with each other. It reminded him of those off-nights back at college when they would sit around at loose ends in the dormitory, restless and sodden, unable to bring each other to life. It would be happening too in every bivouac and on every island where there were soldiers who were unoccupied momentarily with the business of war. It was the other side, he reflected, of life away from women.

Again Walt Anderson started the phonograph and scrabbled behind the bar after the barefoot waitress. "Judas priest," said Burling, eyeing the operation with a flare of interest, "five weeks a bachelor. I could do with a little nonsense myself."

"You bet," echoed the Little Adjutant, hunting meditatively inside his shirt again.

"When I look back," sighed Horanyi, "to some of the wonderful lays which I have had in my life—and which I did not properly appreciate. . . . To think that there were times even when I have pushed a woman from my bed. . . ."

"Cut it out," said Fred Ross.

"What's matter," asked Horanyi, "are we steaming you up?"

"Cut it out."

Yes, a painful subject, thought Harmon—one that down here he had succeeded in putting out of mind. Or had he?

"If you gentlemen haven't heard," declared Burling, "it's an absolute falsehood about Chinese women."

That old chestnut, thought Harmon—inevitable wherever men gathered by themselves.

"Sir," said the Little Adjutant, again crushing a flea, "I'm mighty sorry to hear that."

"I remember once when I was in Alaska . . ." began Horanyi dreamily.

These vague bawdy nibblings—where would they get anybody?
A man, if he had other things on his mind, could do without,
couldn't he?

"Cut it out," said Fred Ross.

"Mister," said Horanyi, "you *have* got it bad."

"I left behind the sweetest little wife in the world," said Ross.
"I swore to God I'd never take a field job again, and here I am."

"Paraguay . . ." interjected Burling, bobbing up from some pool
of thought. "They had so many wars in Paraguay that they wound
up finally with seventeen women to every man. A fellow couldn't
go down the road without being jumped."

From behind the bar Walt Anderson turned on them a wild
bacchantic leer. "Boss," he asked, "if they throw us out of Alba
could we go to Paraguay?"

"That," said Burling, "was in the nineteenth century."

Now, Harmon noted embarrassedly, they were all facing toward
him. Now, as in a minstrel show, it was *his* turn for a little song
and dance. But his lips would not open. Under the circumstances, he
thought with a flush of shame, it would be a fraud, an utter hypocrisy. Tensely he sat in the camp chair and sweated, every eye upon
him.

Luckily the Little Adjutant elbowed forward. "Once," he said,
"I was jumped myself. By two old women. About thirty-five, they
must have been."

"Crones," observed Horanyi, "withered hags."

"I was peddling magazines or something from door to door—
it was a prize contest for a bicycle or something. I ring this doorbell
and it's a mighty hot day, and this woman opens the door and all
she's got on is pants. Little old lacy pants. And inside there's another
woman, and all she's got on is little old lacy pants, too."

"Frightful," said Burling.

"Sir," said the Little Adjutant, "I regret to report they got me."

"Poor little fella," said Burling.

"Now for the rest of his life," said Horanyi, "he has got a complex. He wants to sleep with women."

"Cut it out," said Ross, "cut it out."

"You know," said Burling, plowing ahead relentlessly, "it'll happen sometimes that you get a thing about a little nobody, the most insignificant little creature in the world, and you could do handstands in front of her and she won't even know you exist. You could be President of the United States of America for all the good it will do you. Then, next minute, without your even trying, without your having the remotest expectation, some marvelous little thing will come along from nowhere and just throw herself at you. I was getting off a train once in Calcutta, and there is this perfect little beauty struggling with a suitcase. Not a porter in sight. I ask might I help her to a cab. Nothing in my mind but common ordinary politeness. Would you believe it—one hour later we were in bed and I was learning some mighty fancy things." He smiled richly at the recollection. "And the wife of one of the best-known diplomats in the East. Billyboy, how do you account for a thing like that?"

Again the spotlight. Like every man he had his stories to tell. That woman on the cruise ship—the dancing girl in Havana—and half a dozen others from the days when he had been "all right," marvelously "all right." But now, in the circumstances . . . "I'd just be grateful," he said, "and hope for more."

"Women . . ." sighed Burling. Cigarette in hand, he glanced about for a match. Out came Harmon's lighter. But already three other flints had sparked. Burling took Mercer's as the nearest to him. The others, proudly or apologetically, compared the effectiveness of their own lighters.

"Women . . ." echoed Horanyi. With scientific precision he went on to relate some exotica he had discovered in the connubial practices of the Arabs. It appeared that once in Damascus . . .

"Hell," said Ross, "cut it out."

But on plunged Horanyi with his tale, mercilessly. A Syrian physician, he said, one whom he had come to know very well, had told him that . . .

Harmon no longer was listening. From afar, insidiously, he had begun to sense a presence that was spectral, a fragrance that was night-like.

On and on droned Horanyi with his epic from Damascus. It seemed to involve the harem of a very wealthy emir.

Her eyes, Harmon remembered, were so unexpectedly gray. She had talked longingly of the times past. She had reached out toward him—had she not?—as to a messenger from the years she loved.

Still Horanyi's story reeled on. It had to do, evidently, with philters and potions. . . . .

Her hand, when she had shaken his own, had been so white and silken. He had forgotten almost, in this world of competent women, that such hands still existed. She had striven so hard, he liked to think, for his good opinion. She must have seen him only as whole and strong, the way he wanted to be seen.

"Good show!" roared Burling. The saga of Damascus had come to some thunderous finish. Appreciatively Burling slammed the table with his open hand, then looked about again for a match. Once more the four flints sparked and four flames stood at attention. We're as proud of our lighters, thought Harmon, as our organs. Or instead of them.

With a groan Ross finally stood up. "Hell," he said, "I better get me back near the plumbing."

"Bismuth," urged the Little Adjutant once more.

Again Ross shook his head sceptically and started for the door. Once there, he stopped, on some impulse, and faced about toward Burling. "Boss," he said, "next time I'm in Lorca I'm buying me a gun."

Burling studied him. "What for?"

"Well, I went up the line the other day to inspect the water works in Santa Ana. All the way up in the train"—for an instant Ross hesitated—"all the way up in the train those monkeys kept looking at me and whispering."

"Why wouldn't they? You're a foreigner."

Ross shook his head. "Heck," he said, "a man's got a right to protect himself."

Again Burling studied him.

"He's right," interjected Horanyi. "It's the engineers they always go for first."

"Hush," said Burling in a half-whisper.

Ross took this in and swung, instantly, toward Horanyi. "What're you talking about?"

"A matter of simple folkways," said Horanyi, shrugging his shoulders. "The engineer is a man who disturbs the balance of nature. He digs up soil. He moves rocks. He is a profane intruder on the resident spirits of nature. Among primitive peoples the first impulse is to blame all troubles on the engineer."

"And lawyers," added Harmon.

"Harmon, don't be a Philistine! I learned all this from Malinowski in London. Forewarned is forearmed."

"Right," said Burling. "We don't want any repetitions of what happened in Monopaxi."

Another of those sports of men-among-themselves, thought Harmon. You had only to show the barest hint of weakness and they were at you. But Ross wasn't exactly fair game, especially in his present mood, the worry-raddled ox. "Fellow," he said, "they're kidding you."

But Ross, stubbornly, swung to Burling. "What happened in Monopaxi?" he said. "What was it that happened?"

"Skip it," said Burling.

"What's done," said Horanyi, "is done."

"Look," said Harmon, shaking his head, "this guy is a sitting duck."

But Ross was not to be denied his fears. "I want to know," he insisted, coming all the way back to the table. "What happened?"

"American citizens," muttered Burling. "All three of them. But never a word of protest from State Department. Not expedient. Those cookie-pushers."

"Fred," said Harmon, "go home and take care of your amoeba."

"What happened?"

Now Horanyi took over. "You know the oil diggings of Amro Petroleum? A gang of mountain Indians broke into the compound one night. First thing, they went for the engineers. Cut the throats of every last one of them."

"Yes," said Burling, "but before they ever got to that merciful act . . ."

"The stakes?" prompted Horanyi.

"Boys," said Harmon, "you're a lynch mob."

"Yes," said Burling. "Made every man jack sit down on a pointed stake. Their own weight forced them lower and lower. Never stopped till the stakes came clean through their skulls."

"Out of their *mouths*," corrected Horanyi.

"Boys," asked Harmon, "why don't you get together? Fred, don't you know when you're being kidded?"

Ross's lips worked uncertainly. "There *was* an attack on Monopaxi," he said. "Last winter. I was told about it in Lorca."

This was unfortunate. "Maybe," said Harmon, "but nobody was goosed on a pointed stake. And we don't have wild Indians in Alba."

"All right," said Burling, "let's forget it."

For a moment longer Ross looked about and pondered, then broke into chuckles. "I *knew* they were kidding me," he said, "I knew it all along." Even when he had left the *cantina,* even when he was halfway down the causeway, they could hear him laughing.

"The only amoeba *that* guy has," said the Little Adjutant, "is on the brain."

"Well," said Harmon reflectively, "two to one that we've lost an engineer."

"Poker?" suggested the Little Adjutant.

"Hell, no," said Horanyi, "not again."

"We could fish from the dock," said Harmon.

"Not in the mood," said Burling.

This profound, sea-deep boredom—now they were touching bottom. But in a way, thought Harmon, he almost took pride in it, in the same way that the sufferers look admiringly, affectionately, on the record hot spells or cold spells that have laid them low. . . . Through the open door of the *cantina* he saw a man approach the Customs House with a lantern—the night watchman of the port. Around his face was wound a thick muffler, the traditional safeguard against malaria. The watchman pulled on a rope and tolled a ship's bell nine times.

"Lord," groaned Horanyi, "if it were at least time for a man to go to bed . . ."

"Alone?" asked the Little Adjutant.

"By Jesus, even alone."

It was just then that Walt Anderson, still standing off at the bar, smote it with the flat of his hand and gave out a war cry.

"What's up?" asked Burling, all attention. "Did your barefoot girl say yes?"

"The hell with her," said Anderson, "the hell with that Queen of the Incas. I just found out they're having a *verbena* tonight at Rosales. A dance in the public gardens."

"What," asked Horanyi, "is there to drink?"

"Brandy, she says. A buck a liter. It comes from over the border."

"Rosales for me," said Horanyi.

"Also," said Anderson, "there ought to be plenty of this-and-that." He wrapped his jacket tight about him and strutted. "Burling?"

"Not me."

"God Almighty," said Anderson, "after all that talk!"

"Not in the mood."

"Those clapped-up monkeys!" chimed in the Little Adjutant.

"Harmon?"

Anything, he thought, anything to break out of this cage. "I'll get the car," he said. The truth, it then struck him, was that at Rosales he might catch a glimpse again of that girl with the gray eyes.

CHAPTER NINE

THE night, and the lanterns glowing in the palm trees, had made soft and elegant—a court of Moorish kings—what he knew to be withered and drab by daylight. The sky sheen over Alba was continuous, like that of a length of satin; in spaces that until now he had thought deserts among the constellations burned new hosts of stars. The night could almost be tasted on the tongue, as a bland and succulent melon.

Not one but two dances were going on in the public gardens, by rotation. In the center bandstand sat a quintet of youths in blue silk slack-suits who played—from scores—American jazz, Spanish two-steps and Cuban rumbas. As the inscription on their bass drum indicated, they had been imported from Lorca for the occasion. But off in a corner, hunched on stools, sat a group of *criollos,* native Albanese, who played from memory upon guitars, tabors and Pan-pipes. Their songs were all in a minor key, fandangos and Indian lamentations.

As there were two bands, so were there two publics. Around the center bandstand sat the *gente decente,* the respectable folk. The men all wore jackets. Their women had flowered out in summer prints, New York style, and high-heeled shoes. Among these the Indian blood was faintly dilute. But on the margin of the park, among the *rotos,* the down-and-outers, the skin was darker, the features broader, the eyes more slanted—in the mold of those brother Polynesians across the Pacific. Men and women alike wore fiber sandals or no foot covering at all. They danced at arm's length from each other, somberly and ritualistically.

"Señor Asociado! Caballeros!"

It was as they stood on the border of the two worlds, between *gente decente* and the *rotos,* uncertain which way to cast their lot, that they heard themselves called. A sparkling white-clad man, of a size no larger than a boy, was beckoning from a table near the bandstand—Dr. Solís, the resident surgeon of the Rosales hospital. "Do us the honor of joining us!" he cried.

"Well—for a minute," whispered Anderson, gazing all the while in the direction of the *rotos.* "Hey, man, take a peep at that daughter of the Sun God! Some knockers . . ."

Seated with Dr. Solís was another young man, squat and broad-shouldered, through whose open collar peeped up curls of chest hair. Dr. Larrea, the resident from Santa Ana. *"Señor Asociado,"* he sighed, desperately but affably, "what a month it's been. Four new cases of typhus. A new onset of tertian malaria. This is my first night off in weeks." He spat on the ground. "Anyhow, who can call it a hospital?"

"At Rosales," broke in Dr. Solís, "I order sterile sheets for the surgical table. Then they lay out the patient in her own filthy rags."

"Last week," added Larrea, "the Sisters refused to sanction an ovariotomy. The patient is whole, *Señor Asociado,* but dead."

Not once did they take their eyes from Harmon. They were pleading with him as with a father in whose means lies all bounty. "I know," he said, "I know. Our medical officer will be arriving from the States any day now. One of the best."

"Somebody with authority," begged Larrea. "Somebody who will remind us what medicine is supposed to be. Every day I am being pushed further and further back to the medicine of panther blood and lizard dust. We need some standards."

Yes, Vicente Hidalgo had said something like that. But he had spoken with despair. He had predicted so pessimistically that . . .

"My throat!" cried Horanyi, breaking in on his reflections. "The sands of the Sahara!"

Dr. Solís stood up and snapped his fingers smartly. "Waiter!" he called. From out of the dark materialized a tattered old gnome whose clothes were patches on patches. But all that he had to offer was soda pop, orange-flavored.

"Five times?" asked Dr. Solís lavishly.

The high life—thought Harmon. But promptly Anderson took command. He whispered something to the tattered gnome and passed him several bills.

With the orange pop, the waiter brought back two other bottles, wrapped in a newspaper, which he begged the *caballeros* to keep out of sight under the table.

"Patriots," muttered Horanyi, refilling his glass for the fourth time. "By day they curse the Invader. By night they smuggle his booze over the border." On each of Horanyi's cheeks burned a patch of crimson.

"*Señor?*" asked Dr. Solís, looking up smartly. It was evident that he had a smattering of English.

"A philosophic reflection," said Harmon, nudging Horanyi with his elbow.

"I'm an American," mumbled Horanyi, paying no heed, "free, white and American."

"There must be dozens," said Anderson, his eyes still on the rove, "dozens and dozens."

Now the young men in the silk slacks unleashed a rumba; in the storm of their music all conversation ceased. Ernestina Manriquez, thought Harmon, looking everywhere about. A swarm of little dancers frothed up to the very edge of the table. "Man, oh, man," said Anderson, his glance running greedily over the sinuous hips and tossing breasts. But so far he had made no practical moves toward any of the ladies of the *gente decente*.

From the direction of the park gate, all the while, a large party moved hesitantly up the aisle, led by a man with a shapely gilded head. Marcos Montalvo.

"Señor Gobernador!" cried Dr. Solís, again springing up. "Do us the honor!"

Ernestina Manriquez? No, she was not among them.

The table was not large enough to accommodate all the new-comers. There was a melee of plans and hesitations. Finally a second long table was drawn up and the Governor introduced his retinue, provincial officials and their wives, men of solid physical substance —almost the first that Harmon had seen here in Alba—and ladies whose coiffures were towers of black curls held together with many combs. "Engineer and Señora Gomez," said the Governor by way of introduction. "Welfare Superintendent and Señora Molina. Railroad Director and Señora Egas." For Harmon the Governor had a warm smile. "The Associate Director." Horanyi, embarrassingly, had failed to rise. With a pull, Harmon got him to his feet. "And Economist Horanyi." In the flurry, Agriculturist Anderson had murmured an excuse and made off.

Now the silken boys began a waltz and the ladies were taken off to dance. In the soft jeweled light of the lanterns Harmon and the Governor sat alone, save for Horanyi.

"Well," said Montalvo with a melancholy smile, "you were the victims of a little ambush the other day, weren't you?"

"The statement of the Ministers?"

"I hope none of you has a skin which punctures easily. My father in his day was denounced as the Anti-Christ from half the pulpits in the Republic. It was stated that he had stolen all the gold of the Treasury and shipped it to Paris. It was declared even that he had met my mother in a house of ill fame."

Horanyi, reaching under the table, poured himself a fresh drink. "I'm American," he mumbled defiantly, "American."

The Governor darted a quizzical glance at Horanyi and bottle both. "I had made him out," he said, "as Hungarian."

"Hungarian *born*," said Harmon. And Horanyi carried it, he reflected, like some secret shame.

It was an instant later that he heard himself called by a familiar voice, one that was deep and regal. "Good evening, my dear young Colossus." From behind the Governor a large disheveled form was weaving toward the table.

"Good evening, Señor Hidalgo," said Harmon, rising.

Swiftly the Governor glanced about. *"Tu . . ."* he said, "you . . ." using the familiar form of address, but distantly.

Ironically, patronizingly, Hidalgo returned the Governor's gaze. "Yes, I."

"Well, do me the favor, Vicente, of going away."

"Señor Gobernador," was the instant rejoinder, and again it was with a lilt which turned the title into something ponderously absurd, laughable. "I was not talking to you."

"Tu—drunk again."

"He's a *pretty* fellow," said Hidalgo, "but such bad manners . . ."

The Governor bolted up. Rigidly, an arm's length apart, they stood then and faced each other. Between them boiled the hatred of two men who cannot endure the fact that the other exists. But it was a hatred, thought Harmon, that was profoundly intimate, between brothers.

"Stop it, stop it," whispered the Governor with desperate quiet, "or I shall turn you over to the Carabineros."

"Yes," said Hidalgo, "as a child, too, you used to threaten everybody with the Carabineros."

The Governor glanced about in every direction, but in vain. *"Tu— tu,"* he repeated, "you walking corpse."

There was a flash again of that white, bitter grin. "Your Excellency," said Hidalgo, "I was hoping to have a word with Señor Harmon, but if you insist on making it impossible . . ."

Instantly the Governor sat down and folded his arms. For a

moment Harmon stood half-bent over the table, caught in the cross-fire of their hatred, glancing from one man to the other. Casting his lot perforce with Montalvo, he slowly sat down, but kept smiling all the while in the direction of Hidalgo. "At some more opportune time," he apologized.

"Is he gone yet?" asked Montalvo, looking stonily away all the while. "Is he gone?"

"A brat," said Hidalgo cheerfully.

"Listen," said Montalvo, but with his face still averted, "I have not come to Alba to start the same wrangle all over again. If you insist on making trouble . . ."

"No, Marcos," said Hidalgo, "there will be no trouble. I am no longer that important." Then he nodded pleasantly to Harmon and said, "My apologies. It was gross of us to turn you into an innocent bystander."

"Is he gone yet?" repeated Montalvo. "Is he gone?"

Slowly, cautiously, Hidalgo wheeled himself about. Back, without another word, he went in the direction whence he had come, the corner of the *rotos*.

"Once," said Montalvo, instantly all smooth and airy again, "that man had great possibilities. For himself. For the Republic. He drowned them in a sea of alcohol. Hidalgo was one of my father's few failures."

That sad satanic giant. What had those "possibilities" been? And why had he drowned them?

"A tragic case," said the Governor, and with that he ended the epitaph.

The music had stopped, and down upon the table descended the returning dancers. But now in their midst they enfolded a new-comer, a broad-shouldered man in a white linen suit who towered over all their heads.

"Ramón," called the Governor.

Following behind the young seigneur, hard-pressed in the swarming horde, was Ernestina Manriquez.

The young seigneur marched nearer, and it was as though all who surrounded him were his liegemen and servitors, pressing in upon him for a touch of his person. But he walked among them with a melancholy aloofness, unnoticing of their homage.

Ernestina . . . But a shift in the throng had suddenly blocked her out. How, wondered Harmon, was she dressed tonight?

Manriquez reached the table. His hair was black and curling, his sidelocks grew half down his cheeks in the old Spanish fashion, but he looked powerful and commanding. What kind of woman, in the presence of this husband, was Ernestina Manriquez?

All at once Harmon was being introduced to them, the black-haired handsome couple. He hoped that she would smile, show gladness to see him again.

"*Tanto gusto,*" she said, acknowledging the introduction—but reservedly, with distant formality. A gown of sea-green chiffon she wore, that flowed with pale luminescence from shoulder to ankle. But why had she addressed him so formally, and in Spanish?

"*Para mi también, Señora,*" he replied, falling in with her own reserve. But why, why had she failed to recognize him?

Now his hand was meeting that of the husband. He gave the appearance, Manriquez, of being dangerous. Probably he had once "killed a man," or several. But his hand took Harmon's limply, with that same pensive apathy with which he had walked among his adorers.

"*Tanto gusto,* Señor Harmon."

"*Para mí también,* Señor Manriquez."

He was moved by some primitive, involuntary design to measure himself against the height of Ernestina Manriquez's husband. Identical.

"Greaseballs—niggers," mumbled Horanyi. He was weaving oafishly in his chair.

Worse and worse, thought Harmon. Wildly, helplessly, driven by the pain of some wound, Horanyi had found for himself an unguent —and was wallowing in it. . . . Cautiously Harmon reached under the table with his toe and tipped over the one remaining bottle.

At his left a short stout lady whose husband was the provincial director of railroads fired a cheerful volley of table talk at him. Indeed, he replied, the climate of Alba had turned out far cooler and pleasanter than he had expected. Oh, yes, he had been informed already that it had to do with the Humboldt Current, that mysteriously chill wave which ran through the Pacific off the coasts of the Republic. . . .

Ernestina Manriquez—only once, through the long thicket of heads at the table, had he succeeded in catching her eye, but again she had stared back unknowingly. Had he offended her in some way? At their first meeting she had appeared so friendly, she had leaned forward to him. Was there something he had said? Or—or had she chosen to engage here in a kind of conspiracy? Indeed, he agreed with the Señora of the Railroads, the fruits of the province were matchless—*riquissima*. . . . Once again he tried to throw a glance at Ernestina Manriquez which should strike her like a tangible object and rouse her to notice of him.

Instead, his eyes met those of her husband.

Ambushed.

If Manriquez wanted to make an issue of this . . . But no, there was something in those deep-set, contemplative eyes that was utterly unreachable. They looked out with the same mournful apathy with which the Spanish captains of old must have regarded their domains, never assuaged, ever self-driven, planning always on some newer conquest. He was the richest man in Alba, Manriquez, but it must be that this was not enough. It was the way they were made, those somber captains.

"Señor Harmon . . ."

"Señor Manriquez?"

"Is it correct"—and Manriquez's tone was unexpectedly casual, ordinary—"that the Mission intends to acquire a tract of land?"

"Quite so. One of our first projects is a demonstration farm."

"I know just the site for you."

"Yes?"

"A tract from my own hacienda."

From his own lands. Harmon's ears pricked up.

"Good soil. Plenty of water. And easy access."

Access, thought Harmon with a flare of excitement, easy access.

"How many acres do you think the Mission will want?"

Under the cover of reflection, Harmon stole a glance at Ernestina Manriquez. Pale she sat, and withdrawn, her eyelids lowered. "How many? Three or four hundred, I should imagine."

"Take them," said Manriquez, "as a gift."

"Oh, no," said Harmon, "you're much too generous." But even in this lavishness there was no warmth, only apathy. And some deep design as well? "The Mission certainly is in a position to pay."

"As a gift. I insist."

Access, thought Harmon again, access. He was straining himself, the grand seigneur, to open his own gates. "Thank you, Señor Manriquez," he said. "In behalf of the Mission, thank you."

Suddenly across the still face of Ernestina Manriquez, across the slanted cheekbones, went the faintest shadow of a smile. It was startling how wanton she looked.

"Niggers!" cried Horanyi in a new and more ferocious outburst. "Why are we sitting here with this bunch of niggers?"

"*Que dice*—what's he saying?" asked the Señora of the Railroads.

Under the table Harmon clutched Horanyi by the forearm. "Mister," he muttered, "we're not the only ones in Alba who understand English."

For an answer Horanyi bolted up and began to run.

"What's happening?" asked the Señora of the Railroads.

"*Ai,*" said Dr. Solís indulgently making a cup of his fist and tilting it toward his mouth.

"The *Economista,*" said Harmon rising, "has not been well."

At the park gate he caught up. "Horanyi," he said, "nobody has to get *that* drunk."

"Go screw. It's not in my goddam contract that I have to put my feet under the table with greasers."

For a moment Harmon studied him. "What the hell happened?" he asked finally. "Did you teach in one of those tank-town colleges? Were they always calling you a Hunky behind your back? Or did a girl do it to you?"

"I'm not a Hunky, God damn it! I'm an American! I'm a goddamn American!"

"It's a cinch," said Harmon. "Take my word for it."

Horanyi clawed at his hand. "Let me go!"

"Where to?"

"Back to the port."

"I can't drive you just yet."

"I have my own two goddamn legs."

The high-backed road led straight to the port. The jungle veteran would have no trouble finding his way. Harmon released his grip and Horanyi started running.

In Washington, in those first encounters, Horanyi had shown himself only as the tolerant anthropologist, the friend of all races. This parvenu hatred of all foreigners—behind it must surely lie a thousand rebuffs, and a fever to prove himself one with those who had rebuffed. But only outside the borders of America could he feel himself an American. It was there only that . . .

Across Harmon's mind there flashed—he tried to hold them back, but he could not—there flashed those sharp clairvoyant words of Vicente Hidalgo: ". . . because it is only here, alongside a people even weaker and sicker than themselves, that they can come to feel like men." And Tom Mercer? And Burling? Anderson?

In Washington—it struck him—we were wearing disguises.

Now the orchestra was playing a slow foxtrot, sinuous and feminine. Once, twice, Harmon started up from his chair, then fell
back. Bracing himself finally, he stood up and marched to the far
end of the table. "Señor Manriquez," he asked, "may I have the
pleasure of dancing with your lady?"

It was now finally that she glanced up.

"Naturally," said the Spanish captain.

Don't—thought Harmon in a surge of irritation—don't be so
damned sure of yourself.

She came to him yieldingly, the good dance partner. Because, in
a sudden fever, he was minded to crush her in upon himself, he held
her off instead at utmost length. They danced then in the loose
feathery style of tense indifference which he had learned at college.
The music was suave. And the girl before him—gone were all traces
now of the campus tomboy. The saddle shoes had given way to
silver slippers. She was the woman, all grace and fragrance, of
whom men thought when they thought of "woman." Hers were the
hands. Hers was the flesh.

"Mr. Harmon," she said, speaking English again, and in that
strange substanceless voice.

"Yes?"

"You don't like my husband, do you?"

It startled him. Her thoughts had a way of bursting out so full
blown, as if they had been long in gathering, in winding up inside
her. "Was it so obvious?"

"To me it was."

"Did *he* notice?"

"Ramón? Oh, it would never occur to him."

Yes, that lordly apathy.

"Why," she asked, and again on her lips there was a flicker of
mischief, "why don't you like him?"

"Because . . ." For an instant he pondered. "Conquistador." Yes, of that type Manriquez seemed classic, an example preserved pure from centuries ago. "The master of all he surveys." Her eyes flashed upward. "Of you too." It burst out of him unexpectedly, this last. Why had he let it?

"Was it"—mimicking him gently—"so obvious?"

"All that I meant . . ."

But her gaze had already turned away, to something off at her right. "Yes, I know what you meant," she murmured. Still she was staring, fixedly, almost bitterly. "In these countries a woman is a possession—first of her father, then of her husband. A woman is something that belongs to a man. Not much more."

Inquisitively, Harmon followed the line of her gaze.

"Don't underestimate him," she whispered. Yes, it was at her husband she was staring. "Ramón has intelligence, oh, lots of it." Aloof still, pensively, he sat among his liegemen. "And terrible determination. Hernán Cortez. Yes—and Gonzalo Pizarro who could march five thousand animals through the snows of the Andes."

A girl of petals—but with hidden barbs . . . It was just then that Ramón Manriquez glanced up. "The land," she murmured, "is everything he says. Good soil and lots of water and . . ."

Upon him, all at once, Harmon felt the conqueror glance—languid and insolent. "And access," he added defiantly.

"You—you're really accepting, Mr. Harmon?"

Through him instantly surged a wild exuberance, all male and all lawless. "Yes!" he said. Here, with this one word, he making his declaration. "Yes!" Determinedly he pressed her to a halt among the swirling dancers, in the quiet epicenter of the maelstrom. "May *I* ask a question?" She smiled her assent. "Why did you pretend not to recognize me?"

Her lips parted. She seemed suddenly to lean toward him, or so he thought, so he hoped, the lithe tropical bloom. "It—it seemed simpler that way," she said.

Simpler? Then she must have taken their first meeting as something larger, more intimate, than just a meeting? Something of which she felt guilty. Something which must be concealed from her husband. Her desires then must be running even with his own! He went blind instantly at the thought, as before a sun glare. . . . He was tempted to seize her—call her by name—kiss her on the mouth. He . . .

But the music, just then, stopped.

With anger he gave her back to her husband.

Now the Señora of the Railroads, the cheerful chatterbox, was telling of the fabled country upland where the royal palms grew to a height of fifty meters, where there was rubber to be gathered, and quinine, even.

Access, he kept thinking, access.

If some time the *Señor Asociado* wished to make the trip and see for himself . . .

Ernestina, Ernestina, Ernestina! He wanted her ferociously.

At the terminal of the railroad, said the Señora, mules could always be arranged for. One had only to telegraph ahead and . . .

Because he wanted Ernestina—*her* flesh, *her* body—he wanted a woman. Any woman. A woman. He knew, savagely well, that he was "all right" again. He had to have a woman. If only it could be Ernestina . . . But again she was so far from him—down, down the full length of the table—again enchained to that conqueror husband. Again she sat pale and unseeing and withdrawn. Access, all access, was gone.

"Hey, Billyboy."

At his elbow, bending over conspiratorially, was Walt Anderson. Not the flinty little farmer of Washington, but a wicked tomcat. And he smelled strongly of brandy.

"Excuse me, Señora. . . . Walt, where've you been all night?"

"Prospecting. What's happened with Horanyi?"

"Gone home."

"Well"—in a miscalculatedly loud whisper—"pick yourself right up and follow me out of here."

"Where to?"

"Man—man—I been burning down a field for plowing. Two of 'em." He motioned with his thumb to the faraway corner of the *rotos,* whence was issuing now the lamenting music of the beggars' orchestra. "I got two babies over there just crying to be freshened!"

Down, down the length of the table, past all the black glistening heads that would bar his way, went Harmon's glance. But Ernestina Manriquez would not look up. Again she was denying him.

"Come on," urged Anderson.

"I—I don't know, Walt." It would be a betrayal, he thought anguishedly. How could he?

"Mister, what are you, a boy or a girl?"

A betrayal. But not, strangely, of Laura, not of his wedded wife. (He did have a wife, didn't he?) It was to Ernestina, by some logic, that this would be an infidelity. He didn't want to, and yet . . . Longingly, bitterly, he implored her to look up at him, to save him. A glance, just a single glance, might do it.

"Mister," warned Anderson, "this is the last call."

Abruptly then he stood up—in order to commit himself beyond repair. It was only then that Ernestina finally turned his way, but with a face all blank, not knowing him at all.

"Sósena—Maruja," called Anderson as they reached the corner of the *rotos.* They turned simultaneously in their chairs, tawny girls, both of them, with large gentle features and flashing white teeth. In their orange calico frocks they were like Polynesian women, soft and languid and sunny.

"*El Asociado,*" said Anderson, by way of introducing Harmon. Impressedly the girls gazed up. But then, pointedly, Anderson ran his fingers through the straight black hair of the one called Maruja. By agreement then, the one called Sósena leaned toward Harmon and smiled. "Let's go," said Anderson.

It was as they were helping the girls into the car that a large rumpled man staggered by. He went two or three paces past them, then lurched heavily about. "Conquistadores," he said in a voice that was disconcertingly familiar, "go on and gather your loot."

Instantly Harmon looked away.

"Altruists! Brothers from the North!" Now he spat on the ground, Vicente Hidalgo.

Bolting into a fury, Anderson planted himself before the huge drunkard like a gamecock. *"Hijo de veinte mil putas—son of twenty thousand whores!"* he cursed. "Mind your own lousy business!"

Again Hidalgo spat. "Bearers of light," he said. "Philanthropists." Then he turned about in a wide swaying arc and staggered off.

"Let's go, let's *go!*" said Anderson feverishly.

They drove off with Harmon at the wheel and Sósena pressed against his side. It was good, he thought, that at the moment of climax a man was blind. He could pretend then that he was taking any woman of his choosing—any woman in the world.

CHAPTER TEN

HE LAY on his side under the mosquito netting, his legs drawn up, his forearms crossed in a foetal embrace of himself. The world outside was but a dim effulgence, of no consequence. Here inside the white cocoon was a republic of harmony. Nothing was asked of him but that he breathe. He had no exact notion of what part of the world he lay in.

But then from some far horizon came a shattering intrusion. An insect buzzed. He tried to pretend that it had not happened. But again the insect buzzed.

Inside the netting or outside?

The difference, in its implications, was enormous. If inside, then something, eventually, might have to be done.

From the infinitesimal bugle came another blast. Unhappily, Harmon opened his eyes and looked up. High above him in the conical spire of the mosquito netting, a large horsefly was dashing itself against the gauze walls. With a sigh Harmon propped himself up on his elbow—then thought instantly to look for Walt Anderson.

The cot on the right was empty. He recalled then how he had driven back alone from Rosales in the blue light of before-dawn, how Anderson, fierce and insatiable, had refused to be torn away. "*Que hombre mas valioso*—what a man," the girl had said.

Sósena—he thought next. That docile girl with her harem arts, an instrument for him, accommodating every whim, serving him every instant, not *taking* him. . . . I was "all right," he cried to himself joyfully. Marvelously all right! No fiascos! A four-star performance!

It was precious, this thought—something to tuck away under his pillow like a child's treasure until he was ready later to pick it up again and fondle it. Meanwhile, since it was Sunday morning . . . He closed his eyes and prepared to drift again into sleep.

Across his face tramped four prickly feet.

Angrily he slapped out—against his own cheek.

Missed.

The horsefly, trumpeting indignantly, spiraled rapidly upward. How on earth had it managed to break in? He followed its upward flight until his eyes tired; then he fell back again on his pillow.

But harmony now was gone. Laura—he was forced now to think. Laura. In all the years of their marriage it was the first step off the reservation. Twinges . . . Of conscience? Not exactly, he thought anxiously. In her own way Laura had given an advance consent for last night, hadn't she? There was that last-minute stammered conversation over the telephone—the shooting license which he chose to believe she had presented to him. Good only for the year he would be away. For therapeutic purposes only. But a shooting license definitely. Modern woman.

But where, last night, had *Laura* been? His wife, as any husband tended to forget, was young and good-looking. There must have been more "friend" than one who, commiserating him on his departure, had waited only for the coast to clear. Son of a bitch! And the Penelopes these days did not stay home with their knitting. That shooting license—were there clauses in fine print that he had neglected to examine? Was it meant to work both ways?

So damned modern. When he got back to New York next year he would be listening always for secret laughter. He would bridle every time Laura was called to the phone. He would burn to rifle her mail.

With what man? Johnny Reeves? Pete Goldsmith? Chuck Maney?

Oh, not in their own marriage bed, he prayed, not leaving behind the ghost of another man's weight. . . . Well, not much chance of that, he supposed. There was his mother, always likely to blunder in. And the kids, always likely to wake. No, the crime would be committed on other ground. But how inevitable. Son of a bitch! "A nightcap, Laura? At my place?" The nightcap is lifted in reverent toast to the distant husband. "A swell guy, your Will. Plenty of guts to bury himself in that swamp for a whole year. And—and tough on you too, Laura." A tender patting of Laura's shoulder, a noble fondling of her hand. Out of sympathy, of course. Everything out of sympathy. And in the name of Poor Will. Son of a bitch! And then, after the blackout, a little charade of remorse. "Oh we shouldn't have, we shouldn't! Why, why did I come here?" "All my fault, Laura, I've been a heel. Though, after all . . ." "Awful! How can I ever forgive myself?" "Though, after all, Laura, we're only human and if that husband of yours decides to march off and leave you all on your own for a year . . ." "Yes, I don't suppose Will is just sitting and twiddling his thumbs for a whole year, is he?"

Damn them. Damn their wet-eyed hypocrisy. He'd strangle Laura for this, Laura and her lover both!

What, after all, did he know about Laura? Nothing!

Buzzzz . . . Halfway up the filmy steeple the horsefly was spinning in perfect and desperate circles.

Shooting licenses were dandy, but not the clauses in fine print. Damn it to hell! A man should be able to trust his wife. When a man went off on a job like this he was entitled to know that she. . . .

Buzzzz!

Instantly then, embarrassedly, he recalled something Sósena had said the night before in an interlude of resting. "Ramón Manriquez? *Ai,* around Rosales alone there are four little children who bear his surname. Every Christmas His Lordship sends out little dresses and little suits of clothes. He makes himself heirs with everybody but his own Duchess."

Ernestina . . . "Does the Señora know?"

A wise and languid smile. "What wife does not?"

"And don't they ever ask for a divorce?"

"Señor Asociado, we are all Catholics!"

"And the wives . . .?"

"Oh, Señor, their husbands would kill them!"

For men only. For men it was a royal realm down here, and the flag that whipped in the breeze was the Double Standard. But for Ernestina, the girl who had lived four years on the campus, who had relished the even companionability of the soda fountain, who clung still to those tomboy shoes . . . How could Manriquez do it to her? He ought to have his face bashed in! These Latino roosters who thought that sunshine came out of their bottoms. . . .

Buzzzz.

Harmon, meet Harmon. One eye gleams for the swing of any new pair of hips, and the other weeps for the infidelities, real or imagined, of the Girl You Left Behind. How the soldier boys groaned these days in their letters from overseas. But since when had chastity belts been Government Issue? Answer that one!

You can dish it out, Harmon, but you can't take it.

Harmon, shut your big mouth.

Thinking, he finally concluded, was a waste of thought. To sleep —back to sleep. Turning over on his stomach, he burrowed with his face into the pillow.

Instantly there was a prickle of hairy feet on the back of his neck.

Savage mandibles, all at once, tore into his flesh.

From then on his entire being was dedicated to murder. His arms were flailing in all directions. He was scrabbling, on hands and knees, all over the chamber of gauze. He was leaping from the cot altogether, yanking down the whole mass of the netting from the hoop overhead, bunching it together and pounding it, then taking it apart with cold precision and searching each fold separately for that black and vicious mote. . . .

"Harmon."

His door had flung open.

"Harmon!" Nowadays Burling called him by his surname only when displeased or overwrought. Otherwise it was always "Billy-boy."

"Yes?" He was aware, but didn't give a damn, that the mosquito netting was enswathing him like a raffish bridal veil.

Wordlessly Burling thrust forward a sheet of paper, blue and sleazy. On it, inscribed in the ornate Spanish hand of the port telegrapher, was a single sentence of English. "You and Harmon will proceed by quickest transportation for consultation with me at Embassy. Warren Joab Henderson."

"That was fast," said Burling. "The answer to my love letter to the Ministers." On his face was the look of a prizefighter who has strutted from his corner only to be stopped by the first punch. His hand shook as he lit a cigarette. Sagging down to the very small camp chair alongside Harmon's bed, he puffed jerkily on the cigarette.

Was this the man, thought Harmon, who in Washington had

looked as big as a father? A surge of irritation went through him. Crumpling the telegram, he threw it on the floor.

"Why, Tarzan . . ." said Burling, his small eyes turning round.

"Hell," said Harmon, feeling marvelously tall of a sudden, marvelously muscular. "I don't care for Henderson's tone." After all, he was a father himself—wasn't he?—twice over. And last night . . . Well, he was certainly "all right" again, on top of the world! Let everybody take warning.

CHAPTER ELEVEN

LONG before the the little side-wheeler was to take off for Lorca, on the night tide, its promenade deck was covered over with the recumbent bodies of the third-class passengers. They had come aboard, the *rotos,* carrying hens and geese and suckling pigs in little crates or baskets, and fallen down instantly wherever a space offered itself, as if murdered by some violent plague which hovered at the juncture of gangplank and deck. The food-hawkers on the dock kept shouting, the rusty winches kept shrieking, and late arrivals came treading again and again from the gangplank, but nothing stirred the carpet of exhausted bodies. They lay in their various mannerisms of sleep: some huddled into balls, some straight and stiff, as if composed in coffins, some hugging the deck floor with hands and ears as if eavesdropping on a conversation below.

What a weariness, thought Harmon, as he and Burling picked their way gingerly across the human mosaic to the ladder that led up to A-deck, an existence that was self-defeating. Between dawn and dusk they were worked into animal exhaustion. From dusk to dawn they lay in suspended animation, gathering strength enough in the dark to start the same round all over again by daylight. It was from the labor of thousands such as these, the human work

machines, that Manriquez was a rich man. No wonder that Ernestina had felt stricken, no wonder that she had talked so penitently
of the cruelty of life in these countries. . . . On across the deck
Harmon threaded his way. A funeral barge, he thought. Only the
little animals in their cages seemed still to be alive, legatees of a
world where all that was human had been struck down. "Damn,"
winced Burling, as involuntarily he trod on the shoulder of an old
man wrapped mummy-like in a blanket. But the old man did not
stir. From between the slats of an orange crate, a piglet looked out
and squealed. But in some of these, the massacred, still glowed a
spark of hope, thought Harmon. There was the little porter, Teofilo,
he of the resplendent Greek name, and his desperate willingness to
believe, in spite of all, in the possibility of a "new life." He must not
be cheated. Something must be done about that "new life," *something*. It was not right that evolution should be reversed and that
men should be pressed down again to all fours. It was unbearable.

On A-deck they were received by a boy of fourteen or fifteen, barefoot and shirtless but wearing a crisp white yachting cap. A cabin
for two, asked Harmon. *Ai,* replied the boy purser—an evil situation.
There were only four private cabins on the ship altogether, and all
of them had long been reserved for a party traveling to Lorca for a
wedding.

"*Norteamericano,*" barked Burling. "*Comprendo?* Technical Mission. *Comprendo?*"

What Spanish, thought Harmon.

The boy purser shook his head woefully. On all the ship the only
sleeping accommodations left were those of the second-class saloon.

"*El capitán!*" brayed Burling.

"Don Carlos? He is all over the ship, Señor, making ready to
sail."

"*El capitán!*" insisted Burling.

The boy threw up his hands helplessly. Instantly Burling reached
for him.

"Christ," said Harmon, "pick on somebody your own size. Pick on Ambassadors."

They were assailed, at the door of the second-class saloon, by the odor of soiled flesh, by vapors from a human zoo. In the blue shadows of the night lamps could be discerned two layers of reclining men, one at knee height and the other at eye height. On the floor had been laid out a thicket of cots. And on high—it took another instant to make out that the flying men were perched, after all, in hammocks. But the hammocks had not been suspended in orderly rows and aisles, perhaps because here and there some of the sustaining hooks were missing from the ceiling, and each man in affixing his own hammock had fended for himself. Disorder had been compounded by further disorder. Some of the hammocks hung lengthwise, some breadthwise, and still others diagonally. It was like a huge spider web gone mad.

"God, oh, God," fumed Burling.

An aged hunchback came up and indicated a dwindled pile of hammocks near the threshold. *"Caballeros,"* he invited, "help yourselves."

But the hammocks, like the cots, were of a length for children. And from the packed-in sleepers came an unhappy tune-up: wheezing, groaning, coughing, hacking. All over the floor lay nipples of sputum.

For a moment longer Burling's jaws champed in silence. *"El capitán!"* he roared finally.

The hunchback motioned toward a round table at the far end of the saloon. From a shaded lamp on high fell an orange light upon the grave tight faces of half a dozen card players. Standing by inquisitively was a squat man with a sweatshirt, a Panama hat and a muffler wound twice around the neck.

"Capitán!" called Burling.

With bent fingers the captain saluted him from afar, cast one last lingering glance into the card game, then picked his way forward through the jungle of cots and hammocks. "*Ai*," he sighed, making the obvious guess, "there is not one single cabin left."

"Ask him about his own," snarled Burling. "He'll be on the bridge all night anyhow."

Harmon translated.

In a curious gesture, Don Carlos removed his Panama hat before answering. Was it because the hatband had carved a scarlet worm on his forehead, or because of awe before the name which he then uttered? "It was bespoken three days ago to Señor Manriquez and his lady."

Ernestina!

Abjectly Burling sat down on his suitcase.

Ernestina. Borne on the same ship with him.

"Harmon," said Burling wanly, all the fight now gone, "I put it on you to find me a berth."

Don Carlos sighed. Hereafter, he swore, a cabin would be reserved automatically for the Mission on each and every trip. Never again would this scandal happen, word of a seafarer. Ultimately, under Harmon's prodding, a recourse was found. There was a storage closet just beyond the saloon, regrettably without a porthole but it did have a ventilating tube, and room enough exactly for one cot. A barrel of drinking water would have to be moved but this would be done instantly, word of a seafarer.

Burling nodded relievedly. As an afterthought he asked, "Billy, what about *you?*"

His thoughts were on other things. He did not expect that he would sleep much this night in any case. "I'll manage," he said.

They stood at the rail as the little steamer cast off, as with grunts of pain she turned away from the splintered dock on which all the town stood and silently watched the departure—cut off for another half-week from all the world beyond. From the dock's edge two or three men waved to him, and he was pricked suddenly by a feeling of guilt at thus sailing away, if only for three or four days. Alba had become his personal charge somehow, his private responsibility.

The lights of the dock drew together into a single glimmering rod. Dimmer and dimmer burned the rod, shorter and shorter on the black moonless air. Then abruptly it vanished as the ship turned the bend of the bay and headed north up the coast. From the night-cloaked shore came a heavy jungle scent, compounded of flora and fauna, musky but provocative, like that of a woman moist from dancing. He wondered what eyes looked out from that hidden coast.

"One thing," said Burling, sagging down to the rail bench, "I'm not going home with my tail between my legs. If the Ambassador bounces me, I'll see that this gets on the front page of every damn newspaper in the States. Boon-doggling. Pampering of Hottentots."

Hottentots! Where now was the self-proclaimed friend of the underdog—the humanitarian who had dreamed some day of being known as "Burling of Alba"? For every occasion he could pull out a new and suitable personality, like masquerades from a closet.

"Hell," said Harmon acidly, gazing away all the while at the black calm sea, "you wouldn't be the first crusader who faded out with one big paragraph in the newspapers. There happens to be a war on. In the States they don't even know we exist. Or give a goddamn."

The thought seemed to stop Burling short. For a long time he rocked back and forth in reflection. "All right," he said finally, "I've got it."

Another trick?

"We beat the Ambassador to the punch. Bad temper? Sorry, Mr. Henderson, but do you realize what we've been up against? No support from Washington. Nothing to work with. And on us the eyes of fifty thousand people."

It had the merit, thought Harmon, of being true.

"Fine, decent, suffering people who have been led to expect something of us . . ."

What—Hottentots no longer?

"Those people, Mr. Ambassador, must not be let down. I tell you . . ."

But it was just then that a door—the door for which all this while Harmon had been waiting—opened at the steamer's bridge. "Come," said an expected voice, one with a tone of languid authority. "A breath of air before we turn in."

"We beat Henderson to the punch!" repeated Burling, now all revived, bubbling with self-satisfaction. "Before he can even open his jaws . . ."

Harmon was no longer listening. His eyes were fixed upon the open doorway and the amber light which fell upon it from a deck lamp above. When Ernestina Manriquez came out, what would she be wearing? What costume? What colors? He was greedy for all the possible varieties of her.

"Come," repeated Manriquez from the threshold.

A linen suit, she was wearing, molded smoothly over her breasts and her hips. She had stepped into the doorway as into a picture frame. Over the distance his gaze groped for hers. He prayed that she would look up and smile at him.

It happened. "Mr. Harmon!" she called out, and with frank pleasure. For her the meeting had been so sudden, so unexpected, that she had not had time to consider whether again she ought to engage in concealment.

Now *he* strode up, the somber seigneur, placing himself between his wife and Harmon. For some purpose? Or simply from the rudeness of the high-born? But in another moment they were standing four together. It was to be hoped, said Manriquez, that the Director would make no fuss about that little patch of land which it was his privilege to present to the Mission. Colonel Burling, in the name of his Government, had the honor to accept. He hoped ultimately to find a way of reciprocating. The North American gentlemen were visiting Lorca? Ah, Chimboya. Beware of the altitude. Not too much exertion the first day. Otherwise they would be overcome with *siroche,* that vertigo caused by scanty oxygen.

With each exchange of pleasantries, Ernestina Manriquez glanced back and forth. From Burling to her husband. From her husband to Burling. In every direction, thought Harmon, but his. He felt so left out.

Was the Director, asked Manriquez, drawing Burling off, aware of how rich Alba was in timber? Mahogany, balsa, teak—to mention only a few of the fine lumbers for which the warring Allies were crying. It would be his pleasure to indicate certain extraordinary stands on his very own estate. . . .

All the while they kept drifting off, the two men of affairs, farther and farther away toward the bow. And, said Manriquez, in regard to the Mission's program for developing new local industries . . .

Now finally they stood alone, he and Ernestina, abandoned superciliously to the solitude for which he had burned. "My husband," she murmured, and again it was with a trace of a barb, "is a man of ideas."

Harmon braced himself. "Ernestina . . ." he whispered, ever so faintly, calling her by name for the very first time.

"Sometimes," she went on, unnoticing, "I think that not even Ramón knows how many irons he has in the fire."

"Ernestina," he repeated. Boldly now.

Her lips parted. She darted a glance, instantly, toward the bow, toward her husband still deep in his talk with Burling. "Oh, please," she said, but it was pleadingly, not chidingly.

It was all he needed. "Ernestina!" he said again. Defiantly now. He reveled in it, the speaking of her name, the sphere of intimacy into which thus he snatched her.

"Please, please," she whispered. "This is dangerous."

Dangerous? The thought filled him only with elation. "Ernestina —Ernestina!" he repeated. Joyously now. It was a way of having her. He sensed, he guessed, he knew it for an absolute certainty now, that she wanted him as he wanted her.

But still, fearfully, she hesitated. She shook her head and the long black tresses tossed from side to side. "Oh, please," she whispered. "What good can come of it?"

He grinned wildly, indifferent to all practicalities, all hazards. Here finally he had found access, the first access. Under his feet the ship was rocking as if the whole planet were erupting. Never before had he felt such a sense of recklessness, the grandeur of being a man, being male. It was she who had brought this out of him, Ernestina. "You're so beautiful," he said, "everything you do."

"Please—please," she said, again shaking her head. But not once had she said that she found this distasteful, only dangerous. "Beautiful," he repeated. "Beautiful."

Back and forth, nervously, from her husband to Harmon, from Harmon to her husband, she glanced. Over the taut slanted cheekbones, came finally a smile. "Am I?" she asked.

"Don't you know?" It could be that she did not. It could be that her loveliness had long ago ceased to have a use for her. She wore it so negligently.

"This isn't," she said with a sweet woefulness, "how I wanted to look. I wanted to look—sunny, healthy. Like those lovely girls from the West."

The girls who wore saddle shoes? The girls who looked like—like Laura? He shook this thought off irritatedly. He wanted no part of it.

"Really," she said, "I could tell you so *many* things about myself that I don't like."

Covertly, all at once, he snatched at her hand, that white and lovely hand.

"Oh, please—please," she protested. But she did not make to free her hand, that silken token of her flesh, all that it was possible for him in this moment to have of her. "Please . . ." Again her glance went toward the bow.

"Would he kill us?" asked Harmon mockingly. "You think he really would?" It was the first time in ages that he had been able to draw so much enjoyment from himself, that he approved of himself.

"Mr. Harmon . . ." Her lips twisted with some thought that she hesitated to pursue. Her forehead puckered with a little chevron of anxiety. Then, suddenly, she wrenched loose her hand. "Ramón!" she cried.

How could she do this to him? How, when they meant so much to each other, could she . . . ? Doubling his fists, Harmon wheeled about.

"Yes?" called Manriquez from the bow.

"I—I'm dreadfully sleepy, Ramón."

Minx. On the curved lips flickered a smile, but one that was waspish, girlishly malicious.

"Go ahead," called Manriquez. "I'll join you in a few minutes."

Such husbandly indifference. How could a man who owned all the rights to that wonderful body bear to forgo them?

"Good night, Mr. Harmon," she said, her face as blank again as a plate. Cruelly, she withheld from him even the formal handshake.

"Good night, Señora Manriquez."

Back down the deck toward her cabin she walked—in a narrow and delicate sway. He longed, in a new flash of fever, to be the shoes on her feet, the silk on her flesh. He prayed, as she reached the cabin door, that she would turn and give him one last glance.

But she did not.

Wrapped in his topcoat, he lay all night on the ribbed wooden bench outside the cabin. It tormented him that she should be sharing it with another man.

CHAPTER TWELVE

Up they flew, up over the steep slanted fields where Indians in crimson *serapes* harvested the wheat, and columns of sheep followed after to feed upon the stubble. Beyond the golden meadows stood moon-dead silver peaks—extinct volcanos with thunderous Inca names, Monopaxi, Rumbala, the frozen incarnations of legends about maidens who had died of love or young warriors who had wrestled with the heavens.

Still the plane climbed, now above black, terraced hills where the children of the Incas tended the rich root they had given to all the world for food, the potato. The terraces leaped toward the brilliant blue sky, mile after mile, like a stairway for giants.

And next the plane was shuttling jerkily through passes in the mountain, among great cathedral walls and tall sharp spires. The passengers gripped the arms of their chairs with each crucial turn, each scant evasion of collision and death. They were passing through a world of permanent crisis, among aerial shoals where the flight of an aluminum shell was an insolence, and each extra moment of life was something snatched from the fire.

"*Cosa fantastica*—it's a lulu!" said a genial young man who sat across the aisle. "And I've made this flight fifty times." He spoke English in American style.

Out from the black rock into the bitter white sun, in the clear again. Now they were soaring over a high flat plateau—the roof of the world, the genial young man called it—where horsemen raised screens of yellow dust behind them on the roads and where lay brown lakes without fish or vegetation, said the young man, a world scorched and poisoned by ancient torrents of lava from the volcanos now extinct, the glacial tombstones of the maidens and warriors. . . . The horsemen rode over this land as if to flee it.

Up, still up. Now they were skimming over a sea of gray crags, of stone lashed in former aeons into waves and rollers. Nowhere among the rocky undulations could the eye find a patch of the more friendly earth. If suddenly the heart of this metal bird should stop beating, if its forward propulsion should cease, and together with its passengers it should become its many tons of dead weight . . .

"*Algo raro*—it's a nifty," said the young man with genial excitement. His Spanish, like his English, was utterly without foreign accent. He had a deep love, evidently, for the Andes, or their dangers.

Now a ball of fleece hurled itself at the plane, and passed on. Then a second, which also went harmlessly by. Then too many of them to count. And finally the plane was enveloped totally in a cloud bank. "I've known times," said the young man, "when a fog would come up and we couldn't locate the last pass into Chimboya, and we'd circle around for hours and just have to go back to Lorca." This troublesome phenomenon pleased him immensely.

"You can have them, your rock-lined clouds," said Burling, wheezing heavily. In these upper altitudes he had begun to wilt.

The genial young man finally introduced himself. His name was Elliott Reeves and it turned out that he worked at the Embassy as Second Secretary. Harmon, with a certain expectancy, completed the introductions.

"Oh," said Reeves, "the Lost Battalion."

Burling glanced up belligerently. "Is that what they call us?"

"The Ambassador," said Reeves, "calls you worse than that. His Dead End Kids."

Burling's irritation gave way suddenly to pride. "You bet," he said, "the toughest little bunch of rootin', tootin' roosters anybody ever saw."

"We chew crowbars," added Harmon lackadaisically, "and spit nails."

"If His Excellency," said Burling, "would leave his teacups long enough to come down to Alba and see what we've been up against . . ."

"*Ya lo sé*—I know," nodded Reeves, and it was hard to tell which of his two identities was the definitive one. "I was born in this country. Of missionaries."

"We live worse," said Burling, "than coolies in China. The food. The quarters. Not a night that two or three of us don't find snakes in our beds."

"Yes," said Harmon, "absolutely."

"Half of us down with malaria. My chief engineer dying of dysentery."

"*Doloroso,*" said Reeves, "tough going."

Burling pointed a forefinger in deadly menace. "Reeves," he warned, "if His Excellency has any notion of rapping our knuckles, if he thinks we're going to take it lying down . . ." He broke off with a sinister jerk of his head. "Dead End Kids? You bet!"

"Absolutely," said Harmon. He recalled, tartly, the suddenness with which Burling had collapsed before the Ambassador's telegram. He wondered how well this revived belligerence would hold up in Chimboya.

"Well," said Reeves, backing off amiably, "Mr. Henderson has plenty of headaches on this job. The tin horn who runs this country . . ." He lowered his voice discreetly. "Rivera gets a great kick out of being called the *Constitutional* President. Proud as a whorehouse madam with a pew in church. Once in a while it's even permitted for a deputy to stand up and say boo. But Rivera runs this country through the Carabineros. The *real* Congress are the boys with the guns."

A bad taste came instantly into Harmon's mouth. He had not had occasion before this to think much about the Republic's politics. He had accepted, willingly, desperately, Frank Rhodes's assurance that the job was "clean," and let it go at that. But now . . . "Rivera," he asked, "was elected, wasn't he—one of the few Presidents who came in without a revolution, wasn't he?"

Reeves winked. "You bet. He won the cemetery vote unanimously. Have you heard the latest one? Why is Rivera like an airplane—like the sun—like a cook? One, he's always up in the air. Two, you can't bear to look at him. Three, he's always making love to the cops. At that, Rivera is one of the best. In Rivera's time, at least, nobody has been dragged around behind mules."

"At least," said Burling, "he's kind to mules."

The clouds raced away, and into the plane burst streamers of sunlight. Alongside Harmon's window a black object dashed up imperially—an eagle. It convoyed the plane for the barest instant, then vanished in the wake.

Up ahead now loomed a great black rampart, its base lost in a rolling sea of cotton-white clouds. "Cotolunga's Wall," announced Reeves. Already the plane was winging over westward in a wide arc before the towering rampart. The motors slowed—and straight ahead lay a gateway which was only a wild gash in the black rock, as wide perhaps as five wingspreads. Slowly, cautiously, the plane drifted through.

Then, this last crisis passed, the plane was looping earthward in wide spirals. Below, like sugar cubes in a bowl, lay Chimboya, white and gleaming. The plane leveled off and the city rushed by only a few hundred feet below. "The Presidential Palace," Reeves called out. "Church of the Benedictines. The Montalvo Gardens."

Then a long straight road leaped at them, a road lined with tall, tall eucalyptus trees. Indians in brilliantly colored *serapes* looked up from their burros and waved.

Up forward the indicator flashed notice to fasten safety belts. And there before them, an ordered square on the tawny plateau, lay the Chimboya Airport.

"Don't," warned Reeves as the plane swooped to a landing, "don't take the Ambassador for a pushover. *Un hombre capaz*—he's one tough baby."

The crisp young woman in the tailored suit came back to the reception room. "Mr. Henderson's dictating cables," she reported. "I'll get his attention the minute he's free."

From Burling, sunk low on the sofa he was sharing with Harmon, came a melancholy groan. His skin had turned gray. Once again he resembled a large woebegone baby.

"Gentlemen," asked the young woman, "have you brought any written reports?" She stood provisionally in the doorway, her hands tucked into the pockets of her crisp gray suit. She wore a crown of ash-blonde curls of which each strand was fixed tightly in place. Junior executive, thought Harmon, dynamic. "Mr. Henderson likes to be thoroughly briefed before receiving callers."

"Oh, he's briefed," said Harmon wryly. A moment before he had bent to tie a shoelace and all had gone black. It was only with a real effort that he had managed to haul himself back. His limbs and head hung from him like dead weights. And everything up here was cold to the touch—the stone, the wood, the leather, even the people. Three times he had lit a cigarette but had been unable to keep it going. This rare mountain air was meant for birds, not humans.

Again Burling sighed.

"Altitude?" queried the young woman. "What gets *me* is the cold. Like late November all year around and nobody ever heats their houses." She was pretty, thought Harmon, but there was something about her features which affected him disagreeably. "How's it in Alba? Terribly awful hot?"

"Only in the afternoons," said Harmon. "Mild enough the rest of the day."

She tilted her face as toward the sun. "Mmm," she said, "that's for me."

He wondered mildly at her preoccupation with weather.

"Long is my name," she said, sauntering over, hands still tucked in her pockets. "Rosabel Long."

"Delighted," said Harmon. He started to rise.

"Oh, don't," she said.

Burling, for a greeting, merely groaned.

Miss Long seated herself on the sofa arm next to Harmon. Neatly she crossed her legs and adjusted her skirt to a point an inch below the knee. "Cross your heart," she said, "just how bad *is* Alba?"

"Awful," he said, with a half-conscious flutter of pride. For contrast he gazed pointedly about the reception room with its red-plush furniture, its white walls hung with Inca tapestries, the Spanish ironwork of the fireplace and the polished hardwood floor decked with animal skins and deep-pile rugs.

Miss Long drew on her cigarette and ejected a neat little javelin of smoke. "Mr. Harmon," she said, "you wouldn't be putting it on just a little, would you?"

Damn her. He discovered simultaneously what was disagreeable about her features. Her forehead bulged a bit too much, and her chin was a trifle too sharp and small. It gave her head the topheavy look of an embryo, a pretty and clever embryo.

She stood up and smoothed herself out crisply. "Gentlemen," she said, "I'll see what I can do."

They were seated now, a pair of delinquents in the headmaster's study, on a handsome cowhide-covered sofa.

"Demn it," said the Ambassador, *"demn* it." He pronounced the oath stylishly and frostily. He, too, was cold to the touch. A lean man, he wore long sideburns which gave him a resemblance to the nineteenth-century statesmen, one which he seemed intent on cultivating. "Burling," he said, "you have all the graces of a mad rhinoceros."

"I'm an administrator," protested Burling wheezily, "not a dancing master."

"Shut up," said the Ambassador, but without heat. Glacially, in fact.

Burling fell back like a panting fish in a basket. If hauling him up here to this thin atmosphere had been calculated to take the fight out of him, it was succeeding. His was a temperament that burned copious oxygen.

"An hour after your letter reached the Ministers," said Henderson, "the Palace had me on the phone. Rivera wanted your passports. It took me two days to talk him out of it. Burling, just why do you think you were sent here?"

"To do a job . . ." said Burling, but growing fainter all the while. "To show these poor suffering people that the Good Neighbor Policy is something more than a lot of Washington talk . . ."

"Hmmm," said the Ambassador. A brilliant light played from his eyes, but icily. He stood up from his blond-mahogany desk, strode over to a wall rack of maps and pulled one down testily. Like a schoolmaster, thought Harmon, one who hates teaching.

With his lean forefinger extended, the Ambassador swooped down on a pinpoint of black in the Pacific blue. "Pearl Harbor," he grunted. (A long way from Alba, thought Harmon.) "After December Seventh . . ." The Ambassador wrinkled his nose distastefully. His forefinger then skithered due east across the ocean blue and found a landfall well short of the coast of South America. "The Porpoise Islands—an insular possession of this Republic." (But when, thought Harmon, do we get to Alba?)

Superciliously, however, the lean forefinger over-leaped the coast, the Republic too, and several other countries—and landed instead at the narrow waist of the hemisphere. "The Panama Canal," said the Ambassador with a certain respect, even reverence. "After December Seventh all this lay open to the Japanese fleet like a Cook's tour. Do you follow?"

Burling, still fighting for air, just barely nodded.

"Harmon?"

He found himself flushing savagely. He could think only of Vicente Hidalgo and that tart sceptical warning at their first meeting. Every Conquistador, Hidalgo had warned, has his purposes, and altruism is not one of them. "Yes," murmured Harmon, "I follow."

The Ambassador let the wall map snap back. From his desk humidor he took a short fat cigar and lit it. "The significance of the Republic," he said, and so coolly, "is that it constitutes the western doorway into the hemisphere. After Pearl Harbor we had to have bases. At once. In the islands and on the mainland. We had to have an end of the Border War. The door had to be closed." The Ambassador looked at his cigar and frowned disdainfully. "Rivera? But he did give us bases. He did end the Border War. He did expel the Axis nationals." The Ambassador deigned frostily to forgive his cigar and take another puff. "There are elements in this Republic who are hostile to Rivera. Because of the war settlement—for other reasons. But if Rivera goes, he will be succeeded probably by someone worse. By some out-and-out Axis man."

Harmon bit his lip.

"Washington," said the Ambassador plainly, "wants Rivera to stay in the Palace. Your function is to help keep him there. Other missions are on the way. Also a very large loan from Export-Import Bank."

And what of the "new life"? Nothing about the "new life"? This was not the way it had looked to Frank Rhodes in Washington. Nor the way it had been heralded to the weary, dying men in Alba. Up here everything looked different, as cold and thin as the air itself. But he must, all along, have suspected something like this. He could not have been *that* naïve—except that he had chosen to be. In the words of Hidalgo, for the *private* purposes. He had wanted to run away, he had wanted a new start, and there was nothing, probably, that he would have let stand in his path. Inside him, now, gathered a bitter rage—against the Ambassador, against stratagems, and against himself.

"Mr. Henderson . . ." he found himself saying.

"Yes?"

"Our job then is to play a high-class shell game." The words jetted clear and cold from his mouth, he noted, like a shower of icicles.

The Ambassador sniffed. "Harmon," he said, "your country happens to be engaged in a war for its survival. Most Americans your age are carrying guns these days, or preparing to."

Harmon smiled thinly. "They wouldn't give me a gun," he said. Elsewhere, at sea level, anywhere but on this mountain peak, his

answer would have been hotter. He was becoming one with the
terrain.

"Sorry," said the Ambassador. His cigar had almost died, and he
huffed and puffed at it a while. "The money spent in Alba cannot
do it the slightest harm. A considerable amount of good, in fact.
But it won't help *any* of us if Rommel should be ferrying tanks
across from Dakar next year. Harmon, keep your eye on the world
picture."

To the men lying death-weary on the ship's deck what was the
world picture?

"First and foremost, your objective is to keep on friendly terms
with the regime. They may look like crooks at times, but don't antagonize them. Diplomatic consideration first and foremost. Understood?"

"Understood," wheezed Burling wretchedly. All he seemed to care
about now was to get back to sea level.

"Harmon?"

In his mind, once more, Harmon heard the imprecations of that
grief-blinded drunkard. "Altruists! Brothers from the North! Philanthropists!" In his mind, once more, he saw a mirthless grin that
flashed from white, incorruptible teeth. Suddenly he found himself
standing up.

"Well!" said the Ambassador, lifting an eyebrow. "If the policies
laid down by the Congress and the Department of State do not
coincide with your own views, Harmon, there is always an alternative."

Alternative? He bethought himself instantly of those law texts in
New York. Of the petty skirmishes between Finch and Finch which
did not in the least interest him. He thought how it would be to
return once more to that house of sovereign women. Of Laura and
her endlessly inquiring eyes.

"Harmon," croaked Burling, "the Ambassador's talking to you."

He bethought himself, contrariwise, of that joyous, manly moment in which he had killed a snake—of the title plate which read "Associate Director"—of the overlordship that had come with it, the deference, the esteem. And also of that soft, scented girl with the gray eyes to whom he looked so whole, so strong—whom he had come so close already to taking in his arms. But still that sardonic grin of Hidalgo's flashed before him. "Bum!" he cried out in his mind. "Rumpot! Mind your own lousy business!"

"Well?" asked the Ambassador.

His knees, all at once, gave way.

"Considering the world picture . . ." he said, lamely and self-derisively. He sat down.

"Right," said the Ambassador with a lingering glance, as if to keep Harmon in mind for future reference. "From now on no more mash notes to the Ministers. Understood?"

Burling sighed penitently.

"Ready to go back now and do a job that won't discredit the country you represent?"

"Right," said Burling.

How boneless he had turned, that fighting bull. Was it only because of the altitude? Or had there never been any bones inside that mighty bulk in the first place?

"Good," said the Ambassador.

He had swallowed the camel, but it was left to him still to strain at the gnat. "Mr. Henderson . . ." he said, breaking determinedly through the icy languor with which this cold high city had begun to ensheathe him, "I don't believe it was the intent of the Congress that we should make jackasses of ourselves."

The Ambassador glanced up sharply.

"The Mission," Harmon went on, "is a farce so far. We have almost nothing to work with. We're going through motions, and not much more." These were the things, it occurred to him, which Burling all along had threatened to say, and had not—not a word.

"Harmon," snapped the Ambassador, "there happens to be . . ."

"Yes, sir, there happens to be a war on. But if the Alba Mission is of military significance, then it should be entitled to military priorities."

The Ambassador smiled. "Very neat," he said. "There speaks the legal mind. Just what do you need, Harmon?"

"Iron pipe and locomotive parts. Motors and chlorinators." He rattled it off bitterly. "Heavy-duty trucks. Powdered milk and surgical equipment. Disk harrows and wire screen. Before anything, a first-class medical officer."

The Ambassador squinted at a sheaf of papers on his desk. "Your medical officer," he said, "leaves Washington in approximately two weeks."

"Good show," wheezed Burling.

The Ambassador turned back to Harmon. "Get up a list of everything you want. I'll forward it with my personal endorsement."

"Thank you," said Harmon, but glacially. He wondered whether he could be considered to have squared himself. With Hidalgo. And with himself.

"One other thing," said the Ambassador. "From now on I want to be posted regularly on all Mission activities. Weekly progress reports."

Burling groaned.

"Frankly," said Harmon, "we're not set up for weekly reports. We haven't got the clerical staff."

"I can remedy that."

Instinctively Harmon glanced toward the door.

"Miss Long, my administrative assistant," said the Ambassador, "has requested a transfer. For personal reasons."

Instantly, like a metronome, Burling's head went swinging from side to side. It was his first real gesture of obstinacy since he had entered the room. "Alba," he said, "is mighty rough going."

"Miss Long knows that."

"We just don't have the accommodations for women," said Burling.

"Then make them, *demn* it, make them! I'm offering you the

most capable member of my entire staff, Burling, a brilliant young woman, *demn* it. I expect you to be grateful, *demn* it."

Brilliant young woman . . . Into the preserve that had been walled off for men only, the haven where he had stopped feeling the cracks in his bones, a "brilliant young woman" would now come striding. He'd had enough of them, the clever Amazons, enough. Burling, he wanted to shout, don't give in.

Burling bit his lip. The objections of Burling, obviously, lay in the fact that Miss Long would be coming to Alba as the Ambassador's personal observer, as his spy. Burling bit his lip but said finally, "Thank you, sir. That's very kind of you, sir."

Now the wall was breached.

PART THREE: *The Eaglets*

CHAPTER THIRTEEN

On the surface, Harmon thought as he talked with Editor Donoso, things did seem to be looking up, though in the two weeks since Chimboya no word had come through yet about the requested priorities.

Donoso, like so many Albanese, was heavily pock-marked, but the effect was not unpleasant, rather like hammered bronze. Tiny enough to be almost a grotesque, the editor wore a black suit that was sharply pressed but notably spotted. Throughout the interview he kept taking notes on the backs of old envelopes which several times he returned to his breast pocket only to have to bring them out for further jottings as new ideas occurred to Harmon. He was eager, obviously, to get on to some matter closer to his heart.

But Harmon was determined. "The apprentice engineers," he continued, "are working out most satisfactorily. Right now we have them surveying the new all-weather road to Rosales and also designing schoolhouses. Our economist, Dr. Horanyi, has begun this week to receive applications for business loans. In a few days he will start a census of the province, the first complete one in all its history."

"Most stimulating," said Editor Donoso, "most animating." He made again to return the sheaf of scuffed envelopes to his pocket.

"Now, if the *Señor Asociado* will permit me to allude to a personal matter, one of an economic nature, incidentally . . ."

Harmon had a strong hunch as to where this "personal matter" would point. Was the worthy editor, he interrupted in a certain spirit of mischief, aware also of the many experimental plantings which had been started at the demonstration farm? Of the establishment of the new center for processing cactus fiber? And the plans to bring in blooded stock from abroad?

"Efforts without parallel," said Editor Donoso, but patently restive. "A renaissance!"

"Well," said Harmon, "I wouldn't go that far."

"Absolutely!" insisted Editor Donoso. "These are accomplishments which should be broadcast throughout the province. And will be." He stuffed away the wad of old envelopes in his breast pocket once more and buttoned up his jacket with an air of really final finality. Was the Mission fully cognizant, he desired to ask, of the high professional caliber and the strong spiritual self-dedication of the Alba *Messenger,* of which weekly journal he had the honor to be both editor and publisher?

"Absolutely," said Harmon.

But every enterprise, naturally, had also its practical side. In order for the *Messenger* to be able to carry out successfully its role of intermediary betwen the North American Mission and the people of Alba . . .

The door opened and Ross poked in his head. "Hey," he said, "Santa Ana is ready to go. Don't forget to tell this editor guy about Santa Ana."

"Are you sure?" asked Harmon. "I'd rather not get us out on a limb."

"Mister," declared Ross flatly, "tomorrow night everybody in Santa Ana will be taking a bath. I'm on my way there right now for a trial run."

He closed the door and went down the hallway in a heavy, happy jig.

"Something about Santa Ana?" asked Editor Donoso reluctantly.

"Tomorrow afternoon," explained Harmon, "the water system of Santa Ana will be restored to operation. With appropriate ceremonies."

"Most inspiriting," said Editor Donoso. He made one further note, grudgingly. But to resume the thread of his discourse . . . In a province of such low literacy it was no small feat to keep a weekly journal going. And the temptations were very great. For instance, before the Constitutional President last winter drove out the Axis dogs, it had been the custom of the German and Italian embassies to offer large subventions in return for editorials favorable to the Axis cause. As if the free press of Alba were on the auction block! The Axis dogs, thank heaven, were gone now, but there were still many *native* elements at large, moral derelicts, who hoped to revive the old and foolish bugaboo of *yanqui* imperialism. Such men must be fought tooth and nail. The columns of the *Messenger* would be open therefore at all times to the Technical Mission—hemisphere unity!—so that its acomplishments might be set forth in their true light. It was probable that the Mission would want to reserve a moderate number of copies each week, not only to study this sincere journal for themselves but also to pass along examples to interested parties throughout the Republic and even to higher authorities back in Washington. Say, a thousand copies a week?

Harmon smiled. Commiseratingly.

At the bulk rate, calculated Editor Donoso, this would come out to no more than five hundred pesos weekly—fifty North American dollars.

"Most provocative," said Harmon. All this, of course, would be independent of the editor's plans for reporting the Mission's activities?

"Absolutely."

In fact, hazarded Harmon, to print such news factually, honestly and impartially should of itself bring many readers to the paper and improve its economic position perceptibly.

"Well," said Editor Donoso, "to a degree."

"In any event, the Mission will naturally want to take a certain number of subscriptions. Say . . ."

"Seven hundred and fifty?"

Pityingly Harmon gazed at him. That stained and spotted suit, so wistfully well-pressed . . . The natively keen intellect, but so fly-blown, so heart-breakingly shabby, tropical. The shifts and stratagems to which poverty had reduced him. "Twenty-five," said Harmon.

Not a line altered in the hammered-bronze face. Was it possible that the Mission was not interested really in observing how its activities would be interpreted to the people of Alba?

"Most enthusiastically interested," said Harmon. "Unhappily there is no provision in the budget for spending—spending approximately two thousand dollars a year for the pleasure of reading about ourselves. For that sum we can equip a modern surgery, build an entire new schoolhouse."

The little bronze idol tilted forward. "But of what use to equip a modern surgery if there is no *Messenger* to explain the import, to elucidate that no longer is it necessary to fear the hospitals now that the *gringos*—eh, the North American technicians . . ."

"Twenty-five copies," repeated Harmon with a sorrowful smile.

Donoso stood up. Let it be understood that he admired the caution of the Associate Director wholeheartedly. Perhaps in good time, after due consultation with Colonel Burling himself, it might be considered whether, say, five hundred copies were not within the capacity of the Mission, after all. Well, this was no time to discuss future eventualities.

Poor crooked starveling . . . As Harmon saw him to the door, it opened from the other side. Hector Serrano, the office manager, as dapper as ever in his gleaming white trousers and polo shirt.

"Ah, Señor Serrano!"

"Good morning, Señor Donoso!"

They embraced each other delightedly and pounded each other

vigorously on the kidneys in the standard greeting of Latin American males.

"The wife?"

"Fine! How's yours?"

"Equally!"

"The children? Mine are splendid!"

"The same!"

They stood off and gazed at each other emotionally.

"So good to get together again!"

"Heartwarming!"

Serrano closed the door. "That crook . . ." he whispered instantly. "Whatever he proposed, *Señor Asociado,* I presume you did not accept his first offer."

"I didn't make *any* deal."

"No?" With amazement.

"If he's a crook, why make a deal?"

"But who has to make deals with *honest* men?" It was a new slant, thought Harmon, the tropical one. "By the way, *Señor Asociado,* I have a message for you. At Rosales I ran into Vicente Hidalgo."

"Did you?"

"He sends his best regards. 'To the Innocent Colossus.'"

Harmon smiled, but uncertainly. Innocent? After that talk in Chimboya with the Ambassador, after the concessions he had made, it was not a compliment he was sure he merited. "How well do you know him, Hector?"

"In this country the number of men who can read a book is very small. We knock against each other all the time. That knight of the broken lance—never do I see him but that I want to offer a requiem."

Again Harmon found his curiosity stirred. "Why do you say that?"

Serrano shrugged his shoulders. "Once Hidalgo was on his way to becoming a very big man in this country. You've heard of Montalvo's 'eaglets,' the youngsters whom he kept about him all the time to train? Of these, Hidalgo was his absolute favorite, the one in whom he set the greatest store. You know, Hidalgo might even have been sitting today in the Presidential Palace, except for a serious defect. He could never"—Serrano smiled ruefully—"he could never learn how to make a deal."

Yes, that Incorruptible . . .

"To survive a defect like that," said Serrano, "you have to be a Cesar Montalvo. And you know, *Señor Asociado,* to what a horrible end Montalvo himself finally came. It was not only our reactionaries who roasted his body in the public gardens that day. And carried his head on a pole. He had enemies enough in his own party—men for whom power and the national treasury meant the same thing." Serrano rubbed thumb and forefinger together disdainfully. "Hidalgo they left to mourn by the coffin. Themselves they headed straight for the Palace. In due time, of course, they offered Hidalgo a ministry. His task would be to spread his fine young wings over their dirty work. Among the other eaglets there were plenty who gave in. For instance, the man who today is the Minister of Mines and whom everybody calls the 'Minesweeper' for the clean sweep he has made of his bureau's funds. After all, *Señor Asociado,* the difference between an eagle and a buzzard is not very great—only that the eagle goes for living game, the buzzard for carrion."

"And Hidalgo?" asked Harmon. He found himself awaiting the answer with a certain odd excitement, as though the years had rolled back and the young giant of then were again standing at the fork of decision.

"He fought them. In the House of Deputies. In the newspapers. On street corners. Thugs went after him and beat him up. Bullets were fired into his window. He fought very bravely, I can tell you, but it was a losing battle. In a very short time most of Montalvo's work was swept away. For this Hidalgo blamed mostly himself.

A failure—because he could not match a man we know today to have been a genius. Hidalgo began to drink."

A pilgrim himself, then, on the ceaseless quest for manhood. . . .

"Once while he was in his cups," said Serrano, "his home took fire. About twenty years ago that was, up in Chimboya. It cost him his wife and his only child. How the fire broke out . . ." Serrano shrugged his portly shoulders. "The buzzards, of course, made the most of it. The scandal drove Vicente all the way down to this swamp." Serrano twitched his nostrils. "Today, in a manner of speaking, Vicente does not smell so good. Today we have a new species of idealist, young men trained on party dogmas. Clean-living, athletic, disciplined. Hidalgo? A has-been, a stewpot. But I have never known a more innocent spirit in my life, *Señor Asociado*. He has been to hell and the Devil never even left a soot mark on him."

That lonely heartbroken warrior, hopeless of victory, but impelled still to go on giving battle . . . Across Harmon's mind there flashed a picture of that odd, murderous confrontation at the *verbena* in the light of the lanterns, that fratricidal bout. "By the way, Hector," he asked, "do you know the Governor, Montalvo's son?"

"Not very well. He was away for many years in our foreign service. A kind of national orphan whom all parties have felt obliged to look after. He and Hidalgo don't care much for each other."

"Yes," said Harmon. "It's what I wanted to ask."

"Oh, some personal matter. Even in an eagle's nest there's bound to be a certain amount of scrabbling, *Señor Asociado*. Especially."

The door, just then, was flung open. In stalked Rosabel Long, heavy-laden with documents. "Oh, brother!" she groaned.

Harmon glanced up quizzically.

"I don't mind sitting up half the night to type Ross's reports for him," said Miss Long. "I don't even mind translating them into King's English. But an engineer ought at least to make sense on his engineering, shouldn't he?" She came up to the desk and dropped a sheaf of the papers.

Serrano, with an oblique glance, a covert roll of his eyes, excused himself. For him, he had said privately, the Señorita Long was a rather baffling type, an *exotique* to Latin America.

"Well," asked Harmon grouchily, "what's it all about?"

Standing alongside him, Miss Long shuffled through the offending document. "There—where he toted up his budget for the rest of the year. One million dollars, he has it. Even a moron ought to know it's one million *pesos*—just a tenth as much."

How quickly she had found the weakest spot in all the staff. "All right," he said, "anybody's pencil can slip."

"Oh, brother," said Miss Long, "his pencil slipped for five pages straight."

"Ross has too much to do." He would have been perfectly willing to admit Ross's shortcomings to a man—they were there, all right.

"Now, Bill," she said softly, passing over casually the fact that she was calling him by his Christian name for the first time, "Fred Ross is just about smart enough to carry a surveyor's tripod, and you know it."

He wondered what, behind his back, she said about him. "Nothing of the kind," he grunted.

A faint tart smile lifted her lips. It had that same private in-looking quality as when Laura—his wife Laura—wished to indicate that it was time for him to stop playacting. "Well," he said grudgingly, "the war took the best engineers a long time ago. Ross came from the bottom of the barrel."

She dug into a pile of papers again with her quick white hands. "And Anderson . . . !" she said.

Enough was enough. "If anybody around here's on the ball," he said, "it's Walt Anderson."

"Really? I was at him three days for his progress report. Look what he gave me." She passed over a single sheet covered with pencil scrawls.

"It's short," he snapped, "but it's all there."

Again she smiled. That bleak, unlovely gloat. "Bill," she said, patting him lightly on the shoulder, "I know these tropical tramps. From 'way back. Don't be so scared to crack the whip over them."

You and I—two against the world. She wore a perfume, subtle and tantalizing, that was exactly what the flesh of a beautiful girl ought to smell like. But on this office Amazon—he felt almost grieved for the misuse to which the lovely perfume had been put.

"All right," he said grudgingly. "If you'll dummy out a standard progress report, I'll see that it gets around to all department heads for their guidance."

"Swell," she said. "Thanks, Bill." Her sharp hands darted of a sudden toward his head and ruffled his hair with a kind of affection. Then, briskly, she shoveled together all her papers and strode away to the door. It flashed through his mind—it made him wince in retrospect—that another woman had once put hands on him in this same way, with the same kind of roué condescension. Yes— Miss Ruby Hopkins, the two-fisted Portia.

"By the way," called Rosabel Long from the doorway, "do I understand there's going to be a big show tomorrow at Santa Ana when the water starts again?"

"The Mayor insists."

"Well," said Rosabel, "I wouldn't put too many eggs in *that* basket. I'd sneak up to Santa Ana *today* and see if Ross knows what he's talking about."

The door closed.

For a moment Harmon sat staring. His fists clenched and unclenched. The horror, he thought, was that she might be right.

CHAPTER FOURTEEN

HE HAD hoped they could steal into Santa Ana quietly, but street urchins spotted the Mission's car immediately and pursued it with shouts. *El Director* was in town, and the *Asociado!* A moment after he and Burling reached the pumphouse at the river bank, a crowd began drifting up. Dr. Larrea dropped over from the hospital, a cattleman rode up on his dying horse, and the Mayor himself came from his cocoa-drying shed to pay his respects.

Ross, they found, was having the wooden frame knocked from the newly hardened concrete base on which sat the pump, the hero of the occasion, its black enamel skin glistening brilliantly. A *mestizo* mechanic, a sliver of a man with a tight grave face, who wore a torn blue coverall, was pouring in gasoline.

"Man, oh, man," mumbled Ross happily, "tomorrow night everybody in Santa Ana takes a bath." His trouser legs stuffed into leather puttees, he strode about the pump-house giving orders for the tightening of a bolt here, the greasing of a part there.

"Never mind tomorrow night," said Burling. "Let's see what it can do right now."

"You bet!"

Burling's gaze, Harmon noted, was traveling back and forth between the pump and the water tank that squatted outside beyond the door like a huge washtub on its tall iron stilts. He seemed to be making a mental calculation.

"Men, women and children," mumbled Ross exuberantly, "a bath for one and all."

"Get going," said Burling.

"You bet." But then Ross found yet another part that needed adjustment.

Inside the pump-house, and far beyond, the crowd of spectators continued to grow. From the foreground a whispered commentary was flashed backward, growing louder and louder in transmission like a reverse echo. "Now the *gringo* engineer is looking inside the motor . . . He asks for a monkey wrench. . . . The other two *gringos* are whispering between themselves. . . . The fat one keeps looking out at the water tower. The tall one calls him back. . . . The fat one makes a face. . . . Ah, they're ready now to start!"

"*Olé!*" cheered a small boy.

"Not yet!" corrected a better-situated spectator in the foreground. "Not yet!" came the louder echo from the rear. It was like the feverish reconnaissances which precede the arrival of a parade.

Mayor Padilla, taking advantage of the momentary lull, stepped forward. A short, stout, square-rigged man, he smelled strongly of fermented cocoa beans and his hands were tinted a charming beige-pink. This was a glorious and unforgettable occasion, he declared. Who in Santa Ana would have dreamed that it would be the *gringos*—eh, the North American brothers—who would come some day to restore to its people the sunny waters of the Jivaro? But the brothers from the North had proved their hearts to be as large as the land they inhabited. Never would it be forgotten by the sufferers of the Martyr Province how on this eighteenth day of September in the year 1942 . . .

"Harmon," whispered Burling.

"You want me to reply?"

"Inter-American unity. The usual. But emphasize, for Christ's sake, that it's only a trial run."

The Mayor finished and Harmon stepped forward. Behind his back Burling had begun to goad Ross anew. "Get going, Mister, get *going*." Ross sent the mechanic clambering up the water tower to open a spigot in the tank so that the reach of the water would be perceived immediately when it started to flow.

. . . Naturally, concluded Harmon, the present occasion was only in the nature of a rehearsal, and such performances did not always go as smoothly as might be desired. The worthy citizenry of Santa

Ana could be relied upon to understand that. But, one way or another, in the name of the President of the United States and of its people, the Mission wished to express its gratitude for this opportunity to make itself of service to the Martyr Province and the brothers of the South as a whole. . . .

"*Olé!*" cried the small boy.

"Such rich expressions!"

"Now—now!"

Now Ross waved everybody aside and took his position alone before the motor. Man of the hour. He whirled a crank. The ignition caught and the motor purred smoothly. The pump pistons rose and fell in reciprocal action. Up came a deep sucking noise, full of promise. Every eye turned upward to the spigot in the water tank outside.

"Now—now!" they chanted.

Loudly and greedily the pump went on sucking—but from the spigot came nothing.

"Now—now!"

From the pump burst a rude explosive belch.

"Mister . . ." muttered Burling, his face elongated with strain.

"Okay, I know just what the trouble is," said Ross cheerily. He halted the motor and went to work with a screw driver, a wrench and a mallet. "Now," he said, and started the motor once again.

Suck-suck. Suck-suck. But still the spigot refused to yield water. Through the onlookers went a wordless murmur.

"Mister," said Burling, suddenly shouldering Ross away to a corner, "just what is the *power* of that contraption?"

"Five horsepower," said Ross, blinking.

All the while the pistons kept pumping up air.

Burling closed his eyes and compressed his lips, as if to keep contained the rage that was expanding within him. "Ross," he asked finally, "did you measure the height of that water tower?"

Ross nodded brightly. "Sure. Thirty feet. That pump should be plenty to raise a three-inch column of water thirty feet."

"And what did you allow for raising it from the river?"

Ross's nose, mouth and chin went instantly into a twitch. "From the river?" he echoed.

"Yes! From the river to the pump-house."

Ross, his back to the wall, stared vacantly all about him. "God damn it," he mumbled, "it's the only goddamn pump I could find anywhere. God damn it, I've had enough trouble in this goddamn country."

"You mean," said Burling, and his whisper was like a hard fierce jet of steam, "you didn't allow *anything*."

All the while the pump went on with its empty dolorous suck. In the vanguard of the crowd a man tittered lightly. The titter stole backward, out of the doorway, on to the water tower and beyond. As it ran it grew into a chuckle, into open laughter, into wild guffaws. "Listen—listen! The *gringos* have presented us with a belching machine!"

"No," corrected another wit. "Not *belching!*"

Irrationally, the small boy again cried, *"Olé! Olé!"*

Suck-suck. Suck-suck.

"Ha,ha,ha,ha,ha! Ha,ha,ha,ha,ha,ha,ha!"

The Colossus had fallen.

Bolting over to the motor, Burling snapped off the ignition. "You!" he stormed at Ross. "Get this goddamn carpet sweeper the hell out of here!"

"They gypped me," maundered Ross helplessly. "They're crooks —everyone of them."

Savagely Burling lunged out with his foot and kicked the pump. From the onlookers came a new explosion of laughter. "Ha,ha,ha, ha,ha,ha,ha!"

"Jesus," groaned Harmon, "Jesús, you could leave bad enough alone." He wished there were some place to hide.

"These monkeys," rasped Burling between gritted teeth. "I could give them a volley right in their goddamn ugly faces. These monkeys . . ."

But now, above the wild tumble of the laughter, suddenly rose a rich and cadenced voice. "*Amigos*—friends," it said with sunny humor, "it would not be the first time that a burro sat down on its rump." The laughter slowed. "Even an iron burro gets a fit sometimes."

Every face turned rearward.

"The *gringos*," continued the unseen voice from a point beyond the water tower, "are men who have built skyscrapers. They have put together a glass and a wire and created electric light. They have sent voices out on the air and they have put metal ships into the sea bigger than all Santa Ana. They will know how to make a little iron burro stand up again."

It was Vicente Hidalgo, of course.

"*Olé!*" cried the small boy anew.

"I ask you, who else has ever come to Santa Ana to make the water run? The Constitutional President? The Ministers of the Cabinet?"

"Right!" cried the doctor.

"Who else has come among you to live in this swamp, to share your mosquitoes? Who but the crazy *gringos*? They have promised that the water will run again in Santa Ana—and it will."

"Long live the *gringos!*" cried the Mayor.

"*Olé, Olé!*" cheered the horseman and the doctor.

"Your wives," said Hidalgo, and again so sunnily, "have the beans on the fire. Go home to your suppers."

"Right!" called the horseman from his bony perch. He yanked the bridle about and clattered off. Slowly, purring with good humor, the crowd dissolved.

Harmon went to the door. "Señor Hidalgo . . ." he called. But already Hidalgo was lost in the crowd.

"Who," asked Burling, "was the orator?"

"A local lawyer."

"Whew," said Burling, "a save on the one-yard line."

Hidalgo—inevitably he would run with the hares, even when they gave the illusion of being as big as Colossi. It was predictable of Hidalgo that he would be generous.

"What," asked Burling with a heavy shrewdness, "is his racket?"

Harmon gazed at Burling pityingly. What terrible dreams he must have, by night and by day. It was a world, his, in which every benefaction could only be looked upon as a bait, a trap. "I assure you," said Harmon, "that it was for free."

But already Burling was staring past him, fixedly and banefully.

"Colonel . . ." mumbled Fred Ross, still shrunk dazedly into the farthest corner of the pump-house. "I'm not a well man, Boss. That goddamn amoeba. I've been ailing from the day I got here." He reached for the wall and pressed a palm against it for support. This, the former "Jack Dempsey," the scowling bullyboy of Washington.

Burling's mouth opened and closed. Inside him a thunderbolt was gathering. "Leslie . . ." pleaded Harmon, getting sick to his stomach.

"That stumblebum's got to go," foamed Burling.

"Can you get a replacement?"

"I had a letter three days ago from a banana engineer up the coast. Lew Masters. A poker-playing, whisky-drinking, evil old man. But he knows his business."

"I tell you, Colonel," stammered Ross, "if that goddamn amoeba didn't get into my gut—if I was halfway myself . . ."

But the tautness, all at once, had gone out of Burling's face, to be succeeded by a look that was strangely, unexpectedly tender. "Sure," said Burling. "Amoebas can knock a fellow flatter than a pancake."

Ross nodded—wanly, uncertainly.

"I'll tell you, Fred," said Burling, still so oddly gentle. "Harmon and I've been talking it over. A man's first duty is to take care of his health. A man with a wife and kids has got to look after his health."

"Right," said Harmon.

Ross's mouth worked silently and weakly, chewing on an imaginary cud.

"What we suggest," Burling went on, "is that you take a short leave, Fred—go back to Washington."

"Washington?"

"Or anywhere else where you can get the right medical care. It's not as if you were running out on the job, or anything—just a question of your getting back in shape."

Still Ross could not make himself look up. What other ways were there to soften it for him? "Take my word," said Burling, "you'll be back here on the job inside a month." What, wondered Harmon, had turned him so suddenly tender? A desire to ward off some such evil from himself? Or was it that Vicente Hidalgo had shed even upon Burling some of his own knightly grace?

In Ross's face, at length, rose a smile. "Hell," he said, "I won't need a month. I'll be back in two weeks."

"You bet," said Harmon. It was good, at least, that Rosabel Long had not been here to see any of this.

CHAPTER FIFTEEN

AGAIN, as he turned the corner of the henhouse, he came into view of the hill, and of the rider who galloped along its crest, galloped sidesaddle, with her hair streaming out.

"Man . . ." pleaded Anderson with mock irritation, "say something. We got that coop up in ten days flat. Five thousand chicks incubating in there right this minute."

"Swell," said Harmon, but abstractedly. "You're all right."

In the administration building the plasterers were now at work.

In the cattle pavilion the roofers were laying the last tiles. In the fields more than half the acreage now was planted—with soy, barbasco and beans, with alfalfa, sisal and Janeiro grass. In the six weeks since Anderson's arrival, an energy of florescence had swept the bare hollow which had been the gift of Ramón Manriquez.

"Yep," said Anderson with a pride that was self-mocking but nevertheless earnest, "I'm the kid with the *cojones*."

Cojones—testes. How much we make of them, thought Harmon, the measure of our adequacy, of our superiority. No wonder, when the ladies got mad, that it was the first place they kicked at. Perhaps, he had to grant, it was their only form of self-defence. Perhaps in the Rosabels too burned a canker. He was a father, after all, of women, two of them, and he should learn how to feel with them— with their hatred of the thought that they were incomplete. . . .

But again suddenly his attention was caught by the black rider on the crest of the hill. She had a way of galloping across the horizon in a wild cavalry charge—then checking abruptly so that the horse reared high and its hooves beat upon the sky—then wrenching it about in a violent waltz and charging back in the opposite direction. This frantic pacing of hers . . . A dark humor must have possessed her to ride a horse like that.

"You know," Anderson was saying, "this Manriquez has turned out to be a very cute customer." He motioned with his thumb toward a knoll on the west where a cluster of white stucco cubes shone in the sun.

"How do you mean, Walt?"

"Not a day that his manager doesn't come over to borrow something. Insecticide. The tractor. Seedlings. All high-priority stuff, worth its weight in gold. Manriquez didn't give us this land for nothing. He's the camel in the tent."

That melancholy schemer. He had intelligence, Ernestina had said, lots of it, but the intelligence of the rapacious. It was the only tradition, of course, that it was possible for him to know. For too many centuries now the scions of the line of Manriquez had been raised to be conquerors—by intelligence now as once by the sword. It was an intelligence which, in the words of Hidalgo, was fostered only for purposes of plunder.

"Something tells me," reflected Anderson, his thoughts running even with Harmon's own, "that I'm building this model farm for Ramón Manriquez."

"Over my dead body," said Harmon hotly.

"The day we pull out of Alba . . ."

"The day we do, it reverts to the provincial government. I fixed it that way in the contract and I'll see that it sticks."

"Maybe," said Anderson.

Now again on the crest of the hill the black rider was plunging toward the sky, as if feverish to leave a planet she had found uninhabitable. But again the horse's hooves beat vainly, and again she turned for a burst in the opposite direction as if more were promised there. What a rebelliousness raged here, thought Harmon. Was it in protest against the Conquistador-husband—a protest that otherwise never dared to rise—save in a barbed smile sometimes and the wearing of those tomboy shoes?

His own daughters, it occurred to him uncomfortably, must feel that way sometimes about him. And Laura, too, beneath the tranquil, patient smile? Perhaps, it came to him, he had not been everything to his women that he should have been.

"Billy," Anderson was saying, and again suddenly in the whispers of a wicked boy, "I'm fixing up a couple of rooms out here for living quarters. You're welcome to move in."

Instantly Harmon's gaze went to the cluster of sugar cubes on the western knoll. Access, he thought, access finally!

"Billy, we can have ourselves a time out here. Just say the word."

Busily his eye was measuring the distance from here to Hacienda Manriquez. A quarter-mile? Feverishly he searched the terrain for any and all possible forms of cover—a cluster of papayas, a lemon grove—where a man and a woman could meet in the dark.

"Sósena . . ." meditated Anderson. "Every time I run into that little tomato, she asks after you. Mister, you must have given her something special."

Harmon grinned—mechanically. His thoughts were all on that horsewoman who plunged at the sky. Solitary and galled with anger. He burned to be with her again, to console her and love her. He envied the horse that she rode so cruelly.

"I can fix us another foursome," Anderson offered, "any time you say. If not Sósena, some other tomato. Alba is full of 'em."

"Thanks," said Harmon, "thanks, I'll think about it."

As he was about to enter the Customs House, a huge mahogany wardrobe teetered down the stairway The porters, one fore and one aft, grunted through their clenched teeth. From behind them, hard and shrill, came the voice of Tom Mercer, "Keep going! Keep going!"

The porter to the fore—Teofilo it was, the little man who had talked so eagerly once of the "new life," groaned heavily. *"Patroncito*—Boss," he asked, "can't we put it down for a second?"

"Hell," swore Mercer from somewhere behind them, still invisible, "you hound dogs've been resting every second step! Keep on going!"

Over Teofilo's face, the ordinarily mild homuncule, went a grimace of hatred, but he struggled forward, his partner too, and the huge wardrobe lurched out to the porch.

"Put it down," said Harmon.

Teofilo shot him a glance of surprise, which changed to recognition. *"Ai,"* he said, *"el Asociado.* Good morning!"

"Put it down."

Gratefully Teofilo lowered his end of the wardrobe. His companion followed suit.

Down the stairway clattered the Little Adjutant, splendid in a great white sun helmet. How, wondered Harmon, can a man wear one of those things without laughing at himself? "God damn it," said the Little Adjutant, "this is my baby."

"Sure," said Harmon, fascinated all the while by the magnificent white casque, "but why the hell kill babies?"

"These apes have been lead-assing around all morning," snapped Mercer. He turned back to the porters. "Pick it up. Load it on the truck. *Pronto.*"

It was an immensely heavy-looking affair, carved with scrolls and flourishes. Ostentatiously Harmon stood gazing at it.

"Mister," said the Little Adjutant sourly, "the Colonel's been looking for you."

Slowly, slowly, the porters raised the wardrobe again, lurched forward with it to the tailgate of the truck. But it froze then on the air, a foot or so under the level of the tailgate. The porters panted and groaned with effort, two Ajaxes pressed down to the earth.

All at once Harmon stepped forward and tucked his shoulder in under the wardrobe at mid-length. "Let's go," he said.

The gap closed. Forward went the wardrobe onto the floor of the truck. Clambering aboard, the porters hauled it into position.

"Sweet Jesus," rasped the Little Adjutant, "I said the Colonel was looking for you."

Harmon gave him a searching look. "Mercer," he said, "this isn't a banana plantation."

Mercer pushed the splendid white helmet back on his head. "If you know anything about native labor," he said tartly, "you know that you've made a bum out of me." He wheeled about and climbed into the cab of the truck.

One of these days, thought Harmon, he would do something about the Little Adjutant.

The truck jolted forward, so abruptly that the two porters were jerked off their feet. Heedless of their cries, Mercer sped up the road to Rosales.

For almost the first time since Washington, Burling was chuckling. "Billyboy," he said, handing over a sheet of the blue paper which betokened, as usual, a telegraph message.

Harmon glanced at it. "Am sailing from Lorca tonight with German-made pump which have bought from black-listed firm. Have paid fifty per cent more than is worth. Any arguments?" He flushed with annoyance.

"That," said Burling, "is Lew Masters." If there was anything Burling loved it was tricks, even those which were directed against him.

"Am I supposed to get sore?"

"Masters figures at this point it's better to buy an Axis pump than have all Santa Ana laughing at us."

Probably. "But the son of a bitch didn't have to put it on paper."

"That," repeated Burling, "is Lew Masters. The most even-tempered man I ever met. Mad all the time."

As he opened the door of his office, a voice called excitedly from within, *"Señor Asociado!"*

Planted in the chair alongside his desk was an enormous hulk tented in black silk. "To what," he asked, with a deep half-derisive bow, "do I owe the honor, Señora Bustamente?"

"You lovely *yanqui!*" she cried. You'll be happy to hear that I have just moved the last of our rags from your warehouse. How can I begin to thank you?"

"The honor," he said, "is all mine—your happy slave's."

She cast at him a sharp, suspicious glance, then smiled amusedly to herself. "Enough of the fringes and tassels," she said. "That does it." Yes, she had a sense of humor after all, this Fatty. "By the way," she went on, "how are you enjoying life in our little province?"

He was in no special mood for small talk, but she had a special sanctity, this Mammoth of Mercy—she was the intimate of Ernestina Manriquez. "Marvelously," he said. "It's the garden spot of the Republic."

"Yes, a garbage dump," said Señora Bustamente, "a rat hole." She made as if to spit. "For me, still and all, it's not so bad. I manage to keep busy. But for younger people ..." She halted and sighed in a way that was surely intended to be meaningful.

Excitedly Harmon leaped at the cue. "And how is your charming assistant these days?"

"Ernestina? A fine life, if you like bananas." She wrinkled her huge face.

"And—and her husband?" For politeness' sake alone. To cover up his anxiousness about Ernestina. Later he would return to this dearer subject and pump Fatty for all she knew. He wanted to hear anything, everything, that anyone had to say about Ernestina.

"Manriquez?" Again, startlingly, the Lady President made as if to spit. "A brute," she said. "The sweetheart of every last Magdalen in Alba."

It made Harmon gape. Yes, there was much more to Fatty than she had at first let on.

"What she has to put up with—my poor Ernestina."

"A—a beautiful girl," he was encouraged to say.

Now Fatty beamed, absolutely beamed. "She thinks well of *you*, Señor Harmon." It came to him all at once what role she had chosen to play. The duenna! The intermediary between lovers! "We discuss you quite often, Señor Harmon."

Even the dialogues were falling into traditional forms. "And—and what do you say, Señora?"

She wagged her head with ponderous glee. "Men," she declared, "so vain!"

Oh, he loved Fatty right now—he simply loved her.

"You won't," she said, "drag it out of me with horses."

The mischievous duenna. And how thoroughly she enjoyed the role. Why? Out of a desire to pay Manriquez back—that "brute"? Or some particular "brute" of her own—the dead husband possibly? Señora Bustamente, it came to him, was a kind of rebel. It was not often that Latin American ladies went about encouraging married romances.

"Really," she was saying, "something should be done about Ernestina." Was this foray some idea entirely her own? Or—it made him tremble to think of it—had she come on the urgings of Ernestina herself? "What a life she leads for such a young and beautiful girl," went on Señora Bustamente. "A little Red Cross work with me. A visit now and then to Lorca and Chimboya. Otherwise Ernestina's only companion in the world is her horse."

Her horse . . . Those frantic pacings this morning on the hill . . .

"I tell you, dear boy, that except for the Wednesday afternoons when she comes to my home in Rosales to help me with my correspondence . . ."

Wednesday was today!

". . . she hardly ever leaves the hacienda at all. Poor darling. I look forward to those Wednesdays, I tell you."

Again he leaped to the cue. "Wednesdays . . ." he repeated.

"Yes!" exclaimed Señora Bustamente. She beamed upon him again and made to rise. Harmon came forward and she let herself be hauled from the chair by her wrists. "Manriquez!" she sputtered. Puffed out with immense indignation, she waddled from the room.

How, wondered Harmon, would he live until afternoon?

CHAPTER SIXTEEN

TEACUP in hand, moody and silent, Ernestina sat on the sofa at the far end of the Spanish-plush drawing room, as far from him as the room permitted. This morning he had seen her as the stately and dashing horsewoman. At the *verbena* she had appeared as a lady-in-a-robe; on the ship as the patrician traveler. But now once again she wore the shirt-waist dress and the saddle shoes—as at their very first meeting. Yes, they must be for her a kind of liberty cap, her garb of rebellion.

Harmon himself sat formalistically in a high-backed, brass-studded throne of leather and mahogany. Between them, collapsed on a velvet settee, lay the magnificent bulk of Señora Bustamente. On and on she chattered, a monologue. Accompanying her as a faint obbligato, a white-enameled refrigerator—yes, in the drawing room—hummed and rattled. In Latin America a modern refrigerator was a mark of position. It was not to be hidden away in the kitchen. All about the room, on the end table, the tea table, the piano, had been set out photos of the two daughters who had married in foreign countries, plump and sad-eyed, but there was none, not one, of the dead husband.

"That small piece of nothingness who is the director of hospitals..." said Señora Bustamente, going on and on. Harmon was glad at least to have so ferocious an antagonist on his own side. " 'I will take the *gringos'* money gladly,' he says, 'but they can keep their feet out of my hospitals.' *His* hospitals!"

When, when would she be done? Ernestina, all the while, continued to stare into her teacup. Again her forehead was puckered with that little chevron of anxiety. If only Fatty would go! But this too was of the nature of duennas, to take for their fee a moment of spite. She was at an age where she could arrange such rendezvous only for others.

"Also"—he would bolt over and grab her by those quivering adder-like ringlets—"I would keep an eye on the director of schools. He has flooded the classrooms with texts printed by his own brother. The worst in all the Americas!"

Ernestina had closed her eyes. Pale and motionless, as if abandoned wholly to despair, she lay against the back of the sofa.

"And the director of railroads..." Enough was enough. He would simply stand up and go, it was too unbearable. But all at once the tormentor relented. *"Ai,"* she said, and for her exit she again took a traditional line, "I must instruct the cook about dinner." Regally she held out her pretty hands to Harmon.

"Permit me!" he said, leaping forward. They locked then as if in some ancient style of wrestling, and in an instant he had hauled the Lady President to her tiny feet. He offered her his arm, to see her to the door. Brusquely, as if to indicate how hollow she knew this chivalry to be, she brushed him aside. "Ernestina," she called over her shoulder in a faint double-entendre, "look after him."

The door opened and closed.

Already Ernestina had risen from the sofa. For an instant—wide-eyed with shock and with joy, dreadfully solemn—they stared at each other down the length of the drawing room. Then, frantically, they were racing for each other. "William—William!" she cried in that voice like a muted bell. They found each other with their lips. On the mouth, the eyes, the ears—they could not kiss enough.

At last, he thought, at last.

"William," she begged, "you'll be good to me, won't you, dear, won't you?" It startled him that she should ask this, she in whose nature lay a stony patrician, a barbed hoyden, a cruel horsewoman. But then there was also that side of her which had looked upon him in humility, had seemed to beg for his good opinion. "Won't you?"

For an answer he kissed her. Gently now, protectively.

"William . . . Is that what I'm to call you, dear, is that what you'd like—William?"

It was a happy thought. Not "Will," which was Laura's name for him, and his mother's. Not "Bill" or "Billy" which were the names by which men called him. "William"—there was nobody else who called him that, nobody at all. For herself Ernestina would be calling into being some new and private version of him, one who felt totally male, totally esteemed. "Yes, darling," he said, "yes." He found her mouth again with his own and she arched up on her toes. It was as though he had lifted her by a sheer magnetism of his lips. "Ernestina!" he cried. No moment of his life had ever had so much worth, so much joy. Then he stood her off, briefly, at the full length of his arms, to behold with all ravenousness what he had won—the moon-pale flesh, the beautiful and bitter mouth, the slanted cheekbones, the black cascades of her hair, and that body, that body. "Ernestina," he thought suddenly of asking, "that *was* you on the hill this morning, wasn't it?"

She clung to him as to shelter. "Yes," she whispered.

"Ernestina, you seemed beside yourself. Ernestina, what were you thinking of?"

She buried her face against his chest. "Of—of this."

It was a blinding thought—that he had been so wildly hungered after. By a girl like this.

Their bodies ground together again, frantic lest anything part them, unable to come close enough. He sensed with a dim grief, all at once, that this probably was to be the best moment of all, now at the start. Later would come hindrances, dilemmas, miseries. But now in the utter newness of their love, there was nothing but the fiercest desire. "Ernestina," he whispered, "we *must—we must.*"

Her breath came brokenly. Her glance darted wildly about the drawing room.

"I know," he said, "but there may never be a better place." Always these moments would have to be stolen.

Once more she huddled against him. Shivering uncontrollably, she whispered something. "Serafina—she won't be back." Resistlessly, unlimitedly conquered, Ernestina let herself be lifted from her feet.

CHAPTER SEVENTEEN

Hᴇ ᴡᴀs standing in his room before a shard of mirror and shaving for supper when he heard Rosabel Long burst onto the porch. "Oh!" she cried, and he could picture her shuddering all the way to her toes. "Oh, it's the most loathsome thing I ever saw!"

"Girly," came the voice of Lew Masters, "I don't care if he's a one-man plague."

"Well," said Rosabel, "we ought to find out, shouldn't we?"

Rosabel in a state of alarm—thought Harmon with a certain satisfaction. It was the first time since she had come to Alba that he had heard her squeal, the first time she had joined her mouse-frightened sisters. Not even the buzzards—not even they—had succeeded in denting her assurance. Inquisitive as to what could now be doing the trick, he went out to the porch, still lathered on one cheek. Despite her agitation, Rosabel found time for a studious glance at him. Good, he thought. Let her see him plain, as the unglamorous man-about-the-house. It would put things on a more prosaic and safer plane—might ward off for good any further caresses from those sharp hands of hers.

"Rosey," he asked, "what's the trouble?"

She wrinkled her nose faintly at the unwelcome nickname. "There's a thing like a crab," she said. "It's sitting under that papaya tree by the Customs House. It crawls around on its elbows and everybody says he's a leper."

"How do they know?"

"Well, he came down from Huelva—with his mother—and everybody says Huelva is full of leprosy."

"That still doesn't make him a leper, does it?" His lawyer's habit had asserted itself of assaying evidence ruthlessly. And this was a cross-examination he especially enjoyed.

But Rosabel shook her head, with its tight-bound tower of ash-blonde curls, annoyedly. "Look, Bill," she said, "he came here to take the boat for Lorca tomorrow—so's he can go to the hospital there. And the whole town runs away from him. They ought to know a leper here when they see one."

Lew Masters, big and lumbering and grouchy, was stretched out in a canvas deck chair studying blueprints. "Shut up," he said, without looking up, "both of you."

"Tell me what he looks like—the thing," asked Harmon.

"Like a crab, I told you. He crawls around on his elbows."

"His face, I mean."

"I didn't go near enough to see. Oh, I couldn't."

"Lepers, they say, get to look like lions. Thick and broad across the face. Like a lion?"

Again Rosabel shivered. "Oh, come on, Bill," she begged. "Come back and see for yourself."

He pointed blandly to his still-lathered cheek.

Next Rosabel shot an appealing glance at Lew Masters, but the old man refused to look up. "All right," she said, gathering her courage in a way Harmon almost admired. "A face like a lion?" Off she ran, letting the door slam behind her.

"Women . . ." grumbled Masters, barricaded morosely behind a huge blueprint which he held out to the full breadth of both his arms.

"Masters," said Harmon, "you're the champ sourpuss of all the hemispheres."

"What a country! What a hole!"

"Who told you to come here?"

"Hell," said Masters, "in a decent country nobody will put up with me. They don't have to."

Grinning, Harmon went back to his room. Friday today—he thought, as he stood again with his razor before the fragment of mirror. It showed him as a fragment of a face, with one eye and half a scalp. Five days more until the *next* Wednesday, the next meeting with Ernestina. She was granted to him so grudgingly, for only two hours of each week. And until the next Wednesday came around— it sickened him, enraged him, that meanwhile her husband might choose to lay hands on her—though she had said no, not for many months, almost a year; he was so busily occupied elsewhere. And since it was strongly evident now that from her he could expect no heirs . . .

Unhappy Ernestina. That that lovely body should be so fruitless— it was as though nature, having produced so fine an exemplar of its kind, had despaired of repeating it. In a land where women were prized by the same standards as other domestic animals, by their fertility, it had been borne in upon Ernestina that she was a failure, a cause to her husband of righteous grievance.

But that lovely face—that scented flesh. He was fired suddenly with a desire to storm the white fortress on the knoll, to smash his way in and liberate what he alone knew how to prize, what was rightfully his. Rightfully? Why not? She was supremely the woman for him, Ernestina, and he the man for her. She had given him a sword again, and armor, and a gage of battle. He longed to cherish her, protect her, fight for her. Why, why had Laura not made him feel that way? If only she could have believed in him, have seen him as whole and strong . . . It had been that way at the *start* of their marriage, hadn't it? "Flex your biceps for me, Will, oh, do. Will, let me feel it. Oh, Will!" Their talk in those days had been mostly of *him*, of the great things he was going to do. But somewhere along the line Laura had begun to edge ahead. Somewhere his self-doubts had begun again to poison him, and Laura had led him to a sickbed. For years now he had been made to accept the role of invalid-of-the-house. Like his father before him. And Laura had hovered over the sickbed with a baneful tenderness—watching him endlessly, assaying him, measuring him. And then finally, on that night of the "fiasco," she had almost done him in. Like Mother . . . Mother with her little knives! He had got away only in the nick of time.

He found that he had finished shaving. Taking off his khaki work clothes, he changed to a fresh linen suit. For dinner Burling insisted always on "Class-A uniform," a hangover from his Army days.

As he reached the porch, Rosabel came running back breathlessly. "Yes!" she declared. "A face like a lion!"

Sardonically, still smoldering at the back of his mind against Laura, he affected a yawn. "A real little old lion, Rosy? With mane and claws and everything?"

Rosabel grimaced with annoyance. "Now really, Bill, from where I stood, he looked exactly like . . ."

"Where'd you stand? Mile away?"

"Oh darn it, even the natives won't go close. The owner of the inn chased him and his mother with a broom. There's not a house in town that'll take them in."

"Girl—girly," grumbled Lew Masters.

"Wait," said Harmon, suddenly taking a new view of it. "Where *will* they stay overnight?"

"It's no business of mine," said Rosabel. "If only they'd get out of town . . ." Again she shivered, then brushed the lapels and skirt of her white sharkskin suit as if to dust off any motes of contamination.

But to Harmon the "crab man" had ceased to be a cause of sport. For a moment he deliberated, then started for the screen door.

"Hey," called Masters after him, "don't be loony. It's no goddamn business of ours."

Halfway along the causeway, he caught sight of it. Sitting under the ragged little papaya tree, it rocked on its haunches. Occasionally it jerked forward on its elbows, dragging stunted legs behind, toward a group of children who watched it with joyous horror. They had made a game, the children, of daring each other to touch "the thing." They would run up, one or two of them, tap it boldly on the matted head, then leap away in delighted fright. But the crab man bore them no rancor. Again and again he beckoned for them to return.

From out of the Customs House, now, Harmon saw a squat figure with a sun helmet emerge. Colonel Burling. He made a wide circle around the crab man and started down the causeway. Catching sight of Harmon he waved him to stop where he was and wait.

"Now *you*," squealed the children to one of their number, a boy who, like so many others in Alba, limped badly. The crab man rocked on his haunches and beckoned amiably with both hands. The boy took one step forward—a second. Then, all at once, his nerve failed. He screamed and ran.

Burling just then came up on the causeway. "Awful," he said.

"We ought to do something," said Harmon, "shouldn't we?"

Burling stared down uncomfortably at his shoe tips. "The old woman," he said, "is going from shanty to shanty." Back on the porch of the Mission dwelling, a houseboy jangled the dinner bell. "Let's see how she makes out," said Burling.

"Burling," said Masters, holding up a chunk of the brown stew on his fork, "I don't mind horsemeat, but why the saddle?"

"Go to hell," said Burling amiably.

Night already had fallen—in the space of minutes, as always, on the Equator. The electric bulbs flickered weakly and the Colonel was forced to order two Coleman lamps brought to the table. Hot and hissing, they cast a pale green light on all the faces, and moss-green shadows in the corners.

"Masters," asked Burling, "when are you going to do something about that power line?"

"The trouble's with the turbines. They're clogged with silt."

"Then when're you going to clean them?"

"When I goddamn well please," said Masters. "Tomorrow."

Horanyi laughed and his gold teeth flashed daggers, but with a gold that was green. Rosabel wrinkled her nose boredly. Walt Anderson fired a stream of some Indian dialect at Masters that was intended obviously to cloak the vulgarest of epithets.

"And the same to you," grunted Masters. "Double."

By their hostilities, thought Harmon, they try to prove themselves men.

Jacinto, the broad-cheeked houseboy with the bartender's curl on his forehead, carried in a huge steaming pudding with such reverence as though it were a sacrifice to the Sun God.

"Burling," asked Masters, "what *is* this trash?"

"Brown Betty," said the Colonel.

Masters sampled it. "It's almost edible," he conceded.

"It's damn good," said Burling. "I made it myself."

"Next," asked Horanyi, "will you whip us up some chocolate fudge?"

"I could," said Burling. "I didn't spend two years at the Army Cook School for nothing."

"I'll have seconds on that garbage," said Masters.

"You ought to be informed," said Burling, "that I made the hard sauce with lard."

"Who gives a damn?"

But Rosabel Long pushed hers away.

Jacinto, returning with the coffee, cast Harmon a meaningful glance.

"Yes?"

"The cook says that nobody will take them in, *Señor Asociado*. They are lying down on the bandstand by the seawall."

"Oh," said Rosabel. "I'll never set foot on that bandstand again."

"Ummm," said Burling reflectively.

"There's a wind tonight," said Harmon, "and the bandstand's wide open." His eyes found Burling's and they looked at each other embarrassedly.

"Burling," said Masters, "pass me another slug of that swill."

Abstractedly Burling dished it out for him. "Jacinto," he finally called. From his pocket he took two ten-peso notes.

"Fine," said Harmon, "but it won't cover their backs."

"Hell, hell," barked Burling, covering up his perplexity with a show of force. "Let *them* figure it out."

"What I say," commented Masters, his mouth stuffed with pudding, "is give this leper a good clout on the head and push him into the ocean. The best thing all around."

"Out of the question," said Harmon wryly. "There's a moon tonight."

"Honestly," said Felix Horanyi, "I do not see that it is the function of a technical mission to wash the feet of every individual leper in Alba."

"Why *can't* they sleep on the bandstand?" asked Tom Mercer.

Masters pushed his pudding plate away satedly. "Burling," he asked, "how good are you on angel cake?"

"Dandy," said Burling, but meditatively. "Peachy."

Harmon, finally, came to a conclusion. "Boss," he said, "I'm drawing a couple of cots and blankets out of the warehouse."

Burling glanced up at him.

"We can burn them later. No great loss. I figure we can set them up in the old gasoline shed, and burn that too later. Masters wants to tear it down anyhow."

Masters shook his fist. "Hey, you buzzard. Keep your paws off my fuel shed."

But Harmon was already on his way to the door.

"Hey," Masters called after him, "what about all the other lepers in South America?"

"Shut up," said Harmon, "shut up, you dirty old man."

They lay fallen, two heaps of rags, on the concrete floor, huddling away from the glare of the overhead lamp, which, as the only outdoor illumination in Puerto Pacifico, was generally kept burning all night. Mounting the steps of the bandstand, Harmon rested cots and blankets against the rail and called to them.

"*Ai!*" cried the crab man, coming instantly awake. He rolled to his haunches like a billikin righting itself. His eyes glared wildly under the matted hair that fell across his forehead like Spanish moss.

His mother, too, woke with a cry. "We will go away in the morning," she pleaded, kneeling before her son to shield him with her own body. "On the morning ship."

"For you," said Harmon, pointing to the cots and blankets.

But the woman's only reaction was to shrink back. "He is *not* a leper!" she protested, speaking in the sing-song dialect of the hills, "only a poor sick cripple. It was done to him by the wheels of an oxcart. He is not a leper!"

"No," said Harmon, "of course not." He motioned toward the gasoline shed by the seawall. "You can go there and sleep."

But the crab man, wild with fear, began to moan and to rock on his haunches. "Leave us alone!" cried the mother, continuing to misunderstand.

"I'm offering you shelter."

But the woman, clutching her son, began to rock with him in his own mournful rhythm. "Go away!" she screamed. There was a flash of metal. From the rags of the cripple had leaped a long thin knife.

"Look," said Harmon, pointing once again. "Cots. Blankets. Shelter."

"It's a trick," said the woman.

"Kill . . ." moaned the crab man. "Kill . . ."

If only, thought Harmon, he could make himself understood.

"Nobody helps anybody," said the mother. "Only for a trick."

His bulk, his height, his health—they were all testifying against him, thought Harmon. They marked him as belonging with the conquerors, a race from which nothing was to be expected. And they could only ask, these slaughtered children of the Incas, "Why does he want to be so good to us?" And put it down for a trick. It was the law of their life—nobody helped anybody.

"Go away!" screamed the woman, beside herself now with fear and rage both, an animal that had maddened itself to become brave. She took into her own hand the long thin knife and stood up.

"All right," said Harmon wearily. He dropped the two ten-peso notes of Colonel Burling to the floor alongside the cots and blankets. Cautiously then, and irritatedly, he turned about and went down the steps of the bandstand.

What irritated him most was that all the others, the tough ones— Masters, Horanyi, Mercer—would consider that they had been proven right.

CHAPTER EIGHTEEN

HE CRUNCHED along the causeway in the dark, followed at a pace by Hector Serrano. Again the white beacon was sweeping over Puerto Pacifico like a scythe and swinging out to sea. In the *cantinas* the phonographs were cackling, and the morning-weary stevedores were converging toward the dock. The *Relampago* this time would be bringing in the Mission's medical officer. And Burling had delegated him to spend the day showing Dr. Gilmore around.

But again it was Wednesday, and in the secrecy of that plush-draped mansion Ernestina would be waiting for him. It would have to be managed like clockwork. In the afternoon he would maneuver Dr. Gilmore to Rosales, keep him occupied there with a staff meeting of all the resident physicians of the province—and slip away, in the interval, to Ernestina.

"Good morning," called a voice from the dark, in Spanish. Up ahead, at an intersection of the causeways, a man stood like a sentinel, tall and thin but not otherwise immediately identifiable.

"Good morning," he replied. By the waning moon he then recognized the man as one with whom he had exchanged greetings on several occasions, here and there in the province, but without ever learning the man's name. "After you . . ." he said, halting to make way.

"Thank you, *Señor Asociado*," said the tall thin man. "I am only waiting."

Harmon passed on, but behind him he heard Serrano draw breath and exclaim, "Largo! Isn't this dangerous?"

"It's all right," answered the man called Largo. "I'll be under cover by sunrise."

There were some further ejaculations, stealthy, from which Serrano broke off to call after Harmon, "Excuse me, *Señor Asociado*. Perhaps you'd rather go on ahead."

"No hurry," said Harmon, going on several paces more, however, to remove himself courteously from earshot. He wondered whether this conspiratorial encounter had anything to do with the tension which had been gathering all week in the province. A national election had been ordered suddenly for a new House of Deputies. Several mornings in succession he had waked to find the port plastered with yellow one-word placards, "Abstain!" Each day the Carabineros had torn the placards down and made severe inquiries.

"Forgive me, *Señor Asociado*," said Serrano, now coming up to join him. They trudged on again over the causeway in their column of two. "Yes," said Serrano, breaking the silence finally, "we are going to see a little fun today."

"The election?"

"I presume you've noticed those yellow placards—what we call the 'mustard plasters'?"

" 'Abstain'?"

"They're the work of the *PORA*—the labor party. Nothing can stop the Constitutional President from declaring another glorious victory for himself, but the *PORA* wants to make it the smallest turnout in history."

Harmon's mind went instantly to the thin calm man at the crossroads.

"Largo," said Serrano, as if reading his thoughts, "is their second or third in command. A case of arrest-on-sight." There was an implication in this disclosure, Harmon recognized, that he was to be trusted. It pleased him that this should be taken so freely for granted. "The *Poristas*," Serrano went on, "are all right. Social-minded. Democratic." He cleared his throat. "But a little irritated right now at—at the Mission."

Harmon stopped short. The palms of his hands were tingling unpleasantly. "Why?"

"Well . . ." Serrano faltered.

"You needn't be afraid to tell me."

"The truth, I suppose, is that the Mission is in the position of an innocent bystander, so to speak."

"Come," urged Harmon, but worriedly, "it's something we have to know."

"Well . . ." Serrano cast a look about in the dark, then plunged right in. "Rivera ratified the Washington agreement by executive decree. The Alba program. The war settlement. The bases. It was never submitted properly to the House of Deputies. Now he wants to legitimatize it all. Everything Constitutional, you know. But he considers the present House of Deputies 'unreliable,' so to speak. Some are old-line *gringo*-haters. Others are plain Axis agents. The *PORA* opposes him on general principles. Of course, you can always shoot distasteful deputies. But when you shoot too many it stops looking Constitutional. So—we have a new election, hand tailored."

A queasy feeling floated in Harmon's stomach. He was sorry to have found out so much, after all.

"The *PORA*," Serrano hastened to add, "is not against the Alba program as such. But they are furious that you have given Rivera an American flag in which to hide."

American flag . . . It was true, you had to admit. The Ambassador had said it in so many words. But the alternative was—the alternative for him was unacceptable. No. He did not want to hear any more about it. The matter was closed. "Why blame Washington?" he snapped, savagely almost. "You should give us a better President to deal with."

"Well—yes," said Serrano. "I was only quoting."

Besides, there was always the "world picture." Yes, he reflected wryly, the world picture. World picture, my arse. But on the other hand it was Wednesday again, and in Rosales Ernestina Manriquez would be waiting for him. The matter was closed.

He was the classic physician, Gilmore, all fresh and antiseptic in a white linen suit. From his breast pocket peeped a small pipe organ: fountain pen, thermometer case and surgical flashlight. He had a crisp auburn mustache, cut in guardsman style, and pink temperate-zone coloring which made Harmon realize how dry and leathery his own skin had turned.

In the light of the rising sun, Gilmore gazed out from the dock over Puerto Pacifico. "Um," he remarked, "a first-class microbe-culture."

"Oh, yes," said Harmon. "There'll be plenty to do."

Gilmore's glance went shrewdly over the ragged horde of porters who squatted on the dock. "A lip cancer . . ." he remarked of one.

"Advanced tuberculosis . . ." of another. "I give him two months. A classic case of yaws over there. Intestinal parasitosis and malaria in every one of them." He shook his head knowingly. "The old tropical story. At any given moment half of Latin America should be put to bed."

From him came that hygienic bouquet—green soap, of course—that was the trademark of all conscientious physicians. "The Mission staff," he asked, "what kind of shape are *they* in?"

"Dysentery in waves. Delhi belly. Guayaquil gut. A third of us are always down with dysentery."

"What's your water source?"

Harmon shook his head ruefully. "Oh, we chlorinate like mad."

"Any dengue? Trichinosis?"

"Could be."

"Skin rashes, of course."

"Most of us."

"Who's been looking after you?"

Harmon hesitated. "I wouldn't want to prejudice you," he said. "The nationals are all willing enough and hard-working, but young and inexperienced. They've been waiting for you."

"I'll bet," said Gilmore, "you don't have one microscope in Alba."

"And not many thermometers."

Gilmore gestured crisply toward the ships hold. "I brought a hundred," he said, "and ten microscopes. A complete pharmacopeia too. Half a ton of stuff altogether."

Instantly Harmon began to search among the porters. "Teofilo," he called, as he found the little man squatting exhaustedly on his haunches.

"Si, Señor Asociado!" Up like a jack-in-the-box.

"Supplies." He grinned gently. "For that 'new life.'" Teofilo returned the grin. "Get all our other porters to help you. And the houseboys."

Teofilo nodded happily. Off he went—with a heavy but uncertain gait. His bare soles pounded down as if to make sure the ground were really there. Harmon caught Dr. Gilmore observing him. "Is it something bad?" he asked.

"A symptom," murmured Gilmore cautiously, "of locomotor ataxia. Could be a paretic condition."

Teofilo—so eager for the "new life." It troubled Harmon. "Could you do anything for him?"

"Bring him around as soon as I'm organized and I'll have a look. About the hospitals, incidentally, what's the nursing like?"

"A few Sisters. Very old."

Gilmore grimaced. "In Lorca," he said, "I managed to locate an old-line American nurse at the plague laboratories. Bellevue training, and Public Health Service. She's coming down in a week to start a nurses' aid program. Also, I'm borrowing their best technician for training purposes. A Cornell man."

"Doctor," said Harmon, boundlessly pleased, "you're a sixteen-inch gun."

"Only par," said Gilmore. "You forget, in the tropics, what good is supposed to be."

The remark made Harmon think. Yes—you got by on much less in places like these. What was routine back home was superlative down here. That glittering title plate that sat on his desk, that read "Associate Director," that had automatically brought him so much deference—it might be that it was more than a little hollow, mightn't it?

On the porch Anderson stopped Gilmore to swap glowing reminiscences about their year together in Costa Rica—from which Gilmore broke off to inspect a boil on Mercer's neck. This immediately brought Horanyi up for examination of a running sore on his forearm of long-standing, and soon Rosabel Long snatched Gilmore away for a discreet consultation in the privacy of her room.

As they sat down finally for breakfast and Jacinto brought in the usual pitcher of orange juice, Dr. Gilmore did something thoroughly startling. He took the pitcher from Jacinto's hands, carried it to the window and poured the entire contents out on the ground.

"Man!" cried Masters with unbounded admiration. "You're even meaner than me!"

The orange juice, hazarded Gilmore, had been squeezed by hand? "Right there is the source of your dysentery. Hereafter nothing but whole fruits in their skins. Also"—he frowned with the benevolent tyranny of the physician—"I want the entire kitchen staff lined up for examination the first thing after breakfast."

Burling slammed the table with the palm of his hand. "Now," he said, "I have a ball team."

CHAPTER NINETEEN

EVERYTHING went slower than he had planned. Gilmore, as he was shown through the Rosales hospital, had so many questions to ask, so many alterations to propose, that it was well past three before Harmon, chafing all the while, managed to closet him with the young residents and break away.

Ernestina, he thought excitedly as he drove off from the hospital— illicit, dangerous, pleasurable. Never had he suspected that there lay inside him such a capacity for lawlessness. Back home he had come to be taken for granted, a man without secrets or surprises. And, worst of all, he had accepted this verdict as just. What would they think *now*, those sovereign women? How it would amaze them to know that in him lay a man who could be thoroughly male—who took his pleasures where he found them—who went to secret assignations—who was ready to risk any kind of danger as its own reward.

Ernestina. But she worried him at the moment. There had been no way to reach her and let her know he would be late. Alba's telephone lines went only between government offices. Ernestina, by now, would have taken to wondering, growing more and more irritable as she paced back and forth in the musty room of red plush. He recalled, anxiously, those sparks of temper, so Spanish, that flashed from her at times. On the ship that night. On the hill with her horse. Had she decided by now to consider herself slighted—to punish him? Worriedly he saw her stalking from Serafina Bustamente's house and taking herself off, unreachably, to that white fortress on the knoll. It would be more than he'd be able to bear. He would have to follow after in that case to Hacienda Manriquez and find a stratagem for breaking in, for being with her—if only for a moment, if only to brush his hand formally against her own. No—it must not happen that way. He had been waiting seven whole days for the joy of being alone with her. He couldn't bear to think that now . . .

Abruptly he swung the car around a corner into the main street of Rosales.

There, as abruptly, he had to brake.

Hell, he thought, hell. The roadway was packed solid with a crowd that had spilled over from the sidewalk and that murmured sullenly. Over and over he honked his horn, but they refused to move or even acknowledge that they had heard.

Stepping out of the car, he found that the core of the disturbance was a *cantina* over which hung a hand-printed sign, "Vote here. Vote for the Party of National Unity." At the entrance, with fixed bayonets, stood a gauntlet of Carabineros in their smudged pajama-like uniforms and wide straw hats.

"One at a time," ordered a little rooster-like officer, "and vote for national unity."

A well-dressed gentleman waved a cane. "Why," he demanded, "is there only one party on the ballot?"

"Unity," said the officer.

The gentleman spat upon the ground, three times, rhythmically. "All this *for the gringos!*" he cried. "For the enemies of Christian Spain!"

"Unity," said the officer. "Only one at a time in the polling place."

"The Japanese," said the gentleman with the cane, "throw them out of Asia. The Germans won't let them set foot in Europe. So they must come here and run our Republic for us."

"The hell with them all," said the officer. "Unity."

The gentleman, turning away, caught sight of the Mission automobile. "Wait," he said, waving his cane at Harmon, "wait until Rommel gets here!" He spat on the windshield.

Blank-facedly Harmon bowed and drove off.

Anxiously he pounded the heavy brass doorknocker. A moment later the door was opened by a dark stocky maid who wore a shining white pinafore but no shoes. "Yes," she whispered, "the Señora is waiting." She led him to the drawing-room threshold and vanished instantly on her noiseless feet.

He reached for the doorknob. Simultaneously the door was torn open from within.

"William!" she cried. "William!" She flung herself upon him and hugged him tightly, paler than ever, and greatly agitated.

"Darling," he asked, "what's wrong?"

"Just hold me," she begged. She was breathing rapidly, as if she'd been running. "Just let me know that you're here—that I really have you."

Wonderingly he caressed her, kissed her. He had been prepared for temper, but not for this—alarm and gratitude. "Sweet," he began, "the reason I'm late . . ."

"You were held up by your work, I suppose. That's it, isn't it? But I kept having such frightful thoughts, dearest. He doesn't want to come to me any more, I thought."

"Oh, Ernestina . . ." he protested.

She smiled sorrowfully. "Perhaps he's had a letter from his wife, I thought. Or perhaps that girl with the Mission has been making eyes at him—the *blonde* one. Or some other girl." She shook her head ruefully. "You see, dearest, I don't really have any rights to you. I know that."

He framed her face gently with his hands and turned it upward. His whole being, in that instant, was taken with pity. "Ernestina," he asked, "is that what you think of me?"

"Oh, darling, darling," she said, "it isn't you. It's *me*—this terrible love I have for you. Be nice to me, darling, will you, please—will you?"

That she should think she had to ask for that . . .

Slowly, still wonderingly, he drove back to the hospital. She had wanted so much to be the girl-of-the-campus, a companionable tomboy—a Laura. And she had worn those saddle shoes to remind herself of the times when she had almost succeeded, the days when she had been the girl-student among students. But all in an instant, because he had come late and she had not known what to fear, the last of the disguise had dropped, showing only the bondmaid, the woman whose whole kingdom was to love a man and serve him. It had been bold—the revolt against her husband—the boldest kind of revolt that there could be for a woman in lands like this. But Ernestina, in rising, had not struck out for freedom, only for a change of masters. "Be nice to me," she had begged. From now on her whole kingdom—and the thought left him subdued—would be in *him*. This should make him feel tall, yes, as tall as the skies, but was it *right?* Was it altogether right?

Abruptly he became aware again of a disturbance in the street. Again, he found, he had drawn near the *cantina* that was a polling place. But now the sullenness had broken into open violence. Back and forth on the earthen sidewalk lurched a cluster of Carabineros, struggling with some invisible force in their midst, one that they could not succeed in containing but that tugged and pushed them in every direction, the hidden controller of the dance.

"Drunken bum!" cried one of the Carabineros exasperatedly. He raised a short black club and struck smartly down into the vortex of the whirlpool.

A groan came up from within, and then a voice rich of timbre but shouting the roughest imprecations. "Cow dung! Dog droppings! Jackals!"

"Again!" cried the Carabinero officer. Again the club rose and fell.

"Seducers of your sisters! Lovers of your mothers!"

It was a voice which caused Harmon to brake the car and abandon it in the middle of the road. Almost sick with fright, he ran toward the *cantina*.

"Down with your Constitutional President—I spit on him!" The club struck again. "Down with Rivera!" Once more the club. "Down with . . ." Now as the club struck again, the rebellious voice was finally silenced.

Hands on their hips, the Carabineros stood back to survey the results of their labors. At their feet lay a large torn figure. Blood was trickling brightly through the wild gray hair.

"Hidalgo!" cried Harmon.

The Carabinero officer stepped into his path. "Señor," he said, "go about your business."

"But the man . . ."

"*Yanqui,* don't butt in."

He could lift this smudgy rooster from the ground with one hand. He could get him by the neck and . . ."Listen," Harmon pleaded. "I know the man. If you will just let me take him away . . ."

"We know him too. A drunk. A subversive."

He would sail in against the whole lot of them, knock them about like bowling pins. He would . . . "Please, Captain," he begged. "I'll take him to the hospital. I'll . . ."

"*Gringo,*" said the officer, "get going."

He looked all about. He wanted to fight. He wanted to lift up that bloody head from the ground. He wanted to weep. He wanted . . .

Now the Carabineros were ringing him about sullenly with their rifles. If only . . . Against bullets there was nothing to be done.

He had a better idea. Breaking through the hostile ring, he ran back to his car.

Montalvo, fresh as always in a sand-colored linen suit, came forward from the battered desk.

"Mr. Governor," said Harmon, taking the outstretched hand perfunctorily in his excitement, "I realize that I'm only a guest in this country—that it's presumptuous of me possibly to interfere in local matters, but . . ."

"Vicente Hidalgo?" broke in the Governor.

The news had traveled fast. "They kept clubbing him on the head," said Harmon, "over and over again. By now they must have taken him to their barracks. . . ."

The Governor's eyes searched him quizzically. "May I ask why you're so interested? What *is* he to you, Harmon?"

The question, somehow, stopped Harmon in his tracks. Yes—what? A great deal, *whatever* it was. It had driven him here instantly to plead Hidalgo's cause—a brief to which he was giving his heart as never before. And yet he had not met Hidalgo more than three or four times altogether. Later, some time, he wanted to think more deeply about this. But right now . . . "Not that I know him very well," said Harmon, "but what your Carabineros were doing to him—and what more they will do to him in their barracks . . ."

"Vicente was drunk, wasn't he?" broke in the Governor unhappily. "He was creating a disturbance at the polls, wasn't he?"

True, true. And yet . . . "Honestly," said Harmon taken suddenly with contempt, "do you call that an election?"

The thrust struck home. Montalvo bit his lip and looked away. "I was abroad for almost twenty years," he murmured. "In my absence things have been happening in this country that I don't much care for." A sleeve of his immaculate linen suit touched against the battered desk and he brushed it. "The election," he said moodily, "is a rotten election."

His frankness caused Harmon to relent. "Forgive me," he said. "It's not my country and I don't mean to . . ."

Montalvo shook his gilded head. "You *yanquis* are with us whether you choose to be or not. And the Axis as well." He clapped his hands together frustratedly. "Do you know what kind of thing has started already in Argentina?"

Harmon nodded.

"And the Axis considers itself almost ready to take over in *this* country, too. For a year now Franco has been pouring in money to buy out the House of Deputies. The fascists are beginning to hem us in, Harmon."

Yes—there was the gentleman on the street who had waved his cane and spat. And many other thousands like him, no doubt. "But surely," he protested, "in the case of Hidalgo . . ."

"I know, I know," said the Governor. "Vicente is not the danger. But we must have a reliable House of Deputies. It must not be made into an Axis forum. Vicente realizes that as well as I do. Why, at least, couldn't he have stayed home with his bottle? Why, at least, couldn't he have abstained?"

Abstain . . . Again Harmon bethought himself of those mustard-colored placards, and the cautious man he had met in the dark. Tactics. Discipline. Abstention. But as against all these there was a man who knew no caution at all, who would fling himself recklessly against all that he considered to be wrong. Boozer. Soap-boxer. Quixote. Abstention for him was simply not possible.

"We're living in a hideous age," said the Governor, looking down to the floor, "the age of the lesser evil. Stalin rather than Hitler. Rivera rather than Franco. Democrats today have to lie down with some repulsive bedfellows. They have to think"—and it turned out to be an ironic echo of all that had been said up in the icy air of Chimboya—"they have to think of the world picture, Harmon."

The world picture . . . But all that it was possible for him to see, in the moment, was a man lying bloodied in the dust of Rosales, a man dragged by the armpits to the barracks of the Carabineros.

"Consider," urged the Governor, "the situation of your very own Mission. The fascist crowd would snuff it out in five minutes if they came to power. The hospitals. The schools. The model farm. We must have a House of Deputies that will finally give the Mission a legal existence."

But was there no room in the entire world picture for an individual man? Was it made up only of congresses and armies and bases? Meanwhile time was ticking away. "Mr. Governor," he said, bolting up, "the reason I came here . . ."

"Yes, I know. Vicente. Our problem child."

"The Carabineros have him in their barracks." He pleaded now with all the passion that was in him, all the passion he had never been able to bring to a courtroom in New York. "If there is anything wrong with Hidalgo, it's that he's *better* than ourselves. Too much so. Too much for his own good. Unless you do something, and do it immediately, Mr. Governor . . ."

Montalvo shook his head urbanely. "Harmon," he said, "I'm not given to drinking human blood. I've already spoken with the Carabineros, the moment I heard of this. Vicente will be allowed to cool off. Tomorrow morning he can go back to his bottle." The Governor stood up. "But when," he asked, "when will Vicente learn to read the tides?"

Never, reflected Harmon. The thought, all at once, filled him with love.

CHAPTER TWENTY

IT HAD grown constantly hotter throughout October. The baked earth was cracking. Under the bitter sun, the fronds of the little papaya tree turned brown and shriveled. It was doubtful, everybody thought, that it would last until the rains.

Coming back to the Mission quarters for lunch, Harmon fell down on his cot. It was a day so hot that he could not bear the pressure of his watch on his wrist, and put it away in his pocket—a day when tempers were bound to be ragged. He was not surprised therefore to hear Colonel Burling, overhead, begin to blast at Jacinto, the houseboy, in his pidgin Spanish. *"Pájaros!"* stormed Burling. "You're a pack of dirty little crooks! *Todos*—all four of you! *Comprendo?"*

"Señor," protested Jacinto with a certain terrified dignity, "this is an injustice."

"Pájaros—God damn you!"

The essence of it, Harmon determined, as he balanced the brassy allegations and the flute-like denials against each other, was that Burling was missing five packs of cigarettes and a half-bottle of whisky from his closet.

"An injustice . . ." repeated Jacinto with cautious insistence. But then a wordless roar sent him scurrying out of the room overhead.

With lawyer's eye, Harmon appraised the evidence. For one thing, Burling was a notorious misplacer of his possessions. In the mornings his pockets bulged—by evening the entire contents thereof had been scattered all the way to Rosales and beyond. Secondly, it was not only the houseboys who had access to Burling's room. With no lock on the door, there were times of the day when even strangers could steal in. It was the opinion of the court therefore that no prima-facie case had been made, and in the absence of any proof which could be deemed incontrovertible . . .

A knock on his door.

Raising himself laboriously to one elbow, he called, "Come in."

Jacinto, his face creased with woe. *"Señor Asociado . . ."* he began.

"I heard," said Harmon.

"It is not the first time, *Señor Asociado,* that our honor has been questioned."

Honor. In the starved, stunted Inca bodies remained a heritage still from the Spanish knights who had raped and enslaved them.

Even the most ragged of paupers were wont here to address each other as *caballero,* as cavalier, and to sweep their hats from their heads before each other.

"We have been happy to work for the Mission," Jacinto went on. "Good wages. Good conditions. But if we are not to be trusted . . ." Dolorously Jacinto pointed to the ceiling.

"The heat," said Harmon comfortingly. "It will not happen again—*Caballero.*"

Jacinto smiled and bowed deep from the waist. It was lacking only that he should wear a plumed bonnet.

Most cautiously he mentioned the matter to Burling as they sat, half-dozing, over their coffee.

"Their honor . . ." grunted Burling. Heavily he glanced up at Jacinto who was just then clearing the table. "Line them all up here in the mess hall"—he still clung to Army terminology—"in ten minutes. All four houseboys."

Harmon rubbed his eyes sleepily. "Nothing rash—I hope."

"Be good enough," said Burling, "to stand by. And, Rosabel— you too."

From the far end of the table Rosabel Long stole a glance at Harmon that seemed to say, "Whatever he's up to, we'll stick to- gether, won't we?" The frank inclusiveness of her glance almost made him blush.

Stiff and straight in a parade-ground rank they stood while the Colonel paced back and forth before them and glowered. He could never forget, thought Harmon, that once he had commanded a regi- ment. "Tell them," croaked Burling, "that this isn't the first time effects of mine have been stolen from my room."

Rosabel's Spanish, noted Harmon, was fluent and perfectly accented—but she altered the word "stolen" to "missing."

"Tell them I've got too much on my mind to waste any sympathy on crybabies who go around moaning about their damn honor."

Rosabel faltered.

"Go on," ordered Burling, "tell them!"

As she translated, the boys all winced.

"Honor . . ." said Burling, mugging wildly. He stamped his foot on the ground, flung his hands about inconsolably. "Boo-hoo! The Colonel has hurt my poor little feelings!"

Over the four bronze faces, though not a word had yet been translated, went a look of subtlest disdain.

Rosabel stood mute.

"Tell them," said Burling. "Tell them, damn it!"

"The Director says"—she faltered only an instant and then plunged on, choosing the most esoteric of idioms, all of them surely beyond Burling's own range—"that often his own noblest feelings have been outraged, that he feels like weeping to the highest heavens, but that circumstances compel him to exercise the severest control over himself."

A look of understanding passed over the four faces.

In Spanish, thought Harmon, she was such a different woman— warm and melodious. There was *that* to be said for the language.

"We fill your bellies," rasped the Colonel, "we give you cots to sleep on—which you never had before in all your worthless lives. I don't ever again want to hear any more eyewash about your stinking honor. *Comprendo?*"

"The Director says . . ." Yes, what was Rosabel going to do with *this* prize package?

"Tell them!" commanded Burling.

"The Director—it is his deepest concern, he says, to take the best possible care of all who are employed by the Mission, to see that they eat well and have good beds to sleep in. It is thus, in the most practical sense, that the Director tries to assure honor and dignity to every employe."

Harmon marveled.

"One more yelp from any of those baboons," said Burling, "and I'll turn them over to the Carabineros for grand larceny."

It was not the Director's intention, translated Rosabel, to accuse any of them of larceny, or make this a matter for the Carabineros.

"And now they can haul their dirty little carcasses right back to work. *Comprendo?*"

Nothing, said Rosabel, would give the Director greater joy than that they should return contentedly to their labors.

They bowed, all four, like grandees from Castile and departed.

"Good show," said Burling.

He had just dropped to his cot again for a short siesta when his door opened soundlessly and a curl-crowned head looked in.

"Oh . . ." he said, raising himself on one elbow.

Rosabel placed one forefinger over her lips—with the other she pointed upward. Noiselessly she closed the door and tiptoed across the floor. "Oh, brother!" she whispered, rolling her eyes woefully as she sank down on the camp chair alongside his cot. She was wearing a halter-style frock that showed her smooth, enamel-white shoulders to fullest advantage.

"Long," he said, calculatedly addressing her in office style, as fellow to fellow, "that was damn fast footwork."

She shrugged off the compliment with one pretty shoulder, ran her fingers methodically through her tight-packed curls in search of stray wisps. "That awful, awful drill sergeant," she said. "You know, Bill, I ran five thousand miles just to get away from that kind of roaring and bullying. My own darling father. And now I have it all over again."

"Well . . ." said Harmon, "Burling has his problems too. It's a back-breaking job." Drowsily he let his voice trail off, hoping she would take it as a signal to go.

Instead she bent forward, puckering her high forehead with still-unresolved annoyance. "Really, Bill," she said, "I don't go much for the father-image. Back in the States I was engaged three separate times. Each and every time my darling father managed to break it up."

"It's only fair to tell you," said Harmon dryly, "that I'm a father myself." It caused him to wonder again with what notions his daughters would grow up about *him*.

Rosabel, he found, was still bending forward, intently. "Shall I tell you why I left Chimboya, Bill—*really* left? It was true enough about my wanting a change of climate, but there was something else too. Yes, another engagement that went sour. Silly, isn't it?" Still she leaned toward him, but now with her blonde, almost invisible, eyelashes lowered. "This time it was to a man at the British legation. I was foolish enough to let Father know. He wrote back a ten-page letter—oh, a stinker, Bill. What was the character like? Did he have any brains? How soon before I got bored with him? Was he worth giving up my job for?" Her sharp chin quivered angrily. "Of course, it just ruined Joe for me."

Four engagements. Four temporary marriages. Was it because of the autocratic father that they'd been broken off? Or had they been made in the first place only to be broken? As a cloak for a man-like promiscuity?

"Bill . . ." she said, with a certain tremulousness now.

"Yes, Long?"—again, calculatedly, he addressed her in anti-glamorous office style.

Her hands darted out—the sharp white hands—and tousled his hair. "You're a darn good-looking boy," she said, "did you know that?"

In his mind, ruefully, he began to hear that legendary trumpeting of the Queen Bee as she goes into the nuptial flight—the armed female who takes for herself the choosing of the mate. He bethought himself all over again of that two-fisted Portia with her sly pass at him. Of Laura, taking him by the forearm.

"But you *are*, Bill!"

It was a curiosity, he thought, that in their fantasies men always dreamed of zealous, super-heated females who would woo them, pursue them, ravish them—as in the tale the Little Adjutant had told of the two ladies who had "jumped" him. But in real life men always fled the over-anxious woman.

"Thanks, Rosey," he said. If only she would let it go at that. If only she would do a graceful backtrack. But instead she bent forward and kissed him hastily on the mouth. "Rosabel . . ." he said. She kissed him a second time, less hastily. Oh, poor Rosabel, he thought—she had committed herself now to his mercy, all her pride and dignity.

"Bill," she asked, half-flushing now, "was that so awfully hard to take?"

She had thrust him, he thought dolorously, into the role of female It should be his privilege, therefore, to refuse such attentions.

"Bill . . ." she pleaded, "Bill . . ."

But at the same time it was expected of him to "act like a gentleman." It was binding upon him not to "hurt a lady's feelings."

"Bill," she protested, "you *could* show a little interest."

Should he tell her that he happened to be otherwise engaged? Or even—the truth—that she scared him to death, this flustered Queen Bee? "Sweetie," he said, patting the enamel-white shoulder, a lovely one, really, and it deserved to be better appreciated, "this—this isn't exactly the place."

Her glance darted scornfully about the thin cane walls beyond which lay all the potential eavesdroppers. "Oh, hell," she said, girding her courage, "who cares?"

He wanted, almost, to weep for her. "Rosabel," he said, trying a new tack, "I happen to have a wife. And two kids."

She thrust upon him a long steely glance. Her high global breasts rose and fell with gathering anger. "Am I so damn ugly?" she demanded.

He looked away. "No—hell, no," he said, "you're damn goodlooking. I just don't happen to"—and he recognized woefully that he was speaking a parody—"to feel that way."

She crimsoned instantly.

"Why can't we"—a wicked logic drove him helplessly into yet another irony—"why can't we be friends just the same?"

She slapped him across the face. Hard.

"Oh, now, Rosey," he said. "Rosey."

But she bolted up from the camp chair. Frantically she brushed out her dress, as though it were he—any slightest trace of him—that she was dusting off. "You're a homo," she said bitterly, "aren't you?"

The remark set him back. But, then, hadn't Laura once mentioned that women, in similar cases, were often accused of being Lesbians or frigid? It was a last-line defense for humiliated suitors. Poor Rosabel. He reached toward her penitently.

"No—don't touch me! Don't you dare!" Shudderingly she strode away to the door. "A great big beautiful homo!" She let the door slam behind her.

Oh, if only he could have managed less clumsily . . . He sat up on the edge of the cot, head in hands. If only he could have found a way to appease her, to console her . . . Poor outraged Queen Bee—what future was there for her?

In the hallway, all at once, he heard her call out. Gaily—feverishly—half-hysterically. "Hi, Felix!" she cried. "Hi, good-looking!"

CHAPTER TWENTY-ONE

TODAY it was the humidity. The air was sunless and charged with invisible rain. The cane walls of his office crawled with insects, things of all shapes, some tenuous and hairy, some hard-shelled and button-bright. Documents hung down in his hands like rags.

In the next room Burling and Masters were roaring at each other over some fine point of accountancy. To Puerto Pacifico it must sound as though they were at each other's throats. He was tired of their masculine vigor. Dragging himself up from his chair, he went to the wall, pounded on it twice and shouted, "Shut up, you bastards, shut up!"

The surprise factor brought an abrupt cease-fire, but then came a face-saving mutter from Lew Masters. "Harmon, you son of a bitch, I'm coming after you with a chair!"

He was tired, too, of this kind of joke. "Come on," he said, "I'm waiting."

Wearily, then, he went back to his desk and once again took up Horanyi's report on the business loans. On the surface it looked fine—but there was something about it . . . From outside now came a shrill burst of guttersnipe Spanish that had little to do with getting a truck unloaded. He had capped one geyser only to have a second erupt. Wearily he picked himself up again and went to the window. "Hey, you," he called down, "hey, Napoleon Bonaparte . . ."

From under the huge white helmet, Tom Mercer squinted up. "Yeah, what's biting *you?*"

"Man at work," said Harmon. "Pipe down. Can't you pick on somebody your own size?"

Mercer went on shrilling for just a moment longer—to demonstrate, of course, that he was not to be intimidated. It was really time, Harmon reminded himself, to "do something" about the Little Adjutant. That savage nagging of his had put all the warehouse staff into a state of nerves. There was not one of them who did not wince at Mercer's mere approach. And, Hector Serrano had said openly, it was giving the Mission a bad name. But Burling was so devoted to his Little Adjutant—it was not an easy matter to bring up. Still and all, one of these days—or perhaps this very afternoon as soon as Burling was free . . . Heavily Harmon turned back to the report. It recommended the forthwith granting of three large loans for the establishment variously of a brick kiln, a sawmill, a leather factory. Endorsements from outstanding figures in the province were duly affixed. The legal officer of the Mission was urged therefore—was urged to—to draw up appropriate contracts forthwith—and to . . .

Wearily Harmon sighed and slumped low in the swivel chair. This rotten humidity. It was no day for action. Not even for thinking. But there was something *about* this report . . . He could no longer let it go.

Irritatedly he picked himself up again from the swivel chair and dragged himself across the corridor. He found Horanyi sitting Buddha-like on the floor of his office among a mass of printed forms. His Hussar brilliance had all melted into sogginess.

"These stinking crooks," he mumbled. "These mother-loving degenerates."

His contempt for the "natives" had long ceased to be concealed and his work had long settled down to the merely perfunctory. "What's up?" asked Harmon.

Horanyi took a handful of the forms and pitched them into the wastebasket. "For months I have been slaving on this goddamn census of the province," he muttered. "Half of my census-takers are just plain imbeciles. The others . . . What do you think I found out this morning? The bastards have been going around and charging every family ten pesos for enrolling them on the census. They told a story that every family which was properly enrolled would receive twenty pounds of food, a hammock and a machete free from the Mission."

Harmon mopped his face. "All right," he sighed, "we'll turn it over to the police."

"The police," said Horanyi, "were the census-takers."

Hell, hell, hell. "I'll speak to the Governor the first chance I get. Right now . . ." He held out the loan report. "Felix, I'm leary of this."

"Why?"

"The applicants are all small fry. None of them ever handled an operation one-fifth as big."

Horanyi brushed a stalactite of sweat from his chin. "Hell," he said, "I am not in the business of making silk purses out of sow's ears. All I know is that these apes have the highest endorsements. From the bank manager, from Ramón Manriquez and from the Governor. That's good enough for me, Harmon."

"Weren't there any other applicants?"

"All worse. Shell out the money, I say, and get something started."

"It's a lot of money, Felix."

"Suit yourself. From now on, Mister, it's *your* baby."

Yes, thought Harmon, after the first few flurries of interest, of intellect, Horanyi had settled down on a permanent level—the tropical one. From now on not very much could be expected of him. He was dug in for the duration.

Going out, Harmon noted that on his desk lay a green-enameled compact. Rosabel Long's.

Fine, he thought—*that,* at least.

In the hallway he pressed back to make way for a small huddled figure that teetered along with a typewriter in its hands.

"Good morning, Teofilo."

Teofilo halted. "The bugs," he said hushedly. "They swim all over the blood."

Harmon stared at him.

"They carry poison, *Señor Asociado.* All different colors of poison."

Again Harmon studied him. "When you're free," he said, "come to my office. I want to talk with you."

Teofilo blinked. "And sharks," he said. He squeezed past Harmon roughly. "Many, many sharks." Down the corridor he went, stamping his soles heavily on the floor as he walked. Yes, it was time, Harmon thought, to get him to Dr. Gilmore. He had gone down rapidly of late, the little man who once had talked so eagerly of the "new life" that was to come.

Back in his own office he found Masters sprawling in the swivel chair, heels up on the desk. "Harmon," snarled the old man, "where are all those goddamn priorities you were going to get me from Washington?"

Silently, lackadaisically, Harmon riffled through a mass of papers on the desk and extracted a single pink sheet which had come down only a few hours before in the pouch from the Embassy. Masters read it quickly and pitched it to the floor. "Requested priorities still under consideration!" he echoed. He spat ferociously out of the window. "Where the hell is *that* going to get me, Harmon? It don't build a water line."

"Why the hell chew *me* out?" He was sick of every one of them.

"Because"—now Masters clenched his gnarled old fist and shook it in Harmon's face—"because Burling tells me you won't go along on my order for wood-stave pipe."

"You really want to use wooden pipe for that water line?"

"Hell, man, it's unrationed. I can get it from the States, immediate delivery. All I want."

Again Harmon mopped his dripping face. "How long will junk like that stand up?"

"In this kind of soil?" Masters shrugged his shoulders. "Three or four years maybe. With luck."

"And iron pipe?"

"A lifetime. But where do I *get* iron pipe? It's wood or nothing."

From the outside it would look good. It would make, in the words of Burling, a fine "showing." But the moment it was set into the soil it would start crumbling. It was a fake, a fraud.

"Well?" demanded Masters. "Well?"

He was suffocating in this waterladen air. He was going under for the third time and drowning. He wanted only to be left alone. He did not want to have to think, to fight. He wished that it were Wednesday again, and that again he could steal away to that cool dark house in Rosales, to that loving, adoring girl who demanded nothing of him. "Well," he said sourly, "considering the goddamn world picture . . ."

"Good boy," said Masters. "Now we're cooking." He lumbered out of the room contentedly.

Again Harmon sagged down into his swivel chair. The tropics—in every way they conspired to beat you down, to push you lower and lower into the ooze of indifference and mediocrity. In the tropics, as Dr. Gilmore had said, you forgot what good was supposed to be.

His eye, just then, caught sight of the glittering title plate on the edge of the desk. "Associate Director"—another fake, another fraud. Disgustedly he shoved the plate from the desk, letting it clatter to the floor. He should not have let Masters bulldoze him like that. Better to have postponed the pipeline until the war's end, or abandon it altogether, than waste the money on a phony "showing." But Masters had gnawed at him—and he had let himself give in. It had started up there in Chimboya, this corrupt habit of giving in, during his talk with the Ambassador, and from then on he had found himself ready to give in about more and more. He had accepted, too placidly, the role of salesman of a "hemisphere brotherhood" that did not exist. He had helped wrap the American flag around a tin-horn dictator. He had even sanctioned, in a way, the bloodying of Vicente Hidalgo in the dust of Rosales that day. He had not yet dared to have it out with Burling about the Little Adjutant and the dislike which was redounding against the whole Mission.

And all for the sake of that glittering title plate that in reality was so hollow. All because he wanted to feel important. Associate Director? Associate Director my arse! At some point he must begin to make a stand again.

Shamefacedly, then, he glanced up at the inevitable portrait on the wall—the shrewd, white-tufted face of Cesar Montalvo. How, amid all this tropical rot and lethargy and mediocrity, had Montalvo ever managed to fling that marvelous railroad across the face of the Andes? The answer perhaps was that the railroad had begun to fall

apart the very day it was finished, and that now only one train a day
crawled in each direction ... Horanyi and his loused-up census. The
wooden pipe. The loan applications. A stand had to be made
somewhere.

With a heave, he got himself up from the swivel chair, retrieved
the fallen title plate and set it back firmly on the edge of his desk.
Then he opened his door and shouted down the hallway for Hector
Serrano.

Even Serrano was wilted today, all unstarched. His polo shirt was
rumpled and his trousers hung down in rings. Examining the loan
report desultorily, he said, "Well, *Señor Asociado,* I can name at
least two people who would be better than any of these."

"What's wrong with them? *Falangistas?*"

"Oh, absolutely not."

"Do you know for a certainty whether they put in applications?"

"They did."

"And?"

"Well—they wouldn't pay to grease the wheels. The price, they
say, was too high."

Again Harmon sought to mop his face, but by now the handker-
chief itself was too soaked to have any effect. "At what point," he
asked, "did their applications fail? Do you happen to know?"

Serrano shrugged his shoulders, laboriously. "Lost in the night."

"I'd like to have a talk with those people," said Harmon. Now
finally his gorge had risen. Now finally he would make his stand.

"Very well," said Serrano. "Bring them in tomorrow morning,
Señor Asociado?"

It was just then that the shriek sounded outside—one that was
filled with pain and horror both. On the instant it was not possible
to identify it either as male or female, or even human. It changed
immediately to a gasp of hopeless protest. "No—no—no!"

Harmon leaped to the window. Down below a group of laborers
huddled over something on the ground. "What's happened?" Har-

mon called. "Tell me what's happened?" The laborers all glanced up but did not speak.

"Mercer! Tommy boy!" The griefstricken cry came from the window alongside Harmon's own. From Colonel Burling.

The laborers drew back. On the ground, head crimsoned and mouth agape, lay the Little Adjutant. A yard away his splendid white helmet was still rocking on its crown. Already a Carabinero was running up, his rifle jogging from the shoulder strap.

Pay day—thought Harmon. For months now the Little Adjutant had been building toward something like this. But the way his poor slim frame lay there now on the ground, so flung about and yet so still . . . Sick with nausea, Harmon started for the corridor. Ahead of him, there, was Colonel Burling. "Tommy . . ." he groaned as he raced down the staircase. "Tommy boy . . ."

They stood now in a loose wide circle about the body, the laborers, each at a marked distance from the next man, as if to disclaim any common association and common responsibility. They shifted agonizedly from foot to foot.

"Dead," said the Carabinero, rising up from the body.

It was so ferociously slashed, so hopelessly ruined.

Burling, stiffening suddenly, did not stoop to examine the body for himself. Instead he began to stalk methodically about the loose wide ring of the laborers. One by one he slapped their faces. They stood stock-still, each awaiting his turn to be slapped as though acknowledging that it was his due. "Who did this?" asked Burling finally, the first words he had spoken.

Poor Conquistador, thought Harmon, looking down at the agonized death-face in the dust. If only we had sent him home in time.

"Who did this?" repeated Burling. His manner was entirely that of colonel-of-the-regiment, cold but awesome.

Nobody answered. One and all the laborers kept staring down at their bare toes.

"*Muchachos*—boys," said Harmon stepping forward. "It's more than a matter of being 'loyal.' We can't have a killer running loose." Still no answer. The Carabinero lifted his rifle and swung it about threateningly in an arc. Harmon pushed the muzzle away toward the sea. "Come on," he said, "we've got to know."

A hand rose into the sun like a gleaming bronze indicator. It pointed in the direction of the warehouse. "That's where he went, *Señor Asociado.*"

"Who?"

No answer.

"Tell me who."

"The—the crazy one."

He wanted to retch. "Teofilo?"

"*Señor Asociado,* he was out of his mind. He said—he said that the Little Boss pushed him too much."

Burling, already, was running heavily toward the warehouse.

"Careful!" cried one of the laborers. "He still has the machete!"

The Carabinero hung back.

"I'll fix him, I'll fix him—I'll show every one of them!" muttered Burling, still with a kind of cold determination. Just inside the threshold he picked up a long wooden mallet. To Burling, thought Harmon, this was something far more serious than murder. It was an infraction of discipline.

"Wait," said Harmon, taking a grip on the mallet handle. "The man's crazy, and he still has that machete."

Burling struggled furiously.

"Listen," begged Harmon, "he knows me. I think I can manage him." If only he had not waited this long to "do something" about Teofilo. Or Mercer. Or both. In a way it was all his own responsibility. He should have guessed that something like this was going to happen.

Burling hesitated. Instantly Harmon plunged into the dark of the warehouse. "Teofilo!" he called. "*Muchacho!*"

From somewhere to the right came the sound of wild broken breathing, of an animal that has no recourse but to try—hopelessly—to hide, to become invisible. What an ending this was to that "new life" of which Teofilo had once talked so eagerly. "Teofilo," he called again.

"No—stay away! Don't come nearer!"

He was speaking, Harmon made out, from behind a barricade of crates. "I'm unarmed," said Harmon.

Now, from behind the crates, came a burst of weeping. "Is it—is it the *Señor Asociado?*"

"Yes. The *Asociado.*"

"*Ai,*" moaned Teofilo, "my head is burning. *Ai,* the sharks—the sharks . . ."

"Throw out the machete, Teofilo."

"My head—my head!"

"Come, throw out the machete."

Silence.

"*Muchacho,* you know me. I'll see that you aren't harmed. Come on."

Out from behind the crates, finally, flew the long steel cutlass, handle first. It fell at Harmon's feet.

"Oh, my head—my head," moaned Teofilo. Out he lurched from his cave, weeping without restraint. "What will become of me?"

Harmon took him by the forearm.

"Where? Where to?"

He hadn't thought of that before—only that the frightened animal must be calmed, brought under control. "To the hospital," he said, making up his mind on the instant, "to the doctor." It came to him that once again he had taken on the role of counsel to the accused—as he had done with Hidalgo. Again it was a brief that called forth all his passion. Slowly, cautiously, he led Teofilo along the aisle among the crates. "You'll protect me, *Señor Asociado?* You promise?"

In the doorway, silhouetted black against the daylight, stood Colonel Burling. "So that's the little son of a bitch," he said.

Down, without warning, swung the long wooden mallet. It caught Teofilo full on the head. He staggered backward against a crate.

"Burling!" cried Harmon. "I promised him . . ."

But again the mallet swung, smashing this time into the little bronze face. Teofilo fell in a heap. Blood ran instantly from his mouth and nose.

"Burling!" He felt himself torn with outrage through the whole length of his being.

From the peons gathered in the doorway came a moan of anger and protest.

"I'll show those apes!" ranted Burling. "I'll teach them to attack a white man!"

Again he raised the mallet. Instantly Harmon lunged out with his right arm, thrusting with the full force of his fury.

Burling sat plump on the ground, his mouth open with surprise. He could not believe that it had happened.

Two Carabineros stepped in. "The man is ours," said one of them. They lifted Teofilo by the armpits and hauled him off. Behind him Teofilo left a trail of blood.

Laboriously Burling raised himself from the ground. "You bastard!" he raged. "Harmon, you bastard!"

"Bastard yourself!" said Harmon. "I gave him my word this wasn't going to happen. Bastard yourself!"

Unbelievingly Burling glared at him. "You were out there a minute ago. You saw what he did to Tom Mercer—didn't you?"

"Mercer was all wrong for this job. We should have sent him home long ago. And the peon's insane."

Burling's fists clenched and unclenched. He glanced longingly at the mallet that lay fallen on the floor. How he would love, thought Harmon, to let go on *me*. "From now on," said Burling, and this time he must be speaking the whole truth of what was on his mind, "none of us is safe. These apes can kill any white man they want."

The old tropical discipline, thought Harmon—keep the natives in their place. Once in India, for that kind of "practical" reason, they had shot sepoys from the cannon mouths. He was sick of that kind of white-man's superiority. He would not be any part of it.

"From now on . . ." panted Burling.

"Hell," said Harmon, "we're not in the jungle. They have laws down here. And courts."

"The hell with the laws," said Burling. "From now on we're dead ducks. Every one of us. Unless . . ." He broke off suddenly as some new notion seemed to strike him. With surprising lightness, he made a dash from the warehouse.

A trick, thought Harmon bitterly. Always a trick.

By the time he reached the second floor, he could hear Burling on the telephone. "I tell you, Mr. Governor, that unless steps are taken immediately to secure our personal safety, I am withdrawing the Mission! Absolutely!" There followed an attentive pause—and then a shrewd heavy chuckle. "Good show, Mr. Governor! Exactly what the doctor ordered. Thank you, Mr. Governor!"

Harmon flung open the door.

"You," rasped Burling as he saw him, "stay out of this, God damn you!" He jerked the telephone receiver back on its hook with a ferocious clatter.

For an instant Harmon stared at him. "Well, what's it going to be?" he asked finally, boiling over with contempt. "The *ley de fuga?* 'Shot while trying to escape?' "

"Harmon," now Burling was hysterical, "keep out of this! We're going to do this *my* way! I'm giving you a direct order, Harmon— I'm warning you! Stay out of this, Harmon, God damn you!"

For an answer Harmon ran to the staircase.

Anybody in Rosales, he was sure, could tell him where to find Vicente Hidalgo.

CHAPTER TWENTY-TWO

It was a building with classical pillars and balustrades, but all of wood that now was pitted and long unpainted, a decayed palace that had become a rooming house. The woman who answered the doorbell wore a dress of rusty black cotton. In one hand she held a paring knife and a half-peeled potato. Lawyer Hidalgo, she said uninterestedly, was taking his mid-day siesta.

"Then I will have to wake him."

"If you wish to try . . ." She waved him toward the rear of the dank hallway.

From behind the latticed double door came the rasp of heavy breathing. Harmon knocked and called out, "Señor Hidalgo." The heavy breathing continued unbroken. "Hidalgo!" Still no answer. Harmon rattled the latticed doors. They were secured from within, but lightly. "Hidalgo!"

With a sudden jerk Harmon forced the latticed doors open.

It was the room of the indigent scholar. In one corner stood an iron bedstead and night table. All along the walls, to waist height, leaned columns of books. But at the center of the room hung a burlap hammock. On it, in a rumpled cotton suit, lay Vicente Hidalgo, mouth open. His arms and legs dangled over the sides. He looked like a burst sausage. On the floor beneath him was a nest of empty bottles.

"Hidalgo!" called Harmon once again.

The large loose lips quivered, but only an airy sigh emerged from them. Clutching him by one shoulder, Harmon shook him. A mutter now—but wholly unintelligible. Fiercely, angrily, Harmon went on shaking him, then forced open one eye. The eye looked back at him glazedly and cynically. "Up, get up!" ordered Harmon.

Still no response. He took a clump of the wild gray hair in his fist and shook the head from shoulder to shoulder.

The woman in rusty black looked in through the doorway, still paring the potato. "Sometimes," she said, "he can lie like that for days on end."

For one moment longer Harmon stood and stared. Then, with deepest contempt, he jerked the hammock violently with his hand and dumped the great loose bulk onto the mat-covered floor. "You bum," he said, "you lousy drunken bum . . ."

The Governor opened wide his tawny eyes, ran a hand thoughtfully over his smooth gilded head.

"Yes," apologized Harmon, "I know. I seem to be forcing myself on you constantly these days."

Montalvo drummed the desk with his clean white fingers. "This time," he said fretfully, "it happens that you're going over the head of your own chief."

Harmon gritted his teeth. "The porter's insane. And the truth is that he was pushed beyond endurance."

"Well," said Montalvo, "that will be for the law to decide."

Harmon grimaced. "The law of flight?"

"The law," said the Governor with astounding airiness, "is that if a prisoner attempts to escape, all necessary measures may be taken to apprehend him."

That brutal subterfuge? "Oh, please—please," said Harmon, sourly, not troubling to hide his scorn.

The Governor studied him. "Why," he asked, and it struck Harmon that he had asked the same question on that former occasion too, during the plea for Hidalgo, "why does this man interest you so much?"

It was a question that again, for an instant, left him at sea. Why *not*? The truth was that he had assumed, most of his life, that an injustice anywhere, a wrongdoing to anyone, was his own natural concern. There were numberless people, of course—the "sophisticated" ones—to whom such a feeling was inexplicable. But that it should be questioned by the man who was the son of Cesar Montalvo . . . "The Mission," Harmon replied, groping for words, "does not need blood. And the peon had a certain justice on his side."

The Governor, very carefully, snipped off a sliver of fingernail between his even, shapely teeth. "Burling," he said, "makes a practical point. We're an island among savages. And savages, unhappily, understand only one thing—force."

It made Harmon blink. This was identical—wasn't it?—with the arguments of Cortez and Pizarro, the apologia of the blood-soaked Conquistadores. Automatically, Harmon's glance darted beyond the Governor's head to that familiar portrait on the wall behind him— to the grand, benevolent visage of Cesar Montalvo. "Force," said Harmon, "is one thing the Mission cannot afford."

The Governor threw up his hands. "To whom am I to listen? You or your chief?"

"Burling, right now, is extremely overheated. I beg you to disregard him."

"But he threatens that if I do not act by tonight . . ."

Harmon motioned with his head toward the window. "As I came in," he said, "there was a crowd at the gate. In a very ugly mood. They shouted a number of unpleasant things about the *yanquis.*"

"Oh, well," said Montalvo. "That kind of thing we can take care of with a dozen Carabineros."

Again, unbelievingly, Harmon stared. What, he wondered, had happened to the dedicated idealist whom he had met at this very desk for the first time only a few months before? The man who had spoken so eloquently of his compassion for the "poor devils"? Burling had guffawed. They were all alike, he had said. But Harmon had not wanted to believe that. He had chosen, as always, to be "naïve," if he had to. And now . . .

With a frown, the Governor leaned forward over his desk. "Well, just what are you asking me to do, Harmon?"

"To follow normal legal procedure. To guarantee that the man won't be harmed while he's in custody. To submit him to a sanity test—our own doctor can do that—and to handle the case accordingly."

Montalvo picked up the receiver of his telephone. "I must at least talk to Burling about that."

Impulsively Harmon snatched the receiver from his hand. "Please," he begged. "Burling is in no condition right now to be consulted about anything." He replaced the receiver on its hook and stood up. "Mr. Governor," he said, and again he thought dimly how never in New York had he learned to plead a case with such conviction and passion as before this battered desk with the naked pushbell, "there is something more at stake here than the safety of one crazy peon. To the people of Alba the Mission represents not a group of seven or eight technicians but their entire concept of the United States and its people. If they are made to hate the Mission, they will be made to hate the whole hundred and forty millions of us. I don't care to see that happen." Bolstering the palms of his hands on the desk top, Harmon leaned forward. "You're interested, you say, in 'practical' considerations. The fact is that if that peon is murdered in the barracks, the Mission might just as well leave Alba tonight. And you too." The Governor glanced down in thought. "Talk all you want about Carabineros. From the son of Cesar Montalvo, they expect something else."

Instantly there was an astonishing reaction. "Enough about Cesar Montalvo!" cried the Governor, leaping up. His chair teetered and fell over sidewise.

Harmon stared.

"Now you've gone too far, Harmon!" Blindly the Governor backed away toward the wall—and his golden head blocked out the portrait of Cesar Montalvo, obliterated totally that shrewd and imperial visage. "Enough about my father!"

It was a cry of open hatred, startling and awesome—the protest of a son against his own father's greatness. It could only be that that greatness had made the son feel puny himself. For how long had

Montalvo been harboring such a rage? Was it the reason, possibly, that for half his life Marcos Montalvo had stayed abroad, a runaway from all the multitudinous ikons to his father?

"I'm sorry," murmured Harmon. He thought that if only *he* could have had such a *magnifico* for his father—to be loved by him, to be cherished by him and esteemed—he would have considered it a great fortune. Or perhaps he felt that way only because he had never had a father.

"*My fault,*" said the Governor, taking hold of himself finally. "Forgive me." He smoothed back a feather of his sun-flecked hair. He righted the fallen chair and sat down again. "The little murderer," he said, all composed again, smoothly sealed, "will not be harmed."

"Thank you," said Harmon.

What he had just witnessed, he thought, was a second murder. A patricide.

PART FOUR: *The Encirclement*

CHAPTER TWENTY-THREE

The hands of his watch pushed toward eight o'clock. By now, he thought worriedly, she would be on her way. Several times he made a show of turning back to a report he had laid out on the table, but still Anderson would not go. There was no getting rid of him.

"Mister, you could show some appreciation," complained Anderson. Pointedly he let his glance rove about the neatly plastered walls, the brass bedstead, the floor lamp and upholstered chair—the new quarters he had set up for Harmon at the demonstration farm.

"It's fine, it's dandy," said Harmon. "Thank you with all my heart." But by now, he kept thinking, Ernestina must be picking her way through the moonless night to the lemon grove that stood halfway between here and Hacienda Manriquez. "Man at work," he said gruffly.

Still Anderson would not take the hint. He leaned forward confidentially—though they were alone in the room, alone in the entire administration building, and murmured, "My meeting in Rosales won't take more than a couple of hours. I'm bringing back a pair of tomatoes, Billy."

"One'll do it," said Harmon, affecting a yawn. Back in the States,

Anderson had indicated, he had a wife who was large and aging and for whom he had long lost appetite, but who was strong-willed. And back in the States it must be, also, that he had an unshakeable consciousness of his own runty homeliness. Another kind of run-away, thought Harmon. For him the tropics were one long dream, wet and beautiful.

Anderson, meanwhile, was studying him derisively. "Harmon," he declared, "I believe you *are* a sissy."

"Of course."

"Or maybe"—now Anderson leered like the essence of all lechery—"very discreet."

In a few minutes she would be reaching the lemon grove. It would alarm her to find that he was not already waiting for her. Her husband, if she had judged correctly, would long ago have departed for the Governor's home in Rosales to pass an all-male evening in talk—or so he'd pretended. Between now and ten o'clock every moment was precious, irretrievable if lost. "Walt," he rasped, "run along to your farmers."

"My farmers," sighed Anderson, "are ready to lynch me."

Was it something he ought to know? "Why?" he asked, grudgingly.

"For months, kid, I've been yelling at them to grow something their families could eat, not just bananas and cocoa for export. I gave them the finest vegetable seedlings. too."

"And?" Reluctantly.

"Bugs! Billions of bugs. The aphids love vitamins too. Ate up every last tomato and cabbage. Now I got to promise my farmer boys a ton of insecticide. Free from Uncle Sam."

"Can't they furnish their own?"

"Never no cash in hand. And bank loans come at twenty per cent."

"Who gives them insecticide when we're gone?"

"The billion-dollar question. I'll tell you the honest truth. Sub-sistence farming in the tropics is one of those things that look good just on paper." In other words, thought Harmon sourly, another form of empty "showing." Anderson came back to the table. "Put a banana seedling in the ground and a few months later you have a crop. But vegetables take tending—insecticide—cash. And these poor monkeys down here . . ." Damn it, thought Harmon, why did I encourage him? But Anderson, finally, glanced at his watch. "Holy smoke, I better get going."

"You bet," said Harmon.

He waited for Anderson's car to fade away down the gravel driveway. Then he immediately switched off the lamp in his room, and all the other house lights. Downstairs he noticed a machete leaning near the doorway and automatically picked it up.

Swinging the cutlass, feeling himself armed against any possible danger, he strode over the fields toward the footpath which led in the direction of Hacienda Manriquez. He wondered whether Ernestina, too, had had trouble in getting away. It was not customary for a lady to go strolling alone at night, not even on her own acres. He prayed that nothing had upset the plan. It was five whole days since he had seen her and he had such a desperate longing for her. That moon-pale frailty of hers—what strength he drew from it for himself. She was everything that the word "girl" evoked, all that was tender and scented and gracile; she was girlness itself. How wonderfully lucky he was to be loved by her. He wanted constantly to fondle her, cherish her, protect her—make her understand how grateful he was to her. Whatever it was she loved in *him* was her own handiwork.

From far behind him came a mournful low—the cattle in the acclimatization shed. Otherwise the night was still, but treacherously so. In the soil, in the trees, in the very air, life continued to suppurate, to multiply in silence and secrecy. Malevolent life, murderous life. Things that crawled and things that flew. And motes that no naked eye could see but that lashed the body of man with weird and awful scourges. Microbes, bacteria, fungi—breeding exotic maladies like oroya fever, pinto, ainhum, Loa Loa, sprue. He had seen the effects in the hospitals: bodies bristling from head to toe with warts; legs swollen to elephant proportions; nodules swelling on the scalp to the size of baseballs and packed with worms; skin daubed as by a painter with green, violet and crimson; Negroes spattered white, and white men splashed black; toes that dropped off like withered plums; whole bodies that mummified like relics from a tomb . . . And all brought about by the motes which festered in the warmth and the dark. It was a miracle, he thought, that the Incas had endured long enough in this land to be conquered.

He reached the footpath and the cover of a stand of bananas that bordered it on one side. The immense leaves hung down like portieres, among them the huge unclenched fists of the fruit. He owned hundreds of thousands like these, Ramón Manriquez. Their fruits went out over all the seas of the world, to be eaten by children in New York, ambassadors in Paris, ballerinas and commissars in Moscow. Day after day a thousand serfs labored themselves toward death for Ramón Manriquez, never to know any of the riches that grew in these trees but only the dangers. In Alba one saw almost no men with hair of gray.

Something slithered away under his feet, but he did not change pace. On he strode, bent unswervingly on his outlaw mission. There was nothing which he would let keep him from her. Ernestina—she too was coming through danger, so fragile but so bold in her love. He had not wanted to let her do this, but she had insisted. Fiercely. There was nothing else to life now, she had said, but him. *That* part of it, he thought again, made him anxious. It was too great a charge that by some unwitting act he could turn off all sun and air for Ernestina. He wished, in a way, that he could mean less to her.

Through the black of the night, now, a sharp but exquisite fra-

grance came forward to meet him. The lemon grove! It was a bouquet which he liked to think was that of Ernestina's own lovely
flesh. He raced forward now, calling in a half-whisper, "Ernestina!
Ernestina!"

A shadow separated itself from the trunk of one of the trees and
flung itself at him. "Oh, William—William—William!"

Instantly they were locked together, swathed with the wonderful
perfume of the lemon grove, embowered in it, made dizzy with it.
"William—William . . ." He found that she was sobbing. "Poor,
poor darling," he said. "Was I very late?"

"No, no, it couldn't have been more than a minute! And I knew
you'd come. But all of a sudden I lost my courage."

"Because of the dark? Because of *him?*"

"Everything—because of everything." She pressed against him
feverishly. "Take care of me, dearest, will you? Protect me, will
you?"

There was no danger, he thought, which he would not defy for
her.

"William," she said, brightening now, "our peons have been
talking of nothing all week but the wonderful *gringo!* How he went
to the Governor and pleaded for the crazy man and got him put
away safely in the hospital." Tenderly he kissed her again, but her
lips broke free. "No, no, let me talk," she said. "How I loved listening to them. I'd make them tell it over and over again. The story's
grown, of course. They say that you went to the Governor with a
pistol, that you aimed it straight at his head . . ."

"Not exactly," he said.

"I don't care, dearest. You're a legend now, and there's no stopping
it." She hugged him. "Ramón, of course . . ."

Yes—how had *he* taken it, that somber captain?

"All the next morning Ramón sat on the porch oiling his guns.
He was letting our peons know, of course, that if ever any of *them*
got the notion of lifting a hand against the Master . . ." She shud-

dered, and he recalled how at their very first meeting she had been so quick to assure him that she was not on the side of the masters. It was one of the many things that he loved about her.

"Darling, darling, darling," she said, pressing herself against him happily, "you're everything I want you to be."

"I wish I were."

"Oh, I know you are."

He took her head gently into his hands. "There's always too much about *me,*" he said. "Let's love *you* for a while."

"I don't care much about me, darling."

"If I were you, Ernestina, I'd stand before a mirror and look at myself by the hour."

She laughed. "At that bony mask of mine? That death's head?"

Yes, he thought, there *was* something of the death's head in that lovely face. But nobody else would have thought of discovering it; there was nobody so critical of Ernestina as she herself. "Tell me," he asked, "can I make you understand you're beautiful?"

"Oh, I know I am!" she said with a sudden, girlish lilt. "Good," he said.

"But not in a way I like. I've told you—I don't care for my kind of looks."

No, there was that in her which longed to look—like Laura. "Oh, don't," he said, trying again to brush that thought aside.

"What've I said?" she asked.

He crushed her tightly against himself, breathing her in—her and the bouquet of the grove together. Instantly he was intoxicated again. "Ernestina . . ." he whispered, beginning to tremble.

"Yes, darling?" But immediately, she caught for herself what he meant. "Here? Oh, dearest, how can I go back to the house all rumpled?"

He shook his head. "I'm alone tonight. Come back with me."

She drew a sharp breath.

"Please."

"But—but your people are all over the place."

"No, no. The peons' quarters are back over the hill. Please."
She shook with indecision.

"Please," he repeated. "Please."

"Oh, William," she said then, half-happily and half-mournfully,
"you know I can't refuse you."

Spent now, they smoked in the dark, glimpsing each other only
by the ruby flashes from their cigarettes. He had a feeling of wonderful contentment. It was exactly in *that,* he thought, that the
test lay, the difference between good and bad—how you felt in
the moments afterward. And never had he felt so fine.

"William," she asked suddenly, out of the dark, "what's your
wife like?"

Even in the dark he found himself flushing. Laura was a subject
on which he did not want to think. He had mentioned once, in
passing, that he was married, but he had hoped Ernestina would
let it go at that.

"Tell me, William. What's she like?"

"Three," he said, "is a crowd."

"Please," she begged.

He tried to still her with a kiss.

"No," she said, drawing instantly away. "I want to know!"

Why? Was it the curiosity of a penitent mistress? Or an inquisi-
tiveness to know that side of him which was the husband of some
other woman? "Ernestina," he said, "have a cigarette."

Fiercely, of a sudden, she seized his hand and scratched it. "Ugh,"
he grunted. Down the back of his hand ran a long thread of pain.
"Well, *tell* me," she demanded.

Wildcat, he thought. It was a mood of hers he had forgotten,
the Ernestina who had teased him so waspishly on the deck of the
ship, who had ridden the horse so fiercely on the hill. "A fine
woman," he replied.

"Young?"

"Yes."

"Pretty?"

"Yes."

"Do you"—oh, how Ernestina drove herself—"do you love her?"

That sunlit face. That trim and graceful body. That quick mind. But, also, those huntress eyes.

"Do you?" Menacingly, Ernestina pressed her fingernails into the back of his hand, prepared again to gash him. "Do you *love* her?"

Laura too had put her kingdom in him, he thought. But so condescendingly, knowing always that she had only to reach for it whenever she wanted. And yet that was not the whole of it. And yet—it was the first time, surprisingly, that he had let himself face this possibility—he might not have been everything to Laura that a woman had a right to expect. He had married her on the pretense that he was whole and strong, but he had already long been raddled by doubts and self-disbelief and the fears inspired in him by the death of his father and the steely glitter of his mother. It was in the nature of women that they should judge men in terms of their fathers, that they should expect their husbands to stand as high as the first man they had known, the man who from knee-height could not help looking like a giant. And Laura's father, the scientist, had been otherwise a giant as well. . . . It occurred to him, for the first time, that Laura had a right possibly to feel cheated in him, and that she had carried her disappointments off decently enough.

"Do you love her?" demanded Ernestina again

Some day he must try to think it out.

Again suddenly the sharp fingernails tore grooves down the back of his hand.

"She-devil!" he said. "What if I told you that I don't know?"

Contrite instantly, Ernestina flung herself at him and kissed the gashes she had torn in his hand. "Darling, darling," she begged, "forgive me, darling. What makes me think I have any right to ask such questions?"

He reached out to stroke her head. But, again in a sudden change of mood, she flung herself away. "Do you do this kind of thing often, William?" she asked bitterly.

She meant—did he take mistresses? Was she only one of many, to be mingled in his mind with other casual wooings? How she tormented herself, this girl of sorrows.

"No," he said gently. "It's the first time."

Happily, then, she cuddled up against him. "I've been awful," she said, "so horribly inquisitive."

He drew thoughtfully on his cigarette. "Me too," he confessed.

"All right," she said cheerfully, "what do you want to know?"

"Why ever did you marry Manriquez?" It was a question long in his mind, one which he had wanted to ask ever since the *verbena,* when first he saw them together. Between them was such an opposition of spirit.

"Oh, that," she said. She reached for a cigarette and he lit it for her. When she spoke again it was dreamily, in the glow of a time long lost. "They said we were the best-looking couple in Chimboya. Ramón would read to me from Rimbaud and Verlaine. Did you know he'd been educated in Paris? Like all our rich young men. He'd come to my window in the middle of the night with a whole orchestra to serenade me. So poetic. But entirely conventional in these countries. And the poetry stops, of course, at the altar." She drew away her hand from Harmon and went on in a new tone, choppy and staccato. "Father died just after I came back from the States, and Mother was penniless."

He found her hand again and held to it obstinately. He asked what had sent her to the States for her schooling.

Her answer was a leap ahead of his question. "Would you believe it, William, if I told you that I was a marvelous student at college? Honors in every course. Can you believe that of Señora Ramón Manriquez? But in those days it was Miss Chavez. And the boys I strolled to classes with, and had sodas with and went to the proms with—they're doctors now or engineers or scientists. They've all become something—of one sort or another. This morning I was trying to remember something from Kant—a little thing—so ordinary—something nobody ought to forget. And I simply couldn't ... Michigan? Oh, Father was a modern man, a terribly good friend of Vicente Hidalgo's, by the way. I can still remember Hidalgo coming to our house in Chimboya when I was very little. Yes, Father was modern. He wanted his daughter to be more than just a domestic animal. He wanted her to go among men as a person. . . . But it just didn't seem to come out that way, William, with all that I tried. Señora Ramón Manriquez. . . . The traditions were all against me and I didn't have anybody to help me. Not after Father died and I married Ramón." She pressed her face into the pillow and went on in a muffled voice. "You know, once or twice a week the Governor comes to our home for dinner. He and Ramón talk over all sorts of things—and they talk as if I weren't even in the room." Abruptly she seemed to change the subject. "Dearest, do you know the Spanish painters?"

"A little."

"In Spain in the olden days the ladies used to keep dwarfs for pets. They would dress and undress—even the grandest ladies— in front of a dwarf as if the little things were not human and pose that way for their portraits." She laughed nervously. "William, what *was* it that Kant invented?"

Tenderly he leaned forward to kiss her.

"No," she said, pushing him away. "I mean it. Year after year I'm slipping backward. Once I knew so much—felt so strongly about things. I was even going to take a place in politics! William, tell me what on earth it was that Immanuel Kant . . ."

"The Categoric Imperative?"

"Heavens, yes!"

He felt for her. He had known with the same bitterness what it was to slip backward—to become ever more and more contemptuous of oneself. Here in Alba, one way or another, he had managed to find himself again, or an illusion of himself. It didn't matter which, in the moment; one was as good as the other.

"William," she suddenly burst out, "what does your wife do? Does she do *anything*?"

Again he flushed. Why, why couldn't Ernestina let the sleeping dogs lie?

"Tell me, William," she pressed.

"Laura was an architect."

"*Was?* Why did she stop?"

He wished that she would not run past him like this to take Laura by the hand, to make common cause with Laura. "I never asked her to," he said hotly. "It was her own idea."

Again suddenly Ernestina drew away from him, sitting up rigidly against the backboard of the bed. "William," she said with a kind of stony self-reproach, "I had no right to do this to her. It's wrong —terribly wrong."

"No," he said, irritably now.

"Yes!"

"Not at all. Just before I left the States . . ." The shooting license —but how was he going to say it? It would sound so gross, and farcical too. "Laura—she let me know that—that she expected something like this to happen."

"Oh, no!"

"My wife is—modern."

For an instant Ernestina sat stiff with thought. "Why—doesn't she love you, William? Doesn't she care for you?"

She probably did—he thought—in her own special way. And the shooting license was even part of it. But he didn't answer.

"I can tell you, William, that if you were mine, I mean really mine, I'd probably kill myself. And maybe you as well."

How different, he reflected, were the ways of loving—the ways of the North and the ways of the South. And by at least one of the women who loved him (or by both?) he had been put painfully in debt.

"Ernestina . . ." he said, reaching out and caressing her tenderly on the cheek.

"Don't!" she cried, drawing instantly away. "For goodness' sake don't pity me, don't console me!" It set him aback. "You're thinking," she went on in an odd burst of clairvoyance, "of the day you'll be going home. You're expecting that I'll be making an awful scene—sobbing and crying and all the rest. Well, I won't, William. I promise you I shan't."

She would be left on that day with so little—only a secret from her husband. "Ernestina . . ." he called.

"Yes?"

"I—I wonder if I should have started this."

Silence.

"I mean . . ."

"On account of your wife, you mean?"

"On account of you."

"Oh, darling!" she cried, leaping back and hugging him with all fondness. "You've given me a sense of worth for the first time in years. Oh, no, darling!"

CHAPTER TWENTY-FOUR

FRESHLY groomed, but all ravaged about the eyes, Vicente Hidalgo sat in the visitor's chair and studied the newspaper headlines that told of the first landings of American troops in North Africa.

"Now," he remarked cheerily, "the *yanquis* don't have to bother being so kind to us. They no longer need us."

It was a mark of acceptance, thought Harmon, but only half-flattering that he was always being singled out from his fellow-Americans.

"*Until* now," Hidalgo went on, "they kept flooding our newspapers with photos of marvelous tanks and guns—but all in Detroit. And all in the absence of any victories about which they could talk. This, Harmon, is more like it. *Cojones.* North American style."

Again and again that word would come up. Did it imply, in this instance, that the Latinos conceded themselves conversely to be peoples who were castrate? It might well account for the awe that they mingled, grudgingly, with their dislike of everything North American—and the glee that day in the pump-house at Santa Ana when the Colossus had fallen so flat on his face.

Blandly Hidalgo asked, "How soon will the Mission be leaving us?"

Just as blandly Harmon smiled and said, "Señor Hidalgo, you know better than that. The day is over when our Latin American policy can consist of a brigade of Marines."

"Ah, yes," said Hidalgo, with the sunniest of grins, "the Good Neighbor Policy! It has been succeeding admirably, let me tell you. Now, instead of hating the *gringos,* we merely distrust them."

From Hidalgo it was hard to take offence. "Little by little," said Harmon.

Hidalgo lowered his eyes and a somber shadow went across his craggy features. "Why I came to see you this morning—I came to apologize." It was a moment of anguish for Harmon as well. "I can only say that you managed magnificently well *without* me that day. In the matter of that poor little monkey who ran amok, I mean."

Harmon nodded his thanks.

"But on the other hand, William . . ."

A flush of delight rose in him. It was the first time Hidalgo had called him by his Christian name. And only one other person— Ernestina—knew him as "William." He was happy to be shared this way between these two.

"On the other hand, William, the chances are that you may have prevented a revolution from happening that day. Had the little porter been murdered, the *Poristas* would have rioted. They've been waiting for just such an opportunity for a very long time."

Opportunity—he thought with a certain annoyance. "From the tactical viewpoint then," he asked, "it would have been better to let the man be beaten to death?"

Hidalgo shook his massive head and smiled. "William," he said, "cynicism doesn't suit you. As a matter of fact, it wouldn't have been the right kind of incident anyhow. It was all wrapped up with the Mission and the American flag. The *Poristas* prefer to catch the regime naked if they can. They'll bide their time."

Tactics. Discipline.

"Largo, by the way, sends you his regards," said Hidalgo. "He promises that when the moment comes your Mission will in no way be embarrassed."

Harmon nodded. "What Largo wants," he murmured, "is that I pass along word to Washington that his people are willing to be pro-American."

Again there was a flash from the pure white teeth. "I tell you, William, it's a myth that the *gringos* are all stupid. If that were so, they wouldn't be on their way to owning half the world."

"Thank you. Thank you, Vicente."

It was just then that Rosabel Long pushed open the doorway. "You might want to know," she called, not moving a step beyond the threshold, "that the Ambassador is on his way here."

Harmon looked up sharply. The Ambassador?

"Ah," said Hidalgo triumphantly.

Harmon shook his head. "Vicente," he said, "I wouldn't jump to any conclusions."

With a firm handshake for Harmon and a courtly bow for Rosabel, Hidalgo went.

"The Customs people," Rosabel went on, "just sighted the Ambassador's yacht rounding the Bay. He'll be tying up in about ten minutes. The Colonel wants everybody looking frantically busy."

"Any notion of why the Ambassador's coming?"

She shrugged her shoulders and started to go.

"Rosabel . . ." he called after her.

She wheeled about on the instant and presented a face that was totally blank.

"Rosabel," he said, "about what happened that time . . ."

"Oh, go to hell," she said.

They stood on the dock in silence, Burling and he, as the hawser was thrown from the white wing-like yacht which was named Columbia III and was said to have been loaned to the Ambassador by an American oil man in Lorca. In the week since Mercer's death, Burling and he had not spoken much with each other.

At the rail of the yacht now appeared the genial young man they had met months before on the plane to Chimboya. Elliott Reeves. He waved affably. They waved back and Reeves disappeared below.

Over Burling's face now came a dazed sleepy look. "I know damn well," he said, "that they're bringing me my walking papers."

Instantly Harmon became uncomfortable for him. "Hell," he said, "where would they ever get a replacement? Who would want the job?"

Burling took a grip on himself. "Harmon," he said, "let me bore you with a bit of military history. In the Civil War, General George B. McClellan spent years, broke his back, organizing the army of victory. But they never let him lead that army. When the time came to take it into the field and finish the job, they replaced him with U. S. Grant." He lit a cigarette. "I'm certain," he said, "that Rosabel has told the Ambassador all that there *is* to tell. And more."

Down the gangplank, snowy to his shoe tips, came Elliott Reeves. "Well," he asked, "how've you Dead End Kids been making out?"

Burling did not answer.

"The Ambassador," said Reeves, "is staying for only a couple of hours. He wants . . ."

"If he's come for an inspection," said Burling, "I can get him up to the end of the province and back by nightfall."

"His Excellency," said Reeves, "is not coming ashore."

"His Excellency," said Burling, "is not crazy."

"Absolutamente no," agreed Reeves, unperturbedly. "He wants to meet with every member of the Mission staff. One by one. Will you see that they're all rounded up?"

"Harmon . . ." said Burling.

"Right."

"Colonel," said Reeves, "you first."

Burling braced himself.

"Harmon—you last."

Why, he wondered.

"Let's go," said Reeves. Heavily, sleepily, hauling himself along the rope rail by both hands, Burling went up the gangplank.

All the while that they waited under the striped awning on the aft deck, Dr. Gilmore kept fretting. He had launched a project in the last week for sampling the health levels of the Alba population, and he wanted to keep it under his personal observation at all times. The incidence of intestinal parasitosis, he said, was the highest he had ever observed among children. And their haemoglobin content was so *low* that he was forthwith starting a free distribution of powdered milk.

How, Harmon inquired, was he managing these days with the Sisters?

"Fortunately," said Gilmore, "I was able to relieve the provincial prelate of an acute case of gas pains."

Colonel Burling, just then, emerged from below, looking more sleepy than ever. "Miss Long," he called out, and conspicuously he kept his eyes averted from her, "they want you next."

She marched away, without a word, over the teakwood deck.

"I hope," rasped Burling over the clatter-clatter of her spiked heels, "that none of you lets himself feel constrained by any schoolboy notions of loyalty." He turned and went down the gangplank.

"That crazy coot," said Lew Masters.

"The Wild Man of Borneo," said Horanyi.

Rosabel returned under escort by Reeves, who next asked Dr. Gilmore to go below. But Reeves himself lingered behind and maneuvered Harmon away toward the rail. "The reports," he commented, "have been coming through in fine shape lately."

"Credit that one," said Harmon, "to Miss Long."

"A keen apple."

"That she is." His attention was caught for a moment by a gull that swooped into the gray-green sea and rose, exultantly, with a fish flapping in its bill. He thought that down below Burling must have flapped in just the same way in the clutch of the Ambassador.

"How," asked Reeves, "has Gilmore been turning out?"

"Gilmore's a real find. A doctor from the story books."

"Good on administration?"

"And crazy to cure people. He has a standing order to call him day or night if a tough one comes up. My mother's a doctor. I know a good one when I see him."

Reeves lit a cigarette, then remarked casually, "There's been a little grousing about Gilmore here and there."

"From the local quacks? Naturally. They don't stand a chance before a Hopkins man. Everybody's going to the public clinics."

"That's right," recalled Reeves. "He *is* a Hopkins man."

The Ambassador, down below, was ensconced on a leather lounge amid mounds of briefcases. *"Demn* good," he said without further introduction, *"demn* smart, Harmon."

Reeves smiled at his puzzlement. "The Mercer trouble," he elaborated.

"Thank you," said Harmon. What he had done, he had not at the time considered in the light of the "world picture," only in the light of what was demanded for an individual man. It was nice that for once it had coincided also with the "world picture."

"I may say," the Ambassador went on, and the descent to sea level seemed to have thawed him out considerably, made him glow even, "that the *Presidente* is also grateful to you. There were many elements about the Republic who were ready to take advantage of the situation."

"Well," said Harmon stiffening instantly, "I'm not sure that would have been so bad."

"The fascists, for instance?"

"They're not the only Rivera-haters in the Republic. There happens also to be the *PORA*, and as far as I can make out . . ."

"*Demn* you, *demn* you," cried the Ambassador, "I'm trying to praise you, Harmon!"

Yes, he sensed, there was some scheme going on here to draw him in, to make him one of them. It might be something that would have to be resisted. "Thank you, sir."

The Ambassador and Reeves exchanged a glance. Like two merry schemers, thought Harmon. "About Colonel Burling . . ." the Ambassador began, coaxingly.

A cue—wasn't it?—to begin running Burling down. Harmon stood mute.

"A *loco*—a screwball—isn't he?" prompted Reeves more openly.

He had not known, exactly, on entering the room how he ought to feel toward Burling. But again, as often, he found himself suddenly in the position of counsel to the accused—to a client with a bad case, but pitiable.

"Come on," urged Reeves, "we're among friends."

Amusedly now, Harmon reached for the mahogany box on the coffee table and took himself a cigarette. Reeves came up instantly with a light. Like a pair of Gestapo men, they were—in the first stage, the jovial stage. "I haven't any opinions," he said blandly, "about Colonel Burling."

The Ambassador squinted. "Burling," he said encouragingly, "is a very objective man. He describes himself as a sort of . . ."

"General McClellan?"

"Would you call the analogy incorrect?" Eagerly the Ambassador searched his face for any smallest sign of capitulation.

"I'm not sure," he said, "that I'm equipped to judge."

Now the Ambassador and Reeves twinkled at each other, positively twinkled—appreciative professionals in the art of evasion. "I must say," remarked the Ambassador, "that Miss Long is far more out-spoken than you."

"Miss Long may not be entirely without bias."

"Well," said the Ambassador, and instantly it became evident he was going to turn up an ace, "she speaks well of *you*, Harmon."

It *was* a surprise!

"Extremely well," added Reeves. "She says you're hard-working, intelligent, imaginative. She says you're about the one member of the Mission with any real diplomatic sense."

All this from Rosabel Long! Gallantly she had repressed in her-self all the natural fury of the woman scorned. She had striven, with real magnanimity, to copy that which was considered best in a sex she did not even like. "Miss Long," he said, and they could not guess how thoroughly he meant this, "is a very gracious woman."

"And keen!" added the Ambassador. "When the Mission is fin-ished, I'll see that she gets a vice-consulship out of it."

"Fine," said Harmon. But the men who would be working with her would be on their toes every minute.

"Harmon," asked Reeves, and now a bluntness came into his voice, "do you really believe that Burling is the man for the job?"

Now the Gestapo men were moving into the second phase—firm-ness, austerity. "That depends," said Harmon, still fencing, "on what prospects you can offer. For instance, we made a request weeks and weeks ago for priorities on certain essential equipment."

From among the mounds of hard-leather briefcases, Reeves ex-tracted a copy of a newspaper. It bore the same news of which Vicente Hidalgo had made so much—the landings in North Africa.

"From now on," said Reeves plainly, "the prospects are *regular no más*. Just fair."

Could it be that Vicente had guessed perfectly? Harmon gritted his teeth. "You mean—we're getting ready to pull out of Alba?"

"Nothing of the kind—*demn* it," said the Ambassador. "It means only that Washington will be less disposed now to regard the Alba Mission as entitled to military priorities. The world picture has changed."

Again the world picture. And again he felt himself nudged by the hand of Vicente Hidalgo. "Sir," he asked, but suavely this time, blandly, "you mean we can stop paying the Latinos a bribe?"

The Ambassador bolted up—absolutely stung. *"Demn* you, Harmon, *demn* you!" he cried. "Why all these fierce moral constructions on everything?" But, instantly, he regained his composure and sat down again. "The fact is that overnight the focus of the war has shifted. Instead of defending the Americas, we are invading Africa. Materials will naturally have to follow the troops. There cannot be as much for Alba as we'd hoped. But there *will* be something, more than ever before."

Harmon looked down at the floor in thought.

"After all," continued the Ambassador, "we still have our national reputation at stake. When the Mission leaves here next summer, it must retire in good order. It must leave behind a water system that works, crops that grow, hospitals that cure." He gave Harmon a brilliant and penetrating glance of a sudden. "When the Department accepted Burling last June," he said, "it was only because there was no alternative. Now we're in a position to do better."

Suddenly they were beaming on him, the Ambassador and Reeves both.

The blood rushed to his face.

"For Burling," murmured the Ambassador, "there'll be an opening back in Washington. It carries a lovely title."

His pulses thumped wildly, all of them.

"The Department," said the Ambassador, and now in the gray cautious murmur of a diplomatic dispatch, "takes considerable interest in you, Harmon. What with your legal background and your proven abilities in the field, you might go far."

Could it be that he had really become that good? Red with embarrassment he hauled himself up from his chair, went over to a porthole and stared out. Could it really be that here—in this benevolent atmosphere of esteem—could it be that all those capacities had finally bloomed in him which had so long been awaited and then despaired of? And how close, in that house of royal women, he had come to final obliteration. . . .

"Harmon," said the Ambassador softly, "I won't press you for an immediate answer. Think it over, if you want. Take a week, two weeks, if you wish."

But then, suddenly, he remembered that dazed and sleepy look on the face of Leslie Burling as he had talked of his "walking papers."

"It's a big opportunity," coaxed Reeves. "And it mightn't come soon again."

A big opportunity. An end for good to those deadweight law texts, to the squabbles of *Finch vs. Finch,* to the anguished self-weighings and dreams of escape. This was man's work.

"Well?" asked the Ambassador.

"Has—has Colonel Burling been informed?"

"Not yet—not exactly."

"I don't know," said Harmon. "How can I?"

"Burling," said Reeves with a shrug, "is a dead duck. If you won't take it, we'll look elsewhere."

"I promise you," smiled the Ambassador, "he'll have a lovely title in Washington."

"For how long?"

"That sort of thing," said the Ambassador shortly, "must not be overdone." He pushed away the mound of briefcases and stood up. "Think it over, Harmon."

"Thank you, sir, I will."

But again, as he went up to the deck, he bethought himself of that sleepy look on the face of Leslie Burling, a man about to be confronted with an ultimate proof of his inadequacy. It was of no pleasure, just now, that in his own bones all the cracks seemed finally to have mended.

CHAPTER TWENTY-FIVE

IT WAS a day when everybody was after him at once, as though he were the missing part in each operation of the Mission. Hardly had he asked the two young doctors, Larrea and Solís, to sit down than Lew Masters trundled in. "Mister," demanded the old man, "what's the score on my two-ton truck?"

"We've been phoning Huelva for an hour, Lew. All we get so far is that it was impounded by the border police."

"The hell you say!"

"They claim there was an irregularity about the load your driver brought back over the border."

"I sent him to get cement," said Masters. "He's been doing just that same thing for weeks now. Irregularity, my ass! What the hell do they mean holding up an official vehicle of this Mission?"

Harmon sighed. "Look," he said, "I'm working on it. I'll clear it up just as fast as I can."

"Hell, hell," grumbled Masters as he lumbered out. "It's cost me two days' work on the road already."

All the while Dr. Larrea and Dr. Solís were waiting for him anxiously. And on his desk was a summons in Burling's belligerent scrawl. Leaning provisionally against the edge of his desk, he asked the doctors to what he owed the honor of their visit.

Larrea took the lead, the stocky and gentle resident from Santa Ana through whose open collar peeped curls of chest hair. "Believe us, *Señor Asociado*," he said, "to work with Dr. Gilmore is an immense opportunity. A medical education all in itself."

"Animating," added little Dr. Solís, "inspiriting."

"All the more unfortunate," went on Larrea, looking down wretchedly, "that a crisis of an economic character has had to intrude itself."

When, thought Harmon, would Latin Americans ever learn the art of directness. "A money matter?"

Under his olive skin Dr. Larrea blushed. "I believe—" he stammered, "that the *Asociado*—that he is well acquainted with the basis on which the resident physicians have been—been compensated all along?"

"Fifteen hundred pesos a month?"

"Half from the provisional government," Larrea elaborated, "and half from the Mission."

It was the Mission's intention, Harmon assured him, to continue its contribution for the duration of the program and one year beyond.

"The villain," sighed Dr. Solís, "is the provincial government. From next month on, it stops paying *its* share."

No matter how hard you worked, thought Harmon, there was always a prop falling away somewhere. Irritatedly he picked up his title plate and hefted it in his hand like a club. "Why?" he demanded.

Again Larrea blushed. "It is their contention, *Señor Asociado*, that we are being grossly overpaid."

It came out, Harmon calculated, a hundred and fifty dollars a month at the full rate. "Are you? Could you manage on half?"

Larrea shook his head. "We have families, most of us. It would be a disaster."

Serrano just then came back. "Colonel Burling wants you at once," he said. "In his quarters, *Señor Asociado*."

"I know, I know. Anything new about the truck?"

Serrano glanced about meaningfully. The doctors, taking the hint, withdrew to a corner. "The truck," whispered Serrano, "was carrying more than cement. In half the bags was contraband brandy."

"Damn it," said Harmon. "So somebody has turned us into rum smugglers."

"It's been going on for weeks, I gather."

Again Harmon hefted the title plate in his hand as though ready to hit somebody with it. "Who's responsible? What are the customs people doing about it?"

"The truck and driver have suddenly been released. It seems that early this morning a gentleman turned up and paid the full duty on the booze. It was arranged also"—Serrano winked—"to pre-date the customs receipt as of two days ago. Now all is as white as the snow."

"Who was it who paid?"

"A type by the name of Elóy Ruiz."

"Who is he?"

"Oh, a famous jack-of-all-trades in these parts. Dope peddler, pimp, gunman. Until now there was no trouble about the brandy. But it happened this time that there was a new guard on duty, a farm boy they'd forgotten to take care of. The mistake, I'm sure, will not be repeated."

"Damn it," said Harmon. "In a Mission vehicle. Talk to the driver the minute he gets back—and fire him."

"Absolutely," said Serrano. He started to go, then turned back. "About those business loans, *Señor Asociado* . . ."

"Yes—where are the people you were going to bring to see me?"

"They beg that you let it drop."

"Why?"

"They say they've had trouble enough."

Exasperatedly Harmon banged his desk with the title plate that read "Associate Director." He would like to bang a few heads instead. Everything around him was being sucked down into the stinking tropical ooze. There was nothing that they would not try to adulterate, contaminate, ruin. Hardly was a new project born than they . . . He recalled, then, that the two doctors were waiting.

"Gentlemen," he asked, turning to them, "what are your intentions if we cannot stop the salary cuts?"

Larrea shrugged his shoulders unhappily. "To continue with Dr. Gilmore as long as we possibly can."

"In six months," said Solís, "we will all be broke."

"Finished," said Larrea.

Burling, he found, was entertaining a guest, none other than the Governor. They sat around a coffee table on which stood a bottle of brandy—with a suspiciously foreign label—and several bottles of vanilla soda pop which was being used as a mix. In rare good humor, Burling was engaged in telling once more the saga of how he had taught the Young Marshal to swim, but now with new embellishments. "The crawl and the overhand—the breast stroke and the side stroke. He filled the bathtub, Mr. Governor, stripped down to his shorts and . . ."

Poor Burling. He had no notion yet, of course, of that secret conversation on the yacht, and of the sword that ever since had been hanging over his head by the thinnest thread. It would take but a single word to bring it down on him—a word Harmon had not yet been able to make up his mind to speak.

With a lingering smile of appreciation over his own anecdote, Burling looked up. "Harmon," he asked, curtly, "when am I getting those loan contracts?"

The Governor had turned studiously away. Ever since the day he had bolted up before the portrait of his father, and sought to obliterate it, there had been an awkwardness between him and Harmon.

"Well?" insisted Burling.

"Sorry, Boss," said Harmon, "but there're still a couple of commas and semicolons to work out."

"You lawyers," said Burling sourly, "you Philadelphia lawyers."

The Governor cast a sidelong glance. "Harmon," he said, "if what concerns you is the good faith and reliability of the various applicants, let me assure you that our own local bank does not have the

same reservations. It has already advanced a sum of money to each
of the men from its own private funds. On a smaller scale naturally
than the Mission can afford. It was our hope that the Mission, being
charged with promoting new local enterprise . . ."

"Harmon," said Burling sternly, "I want those contracts on my
desk by five this afternoon."

"Right," said Harmon. But simultaneously he found Burling's eye
and winked. Burling took it in and replied with the barest twinkle.
If it had anything to do with intrigue, thought Harmon, it was sure
to be Burling's baby. "By the way," he went on, "I know that the
Governor will want to hear that Dr. Gilmore is extraordinarily
pleased with the work of all the resident doctors."

"Splendid," said the Governor.

"In fact, he wants every possible effort made to keep them on the
job for at least two whole years. By then he expects each to be
equipped to run such a program all by himself."

"Excellent," said the Governor.

Lackadaisically, Harmon sat down. "Well, then," he asked, "do
you think this is a strategic time to cut their salaries, Mr. Governor?"

Montalvo's reaction was a quick, amused smile. "Oh," he said,
"so they've already started a campaign."

"As they put it to me . . ."

"Untenable!" said the Governor, now less airily. "As things stand
at present, they are receiving three times the pay of my welfare director. Twice that of the railroad superintendent. In fact, two hundred pesos a month more than any Alba official whatsoever."

Harmon found his eye. "Than the Governor himself?"

Montalvo reddened. "Not that I intend to engage in recrimina-
tions," he said, "but the ill-considered generosity of the Mission has
thrown our entire wage structure out of balance."

Burling, like a tennis spectator, glanced from one to the other as
they spoke—with relish.

"Mr. Governor," asked Harmon, "are these men seriously expected
to look after themselves and their families on a salary of . . ." He

turned to Burling. "It would add up to seventy-five dollars a month with the cut."

The Governor smiled broadly. "Who says they will have to?"

"It seems obvious that unless you rescind . . ."

"I assure you," said Montalvo, now all hints and innuendoes, "that neither the good doctors nor their families will go in want. There are certain long-standing customs down here—not that I approve— but in the so-called free clinics it is expected that the patients now and then will scrape up a grateful offering to the men who heal them. And if occasionally drugs and other supplies find their way from the hospitals to the shelves of private pharmacies, well . . ." Montalvo threw up his hands in cheery despair.

"I propose," said Harmon, standing up, "that we keep our doctors from becoming crooks."

Montalvo, too, stood up. "Absolutely untenable," he protested, "that half-baked medical students should get a higher salary than the chief official of Alba!" He was openly enraged now. What fierce devotion to form—thought Harmon—to pomp and to self-reassurance.

"Well," said Burling, "let me think about it."

There was a knock, just then, on the door and Jacinto looked in. "There is a gentleman," he said, "to see His Excellency."

"Not now," said the Governor. "We're busy."

"A thousand pardons, Your Excellency, but Señor Ruiz says it is a matter of the highest importance."

"Ruiz . . . ?" The Governor wheeled about.

The name also brought Harmon to.

"All right—all right," said the Governor hastily. "I'm coming." He did not even pause for the traditional handshake.

Fascinatedly Harmon watched him make his way down the shaky staircase. So it had come to this. . . . "Colonel," he said, thoughtfully closing the door, "would it interest you to know that the son of Cesar Montalvo is probably a—bootlegger?"

Burling's glance darted instantly to the bottle on the table.

"And that he's been running the stuff over the border in an official vehicle of this Mission?"

Carefully, silently, Burling let himself down into his armchair. Then, suddenly, from his mouth broke a storm of laughter. His belly quaked. His eyes dripped tears. "Oh, the son of a bitch!" he howled. "The cleverest little bastard I've ever met!"

Well, thought Harmon, that was *one* way of looking at it—the tropical way.

CHAPTER TWENTY-SIX

SLOWLY they walked down the hallway of Serafina's cool, dark house—step for step, Ernestina's head against his shoulder. "Oh, I love you so," she said, unwilling to let him go, grasping for each extra moment.

He kissed her as they walked.

"William—William . . ." she said, as if reveling in him. They reached the door and still she clung to him. But now, of a sudden, there passed over her forehead that little chevron of anxiety. "Darling," she asked, "do you ever think of me from one time until the next?"

"Ernestina!" he protested. He could not bear to see her humble.

"What if we were just to sit and talk sometimes—or just go walking—or be together and not do anything at all?"

He grasped her tightly and kissed her again. "Don't talk like that," he begged. "I won't have it." Except for an occasional spark of temper, she had become so entirely submissive of late. It was what he had always longed for—this kind of adoration—wasn't it? But nowadays it left him only uneasy. He would not ever want, he thought, to see his own daughters so humble. Or anybody. But on this entire continent there were few women who were not.

"William," she said, her thoughts turning apprehensively in another direction, "there was something I meant to tell you. Manriquez seems terribly displeased with you these days."

She had referred to her husband by his surname, he noted dimly—as if pushing him away to the status of a mere acquaintance. "Why?" he asked. "Has he begun to guess?"

She smiled wanly. "Oh, no," she said, "or I'd be dead by now. His sacred honor—you know. No, it has to do with some scheme of his. And he seems to think that Vicente Hidalgo is having a bad influence on you."

"What do *you* think?"

"Vicente? Oh, he's lovely. What marvelous stories I used to hear from him when I was a child. But he's awfully disappointed in me, I suppose. When I married Manriquez he wouldn't come to the wedding, you know. He said"—and now she seemed shot again with penitence, as at their very first meeting—"he said he never expected that I'd go with the Conquistadores."

This girl of sorrows. He would have loved to know her when her spirit was in full bloom, in the days when she was still half a tomboy and had no trouble remembering the Categoric Imperative. Year by year, ever since . . .

From the end of the hallway, suddenly, came the pad of heavy bare feet.

"The maid!" whispered Ernestina. But she clung to him until the last possible instant.

As he stepped through the doorway, a green sports car drew up sharply at the curb. At the wheel a black-haired giant noticed him and called him by name.

He found that he had absolutely no inclination to retreat. "*Hola,* Señor Manriquez," he replied.

Pensively Manriquez ambled up the steps. He wore a white shirt, riding breeches and dusty black boots, and from his hip sagged a heavy pistol holster. He must have driven here straight from his

lands. Always they wore pistols, these sons of Cortez, when they
went over their domains.

"You visit here often?" asked Manriquez. Again he spoke with
that tristful apathy, as though his mind were on matters far more
vast—and again Harmon found it irritating. He was filled with a
desire suddenly to shake Manriquez, push him, punch him, anything to arouse him from that supercilious reverie. "Red Cross business," he replied. And then, deliberately defying the lightning, "I
had the pleasure of taking tea with your charming wife."

For an instant Manriquez studied him, but from afar, from a
mountain peak. It's a certainty, reflected Harmon wryly, that whatever he may be thinking, he's doing me no injustice.

"Harmon," he murmured finally, "I have something to show you."
He sauntered back to the automobile, then returned with a yellow-
ish tabloid newspaper. "Have you seen it?" he inquired mildly. "It's
the latest issue of the *Messenger*."

Was that all? "I've not had the pleasure."

On the second page Manriquez found for him a short editorial.
It was signed in the name of Aristides Donoso, that same little editor
who months before had come canvassing subscriptions from the
Mission. The essence of it was that in spite of all obstacles the Technical Mission could confidently be expected to bring great blessings
to the Martyr Province. "It is unfortunate, but only to be antici-
pated," wrote Editor Donoso, "that of the five seed bulls imported
by the Mission recently from Ecuador two should have proved to
be sterile and two should have died of anthrax."

Harmon glanced up. "That doesn't happen to be true," he said.
Manriquez' deep-set contemplative eyes gazed past him.

Flushing irritatedly, Harmon went on reading. "Nor should too
much be made of the fact that at Rosales the Sisters have been compelled to dismiss three of the nurse's aides for immoralities with
the patients. Any experiment, as we all know . . ." He must try not
to show his anger; he must not give Manriquez that satisfaction.

"Nobody," he said, forcing himself to speak lackadaisically, "has been dismissed from anywhere."

"I'm relieved," said Manriquez, "to hear that." To his lips, for the first time, came a smile.

If you knew what I know, thought Harmon savagely, you would not be smiling. On his shirt was still the scent of Ernestina's hair.

"Well," said Manriquez, taking back the newspaper and stuffing it into a pocket of his breeches, "at least the *intention* was friendly."

"Oh, yes," said Harmon, making himself yawn. "Unity of the Americas."

Manriquez went up the stone steps—but at the iron-bound door he looked back once again. "Harmon," he said, "I take it that your faith in my endorsement is not altogether complete—mine and the others'."

Steadily Harmon gazed back at him. "In the matter of the loan applications?"

"Exactly." Gone instantly were all signs of the pensive apathy. "They were to be acted on weeks ago, Harmon, weren't they?"

"Well," said Harmon, "put it down to red tape. The usual Government caution."

Manriquez lifted the door knocker. "I wonder," he speculated, "what has happened to that famous *yanqui* boldness."

"Our *yanqui* boldness," Harmon shot back, and with a savage satisfaction, "is doing all right."

On his way back to the port he picked up Dr. Gilmore. Cautiously he asked, "Have you seen the newspaper?"

"Bilge," said Gilmore crisply.

"It may get worse."

Gilmore stroked his neat auburn mustache thoughtfully. "Let's talk about something *important*," he said. "Are you all inoculated against typhus?"

"Before we left Washington. Why?"

"We're getting three and four cases a day lately around Rosales and Santa Ana." Gilmore lit a cigar. It was almost the only way in which he relaxed from the perpetual doctor—with his heavy cigar smoking. "What kind of liaison do we have with the Army base?"

"Tell me what you want."

Fluently Gilmore called off a long and cumbersome name. It was a brand-new delousing agent, he said, one which had not yet been released for civilian use—called DDT for short.

"Just how serious," asked Harmon, "*is* the typhus?"

Gilmore drew meditatively on his cigar. "In ten days," he said, "we'll have an epidemic."

Instantly Harmon pulled over and braked, finding himself alongside the knotted and scummy swamp from which—always so incredibly—rose the white dazzling flights of herons and egrets. "I'll telegraph the base the minute we reach the port," he said. "How are you set up otherwise?"

Gilmore rattled it off crisply. "The nurse's aides are far enough along now to take care of all nursing needs. I'll make Rosales my isolation center. I'm sending delousing squads into every settlement in the province. And free inoculations starting tomorrow." He drew again on his cigar. "That for a starter."

Good, thought Harmon. Another kind of *yanqui* boldness.

Beside his plate at dinner he found a letter from Laura. He got as far as ". . . and it's so exciting, Will, about the Ambassador's offer! You're going to accept, aren't you?", when Burling called to him. "Harmon," he asked, "what do you make of that stinkbomb in the newspaper today?"

Quickly, Harmon put Laura's letter away into his pocket. "It's pretty obvious, I think, that we're being pressured on those business loans. And I think you know by whom."

"Well," said Burling indifferently, "then we're going to let the bastards *have* their loans. My instructions were to avoid trouble. And that's what I'm going to do, avoid trouble."

He spoke, thought Harmon pityingly, as though the buttons were still all his to push. It had not come to him yet that he was a goner, or about to be. But until the inevitable happened it might be just as well to keep him on the guide lines. "Colonel," he said thoughtfully, "today in Rosales I picked up a little piece of information you ought to know about. Something right interesting."

"No, I don't want trouble," repeated Burling.

"I've invited somebody to come here tonight and tell you about it. Vicente Hidalgo."

"Oh—the orator?"

The characterization made Harmon wince slightly. "One thing you'll grant. Hidalgo never went to you for a payoff."

"That's a fact!" admitted Burling, much surprised.

"Well, he has a story to tell, and I think we can promise you a new little something in the way of skulduggery."

Burling's face lit with interest. "Good show," he said. "I'm always ready to learn."

Lingering behind at the table, he went on reading the letter from Laura. " . . Of course it's very charitable of you, Will, to be concerned about Burling and how he would take it. But if he's going to be replaced in any case, wouldn't it be foolish to refuse the promotion? It's the kind of thing you've always really wanted, isn't it? But when the program is finished in Alba, I do hope they'll send you a place that's not so impossible. Next time, we hope, it'll be somewhere that you can take us with you. There isn't anything special, after all, to keep us here in New York; the children would just love going to places like Rio or Lima or Buenos Aires. I know there's always been talk about my returning some day to Harlan and Burton, but, darling, a leave of absence that's lasted seven years can be considered to have run itself out—don't you think? What's important is that you should be able to work at something that keeps you happy, dear. All our love. Laura."

Also there was a postscript. "Going through my desk today I ran across a few sketches I did just after Ann was born. A model community it was supposed to be, but everything looks so horribly square and white to me now, a collection of icebergs. Stinkers, all of them. I threw them down the incinerator."

He found himself flushing hotly. . . . No, they had *not* been icebergs, not in the least. The most graceful designs probably that Laura'd ever done. And she had thrown them away. Now it was final that to him she would be totally a wife, and to herself nothing. And her talents, always, had been larger than his own. . . . But he had never asked her to do this, had he? No, damn it. He hadn't, he hadn't. . . .

It was just then that one of the houseboys announced Vicente Hidalgo. Good. There was work to be done.

Smiling cheerfully, he sat on the edge of the rattan chair and held aloft one of those long cheroots that were like burning scepters. "Yes," he said, "my client was among the very first to make application. Soon afterward he received a visit from a type of some fame in these parts. Elóy Ruiz, he is called. A kind of underground statesman."

Burling glanced questioningly at Harmon.

"The same," said Harmon. "The Governor's errand boy."

"My client," continued Hidalgo, "was informed that his application stood no chance whatsoever unless it could be made to win the endorsements of certain outstanding personages in the province upon whose judgment the Mission relied. Naturally, these exalted characters would require a certain compensation for their endorsements."

In a way, thought Harmon, this kind of thing had been brought upon the Mission by Burling himself. Had he not, at the very first meeting with the Governor, months before, indicated that he expected the Governor to play that kind of game? The only way to operate in the tropics, he had said, was through the *mordida,* the bite.

"Is that all?" Burling asked now, pouting disparagingly. "Old stuff. And for ten per cent it isn't worth all the trouble of . . ."

"Not *ten*," said Hidalgo with a smile. "Thirty-three and a third."

Burling stared at him, then shook his head unbelievingly. "It doesn't make sense," he said. "On that basis no man can stay in business."

"Exactly! It was just the point which was raised by my client. Well, he was told not to be so serious-minded. All he need do is throw together a few boards for a factory and show a sample product every now and then. By next summer the Mission would be gone, and the debt would be assigned to the provincial bank for collection. And at that time . . ." A smile lit up the craggy features like a sunray.

"And at that time—your client could cover up with a fake bankruptcy?"

"Yes, something like that."

Instantly Colonel Burling stood up. Three separate times he pounded the coffee table with his fist. "Goddamn, thieving, mother-loving, swill-eating, louse-bitten degenerates!" he roared. "I'll fight the sons of bitches from here to the South Pole!"

"Good show," said Harmon, pleasurably, borrowing the Colonel's own favorite phrase for the occasion.

"What the hell kind of sap do they take me for anyhow?" demanded Burling. He snatched his lighted cigarette from his mouth and flung it on the floor. "Thirty-three and a third? Not one goddamn penny!"

At anything up to ten per cent, reflected Harmon, Burling would have been merely amused.

CHAPTER TWENTY-SEVEN

IN THE villages, when it first appeared, they called it the "spotted fever" and insisted it was caused by "bad vapors," nothing else. To counter these vapors, said the old people, it was necessary to wear a thick scarf about the mouth and nose at all times and to burn smudge fires inside the shanties. The smoke must be heavy enough to bring tears to the eyes, otherwise the effect might be completely lost—which was the reason, for instance, that a family of six had all been laid low at Huelva. But even when the spots erupted over the entire body, even when the sick one lay open-mouthed and floating in his own sweat, all was not yet lost. It was necessary only to anoint the spots with a mixture of lard and rooster blood. Not beef fat, not hen's blood. It was inexactness such as that which had wiped out a family in Santa Ana.

They only sniggered at first when Dr. Gilmore had placards posted in every settlement with an enormously magnified photo of the body louse and the warning, "This is the carrier of typhus! Kill him before he kills you!"

At Mancha derisive legends were scribbled on the posters such as, "Uncle Sam, bloodsucker!" At Barrio, when a nurse's aide came to offer inoculations, she was hooted out of town. Bad vapors—didn't she know? When the delousing squads came with their spray guns and DDT powder, they were set upon and their equipment was smashed. Thereafter they were accompanied always by Carabineros, who sometimes had to fire into the air. It was Gilmore's joke that he would stop the typhus if he had to shoot everybody in Alba.

Along the railroad line, day and night, ran an ambulance car, taking moaning cargos to the isolation center at Rosales. It was regrettable but unavoidable that trouble was evoked thereby with the Rosales resident, Dr. Solís. On the fourth day Harmon, on a tour of inspection with Gilmore, dropped in at the isolation center only to find Solís absent from his post. When they tracked him to the local inn, where he kept a room, he was packing a bag.

"Planning a trip, Doctor?" asked Gilmore.

"Solís sighed. "Bad news from Chimboya," he explained. "My father is on his deathbed."

Gilmore lit a cigar.

"Angina pectoris."

Gilmore puffed in silence.

"The captain of a banana boat was kind enough to offer me a berth," said Solís. "A last-minute matter. I was going to leave you a note, Doctor."

Gilmore put down his cigar. "Carlos Finlay," he said thoughtfully. "Oswaldo Cruz. Eugenio Espejo." They were the names, Harmon recalled, of the giants of Latin American medicine.

Solís crimsoned.

"When yellow fever broke out in Rio," said Gilmore, "Oswaldo Cruz did not pack a bag. His father's health remained perfect."

"I am being affronted!" cried Solís.

Meditatively, Gilmore sauntered over to the bed where Solís's valise lay open. "So are your patients," he said. He lifted the suitcase, open as it was, and carried it to the window. Puffing still on his cigar, he pitched it out.

Solís charged up with shaking fists.

Gilmore stood his ground.

"I shall report this in Chimboya!" cried Solís. "I shall demand . . ."

"Hurry," said Gilmore. "Your father is dying."

But, as a result, Gilmore had to take over the isolation center personally, in addition to all his administrative duties. His burden became even heavier when Dr. Larrea succumbed to the typhus at Santa Ana. Miss Osborn, the American nursing supervisor, had then to be shifted to Santa Ana, and her Rosales duties divided among three nurse's aides. However, the Lorca plague laboratory finally came to the rescue by loaning another nurse, and a Chimboya specialist flew down as further relief.

Farther and farther into the province went the hypodermic corps and the delousing squads. All public assembly was prohibited by law and the peons lay idly in their huts. But for the first week there was no stemming the tide. Still the railroad ambulance hauled larger and larger cargos to Rosales. Gilmore puffed calmly on his cigar. The incubation period for typhus, he said, was ten to fourteen days. They were still reaping an old harvest.

In the second week the toll dropped steeply. In the third week there were days when not one single new case was reported.

By then a full twelve pounds had melted from Gilmore's neat frame, but not for one day had he neglected to keep that guardsman's mustache in trim. A medical colonel, coming from the Base, reviewed all he had done and pronounced it a classic operation. It happened, he said, to be one of the first mass demonstrations of DDT ever undertaken and he urged Gilmore to do a paper.

Burling, incidentally, took advantage of the situation to notify Governor Montalvo that because of unsatisfactory guarantees the Mission was suspending all loan applications.

It was in the flush of Gilmore's triumphs that the white wing-like yacht again rounded the Bay and brought in Elliott Reeves. He was on a fishing trip, he explained to Burling, nothing official. But, closeting himself alone with Harmon, he remarked, "Washington okays your appointment."

Harmon looked down in thought.

"You're accepting, of course."

"All right," said Harmon. The decision burst from him as suddenly as that.

Reeves shook his hand warmly. "It'll take a couple of weeks to regularize the promotion. Not a word meanwhile to Burling." Casually then, Reeves added, "By the way, don't let too much hoopla get worked up about Gilmore."

It was an odd remark.

"We'd rather," explained Reeves, "that they didn't go too manic-depressive about us *gringos*. Too much love one day—too much hate the next. Besides we've had a little backfire on Gilmore in Chimboya."

"From Solís?"

"Solís has lots of friends. The story he tells . . ."

Harmon smiled wearily. "That Gilmore was gross to him? That Gilmore affronted the national honor?"

"Something like that."

Harmon shook his head firmly. "I was a witness to what happened," he said, "and I'm going along on that with Gilmore."

"*Bueno, bueno,*" said Reeves, backing off genially. "One other little kink. It's very trivial and I know that Gilmore can explain. The Civil Service investigators have run into a little snag on him."

"He's a Nazi spy?"

"Don't be a clown, *hombre.* Civil Service confirms his twenty years in tropical medicine, and a whole string of foreign studies too. The joker—I don't want to make too much of this, and I'd rather leave it to you to take up with him. Gilmore's appearance, they say, doesn't jibe too well with the photo they dug up from his medical-school yearbook."

"Why should it—twenty years after?"

"You have a point, but the eager beavers in Washington . . . How does a long chin turn short—something like that. Get his explanation and wire it to the Ambassador when you can."

"If you're looking for *real* worries . . ." began Harmon.

"The Governor?" Reeves' face clouded. "Don't start any more bonfires right now. We'll take the matter up directly with the *Presidente* in Chimboya. The son of Cesar Montalvo—you know what a ticklish business *that* can be."

"Oh, yes," said Harmon.

Reeves held out his hand. "Well, *Señor Director,*" he said, letting the new title roll grandiosely from his tongue, "you ought to be happy."

Happy? There was no use hiding it from himself—he *was*. What a change had swept over his life in this past half-year. Finally all the possibilities in him had bloomed. Finally he was somebody.

He found Gilmore lying in his quarters at the Rosales hospital, alone and all spent. "Harry," he said gently, "you've certainly been through the wringer."

"Yes, Bill. I'm just finding that out."

On the wall above his daybed marched a phalanx of parchments: the diploma from Johns Hopkins and the graduate certificates from London, Hamburg, the Sorbonne, all in neat black frames. Also there were several group photographs—all of white-clad men sitting together under palm trees.

Gilmore took note of Harmon's curiosity. "That one," he said, raising himself to an elbow and pointing to a photo just immediately above his head, "was taken at Tumayo Petrol in Venezuela. I headed a staff of fifty-three. My medical budget was as large as the entire Alba program." He sagged back wearily to his pillow. "Did you want to talk about something, Bill?"

"Nothing important," said Harmon uncomfortably. "About a photo, as it happens, a different sort of photo. The Civil Service people . . ."

"When," asked Gilmore, "will I hear the end of that photo? You mean the one in my college yearbook?"

Harmon nodded, a little surprised at the quickness of the guess.

"I wonder," said Gilmore patiently, "why grown men can't deduce for themselves the simple fact that . . ."

"I did say that in twenty years a man's face is bound to change."

Gilmore shook his head. "That's not it, not at all. It came about through a mix-up. The printer of the yearbook simply used the wrong photo—one of a lower classman. And the damn thing's been hounding me now for twenty years."

"Okay," said Harmon crisply, "that does it."

Gilmore drew on his cigar, then blew out a screen of heavy blue smoke. "Is the Civil Service," he asked, "acting on the theory that I'm a quack? Has anybody informed them about a certain outbreak of typhus in the province of Alba?"

"I damn well will, Harry."

Gilmore turned away wearily toward the wall. "A printer's mistake. That's simple enough—isn't it?"

"You bet," said Harmon. Softly he walked from the room. It was only when he got outside that he took to wondering whether it might not be too simple.

CHAPTER TWENTY-EIGHT

WHEN again the trouble started, it was in a new form. One by one, complained Walt Anderson, peons of his had quit their jobs at the farm until suddenly he was a dozen hands short—and in the midst of a harvest, too. When he tracked some of them down and talked with them, they offered excuses that obviously did not hold water. Next, on the half-finished road to Rosales, four laborers and the bulldozer operator left their jobs in one day. At the new hospital in Huelva, several carpenters and plasterers did the same.

A strike, obviously, was going on against the Mission. Why? Pay and working conditions were admitted to be excellent.

Serrano, put to investigating, flushed up what must be a manifestly absurd explanation. The men had said, some of them, that they'd become worried that employment by the Mission made them automatically liable to forced labor service at the American naval bases in the far islands. They were afraid of being torn from their families and subjected to the rigors of military discipline.

Masters and Anderson laughed this off. Nobody they said, could be *that* dumb. But a few day later there appeared a "dispatch" in the Alba *Messenger* on exactly the same theme. Albanese who had been transported to the islands, it said—putting the matter on a cheerful basis—had found conditions there much better than they'd expected. The barracks, it was reported, had finally been made rainproof; the diet had been improved by the addition of fresh meat once a week. And at the end of a full year's service the labor conscripts would be permitted to rejoin their families on short furloughs.

That afternoon Harmon sought out Editor Donoso in his black little printshop at Rosales.

"I trust," said Donoso, showing Harmon to a rickety stool alongside the huge desk, "that the *Señor Asociado* has observed the pains to which we have gone to correct certain widespread misunderstandings."

Yes, and the *Señor Asociado* was deeply grateful. Might it be inquired, incidentally, at whose instance the *Messenger* had taken this step?

"Friends of the Mission."

A sour taste came into Harmon's mouth, but it might be interesting to put out a little feeler. "Señor Donoso," he said, gazing thoughtfully toward the stained, cracked ceiling, "some months ago you suggested that it might be advisable for the Mission to take a certain considerable number of subscriptions to your excellent journal."

Donoso, tiny in his huge leather chair, brought his finger-tips together in five Gothic arches. "A most ill-considered proposal," he said. "On *my* part."

"Not at all."

"Yes, indeed! Unwittingly I placed myself in the position of a beggar. The inference might have been drawn by unfriendly parties that the columns of the *Messenger* were open to purchase." Not a single line creased the bland hammered-bronze complexion.

Donoso, then, was no longer in the market. He had let himself be bought, wrapped up and taken home by Manriquez and the Governor. "Well," said Harmon, deciding suddenly to take another tack, "I conclude that the economic position of your paper is now well-secured."

"Exactly as you predicted, *Señor Asociado!* Our circulation has now reached a point where we can hardly cope with it."

"Most animating!" said Harmon. The abundant success of the *Messenger,* he went on, suggested that the saturation point, journalistically speaking, had not yet been reached in Alba. Might it not be fruitful therefore for the Mission to consider granting a loan for establishment of a *second* newspaper in the Martyr Province?

Editor Donoso planted his elbows on the desk, cupped the little metal ball of his face in his hands. Such a journal, he declared, would be taken by him not as competition but only as a second jewel in the crown, if he might be so immodest. . . . It would be required, of course, to adhere to the highest standards of truth and accuracy?

Naturally.

"But in the improbable case," continued Editor Donoso, "that it should sink to the venality of the rags which used to be subsidized by foreign embassies, our Governor can be relied upon to take action. Carabineros might be detailed to prevent its distribution. The editor might be made to stand criminal charges. The anger of the people might result in the destruction of its plant and presses."

Harmon gritted his teeth. If only, he thought, this exquisite subtlety could have been turned to some better use. But it was soaked in an old and fetid tradition, in the wine of corruption that had been brought from Madrid and Seville by the gold-mad cavaliers. With their knightly greed they had devastated this continent as surely as with their swords. Until Pizarro came, the children of the Sun had worn garments of white and bathed each dawn in ice-pure lakes.

"I know," declared Donoso enthusiastically, "that we can rely upon the son of Cesar Montalvo to keep the ideological life of Alba untainted."

Again that sour taste came into Harmon's mouth.

"By the way . . ." said Donoso. He hunted all over the cluttered desk top and finally ferreted out a long smudged paper which was a galley proof. "In our next issue, *Señor Asociado,* I am disproving absolutely that the death of two infants at Santa Ana can be attributed to a nurse's aide."

Now, bursting with fury, Harmon bolted up. "Donoso," he warned, standing to his full height above the hateful little wasp, "you're playing with fire! A report like that . . ."

"False!" interjected Donoso. "Which is why I am making certain to deny it!"

With one punch, thought Harmon, he could smash open that tiny head, spill out all its corrupt stinking contents on the floor. With one single punch he could . . . Oh, how he ached to take advantage at least of his sheer bodily strength, all other resources having failed. But it was out of the question. And before this insolent, shady, crooked David, he had been reduced to a bumbling Goliath—brought to the ground—walked upon and spat upon.

"It was nice," said Editor Donoso, leaning back cheerfully in his huge leather throne, "to talk things over."

When he got back to the port, after attending to some other matters, he found Ramón Manriquez waiting for him in his office. By arrangement, of course—wasn't it?

Manriquez was dressed again in riding clothes, and carrying a short leather crop. Manriquez—the last man, thought Harmon, that he was in a mood to see. Sullenly he sat down in his swivel chair. "Yes?" he asked.

Once more that mournful apathy had enveloped the Spanish captain. *"Señor Asociado,"* he said, "I find that I owe you an apology." With his leather quirt he absent-mindedly nudged the title plate that sat on the far edge of the desk. "I learned only this morning that the dozen peons who quit the demonstration farm were hired away by my own manager."

"Indeed," said Harmon tartly, his eyes all the while on his title plate, his token of office. He wondered, purely as a sporting proposition, just how Manriquez would proceed after this opening gambit of mock apology.

Bit by bit, all the while, Manriquez was nudging the title plate away to the right-hand side of the desk. The peons, he promised, would be ordered back to the demonstration farm at once so that there would be no further interference with its harvesting. And it would never happen again.

"Most animating," said Harmon, his eyes still following the progress of his title plate.

"A matter of common courtesy," said Manriquez. "But these things should work both ways." Still he went on nudging the varnished spar with his quirt—and suddenly it was half over the side of the desk. "With Colonel Burling we might have reached an understanding quickly enough. He knows the local customs. The *established* customs." One more push from that riding crop and the title plate would go crashing to the floor. "The *accepted* customs, Harmon."

Out shot Harmon's hand.

It clutched the tip of the riding crop.

"Yes?" asked Manriquez somberly.

Those deep-set languid eyes, so inhuman in their indifference . . . Reaching out with his free hand, Harmon retrieved the teetering plate and restored it securely to a place in the middle of the desk top. With his right hand, simultaneously, he tightened his grip on the riding crop. Now his gorge had risen. He would smash his way yet through that insolent apathy.

"Yes?" repeated Manriquez.

Conquistador with his scepter—ruler of slaves in a stolen domain —captor of Ernestina.

"Harmon, I would like you to take your hand off my riding crop."

Instead, Harmon jerked it loose and flung it on the floor.

Now Manriquez stood up. Now finally from his veiled eyes came a flash of anger. "That was gross," he said.

"I am sick," said Harmon, "of cavaliers."

The olive skin became suffused with blood. "Be good enough, Harmon, to give it back to me."

"You make me want to vomit," said Harmon.

"Pick it up and give it back to me."

"You and Montalvo both—you make me want to vomit."

"I am asking you to pick it up."

Still Manriquez maintained his pretense of calm. It must be smashed to pieces, that pretense, all of it. He must be made for once, Manriquez, to stop holding himself above all the rest of the world.

Rising from the swivel chair, Harmon walked over to the fallen quirt—and planted his foot on it. "Come and get it," he said. It was primitive, this kind of satisfaction, infantile—but at the moment no other satisfaction was open to him, nothing but what he could wrest with his bodily strength.

Manriquez, all at once, lunged for him.

Fine! thought Harmon. Against that apathy, it was a victory *already*.

Out shot his own hands.

They locked, each gripping the forearms of the other.

It was fine, fine, thought Harmon—the first time he'd had a chance to put his brawn to use since the boyish struggles over a football. It was marvelous to know that his strength was still there.

"Scum," said Manriquez between gritted teeth. Still they stood frozen in their deadlock, neither giving way an inch. He was strong, Manriquez. Not for nothing had his fathers lived for so many centuries on the best of the land. "Excrement." What stylish epithets—the four-letter words of the grandee.

With a sudden heave Harmon broke the stalemate. Deftly he wrenched Manriquez into a hammerlock, twisting his right arm behind him. Yes, Manriquez was strong—but hand-to-hand struggle was not his forte. They were meant to fight only with weapons, the cavaliers, at a distance from each other, untouched by the flesh of the antagonist. Without a whip, without a weapon, Manriquez was castrate.

"Let go of me!" grunted Manriquez. Down his frame ran a shiver of distaste. "Take your hands off me!"

He almost felt sorry for Manriquez—this must be such a repulsive experience for him. But—slowly, slowly—he forced down the twisted arm. And, slowly, slowly, the large powerful body followed—down to crouching, to stooping, to kneeling on the floor.

"Damn you, damn you," grunted Manriquez. "Harmon, you bastard!"

Better and better. Now the grandee was coming down to earth. "Son of a whore!" Oh lovely. . . .

With one last thrust he heaved Manriquez forward on his face. Fine! He had bested the captor of Ernestina. From now on she was all his—his war trophy. He didn't know when, in all his life, he had felt so exhilarated.

Manriquez rose from the floor—panting heavily, his shirt untucked from the riding breeches. This was surely an experience he had never known before, and numberless generations of his fathers. "Harmon . . . !" he cried, wild with rage. "Harmon!" Gone was every last trace of that maddening apathy.

Cautiously—his glance covering Manriquez all the while—Harmon stooped and picked up the riding quirt. Again Manriquez started to lunge toward him. "All right," said Harmon, letting his contempt jet forth freely, "shall we make it two out of three, *Caballero?*"

Silently, Manriquez snatched back his riding crop. He paused only, on his way out, to smash it savagely against the doorpost.

Fine, fine, thought Harmon as he sat down again in his swivel chair. This was the way he liked it. When he took over ultimately from Burling he would let it be known that he was a "Director" in fact, not only in name. Nobody was going to push him around. He was not going to let them smother him in their goddamn tropical ooze. If they had any notion that they were going to play him for their dumb Samson . . .

"Harmon . . ."

In the doorway stood Burling, a perplexed Burling who scratched the sparse remains of his hair. He was holding in his hand a single sheet of paper—the form on which Rosabel Long habitually decoded confidential messages from the Embassy. Burling's "walking papers"? Had they finally come through then?

"Read this, Harmon."

Quickly he glanced it over. . . . The Governor's intrigues had been brought to the personal attention of Presidente Rivera. But he had dismissed the whole thing as a matter of mere political slander on the part of opponents of the Constitutional regime. As a vigorous and effective supporter of the administration, the son of the Eagle of the Andes had naturally made enemies.

"Nice going," muttered Burling.

In the circumstances, counseled the Ambassador, the Mission must try to get along with the Governor as best it could. The applecart must not be tipped by any further conflicts with the regime—pending future developments.

All hot and twitchy, Burling sat down. "Well," he asked, "how do you like it?"

The son of the Eagle of the Andes . . . *There,* thought Harmon, was the real enemy. Not in Ramón Manriquez. Manriquez, in his own way, was merely an "innocent," a natural. He had been bred, over the generations, to the single trait of rapacity—like a tiger—and he played his role with a kind of single-minded purity. But Marcos Montalvo knew better. Deliberately, knowingly, he had corrupted all the good works of his own father. He had chosen to spread his "fine young wings"—in the words of Hector Serrano—over evil and corruption. Yes—*there, there,* was the enemy. And the brief passage-at-arms with Ramón Manriquez had been a sham battle, a hollow victory. It had left him nowhere.

"Well," asked Burling, "what's your notion?"

Absently Harmon picked up his title plate from the top of the desk, the glittering spar that read, "Associate Director." He gripped it so hard that the edges dug deep into his flesh.

"Well," repeated Burling, "what do we do?"

Once—twice—a third time, Harmon smote the title plate down on his desk. "Let them have it," he said finally, in a high thin voice. "Give it to them."

Burling's eyes went round.

"At ten per cent," said Harmon, still clutching feverishly at the wooden spar, his token of office, almost all that was left him to hold to. "Not a nickel more." At ten per cent it would at least be "traditional."

PART FIVE: *The Hour of Truth*

CHAPTER TWENTY-NINE

THEY sat together in Hidalgo's large bare room, the cell of the in-digent scholar—Harmon on a huge rattan chair that swayed and creaked; Vicente on the edge of the bed, helping himself steadily from a bottle on the floor. But the *aguardiente* was in no way stupe-fying him; rather it fired him to a greater glow and clarity than ever.

"*Señor Asociado,*" he said, and this time he seemed to pronounce the title with a rueful fondness, not mockery, "don't suffer so much. If the shame is anybody's, it's our own. For having given birth, after all, to that species of monster. In Latin America, Marcos is no rarity."

Yes, he had used even *that* argument to console himself. Once, long ago, he had raged at Hector Serrano, "Why blame Washington? You should give us a better president to deal with." But still it did not lessen his twinges of shame. The truth was that bit by bit he had let himself be made a part of it, of the whole swindle. The only way was to resign finally, to renounce once and for all the glories that he knew now to be so hollow, so fly-blown. But the thought of going back to New York—to that house of clever women—and going back in defeat . . .

"You must be curious," remarked Vicente, "as to how the son of Cesar Montalvo can go over so completely to the enemy."

Harmon nodded somberly. "He *hates* Cesar Montalvo."

Again a smile flashed from those white incorruptible teeth. "It's false, absolutely false," said Vicente, "that the *gringos* are a race of insensitive mechanics."

Harmon returned the smile, but unhappily.

"In the Palace," mused Vicente, "it was a rule of Cesar Montalvo's that his disciples, the eaglets, should have access to him at all times. Whether he was throwing out a crook by the seat of the pants or planning the trans-Andean railroad, he wanted us about him at all times—to teach us by demonstration. Marcos, the blood son, was younger than the rest of us. He would be told quite often to run back to his room and do his homework. I remember how once, as a group of us were entering his father's office—we, the foster sons— Marcos ran up and pounded us with his fists. It was as simple as that—in the beginning. The door that was open to strangers was closed sometimes to the blood son."

Harmon smiled wryly.

"I'm making too much of this?"

"No. I'm the son myself of a pediatrician. The door that was open to strangers . . ."

Vicente held out the bottle of *aguardiente,* as if in solace. It had become so automatic a recourse to him, thought Harmon sadly, for any and every form of pain. "Not yet," he said.

Hidalgo poured one for himself, generously but firmly. "As a child," he went on, "Marcos would often filch candy and toys from the shops near the Palace. But when they caught him, he'd spit and stamp his foot and scream, 'Take your hands off the son of Cesar Montalvo!' An old, old story, you see."

Inquisitively Harmon glanced toward the bottle, now set back alongside the bedstead.

"Oh, no!" protested Vicente. "I don't buy my booze from His Excellency. Native produce—tax paid." Suddenly he stood up. On his lips still lingered a vestige of a smile, like a parting ray at sunset, but already the rest of his craggy face was in the shadows. "William," he said, "I weep sometimes when I think of how your work will crumble the moment you leave. The new schoolhouses. The roads. The seawall. The model farm. They will drive all the nurse's aides from the hospitals—those fine young people. And the new water system . . ." He shook his head. "Do you realize that there are half a dozen men who make their living from selling water—foul water —in the port? How long will they let your pipe lie in the ground after you're gone?"

A picture went through Harmon's mind of all the new contours which had been fashioned into the gray ugly land—of all the structures and the roads built into it at the cost of so much planning and labor. But the truth, as Hidalgo saw, was that nowhere was the ground firm under any of them. The truth was that they looked good only from the outside, that it was all a swindle. . . . But here he had importance of a kind, and here he had—Ernestina. In New York the outlook was nothing but bleak.

"Yet, I want to tell you," said Hidalgo, brightening suddenly, "that the Mission will be leaving behind one very precious thing after all."

"What?"

"Discontent."

Harmon glanced up quizzically.

"They will always think back, our poor little monkeys, to the fabulous year when the *gringos* were here and did things. They will have been taught that life need not be so hopeless, after all." Hidalgo poured himself a fresh drink, a stiff one. For what, wondered Harmon, was he nerving himself? "William, I am fifty-three years old, and in my own lifetime I have seen nineteen revolutions in this Republic. Nineteen. And only one or two ever gave anything to the *rotos*. The rest were all barracks uprisings, of the kind we have inherited from Spain. Family quarrels among the Conquistadores. Who, after all, murdered Francisco Pizarro? Not the Incas but one

of his own comrades, Almagro. And who beheaded Gonzalo Pizarro?
Pedro de la Gasca." He grinned acidly. "For four centuries, in these
countries, the thieves have been falling out, but it cannot be said—
as a rule—that the honest men have received their due. Except in
Mexico and one or two other places. You know, William, our big
landowners down here don't worry much about Moscow. The Krem-
lin is very far away, and *rotos* don't understand much Russian. But
even in a faraway hole like Alba they have caught whispers about
Pancho Villa and Emiliano Zapata. They have heard that in Mexico
rotos like themselves have actually chased out the *hacendados* and
taken the land."

His hand, Harmon observed with a catch, had begun to shake.
Abruptly Hidalgo bolted down the rest of the colorless liquid in
his glass and started to pace back and forth. "We have got to encourage discontent," he said, in a sharp staccato voice. "Against the
tradition of plunder, we must set a new tradition. That of Cesar
Montalvo. They murdered him—true. They burned his body—true.
But behind him Montalvo left a new mythos—a clean one—a marvelous one." Suddenly Hidalgo ceased his pacing and lowered himself heavily to the edge of the bedstead. "To endure," he said, "a
mythos must be refreshed from time to time."

A tingle of anxiety went across the palms of Harmon's hands.
Marcos Montalvo and Vicente Hidalgo, he thought—the blood son
and the foster son. To each of them the Eagle had left a legacy of
despair, a hopelessness of ever being able to emulate the father's
greatness. In the end they too, both of them, had become runaways
—the blood son a runaway into corruption; the foster son into dis-
integration. But suddenly, Harmon sensed, Vicente was coming to
a new decision, a grim one possibly.

"These past twenty years," said Hidalgo, looking down at the
floor, "I have been going to pieces, William. I have sunk lower,
lower, lower." He pressed his hands together firmly. "In bullfight-
ing, William, they have a marvelous phrase for describing the climax
of the ceremony—that ultimate moment of reality when the sword

strikes the bull. '*La hora de verdad*—the hour of truth.' A man must not waste away into nothing, William; a man must find his hour of truth. Don't talk any more about resigning, William, about going away. There may be things happening here yet that you ought to see."

Worriedly Harmon stood up. "Vicente," he pleaded, "better leave that kind of thing to the *Poristas*. They have plans, tactics, organization."

"Organization," granted Hidalgo, thoughtfully, "is a fine thing. Organization is indispensable."

With three long strides, Harmon went over to him and took him by one of the massive shoulders. "Beware," he said, "beware of Don Quixote."

"A man must recover his innocence," said Hidalgo, again in that grim staccato voice. "Of innocence, you know, there are really two kinds. There is the kind you are born with, the innocence of infancy, of ignorance. And there is the kind which comes sometimes after disillusionment and despair, after you have lived far too much—a kind of *second* innocence—the only one which is worth anything. William, I would like to get clean again."

Oh, yes, thought Harmon. It was true, it was right—every word of it. But it was dangerous, too, and he would rather that the demonstration should be made by some other man, not by this one who had come to mean so much to him. "Careful, Vicente," he begged. "The Quixotes only get laughed at. And unseated from the horse."

"That knight," mused Hidalgo, looking down with a sweet stubborn smile, "knew what he was doing. There was nothing better than him in all of Spain."

"I beg you, Vicente—take care of yourself."

When again Hidalgo looked up it was with a deep wistfulness. "These countries," he reflected, "are all Catholic, William. They are steeped too much in the mystery of the Mass. There is only one kind of idealism that our poor little monkeys will trust."

"Please—please!" Almost frantically he took Hidalgo by both

shoulders and shook him. "Nothing theatrical, Vicente. Nothing foolish."

Hidalgo went on as if he had not heard a word. "They are so terribly demanding, the poor little monkeys. It must be mixed up also with memories of those sacrifices to the Sun God. The only man they can believe in is one who will shed his blood for them."

Montalvo, too, had seen this thing, thought Harmon. He had mentioned it at their very first meeting, and he had run away from it. But Vicente, the foster son, yet always the better of the two, was coming now to another kind of decision—that he would *stop* running—that he would turn around and once more face the Father.

"Vicente—Vicente," pleaded Harmon, becoming sick now with anguish and fright, "there must be other ways to prove that you're a man."

Again Hidalgo looked down. "Is that part of it, too?" he asked. "I suppose that it is."

CHAPTER THIRTY

SUDDENLY they were engaged in a bewildering tug of war in which Dr. Gilmore was the rope.

It began with a telegram from the Palace in Chimboya stating that Gilmore, in view of his spectacular services, would be named honorary personal physician to the President. Within a few hours there followed a code message from the Ambassador that Gilmore was under no circumstances to accept public honors, and that steps were being taken to restrain the President's enthusiasm.

Gilmore, puffing calmly on his cigar, said that he understood perfectly (which Burling and Harmon did not), that honors were meaningless anyhow and that his sole concern was to get on with the job. The situation, Burling wired back to the Embassy, was contained.

But very soon after, without any advance notice to the Mission, there appeared an announcement in the Alba *Messenger* that at the dedication of the new wing of the Rosales hospital—the following day—the entire institution would be re-named in honor of Dr. Gilmore.

There ensued a polite but strained tussle with the Governor, virtually the first conversation with him since his victory in the matter of the loans. He failed, he said most airily, to see any reason why Dr. Gilmore should not receive his well-merited honors.

Burling, himself in the dark, pulled perplexedly at his ear. "My instructions," he said, "are to avoid excessive publicity of any kind."

"This is an expression," said the Governor, "of the will of the people of Alba. I see no reason to deny them."

Harmon winced—it was a long time since Montalvo had chosen to engage in flourishes of this kind.

"You put me into a delicate position," argued Burling. "It was the expressed desire of the Ambassador that . . ."

"Damn your Ambasador," said Montalvo, in a sudden flare. "Since when is he running my province for me?"

This anxiety of the Governor to force a second honeymoon on the Mission . . . Bewilderedly Burling wired a report of the conversation to the Embassy.

The answer that came through the next morning—tardily, as it turned out—was thoroughly disconcerting. "Regret to inform you," wired Elliott Reeves, "that Civil Service investigations show Gilmore to be a nine-dollar bill. Am flying to Rosales with our air attaché first thing in the morning. Keep Gilmore away from the medals until I arrive."

Burling's entire face, and bald crown too, were creased with puzzlement. "Harmon," he said, "this doesn't leave us much time. Take over, will you?"

Wordlessly Harmon looked down at the floor. It was a chore not the least to his liking.

Nor to Burling's. "Billy," he alibied, "if I show my nose in Rosales this morning, they'll move heaven and earth to drag me into that ceremony."

Gilmore, thought Harmon—that calm efficient man with his story-book passion for healing. Story book . . . It began to look suddenly, from hindsight, as though his behavior all along had been really *too* perfect. Nine-dollar bill. Among all the inadequate and half-adequate tropical tramps who constituted the rest of the Mission, it looked now as if Gilmore had been really *over*-adequate.

"Billy," pleaded Burling, "that ceremony is set for eleven. You'll have to step on it, boy."

Reluctantly Harmon got to his feet. It took such a very long time, he thought, to make a man—and so short a time to destroy him. "All right," he said.

Dr. Larrea, thin and haggard after his bout with the typhus, was first out of the surgery. "A lumbar nephrectomy," he said. "Oh, what a work of art!" Gilmore followed, stripping off the white surgical gown and handing it to an orderly.

"Doctor," asked Harmon, "can we talk?"

Gilmore looked at him, and colored instantly. They achieved in that moment an odd but considerable understanding. "In my quarters?" suggested Gilmore. They were forced to elbow their way through a reception committee which had come to escort him to the ceremony.

Gilmore clamped a cigar in under the neat guardsman's mustache. "The way I see it," he commented, "I'm under arrest."

"Not at all," said Harmon uncomfortably. "It just happened that Reeves wired us and asked . . ."

"Bill," broke in Gilmore, "would you say I'd been a good doctor?"

"We all know that."

Meditatively Gilmore began to saunter about the neat hygienic cell which was his living quarters. "The Tumayo Petrol people can tell you all you want to know about my nine years in Venezuela," he said. "About my work in Costa Rica—ask Walt Anderson. We were together for more than a year." He stopped at his neat plain desk and tapped a squared-off pile of brochures. "Nine original publications on diseases of the tropics." He went over to the wall and pointed up at the phalanx of framed parchments. "While I was with Tumayo my arrangement was that I could have every summer off to go abroad for advanced studies. Hamburg. London. The Sorbonne." But somehow he passed over the most imposing of all the documents—the diploma whereby Johns Hopkins University conferred upon Harry Galway Gilmore the honor, rights and privileges of doctor of medicine. "Bill," he asked, and now in a tone unaccustomedly rough, "what the hell do they want of me?"

"I couldn't say," murmured Harmon, looking away. "I'm only following orders." It was the standard apology, he reflected uncomfortably, of the arresting policeman.

Gilmore sat down on the edge of the daybed, dovetailing his fingers together thoughtfully. "Any graduate of a diploma mill," he said, "can sit in New York and prescribe pills. How many medical men, do you think, would be willing to pull up stakes and come to a hole like Alba?"

Not many, of course.

"You'll grant, won't you, that I haven't had one real night's sleep since I got here? I've dropped twelve pounds, haven't I? Once I went fourteen miles on muleback to do a Caesarean, didn't I?"

There was a knock on the door.

"One moment," called Gilmore in Spanish. But the door was pushed open and an elegant white-haired gentleman looked in and pleaded, "The committee is waiting, Dr. Gilmore."

If the *caballeros* might be asked to wait just a few moments longer ... replied Gilmore in his quick, graceful Spanish.

When the door had closed, Gilmore sat down again and planted his feet—so raffishly for him—on top of his desk. "Bill," he said, "you're a professional man yourself. Do you stand on the proposition that a law diploma automatically makes a man a barrister? Or let's turn it around. Until just a few decades ago there was hardly a top lawyer who had not learned his law by clerking in an office. No degrees. No diplomas. Am I right, Bill?"

Harmon nodded.

"And for centuries doctors were made in just about the same way —as surgeon's apprentices—holding the basins—heating the poultices." He tapped his temple. "Bill, it's what you've got up here"— his forefinger descended and tapped his breast—"and inside here that matters." He aimed disdainfully at the parchments that marched on the wall. "Not what you've got up there."

"Right," said Harmon.

"Stop all the *rotos* in Alba and ask who's healed them. The pill-pushers from their universities? Or was it . . ." He broke off and smiled warmly. "Oh, those sweet little monkeys. They want to name their hospital for me."

That calm, efficient healer—thought Harmon. He had worked, he had slaved endlessly. But what fears he must have had to keep suppressed inside that smooth shell all along. Whatever else, it had been an act of highest bravery.

"Let me tell you something, Bill. Cards on the table." There was another knock at the door and Gilmore backed away toward it, still talking as he went. "If Washington puts me on the skids, they are going to have one hell of a time explaining it to these folks in Alba. They're going to want to know, these folks, how it could happen that the great and wise Government of the United States could go and . . ." The knock was repeated. "The laugh, when it comes, won't be on *me*, Bill!"

Grinning, but anguishedly, he opened the door.

This time it was Elliott Reeves.

"Gilmore," he said crisply, "you talk too loud."

Gilmore opened his mouth to answer.

"One thing," said Reeves, closing the door behind him, "don't start telling me what a good doctor you are. I know all about that." He spoke, Harmon observed curiously, without the slightest evidence of rancor. "Hello, Harmon."

"Hello."

Inquisitively Reeves shot a glance about the room with its bare tidy furnishings and found the wall on which marched all the framed parchments. It seemed to magnetize him. Drawing closer he let his gaze focus down on the diploma from Johns Hopkins. "Gilmore," he asked, but it was mournfully, almost with a sigh, not reproachfully, "that one doesn't really belong to you, does it?"

Gilmore turned white.

"Your name is really *John* Gilmore, not Harry, isn't it?"

Gilmore sagged down to the edge of the daybed.

"Harmon," said Reeves, turning about, and again he spoke wholly in sorrow, "this isn't as amazing as it might sound. Not an everyday occurrence but they tell me that one does turn up every now and then. When he was a young fellow, Gilmore worked as a hospital orderly. Good training, too—Bellevue Hospital and Johns Hopkins. Later on . . . Gilmore, you can stop me any time I'm wrong." Silently Gilmore stared down at his intertwined fingers, and Reeves went on, but mournfully still, even with a kind of reverence. "A Public Health Service brass hat who was passing through Chimboya explained the psychology to us, Harmon. Crazy to be a doctor. Crazy to be a *somebody*. In New York he even took a couple of night courses in anatomy and physiology. He just never had the money for college and medical school."

From his breast pocket Gilmore tremblingly took a fresh cigar.

"But he had a cousin who did. When Cousin Harry was admitted to Hopkins, Cousin John followed after. Whenever he found a free moment, he sat in at Harry's lectures. When Harry put up his shingle, John hung around the office day and night."

Gilmore struck a match, but it shook in his hand.

"A couple of years later Cousin Harry died. . . ."

The match could not be made to meet the cigar tip.

"Gilmore," said Reeves turning back to him, somewhat aggrievedly now but still without rancor, "they tell us that when your cousin died you took his papers and set up in a little tank town for yourself. As far as they can make out, you never really harmed anybody and you even helped a couple of people. But it was a hot stove, so you took off finally for South America. Aboard ship you met a man with a bellyache—which you relieved. The man with the bellyache was a field superintendent of Tumayo Petrol and he was very grateful. Correct?"

For a moment Gilmore sat mute, rolling in his mouth the cold unlighted cigar. But then suddenly he sprang up and faced about to the wall hung with the parchments. "As a matter of absolute fact," he said, pointing with the cigar to the graduate certificate from Hamburg, "that one is all my own. And London, too. And the Sorbonne."

"Absolutely," agreed Reeves with a sober nod. "The only trouble is that you're topheavy."

Boldly now, Gilmore struck a match and lit the cigar in a single draw. "Reeves," he said, "there's a committee waiting for me outside in the hall, and you know it. What're you proposing to do—make a sap out of Uncle Sam?"

Reeves smiled. "Oh, yes," he said, "you've got us over a barrel all right—which a lot of people would enjoy hearing about." He seemed now, as a professional schemer, to draw almost a relish from the situation. "I *will* say that before I flew down we had that brass hat from Public Health Service go over all your progress reports. Every single one of them."

Gilmore looked up tensely.

"He says—he says that if he'd known you twenty years ago he'd have been glad to stake you to medical college. He says . . ." Under Gilmore's tense and burning gaze Reeves broke off. "Fellow," he said, "just don't ever try to hang up your shingle in the States again."

It took some time for this to sink in on Gilmore.

"If you do," said Reeves, and the words he chose were a wry self-parody, "the Department will find itself compelled to blabber to interested agencies." He gave Gilmore a look, compounded of frustration and admiration both, of the kind which parents reserve for bratty but gifted children.

Over Gilmore's face, finally, came a sunny smile. "Cross my heart," he promised.

"Some time," said Reeves thoughtfully, "you ought to take four years off for medical college."

"At my age?"

Again there was a knock at the door and the white-haired gentleman called to Gilmore.

"Go on," said Reeves. "Go and get your medal."

With a nod of thanks, Gilmore pulled open the door. *"Caballeros,"* he said with a professional courtliness, "I have the honor of placing myself at your disposition." They enveloped him instantly in their midst and carried him off as in a mass embrace.

"Now," said Reeves, "I can fly back to Chimboya. *Te gusta?"*

"Yes," said Harmon, sighing his relief. "I like it fine."

"Oh—oh," said Reeves, with a certain deep enjoyment of his own predicament, "if this ever got out . . .!"

CHAPTER THIRTY-ONE

THE lecture theater when he got there was conspicuously crowded, and at all the doors were posted Carabineros. He tried purposefully to lose himself at the rear of the hall, but from the dais the Governor's eye found him. Inexorably Montalvo went on beckoning until it was no longer possible for Harmon to pretend that he had not noticed.

"Where's Burling?" asked the Governor.

"Detained by other duties. He sends his apologies."

Displeasure twisted faintly the clean and well-beveled features. "It was my intention," said the Governor, "that he should make the formal reply in behalf of the Mission." Sourly Harmon noted his choice of words. Yes, ever since his victory in the matter of the loans, Montalvo had grown more and more autocratic.

"Dr. Gilmore can do that."

"It's not the same thing," insisted the Governor. "It should come from a representative of the Mission's directorate."

"My Spanish," said Harmon instantly, "is not that good." Why, he wondered, this insistence on protocol—this ardor for a second honeymoon with the Mission?

"Your Spanish," said the Governor airily, "is admirable."

Harmon gritted his teeth, but there was no escape. Firmly the Governor guided him to a place at one end of the dais, which had been embowered with huge wild flowers from Alba's swamps, scentless but brilliant of color and twisted bizarrely like adders and vipers. Yes, thought Harmon again, there must be a plan behind this despotic kindness. . . .

The Mayor of Rosales, as chairman of the occasion, just then began the opening address. In an idiom as cloying as meringues he spoke of the marriage of destinies which, he said, had linked the Americas—the long and shapely continent of the South, the rugged and broad-shouldered continent of the North. Between them, said the Mayor, had bloomed a new understanding, a new love. How soon, wondered Harmon, would he get them to bed?

"Señor Harmon . . ." From the burning forest of flowers behind him came a whisper. It was so close that it felt damp in his ear. He turned half about. Concealed among the flowers was Hector Serrano.

"Yes?"

"They ask you to abstain."

Abstain? Immediately the word brought to mind those yellow

posters of many months before. "Largo?" he murmured. "The Poristas?"

"Their strategy," replied Serrano softly, "is to attack the Governor as a saboteur of the Mission's work. They ask you to refrain from making any statement in praise of him. They beg you not to whitewash him."

Now, thought Harmon, this ardent new courtship by the Governor was thoroughly explained. The Mission must have become exceedingly popular in Alba. Its approval was something worth having, and something that Montalvo was counting upon to use as a cloak.

"If you can abstain altogether, *Señor Asociado,* from speaking . . ."

"I don't know," whispered Harmon anxiously. "Let me think about it."

"We count on you," said Serrano, "to do the decent thing." Instantly he vanished again among the huge serpentine flowers.

Abstain . . . Now the cantonal president had gone to the rostrum. Again there were metaphors in which the southern continent played the role of female before the continent of the North. . . . In the air now, in the intent silence of the audience, Harmon could feel preparations for events to come. Abstain . . . His muscles began to play nervously. What to do? It would be a difficult moment when eventually Montalvo called upon him to speak. Impossible, most likely, to refrain altogether from taking the rostrum. The better course—to choose his words carefully, coldly, to demonstrate his disapproval by subtle omission. They would not fail to get his meaning, these bowed-down half-cavaliers who were the audience. In the Spanish language, as in the Hollywood tongue, anything less than superlative had the meaning of dispraise. Fine, fine, he thought. It would be a chore to his liking. But where, it suddenly occurred to him, was Vicente Hidalgo this morning?

Simultaneously the welfare director had begun to speak, a shrunken little man whose voice did not carry beyond the first rows. But where was Vicente? Anxiously Harmon searched the entire

hall. Across all the rows, face by face, went his glance—back, back
to the standees packed tightly together at the rear.

Yes, said the welfare director, a great new life had dawned for
Alba, and it had been made possible only through the high esteem
in which the North held the Constitutional President and his strong
right arm, the son of the Eagle of the Andes. . . .

From all sides of the hall, dark, intent eyes played upon the dais.
Harmon was taken suddenly with the feeling that he was under
whispered discussion in all corners of the hall, being weighed,
evaluated. But where was Vicente? Across Harmon's mind there
flashed now those sad apocalyptic words of Vicente at their last
meeting: ". . . They are steeped too much in the mystery of the
Mass. There is only one kind of idealism that our poor little
monkeys will trust . . ."

But nowhere about the hall, he found, was there a sign of Hidalgo. Good, he thought. Perhaps once again he was lying in that
hammock like a burst sausage. Perhaps once again Vicente had
drowned his grand intentions in a bottle of *aguardiente*. He hoped
that this were only so. . . .

Now the Governor was stepping to the rostrum, all grace and
light—that spurious mask of himself by which Harmon had for so
long been taken in. He opened, as if by ritual, with the traditional
tribute to the Eagle of the Andes, speaking those same shibboleths
as months before at that scarred desk with the broken pushbell.
"Here in the Mission," said the Governor, "we find an echo of my
father's very own dreams."

"Right!" called a voice from the rear of the hall—the loud leathern
voice of the professional claqueur.

"And here in the Mission," said the Governor, "lies hope again,
and opportunity, for all those whose life has become worse for
them than death."

"Right!" cried the claqueur again. Montalvo was rich these days, thought Harmon wryly—well able to pay for the bliss of hired applause.

The Governor smiled pleasurably. From the day the North American brothers had first set foot in Alba, he continued, it had been his honor and privilege to offer them the fullest measure of his co-operation.

"Liar!"

It was the voice of the same claqueur. But what was he saying? This could not be believed.

Montalvo himself made as though he had not heard. "Together we planned all the projects," he went on. "Together we assembled all the materials and equipment. Together we worked far into the night to . . ."

"At night you smuggled brandy!"

Through the hall went a buzz of amazement. At the lectern the Governor reeled.

"At night you were planning how to steal the money which was a gift to the people!" Now finally the disguise was off. Now finally the invisible heckler spoke with the full golden timbre which belonged to nobody but Vicente Hidalgo.

"Slander!" shouted the Governor. "Stop him!"

From all the doorways Carabineros had begun already to converge on the point, at the rear of the hall, whence spoke the bland, derisive voice.

"At night you were betraying your father and your people."

Oh, Vicente! thought Harmon, seized suddenly with fear and anguish. Far back, amid the crush of the standees, he could now make out that banner of wild gray hair.

"Silence!" cried the Governor, taking hold of himself again. "Order!"

Still the Carabineros were pushing their way to the rear.

"Down with silence!" said Hidalgo, his face still not discernible. "Down with order! In the name of silence and order you are destroying us all."

Nowhere else in all the hall was another voice raised, as though by common consent the scene had been yielded to these two duellists alone.

"Slander!" cried the Governor. "Treason! Stop him! Arrest him!"

"Down with you and all the thieves like you!" said Hidalgo. "Down with all the Conquistadores!"

Suddenly the flow of the Carabineros was stemmed. About the person of Vicente Hidalgo, it could be seen, had formed a wall of bodies, a human casemate. Tactics, thought Harmon instantly, organization. It must be the *Poristas,* of course, who had formed the fortress. From within it the voice still issued, but serenely now, with measured eloquence. "My countrymen," it said, "you will not be led to a new life by buzzards and jackals. You must start anew with men who are clean and decent—leaders from among your-selves. You must not leave it to the North Americans alone to rescue you from your misery."

Sick and shaking, the Governor left the rostrum and staggered away to a door at the rear of the dais. Simultaneously a shot was fired into the ceiling. Clubs flailed at the human casemate protecting Vicente Hidalgo. But his voice swelled yet higher. "You must help make your destiny for yourselves, my unhappy friends. And you must not be afraid to buy it with your blood."

A second shot was fired.

Now a gap was torn in the human stockade. From the dais a glimpse could be caught finally of the face of Vicente Hidalgo—of those dark and massive and life-scarred features. It was a face trans-ported, glowing with its own inner light. "I have not much longer to go on," said Hidalgo, but calm still, unhurried. "I want only to tell you, children of misery . . ."

Oh, turn this way, Vicente, and see me, begged Harmon silently. Vicente, let your eyes find mine. Say some word for me alone!

"I want only to tell you that when finally you have won . . ." A fist smashed into the impassioned mouth, into those white, in-corruptible teeth. ". . . I tell you to remain still on guard. Beware always of the men who love power—especially those who call themselves your friends."

Oh, look this way! implored Harmon. Say something for *me*!

"I tell you . . ." A gun butt crashed against the open lips. "I tell you . . ." Now the massive gray head sank suddenly into a whirlpool of fists and clubs and gun butts.

From Harmon's lips leaped one word that was filled with love and horror and longing all. "Vicente!"

A Carabinero vaulted simultaneously to the dais with his tommygun. "Out of here," he ordered. "Everybody out."

There was time only to see them jerk Hidalgo up by the armpits, at the other end of the hall, and drag him away. Was this what it came to—the hour of truth? Oh, Vicente!

CHAPTER THIRTY-TWO

HE WAS sitting in his office hours later, still dazed, still numb, when the two women came in. Ernestina, shaking nervously, rushed at him and exclaimed, "Is it true?" Serafina Bustamente, he noted dimly, had seated herself stolidly at the door, like a sentry at a post. "Tell me if it's true!"

Confusedly, weakly, he held to her. "What? Is what true?"

"The whole province is in an uproar, William! And everybody says that the Mission will be called back! William, are they really going to send you away?"

He shook his head. "Not that I know of. We did try to telegraph the Embassy for instructions, but Montalvo has closed the wire." And for hours ever since he had sat alone and paralyzed in his office. The others—Masters, Anderson, Horanyi—had gone about their tasks as usual. These "fireworks," as Masters had put it, that old tropical hand, didn't mean a thing. He had seen them sputter on and off for thirty-five years in these banana Republics and they had never seemed to make a hell of a lot of difference one way or another—just the same old game of musical chairs between the "ins" and the "outs."

"Montalvo . . ." said Ernestina with a shudder. "You know, William, he came running straight from the meeting to our house. And he had a long, long talk with Manriquez." Again, Harmon noted, she was referring to her husband by his surname—as to a stranger.

"Hidalgo . . ." he asked chokingly. "What did they have to say about Hidalgo?"

She looked at him distressedly. "Oh, darling, darling . . ." she said. "Vicente means so much to you—doesn't he?"

"What did they say?" he demanded. "Tell me what they said."

She caressed him with both her hands on both his cheeks before she brought herself to answer. "Gone . . ." she whispered.

It felt to him as though his whole mouth were filled with sand. "Where? Gone where?"

All the while she went on caressing him—the tender bondmaid in the hour of her lord's distress. "Manriquez—he said it would be best to get Vicente out of the province at once. He said to put him on the Customs launch—take him away to Lorca. He said . . ."

Harmon fell down into his chair.

"Darling, darling . . ." she said, pressing his head against her breast. "They're just going to send him to prison in Lorca—the idea is just to have him away from the province." All the while he could hear the ticking of her heart, the heart that was beating for him. "I *know* that's all it is. Darling, I had something more to tell you." He glanced up dazedly, hardly comprehending. "William, are you well enough to listen?"

He managed to nod his head.

"I—William, I've decided . . ." But then she broke off.

"Tell me."

Her lips were open but she was unable to go on.

"Come—what is it?"

From her sentry post by the door, Serafina Bustamente went on for Ernestina. "I've told her she can come and live with me. I will take her in as my daughter."

His glance shot back to Ernestina. "I don't know how I can go on living with Manriquez any longer," she whispered. The moon-pale face was wrenched with hatred. "He's so horribly ugly, William. As a husband. As a person. He's everything that Vicente did not want me to marry."

So she was leaving him finally, the Conquistador husband. For a woman in these countries, for an Ernestina, it was an immensely bold step. There had flashed up in her once again a spark of the campus tomboy, the rebel who had wanted to be more than a domestic animal. "Ernestina . . ." he said gently, taking her on to his lap. But immediately then she began to sob. "I'm frightened," she said. "Take care of me, darling, won't you?"

Yes—it came to him once again—in her rebelliousness it was not for freedom that Ernestina had struck out, but only for a change of lords.

"Darling," she said, huddling against him, "you can come to me now whenever you want. It doesn't have to be just Wednesdays."

The loving, worshipful handmaiden. . . . But all that he could see right now, in this cataclysmic moment, was the long prow of the Customs launch cutting its way through the gray Pacific toward Lorca.

"Oh, I love you so," she said. "You're so good!" He wondered whether they had bound Vicente with ropes, whether they had thrown him into the dark hold like inanimate cargo.

She drew his face to her and kissed him tenderly. "Sweet," she said, "if there's anything I can do to make you happy . . ." Outside, simultaneously, he heard the tramp of running feet on the rickety staircase. "You want me to, William, don't you—don't you?"

He stood up, bringing her with him. "Yes," he said dazedly,

"yes." Numbly he returned her kiss, wondering all the while what news was going to be brought by those running feet.

The door, finally, flung open. But still, bold and unashamed in her dependence, Ernestina held to him.

"Harmon!"

It was Hector Serrano, his voice ragged with a fury of some kind.

"Harmon!" It was the first time, in all their relationship that Serrano had omitted the respectful "Señor." It must betoken some catastrophic contempt that had been loosed.

"Yes?" he asked, facing about.

Serrano shoved something at him, a single printed sheet on which the ink still was damp. "A special edition of the *Messenger*," said Serrano, "and oh, how stinking special!"

Harmon snatched at it with both hands, and Ernestina was shaken loose of him. Across the top of the single sheet, black and bold, ran a headline: "Director Burling Acclaims Our Governor."

"And I was beginning," said Serrano, spitting out his contempt, "to become optimistic about you *gringos!*"

. . . In the name of his government, the Director of the Technical Mission was happy to take this opportunity of thanking Governor Montalvo for his unstinting co-operation. Contrary to the lies of certain fascist agitators, it was the Governor alone, son of Cesar Montalvo, who had made it possible to translate the Alba program from blueprints into such realities as the hospitals, the schools and the roads. It was the pleasure of the Director therefore to state . . .

Harmon let the newspaper drop to the floor. "Where *is* Burling?" he asked quietly.

"In his quarters," said Serrano. "Nicaragua and Haiti all over again . . . The same old story. Just how low can you *gringos* sink anyhow?"

Instantly Ernestina leaped between Serrano and himself. "Don't say that!" she cried passionately. "It's not true! Not about *him!* You *know* that it isn't! Not about *him!*" It made Serrano fall back a step.

That fierce loving partisan, thought Harmon. Never, by nothing, could she be made to believe ill of him, though the Harmon that she saw was one who could not possibly exist . . . He gave her a tender fleeting hug—then raced suddenly for the staircase.

Burling, sprawled out in bed, his head bolstered up luxuriously by three pillows, chuckled. "This time," he said, "I knew I had Montalvo by the short hairs."

Was it possible, thought Harmon, that there could actually be a second viewpoint about this? Was it possible that a man could even chuckle about it?

"He dashed in here so excited, the monkey, that I thought he would wet his pants. There'd been a little disturbance, he said. Some agitator had sounded off about bad relations between himself and the Mission. Would I mind saying a little something in denial?"

A *little something,* thought Harmon savagely.

"You know, Billy, the regular hoopla about inter-American co-operation and solidarity of the Hemisphere. Why not? What would it cost me? Only this time I smelled that Montalvo wanted it real bad."

How was he going to find it possible to hear Burling out—*how?*

"I said to him, 'Mr. Governor, that kind of deal has got to work both ways.' I said, 'Mr. Governor, as I understand it, a contract has no validity without a consideration for services rendered.'"

Still he would make himself hear Burling out.

"The monkey asked me what I wanted." Gleefully Burling heaved himself up from the nest of pillows and sat on the edge of the bed. "For weeks now, Billy, that buzzard has had us jumping through hoops. I said to myself now it's *my* turn to crack the whip. 'Mr. Governor,' I said, 'I'm asking you to refund all those business loans. Every last penny of the money.' Billy, I squeezed till the buzzard screamed. But he gave in all right—right down to his own goddamn share of the loot."

Slowly, stiffly, Harmon stood up from the camp chair alongside the bed.

"Right there, Billy, I tied up the neatest little package you ever saw. One, I got the swag back intact. Two, I followed out to the letter every last damn instruction of the Ambassador about co-operation."

Merrily he made to nudge Harmon. Instantly Harmon took a step backward. "Do you happen to know," he asked, "who that 'agitator' was?"

Burling looked up. "No. I didn't think to ask."

"Well, said Harmon, coldly still, stiffly still, "it was a man named Vicente Hidalgo."

"Oh," said Burling interestedly, "that orator?"

"What do you suppose happens now to Hidalgo?"

"Hell," said Burling, "they can fight that out among themselves."

He saw Burling suddenly—in a last flare of thought before his rage exploded—as a kind of tropical growth, a rank melon. Swollen and overblown. Running inside with fetid juices. Nourished and fattened by a sickly heat and an over-fertile soil.

"Harmon . . ." said Burling, his small eyes turning round with wonderment. "Billyboy . . ."

But already his hands had thrust out and clutched Burling by the plump shoulders. "Burling" he cried, shaking the over-ripe tropical body. "Burling! Burling! Burling!" The obese mass quivered and rattled, the jowls, the chins, the belly. "Burling, Burling!" —shaking him all the while in rage and grief and loathing. He could think of no epithet more contemptuous, more expressive of his hatred, than the man's own name. "Burling!"

CHAPTER THIRTY-THREE

HE SLEPT that night at the port—to be near the telegraph office should any message come through from Chimboya. He was certain, once during the night, that there swept through his room that white scythe of light which betokened always the arrival of a ship. But where were the other elements, the *sounds* which always the beacon unleashed—the cracked music from the bars across the mudflat, the tired greetings of the stevedores on the causeways, the cries of the foodhawkers at the seawall?

This time the beacon flashed in silence, or so it seemed.

He fell back into fitful restless sleep. Now and then he floated away into dreams, joyful ones, dreams of extreme power: that he was striding through a city a full block at each step—that he was standing off a gang of thugs singlehanded—that he was lifting an entire building in his own fingers—that he was . . .

The sun suddenly was high. Through the mosquito netting an object like a hairy tarantula was nudging him. "Wake up! Harmon, wake up!"

The object was the fist of—Hector Serrano. Instantly he came wide awake. "What is it? What's happened?"

Serrano, obviously, had dressed in haste. His white sport shirt was misbuttoned all the way down. His uncombed hair bristled in all directions. "The Customs launch . . ." he panted. "During the night it came back."

The Customs launch! This then was the ship which had stolen in so silently during the night. "Hidalgo . . . ?" he asked, all choked.

"They came back without him."

Oh, no!

"The police—the explanation they make is that Hidalgo broke loose during the trip—that he jumped overboard . . ."

The "law of flight"? *That* brutal ruse?

"The police insist that they held their fire—but that the water was infested with sharks and that . . ."

Father!

". . . and that the body could not be recovered. Bastards! Sons of whores!"

Had he not for long now expected some such horror—the hour of truth—the destiny toward which Vicente had knowingly set himself in motion . . . ? But now that it had happened Harmon felt himself completely engulfed, smothered, slaughtered. "Oh, no!" he cried. "No, no, no!" Relentlessly, Serrano nodded yes, yes, yes—over and over again.

Action! thought Harmon. Something must be done! He leaped from bed and yanked on his clothes. He dabbed a few drops on his face from the bowl of gray water and reached for the towel with no thought for scorpions. Something must be done! But—what?

"Largo's come to the port," said Serrano, as if reading his thought. "He's talking it over with his top people."

"Talk . . . And more *tactics?*" He snapped the words out scornfully. Something *large* must be unleashed, he thought, something to match at least the monstrosity of what had been done to Vicente.

"Action," murmured Serrano thoughtfully, "is going to cost lives. What's worrying Largo and his people—the American troops at the Base . . ."

"That they'll intervene for the Government? God, no! Not possibly."

"Nicaragua!" repeated Serrano savagely. "Haiti!"

"This isn't the same thing," said Harmon. "Absolutely not."

In the hallway sounded a heavy uncertain tread. "All very well," said Serrano shrugging his shoulders, "but after Burling's statement what are the people down here to think?"

There was a cautious knock at the door.

"Burling," snapped Harmon, "stay out of here."

From beyond the door Burling's voice came faint and hoarse. "Hold your fire," he pleaded. "I've got something to show you."

"Bastard," muttered Serrano. "Son of twenty thousand whores."

"Please, Harmon," asked Burling. "This concerns you personally."

Coldly Harmon pulled open the door. In his hand Burling held a square of the pink paper that betokened a decoded message. Harmon took it. "General McClellan . . ." said Burling, coming inside. Uninvited he sagged down to a very small camp chair.

Indifferent at first to all its implications, Harmon read the message. "Chimboya papers display a statement by you in regard to local disorders. If this is correct, Harmon replaces you immediately as chief of party. He will refrain absolutely from any further comments on internal politics. Warren Joab Henderson."

Still Burling squirmed on the very small camp chair and sweated. "That's one time," he said, looking down, "that Burling outsmarted Burling."

For a moment longer Harmon glowered at him. But that huge body, slumped so bonelessly on the very small chair . . . It brought to mind the white face and the trembling hands of Fred Ross on the day of that failure in the pump-house at Santa Ana, at his inability to look anywhere but at the ground. It recalled also that tenderness, so unexpected, with which Burling had helped Ross to stand up straight again. . . . Well, thought Harmon, Burling too had found his hour of truth. . . . "A tough break, Leslie," he said.

Burling looked up finally. But his eyes pleaded for something more still.

"There are other hot countries," murmured Harmon. "You'll land something else in no time."

A ghost smile lifted the corners of Burling's mouth. "You really think so, Billy?"

But already Harmon had turned away to Serrano. "Find Largo," he said. "Right away."

He came into the office, the thin calm man, with two escorts, squat and bulldog-like, who obviously wore shoulder holsters under their linen jackets.

In his hand Harmon hefted the pyramidal title plate thoughtfully. "We'll have to talk alone," he said.

"As you wish," said Largo. He sent his bodyguards out to the hallway, then took up, before Harmon's desk, a position which was half of staying and half of going. He held himself as if he had stored in his mind a plan for every possible eventuality.

"What I have to say . . ." Harmon began. He observed all at once that the title plate in his hand was a new one—"Director of the Mission," it read. With a true Spanish regard for form, even on a morning like this, Serrano had already replaced the "Associate Director" plate with Burling's own. Dead man's shoes, thought Harmon, putting it down instantly. "I must have your word, Largo," he went on, "that you will refrain from quoting anything of what I'm going to say. You are not to attribute it to even, say, 'an unnamed North American official.' Not a word—not directly nor indirectly."

Largo studied him curiously—then nodded.

"Well, then, I think I can assure you that Washington"—Harmon took a deep breath before plunging ahead—"will not be lending our flag to *anybody*. Not to your party, naturally, but not to the regime, either." Largo smiled politely. "In other words, the policy is absolute neutrality."

Again Largo smiled—but still no more than politely. "After all," he said, "there's a world war going on. And in the Middle East the British, for instance, *have* used their troops to stop internal disturbances."

Harmon shook his head firmly. "Washington has to operate from a different policy. Take my word for it, there'll be no intervention."

"Fine," said Largo, "but by now Burling's statement has done its damage. And considerable damage. Our masses here are thoroughly frightened. They take it, unless they hear something to the contrary—and something *official*—that at the first shot they will be over-run by the North American tanks. The only possible antidote" —he leaned forward eagerly—"is a *counter*-statement. Public and official."

In wide arcs, from side to side, Harmon shook his head. "You're asking for the impossible," he said. "I am not empowered to make that kind of a statement. My instructions are for absolute neutrality."

Outside just then, in the corridor, a woman's voice rose shrilly in imprecations. "Hoodlums! Stand aside—the two of you! Out of our way!"

"Señora," pleaded one of the bodyguards, baffled obviously by the situation, "I must ask you to wait here for just a few moments."

"Not on your life! Get out of our way!"

Harmon leaped to the door. Behind Serafina Bustamente in the tight-packed melee of the hallway, he found Ernestina. "We can wait," she said, with large staring eyes. "If you're terribly busy right now we can . . ."

He led the women inside. Largo, he found, had turned his face cautiously away to the wall. "Señor," he said, to avoid calling Largo by his name, "there's an empty office just next door." Yes— Burling's.

Largo nodded. As he went, he held one hand over his face. Serafina Bustamente waddled after him to the door, closed it and —as once before—took up her sentry post before it.

Wonderingly, Harmon turned to Ernestina. "Yes?" he asked.

She leaned against the edge of his desk with her hands palm-down, those white and fragile hands—bracing herself. "William," she said breathlessly, "I've had it out with him. I told him I'm leaving him." It was important, he thought, but at the moment there were other things to think about and he wondered why she. . . .

"Oh, that isn't all of it, William." Softly she began to sob. He went to her and put his arm protectingly, consolingly, around her shoulder. As always, he noted what she was wearing. Again it was the shirtwaist dress and the tomboy shoes, her garb of rebellion. "What is it, dear?" he asked. Still she went on sobbing. "Come, tell me what it is."

She swung about then, in the arc of his embrace, and looked at him.

"Oh," he said, and instantly he felt himself crushed again. "It's more about Vicente?"

"The Governor—he came to our place again last night. It was just before the launch was to leave for Lorca . . ."

His fists clenched—but not for fighting, only to brace himself. He was going to hear something, he knew, that would make him ill.

"What they had to say, William—they said it right out in front of me—as always—without the slightest shame!"

"Tell me," he said, but wishing all the while that this were only a dream, something from which he could wake.

"They said . . ." When finally she let it come out, it came out in a rush. "Manriquez said that Vicente must not be allowed to reach Lorca. Something must happen to him on the way. But he must not be shot—not *shot*—under no circumstances." Over her face went a grin of horror that reminded him how she had once compared her looks with those of a death's head. "Oh, the bloody, bloody butcher!" she cried. "He said that Vicente must be *beaten* to death! Not shot. Beaten. Beaten!"

Harmon closed his eyes, but there was no shutting out the picture. It flashed on again, burningly luminous, in the dark of the theater between his corneas and his eyelids.

"Manriquez said that it would be embarrassing—that was the word he used, embarrassing—to have bullet wounds show later if the body should wash up. That is—if—if the sharks left anything to wash up." She clutched Harmon tightly and spoke close to his ear as if confiding a secret. "Montalvo asked if it wouldn't be enough just to throw Vicente overboard. He had certain compunctions—for the sake of old times, I suppose. But Manriquez remembered something, that Vicente was known to be a very strong swimmer. . . . Oh, yes, said Montalvo, quite right. So, *beat* him, *beat* him to death!"

Slowly, dazedly, Harmon withdrew from her embrace. Finding a chair near by he gripped the back of it with both hands. "You heard them say all that?"

"They talked as though I were just a part of the room—a wall."

"You—you said nothing?"

"I screamed, William. I went on screaming and screaming." She opened the dress at the neck and bared one shoulder. It was covered with black bruises. "He held me there until I thought I would faint. He slapped me across the face. He said that if I ever breathed a word of it . . ." She covered her face with her hands and shuddered.

Numbly Harmon sagged down into the chair. His elbows fell to his knees, his face into the cup of his hands. Silently, the solitary unconsolable mourner, he sat there. If only, he thought, he could have been with Vicente in those last moments, with him and alongside him . . . Or if at least Vicente could have spirited away from that murder ship some message for him. . . . A *message,* a *message*— as once he had longed for one from his own blood father, Steven Harmon. . . . In his mind, suddenly, on the screen of his lowered eyelids he saw an image of that great fatherly body floating in the scummy waters—floating face down in the way of the male drowned —the eyes staring down, down, down, blindly to the ocean floor. And the sharks, those buzzards of the sea, cutting white tracks through the waters with their fins. And the flesh, garb of that innocent, incorruptible spirit, being torn, torn, torn by the idiot teeth. If only he could have been there to shield Vicente—to fight for him—to die with him, if he had to . . .

He had no notion of how long he had been sitting there. Action, he thought finally. Finally he stood up again. Finally he was all composed again. "Ernestina," he said, speaking quietly, almost remotely, "I want you to tell that story all over again."

She threw him a startled glance.

"I want you to repeat it to that man who was just in this room."

She backed off a step. "William," she begged, "don't ask me to do that. Please, William."

"I have to," he said gently. "It's something that everybody ought to know about—and you are the witness."

"Oh, don't—don't," she pleaded.

He gazed at her curiously. "I thought Vicente meant so much to you," he said.

"Oh, yes!"

"Doesn't it matter what they've done to him?"

"Yes—yes!"

He took her by the arm. "Are you so afraid of Manriquez?"

She began, in the age-old gesture of despair, to wring her hands—a gesture, he thought oddly, which you never saw in America, which was totally European or Asiatic. "Manriquez? It's not even that. Please, please—it's just that I'm not made for that sort of thing."

For *what* sort of thing? Participation in life? In the realities among which she dwelt? His glance, instantly, went down to her feet, to the tomboy shoes which she wore always as a memento of other times, as a souvenir of the girl who once had strode so freely across the grass, the student among fellow students, an equal in the world and not a vassal female.

"Don't ask me to do it, William! You mustn't—you mustn't!" With the fingernails of one hand she dug suddenly into the back of the other hand and gashed it savagely. Over the delicate moon-pale face, as if to fragment it, went a look of fury. "You mustn't!" Still she went on stabbing at her own flesh, gashing it, bloodying it, as once in a temper she had torn at *him*. "You despise me—don't you, William?" she cried. "Don't you?"

Pityingly, heartbroken for her, he took her into his arms. But automatically he found himself thinking of Laura, wondering what *Laura* in the circumstances would have done. It came to him with absolute certainty that he knew. He saw, in his mind, the image of

her clean strong stride as she went up a mountain road. He saw her
—and it was for the first time, wasn't it?—with a kind of respect.

"Ernestina . . ." he said sorrowfully.

"Please, please, please, William . . ."

From her sentry post by the door Serafina Bustamente cried out
in anger. "What do you want of the poor child anyhow? They
train us down here to pull off their boots—for nothing more."

This high-spirited Fatty—in *her,* at least, still burned some last
sparks of rebellion. They manifested themselves in tragic-silly ways,
in her putterings about as Lady President of the Red Cross, in her
waspish determination to see Manriquez—and all the similar
"brutes"—soundly cuckolded. Serafina, at least, had still not put
down her arms. But Ernestina . . .

"You hate me, William, don't you? You despise me, don't you?"
she cried, clutching at him with her bleeding hands.

These were questions, he was certain, that Laura would never
think to ask. Or was he taking too much for granted? Had she not,
too, over the years been reduced to vassalage? Yes! More and more,
over the years, he had let Laura become his handmaiden—she the
girl of glorious promise. And he had forced it on her not with his
strength but with his weakness. He had reigned over Laura through
his infirmities—as a despotic invalid. Why, why had he never considered the torments which must be raging inside *Laura,* the sorrows over the withering of all her *own* gifts? . . . There came back
to his mind suddenly that haunting scene of his two daughters
falling into his arms at suppertime, all smudged with the dirt of the
afternoon's play but their hair doused bravely with the stolen cologne, half-tomboy and half-coquette, and torn between the roles.
It was not to be endured that they too might plead some day for
the good opinion of a weakling.

"William . . ." begged Ernestina.

"No, darling," he said, all wrung with shame, "I *don't* hate you."
He cupped her face in his hands and kissed her.

"You'll come and see me just as soon as you can?" she asked.

"Now it doesn't have to be only on Wednesdays. Come to me as often as you can, will you, darling?"

More than ever, he thought, she would be looking now for ways in which to serve him. She would pay penances a thousand times over for this one time that she considered herself to have failed him. Never would she think to cast upon him that appraising glance which was Laura's. Never would she call him to account. Once, long ago, he had thought this to be exactly what he wanted—hadn't he?

"Yes," he said heavily, "as often as I can."

When Ernestina was gone he sat down again in the swivel chair and his eye fell simultaneously on the title plate, the new one, sitting boldly there on the edge of his desk. "Director of the Mission," it read. There he had it finally—the full measure of potency, of manhood. *Director*. He could consider himself a success. On all fronts. . . . But from afar a pair of keen blue eyes seemed to search him. If this was what he wanted, they said, if this was what he needed to make himself feel tall. . . .

Abruptly he turned the title plate about.

Vicente—he thought next. Again in his mind he saw those intercepted letters in which first he had become conscious of the man called Vicente, those letters so full of hurt laughter, of bitter innocence. Again he saw that hobo king standing before him at this very desk for the first time and holding aloft the long cheroot that was like a burning scepter and crying ironically, "Oh, my dear young Colossus!", that everlasting penitent who had been to hell and back without even a soot mark, the tortured Danton who had striven twenty years against his own inadequacies and made himself stand up finally to repeat the blood-stained passion of his master. Rumpot. Eccentric. Individualist. Scornful always of tactics and of safety. There must be many others like him in the lands of the world, other such sons of Prometheus, who in the same way chose death, and silently often, unheard of beyond their own villages. They too had managed to achieve that wise and bitter innocence of Hidalgo's, that "second innocence" which could be reached, he had said, only after disillusionment and despair; the only kind, he had said, that was worth anything. Again and again the world would fall to the men of tactics, the lovers of power. Again and again the Conquistadores would trample down the innocent under their boots. But in the crushed, smashed, trampled remains of each innocent would lie the seed of at least one other. There, in the words of Vicente, lay the *counter*-tradition, or the hopes of it. Vicente could surely not have considered that his death was going to mean a total cessation of life, or he would not have chosen to do what he did.

Again Harmon's eye caught the title plate. *Director*. A desk-bound Conquistador of the twentieth century—that was what he was on the way to becoming. It was hard to imagine Vicente content on such a throne. Vicente . . .

Standing up suddenly from his swivel chair, Harmon walked to the wall, knocked upon it and asked Largo to come back.

"In a moment," he said composedly, "I will have Serrano come in and take a statement. You will be free to use the statement in any way you wish."

Largo studied him curiously.

"In this statement, I intend to detail the exact circumstances of Hidalgo's death, exactly how he came to be murdered."

Largo, behind his compressed lips, began to breathe audibly.

"Also, I intend to explain just why Hidalgo let this thing happen to him—why, actually, he chose to bring it upon himself, and how"—he felt himself smile then with a certain merriness—"and how it was Vicente's notion that even the noblest of sacrifices is liable to be turned eventually into a Black Mass."

Under his tawny skin Largo flushed. "Not necessarily," he said.

"I predict," said Harmon, and he felt an irony, an innocent irony, issue from his lips in the voice of a beloved ghost, "I predict that by next year every thievery in this Republic will be committed in the memory of Vicente Hidalgo."

Largo shook his head.

"Nevertheless," went on Harmon, "there's a logic which compels us to do this thing. Cesar Montalvo—Vicente Hidalgo. Already there is starting a kind of dynasty—what Vicente would call the counter-tradition."

"On that," said Largo, "I agree."

He would love, he thought, to come back here in ten years and see how this thin calm man had turned out. "It happens," he went on, "that there's a witness as to how the murder was planned."

Largo bent forward eagerly.

"The name of this witness," said Harmon firmly, "or any hints of the witness's identity cannot be used, must not. However, I don't think that should matter very much. The statement will carry another kind of authority—that of an American official."

Largo stared unbelievingly.

"Yes," nodded Harmon, "I mean to sign it with my own name. Publicly and officially. Will that give you what you need?"

"Absolutely," said Largo. "It's the one last weapon that guarantees success." But then he looked down and began to shift in his chair, torn obviously by some inner conflict. *"Señor Director,"* he said, and the pronouncement of the new title struck Harmon as something odd, as something utterly removed from and utterly alien to himself, "I don't want to take advantage of a mood. I know that the moment word of this gets to your Ambassador . . ."

"Oh, yes," said Harmon. "I'll be sent home in disgrace." Instantly he was seized by a pang. In Ernestina, in that love which burned so fiercely for him, he had found a sheltering warmth at last. To have to turn from her now, to start alone on the bleak journey to the North, to stand and be measured again in New York against the realities of a colder zone . . . Yet it was impossible that he should go on forever accepting her servitude. Or anyone's. In the end it would only corrupt him, as did every form of narcosis. As soon as he got it over with, this last imperative office, he would go directly to Ernestina and try to explain it to her. He wanted desperately for her to know that it was not for lack of love that he would be parting from her. In a private compartment of himself, he would carry a love of her the rest of his life—even for the frailties, *especially* for them.

"*Señor Director,*" Largo was suddenly inquiring, "may I ask why you are doing this thing?"

His eye went instantly to the title plate. Musingly he picked it up in his hand, the mace of office which had come to him only long enough for him to renounce it. "If I stayed here," he said, "I'd have to consort with the Conquistadores." He opened a drawer of his desk and put the plate away. "There are other ways," he said as he closed the drawer, "for a man to feel important. Would you please find Hector Serrano and send him in?"

Yes, it would hurt to leave Alba, that flat, ugly, over-fertile land where the buzzards walked like sparrows—to leave behind the sick hopeful children who had learned to trust him. Here he had come to find that his capacities were not, after all, dead. Here—was it *all* illusory?—he had come for a while to feel whole and strong. He wished that it could have been possible for him to see the work of the Mission through. Somebody else, of course, would be found for that, a successor whose work had assuredly been made easier now because now the Conquistadores would be toppled. And Largo was pledged to see that everything did not crumble later. It would even turn out—though in his first rage the Ambassador would not see it that way—the best thing for the credit of the *gringos* as well. It would have been demonstrated, this once at least, that not all *gringos* hunted with the hounds. And even—this caused him to grin—it might be the best thing for the "world picture."

Musingly he glanced through the window at the gray-green huddle of shanties in the mudflat. Puerto Pacifico—he would take away from this sea swamp a kind of fond remembrance, also, of the runaways who had been his companions here: Walt Anderson, that Don Juan of the cane huts; Horanyi, who could feel himself to be American only outside of America; Masters, who had to nourish himself on bad temper; Gilmore, with his felonious but benign passion for healing, so ardently loyal to a Hippocratic Oath he had never taken; Burling, who would surely manage to stand up again when again he found himself among a people weaker even than himself; and Rosabel, poor Rosabel, who could never be consoled for not having been born a man. By next summer the work in Alba would be done and they would go their separate ways again. He would be hearing from them for years to come, and always from tropical lands, always in flight.

Himself . . . He bethought himself suddenly of an adage—that it was possible, in a single act, to win all eternity. And manhood too. When he got home again he must make Laura understand that he was not to be pitied, not even if he had to spend all the rest of his life over law briefs which did not interest him. . . . Laura—now for the first time it had become possible for him to see her as she really was: gallant, not disdainful; magnanimous, not imperious. And she, in turn, must be made to see that there was no longer any throne for her to serve. He knew it for a fact that now his bones were really whole again, and that now he had height because he was tall and not because those about him had been made to kneel. It struck him that for some time lately he had begun to admire Laura, and now it had become possible also for him to love Laura.

There was a knock on the door. "Come in, Serrano," he called. It was, he thought, his own hour of truth.